TWO LITTLE LIARS

TWO LITTLE LIARS

MICHELLE HARRISON

NO EXIT PRESS

First published in the UK in 2026 by No Exit Press,
an imprint of Bedford Square Publishers Ltd,
London, UK

noexit.co.uk
@noexitpress

© Michelle Harrison, 2026

The right of Michelle Harrison to be identified as the author of this work has been asserted in accordance with the Copyright, Designs and Patents Act 1988. All rights reserved. No part of this book may be reproduced, stored in or introduced into a retrieval system, or transmitted, in any form or by any means (electronic, mechanical, photocopying, recording or otherwise) without the written permission of the publishers.

Any person who does any unauthorised act in relation to this publication may be liable to criminal prosecution and civil claims for damages. A CIP catalogue record for this book is available from the British Library. This is a work of fiction. Names, characters, places, and incidents either are the product of the author's imagination or are used fictitiously, and any resemblance to actual persons, living or dead, businesses, companies, events or locales is entirely coincidental.

ISBN
978-1-83501-510-0 (Paperback)
978-1-83501-511-7 (eBook)

2 4 6 8 10 9 7 5 3 1

Typeset in 10.8pt Adobe Caslon Pro
by Avocet Typeset, Bideford, Devon, EX39 2BP
Printed and bound in Great Britain by
CPI Group (UK) Ltd, Croydon CR0 4YY

The manufacturer's authorised representative in the EU for product safety is Easy Access System Europe, Mustamäe tee 50, 10621 Tallinn, Estonia
gpsr.requests@easproject.com

*For the weird, wise, and wayward who would have
once been called witches*

Part One

A lie never lives to be old
– Sophocles

1

SEPTEMBER 2016

*I*F AN ASSAILANT TAKES YOU *to a second location, chances of escape or rescue are significantly reduced.*

It's one of the things Erin frequently tells herself whenever she steps outside the house. She's thinking it now, while at the same time trying to convince herself that the man isn't really following her.

If you are being followed, find an open place of business like a coffee shop or petrol station and go inside.

Erin steps into Costa Coffee on the high street and joins the queue. She'd been thinking about coming in anyway but she does it now out of necessity rather than as a treat, knowing that the lemon muffin she orders will stick in her throat and the cappuccino she's been looking forward to will taste of nothing.

She'd noticed the man in the art shop. Prior to that it'd been an average sort of morning. She'd popped to the supermarket early, got back, put the shopping away and opened her mail: a bank statement, an invitation to cervical screening and, less depressingly, a cover proof for a forthcoming picture book she's illustrated. She'd spent a few minutes studying it, her mood lifting briefly, as it always does, at the sight of her name and her artwork on the cover of what will be an actual book, in actual shops, in a few months' time. She'd allowed herself a moment to take it in. To feel something like content.

Erin loves her job. It's one of the very few things about her life that is good. She knows she's lucky, luckier than she deserves to be. Seeing the cover prompted her to pick up her phone and check her emails. She's been waiting for a response from Sam, her agent, on a picture book idea she sent him – her own text this time instead of someone else's. Her inbox loaded two new messages, neither from Sam. The first from Tesco Clubcard, which she deleted without reading, and the other through the contact form on her website. The subject line sent her mood, and her stomach, spiralling.

MURDERING BITCH.

She'd clicked on the message only to find the main body of it blank. The field meant for the sender's email was filled with a string of meaningless letters and numbers. With shaking fingers, she'd deleted it. And then she'd put on her coat and forced herself to go out.

It's the last week of September and autumn has crept up stealthily. A few days ago, on Erin's thirty-seventh birthday, the damson tree in her tiny garden dropped most of its leaves, which she has already swept up and disposed of. *Got to stay busy.* There had been a chill in the air when she'd left this morning, which nipped at her despite the faint, pear-golden glow of the sun. She'd walked briskly to the compact but well-stocked art shop on the fringes of town and spent a peaceful half hour choosing some new paints and replacing pencils that have worn to stubs. She has decided to work up three sample illustrations while she waits for Sam's reply. It will keep her occupied.

The man had entered the shop shortly after her and was the only other customer. Erin had looked up briefly as he came in, eyes skimming over him. White, stocky, a shaved greying head, blue jeans, brown corduroy jacket. A bent nose, the result of multiple breaks, his skin heavily pockmarked. Not the usual bohemian type she sees there, or the students with alternative haircuts and piercings.

Always be aware of your surroundings. Know who and what is in the immediate area, and where the exit is.

Passing him to pay for her items, Erin had noticed the man was holding a set of watercolour paints and staring intently at a couple of box canvases. It'd been a small detail, but one that had got her attention. She'd wondered then whether he was a clueless dad or husband picking up a gift for a creative relative, but Erin is not the type to point out that box canvases are for oils or acrylic paints, not watercolours. She doesn't speak to strangers if she can avoid it. In any case it was likely that the shop assistant would alert him to his mistake.

She'd been halfway down the street when she'd paused to look at some boots in a shop window and, on the edge of her vision, she'd noticed someone mirror her movements, stopping abruptly to look in a neighbouring shop.

The man from the art shop, just few steps behind.

Erin looks up from the counter now as the door to Costa Coffee opens, and in he walks. She turns back quickly to the barista, who has moved along to take the order of an older couple behind her. She could say something. Ask for help, say she's being followed. Doubt keeps her silent. Erin has been wrong before, created a scene and drawn attention and it's all turned out to be a misunderstanding. A couple of months ago she'd been returning a supermarket trolley when an abrasive voice sounded close by: 'I know what you did. Liar. Don't think you're getting away with it.'

A ranting woman charging towards her, face twisted. Erin had freaked and launched the trolley at her before seeing, too late, the earphone wires under the woman's hair. Connecting her on a phone call. Her words not meant for Erin… until they were, and more people had gathered by then to hear her being sworn at. Being called a nutjob.

She often thinks she's being followed, being watched, and today the email has left her more on edge than usual. She is used to jumping at shadows, to messages from anonymous aggressors –

MURDERING BITCH…

… You don't deserve to live…

– to fearing everyone and everything.

She watches the man in the mirrors behind the counter. He's picked up a panini and is scanning the overhead coffee menu, paying no attention to her. She risks a glance his way and sees he has no bag from the art shop; nothing was bought there. He must have left right after her. She squashes down a wave of dread. It doesn't mean anything. He could have changed his mind, left empty-handed.

Or he could be following her.

She pays and sits at a table by the window, an equal distance between the counter and the door. Between help and escape. She only starts to calm down when the man takes his tray to the far end of the shop near the loos. He settles at a table with his back to her, taking out his phone to scroll through it. He is not watching her. He is not following her. She stirs her cappuccino. The drink is foamy and perfect and the muffin is soft and fresh. Perhaps she will enjoy them after all.

The woman who was behind Erin in the queue comes to sit at the table next to her, fussing with her shopping bags. Erin studies her, glad of a distraction. She is a people-watcher, always noticing posture and movement and doing her best to capture it on paper. Clients are consistently impressed by how well she draws hands. The woman removes her coat and fans herself. A minute later her partner joins her, setting down a tray.

Erin glances behind at the man with the corduroy jacket – still there, not watching her. As she turns back her eyes seize on the couple next to her.

The man has taken out a tabloid newspaper and is holding it up to read the sports page on the back. The front page faces Erin. She doesn't see the headline at first, only the picture.

A bite of lemon muffin dries up and sticks to the roof of her mouth.

In every high-profile murder there is a photo that is synonymous with the case; an image that etches into the nation's psyche to become instantly recognisable.

The girl's photograph was taken in her final year at school. She wears a green blazer and her thin hair is mousy brown, parted on the side. Her eyes look black in the picture, with no hint of the murky pond colour of her irises. *She looks so young*, Erin thinks. The article will name her as Belinda West, but Erin first knew her as Belinda Webb. She would have been almost thirty-seven now, same as Erin. But she never made it to eighteen.

At first Erin never understood why they used this picture of Bee. It bore little resemblance to her at the time of her death. There's no red hair, no vampy make-up. She's fresh-faced, if a little pale. Her expression is curiously neutral. But the answer, Erin had eventually learned, was a simple one: there were never many pictures of her in existence.

Erin's attention finally goes to the headline. It reads: CHILD BEE.

It's as though someone has pushed an alarm button in her brain. She stares at the two words, trying to work out what's wrong through a growing fog. Because something *is* wrong, even though the image and headline both fit with everything Erin knows. Her eyes drop to the subheading: DEAD GIRL ONE OF THE TWO LITTLE LIARS.

She stands up quickly, her knee knocking the table. Her half-eaten muffin lands on the floor and the man with the paper glances up, concerned. Erin ignores him, tugs on her coat and rushes out on to the street. Her face burns in the cool autumn air. Raindrops speckle her cheeks. The town is busy. People squeeze past her, shaking open umbrellas or diving into shop doorways to escape the rain shower.

She doesn't hear the voice at first. Doesn't hear the approaching footsteps. She's momentarily forgotten the man in the brown jacket until now, when she feels the hand on her arm and whips round ready to run or to lash out. But it's the woman from the coffee shop, slightly out of breath. Erin waits, for what she is not sure. Abuse? A slap? Recognition of some kind, for now the truth is out it will lead to her. It has to.

The woman hands her something.

'You left your bag, dear.'

Erin gazes at it blankly. Her art materials, forgotten under the table in the coffee shop.

'You ran off in such a rush,' the woman adds with a tentative smile. 'Are you all right?' She has a kind face. Erin imagines she has grandchildren that she does puzzles with and takes to farms for wholesome days out.

'I'm fine,' Erin mutters. 'I just remembered I've got a… an appointment.'

She sounds croaky and weird. She tries to smile, meeting the woman's eyes. A forgotten bag, that's all. The woman's smile falters as she looks back at her. It's a look Erin's seen countless times. Where people stare into her eyes, trying to work out what it is about them that's odd. The woman is uncomfortable now. Her hand reaches to the neck of her coat, gathering it tightly as if to protect herself.

Fuck off, Erin thinks viciously, but of course she doesn't say it. She is quiet. A mouse. A hider. She takes the bag a little too abruptly.

'Thanks,' she says in a tight voice, then turns and walks away. The rain gets heavier but Erin barely notices. She heads for home with one stop off in mind. There's a newsagent at the top of the high street, five minutes from her house. She picks up an overpriced bottle of milk she doesn't need, then scans the news stand. Aside from the tabloid she's already seen, there's only one other paper with Bee's face on the front. Its headline is less sensational: 20 YEARS UNSOLVED. Then underneath: ISLAND MURDER BAFFLES TWO DECADES ON. There's no mention of the *two little liars*, but this does nothing to unknot Erin's insides. Tomorrow it'll be on every one of these front pages.

She buys both papers and leaves.

When Erin arrives home she abandons the bag with the art stuff by the front door and goes straight to the kitchen table. She sits, not even bothering to remove her jacket, eyes barely leaving the picture of Bee's face. If she blinks she knows she'll see it behind her eyelids, inverted like a negative.

She begins to read.

2

AUGUST 1990

Erin never wanted to be her friend. When you're a child, though, and your parents tell you to include someone, you do it because you have to. The memory of the first time they played together is frayed in places. She remembers how it ended and how it began, but not really the middle.

It's the third week of the summer holidays. Erin and Aidan are on their bikes, racing each other up and down the street. Erin has already lost two out of three – not because she's slower, but because her stupid pink bike is too small for her. She pedals hard, eyes fixed on Aidan. Her pace matches his but there's no way she's catching up. She's preparing for defeat yet again when a cat shoots across his path. As Aidan brakes Erin swerves, flying past him into the lead.

'Ha!' she yells. She's still grinning when they skid to a halt outside her gate, chests heaving. 'Thrashed you.'

'Only because I let you.' A faint smile is playing around the edge of his lips. He clambers off his mud-spattered BMX and leans it against the wall, then stands under a tree near the kerb. She glances at his bike enviously then joins him. Even in the shade the day is so bright they're both squinting. Erin peels her thin dress away from clammy skin.

'When's Jess back from holiday?' he asks, pushing sweaty dark hair out of his eyes.

'Thursday.'

16

He nods. 'It's been good this week, just us.'

Erin has enjoyed it, too – not that shes likes Jess any less than Aidan. She likes them both, but sometimes she has more fun mucking about with Aidan on their bikes over the field than she does with Jess, who hates getting dirty or doing anything boisterous. Erin's known Aidan for ever. Their mums were on the same maternity ward and, later, in a mother and baby group together. Now he lives a couple of streets away and they go to the same school.

'What about Jamie?' Erin asks. 'What's he up to?'

Aidan wrinkles his nose and reaches out to pull a leaf from her hair. 'You know what he's like. His dad just brought him back a Game Boy from America so he's glued to that. I don't know how anyone can stay indoors when it's like this.' He blows the leaf into her face, grinning.

Erin's mother cuts in unexpectedly. 'Maybe some people aren't as lucky as you two.'

Erin looks up to see her on the garden path, holding a tray with two iced lemonades and a bottle of sun lotion.

'What do you mean?' Erin asks. She and Aidan take the drinks and drain them in deep, thirsty gulps.

Her mother nods to the opposite side of the road. Erin follows her gaze to a flaking, red front door: the Webbs' house. Out of the corner of her eye she notices Aidan respectfully suppress a burp for her mother's benefit, but then her attention is caught by a movement in one of the upstairs windows. A small, pale face watches them from behind the glass.

Erin groans and turns back to her mother. 'Not the Belinda talk again.'

She's rewarded with a stern look. 'It wouldn't hurt you to include her, Erin. The girl has no friends. She's stuck in that house all the time.'

'Whose fault's that?' Erin mutters, looking to Aidan for support. It's pointless – he always turns into a complete goody-

goody in front of her mother. 'You asked if she wanted to come round. She never did.'

She recalls bumping into Belinda and her mother a while back outside the shops. Since the Webbs moved to their street at the start of the year they've only exchanged a few polite hellos from across the road, but that day Erin's mother had attempted conversation and made Erin give Belinda one of her Opal Fruits. Belinda accepted it, unsmiling.

'People call me Bee,' she'd said. 'I'm a witch.' She tilted her head, taking Erin in. 'Your eyes look funny.'

'That was ages ago,' Erin's mother says now. 'Maybe she'll come if you ask again.'

'I don't want her to,' Erin grumbles. 'I bet she's happy playing her witchy games all by herself, anyway.'

'Nothing wrong with having a vivid imagination.' Her mother laughs. 'It's probably something you need if you're lonely.'

'She's mean,' Erin says sulkily. 'She said my eyes are funny. And her legs are all scabby.'

Her mother raises an eyebrow. 'Now who's being mean?'

'Scabby?' asks Aidan, in a way that suggests he wants to see this for himself. Aidan has a strong stomach for things most people find gross. Erin's lost count of the times he's peeled back bandages to inspect war wounds or burst blisters. Last week he'd called her over to point out a mass of writhing maggots in a bin. *Disco rice*, he'd called them, grinning and doing a ridiculous dance.

'It's probably eczema,' says her mum. 'It's not catching.'

'Well, she didn't say thanks for the sweet, either,' Erin persists. '*And* it was a red one.' She glares at Bee's house, hearing her mother sigh. Almost as though she knows she's being talked about, Bee lifts a hand to the window and rests it on the glass. That does it.

'Come on.' Aidan nudges her, his dark eyes soft like melted chocolate.

Reluctantly, Erin puts her empty glass on the tray and endures a few swipes of sun lotion at her mother's insistence until, hot and grumpy, she squirms away.

'You too, Aidan,' her mother says, dabbing his blotchy forehead. Erin pulls a face at him, but he merely winks and stands obediently until her mother is finished.

'Go on, then,' she says, picking up the tray. 'Off you go.'

Erin grunts in defeat. Then they are crossing the road and knocking on the red door, and saying hello to old Mr Baxter who is weeding his already immaculate flower beds next door. Erin stares round Bee's front garden while they wait. It's choked with weeds and rubbish blown in by the wind. There's a clothes horse on the lawn with a tatty Rainbow Brite sleeping bag thrown over it. Halfway down the fabric, a wet stain is drying out in the sun.

Daphne Webb opens the door wearing rubber gloves. The harsh stink of bleach comes out of the house, surrounding her like an aura.

'Can Bee come out to play?' Aidan asks. Some of his chirpiness gives way to a cough as the fumes get down his throat.

Daphne doesn't say anything at first, but looks beyond them to where Erin's mum is watching from across the road. She turns to shout up the stairs. They are uncarpeted and paint-speckled, as though the Webbs have only just moved in.

'Get dressed and come down. There's kids here for you.'

Erin wonders why Bee isn't dressed yet when it's gone lunchtime. The smell of bleach is so strong that even years later, her eyes will water at the memory of it.

3

SEPTEMBER 2016

BY LUNCHTIME THE STORY IS everywhere. Erin sees it on the news and hears Bee's name on the radio. Though she doesn't 'do' social media – not even for her books – Erin has anonymous accounts set up so she can track current events. She makes the mistake of clicking on Facebook and Twitter articles which take her down rabbit holes to more news pieces and a true crime blog. She also finds a podcast about the *two little liars*, though it appears to be obscure – for now. She makes cup after cup of coffee, forgetting to drink them all as she scours the internet for whatever's going to pop up next. She reads each piece and every comment, even though she knows it's the worst thing she can do. The vitriol has not faded with time. If anything, the revelation about Bee's identity has stoked it all up again.

Got what she deserved!

BITCH CAN ROT IN HELL.

Now name and shame the other one.

Erin doesn't move from the kitchen, clicking from one toxic website to the next. Her head is in a fog. She ignores two calls from her mother. She can't speak to her, not yet. An email comes in from Sam. He's keen on her idea, asking if she can come up with sample illustrations in time for the upcoming Frankfurt Book Fair. She won't. Erin no longer cares about the illustrations or the idea and has no intention of going up to her studio, the bright room at the top of her house. The art materials will sit by the door where she dumped them.

The day grows darker around her. *Get up,* she wills herself. *Wipe the coffee spills off the counter. Wash those dishes. Open the blind.* She does none of these things. She wakes up her laptop, and it opens on the last tab she visited. She hits refresh and the page reloads. Bee's face is still at the top, but the headline has changed.

BBC TO AIR WITCH BOTTLE MURDER CRIMEWATCH SPECIAL.

A video has been added under the headline. Swallowing, Erin clicks on it and a newscaster begins to speak.

'BBC1 is to air a *Crimewatch* special on Belinda West, who was murdered on a college trip twenty years ago this October. Fiona Newton reports.'

The camera cuts to a smart, blond woman outside Chelmsford police station.

'Belinda West's body was pulled from the Tithe Estuary on the morning of Sunday, the thirteenth of October, 1996. The seventeen year old had been on a college trip to a remote tidal island in Essex and was last seen alive following a party the night before. What initially appeared to be a tragic drowning quickly turned sinister when it was found that West's throat was slit, with cuts to her mouth and tongue. Her autopsy later revealed pieces of broken glass in her throat from a silver bottle belonging to the island's witchcraft museum. West's killer had forced her to swallow it.

'Two decades on, that killer has never been found. But cold case detectives have released new information which they hope could lead to a breakthrough. It's now been revealed that Belinda West was one of two children, until now identified only as Child A and Child B, who were involved in another notorious murder which took place six years before West's own killing.

'In the summer of 1990, sixteen-year-old Nicky Pemberton was beaten to death by three men including his own father, after false claims by West – then known as Belinda Webb – and another child that Pemberton had molested them. The two children, aged ten at the time, were dubbed the "two little liars" by the press, and were so vilified by the public and media that the courts were forced to grant them lifelong anonymity for fear of vigilante attacks. Here with me now is Detective Inspector Graham Giles. Detective, the question everyone is asking is, why is Belinda West's true identity only now being made known?'

The camera pans out to show a dark-haired man in a plain grey suit.

'It's a fair question, Fiona,' he replies. 'And the answer is a simple one. At the time of Belinda West's death the police chose not to disclose her link to the earlier murder of Nicky Pemberton, as they believed it could harm the investigation.'

'So, essentially,' Fiona interjects, 'it was kept secret that West was Child B, because she was so hated that police thought the public wouldn't help if they knew the truth?'

'Correct,' Giles confirms. 'However, with her murder unsolved for so long we've decided to release that information. Leave no stone unturned.'

'And what's the thinking behind this?' Fiona asks. 'Is it the case that you've exhausted all other leads, and this is all that's left? Do you think people will care now?'

The detective baulks at the naked hostility of the question.

'Twenty years is a long time, and loyalties may have changed. The Nicky Pemberton case was sensational in the way people focused on the lie that West and the other child told. We need to remember that they were just that – children of ten years old. They weren't the ones who chased that boy down, beat him senseless and hung him from a tree.'

'Could it be inferred that the two cases are connected? That

Belinda West's killing could have been payback for Nicky Pemberton's?'

'There's no evidence to suggest that,' the detective replies. 'The length of time between the killings would indicate not, and given the remote location of West's murder and what we know about the complexities of her life, it's unlikely. But we can't rule it out.'

Fiona Newton thanks the detective and turns back to the camera. '*The Witch Bottle Murder Crimewatch* special airs at nine o'clock on BBC1, Thursday the thirteenth of October.'

The clip ends, just short of three minutes. Erin refreshes the page once more. Comments appear underneath. Some are crass, referencing Bee's well-documented personal life; that she'd been 'a slut who was shagging a teacher'. Many rehash details from Nicky Pemberton's murder and how he was beaten unrecognisable. A couple of commenters side with the detective: **Only children... mistake... not the ones who killed him.** They are quickly trolled. **Old enough to know right from wrong, what kind of kids tell lies like that?** Erin continues to stare at the screen until her eyes are gritty. The comments grow and grow until at the next refresh, they vanish. They've been disabled.

At some point during the evening Erin jolts awake. She is slumped over the table, dazed in the dark kitchen with no idea of what time she nodded off. Her phone battery is flat, exhausted from endless scrolling and missed calls from her mum. When she tries to wake up the laptop she finds that it, too, is dead. The clock on the microwave tells her it's almost midnight. She's been asleep for hours. The thought of this sends her into a panic. What has she missed? What else could have come out during that time? She starts to get up to grab chargers for her devices, but a sound stops her.

She sinks back into the chair, suddenly sure it's the same sound that woke her. A scraping, rustling noise. It's coming from outside her kitchen window.

Someone is out there.

Instinctively she slides off the chair, lowering to the floor. The kitchen tiles are freezing, shaking the last dregs of sleep from her. *It's just next door,* she tells herself. *Putting something in their bins.* But it sounds too close for that.

Her heart drums erratically as she crawls to the cutlery drawer. The blind is down, the light is off. Whoever – or *whatever* – is outside cannot know she's here. She slides the drawer open soundlessly and takes out her largest kitchen knife. She holds on to it in the darkness, counting her own breaths, crouched against the wall.

Something crunches outside, a clumsy sound of movement on gravel. Erin stands up then with a rush of relief as she makes sense of the noises.

Foxes. That's all. But her hand trembles as she carefully separates the slats in the blind to peer outside, eyes already accustomed to the dark and expecting to see the mangy brush of an urban fox slinking over the wall.

Instead she gets the briefest glimpse of a brown corduroy jacket sleeve, caught in the glow of the street light before it vanishes from view.

4

AUGUST 1990

Erin is hot, irritated, and bored. The afternoon has stretched out and shadows are lengthening with it, but the heat is still as intense as it was at midday. The journey to the playing field is a slow one. Bee doesn't have a bike and doesn't know how to ride one, so Erin can't even lend hers and sit on Aidan's handlebars. An attempt to get Bee on his handlebars results in her falling off, and scraped knees to add to her other scabs. So they leave the bikes at Erin's and walk, making small talk as they go. Bee stops every now and then to scratch the red marks on her legs. Some are so dry and cracked that they've bled in places. Erin takes care not to brush against her, even though Bee has a way of standing uncomfortably close. She doesn't want whatever scabby disease Bee's got, even if her mum says it's not catching.

The conversation is stilted. They learn Bee is ten, like them, and goes to the other school that's slightly further away. She doesn't have – or want – any pets, doesn't have a best friend, a favourite book or TV show. She lives with her mum and doesn't know who her dad is. Aidan, persistently kind, perseveres long after Erin runs out of things to say. Bee listens in silence, her pale face giving no indication of what's going through her head. The only time she volunteers anything is to compliment Aidan's earring, a silver stud that flashes with every turn of his head.

'Oh, yeah.' He grins. 'I got Erin to do it for me at Easter.'

'Did it hurt?'

'A bit. I had to numb my earlobe with frozen Yorkshire puddings 'cos we didn't have any ice, and then Erin pushed the stud through. Got a right bollocking off my mum, but she let me keep it.' He grins at Erin. 'It's a bit wonky but I'll let you off.'

'You kept wriggling,' Erin reminds him. She'd escaped the bollocking. Aidan had told his mum he'd done it all himself. A week later it had been weeping and infected, giving him something new to pore over in morbid fascination.

The playing field is in a sorry state. A graffiti-covered slide, a roundabout and three swings are all it has to offer but, on days like these, it's usually enough. Soon, the three of them are swinging high, soaring into the cloudless blue and glimpsing the neighbouring gardens ahead and, over the far side, the vast cornfield bordered by a thin strip of woods.

Bee's heels scuff the ground, bringing her swing to a halt. She gazes at the cornfield.

'Let's go over there.'

'Can't.' Aidan stands up on his swing. 'Erin's not allowed past this field.'

'But are you?' she asks him.

'Are *you*?' Erin demands.

'I can go wherever you two go,' Bee says. 'So, if Aidan's allowed, so am I.'

He shrugs. 'I've never been told I can't, but our parents have a rule that we have to stick together. Erin's not allowed, so I can't go without her.'

'Oh.' Bee pouts. 'Well, what about over there?'

She points to an overgrown corner of the field that's fenced off. Years ago there used to be a council building there – probably to store tools for the maintenance of the field – but it's long since been demolished. A wire fence surrounds it, but it's torn in several places and choked with blackberry bushes and nettles. An alley which runs beside it makes it a popular fly-tipping spot.

Aidan frowns. 'In there? It's just junk.'

But Bee has already left the swing and is moving towards it. 'I want to see.'

Aidan and Erin exchange glances. Then, with a sigh, he takes a flying leap off his swing and lands on the grass. 'Better go with her,' he mutters, scrambling off after Bee.

Erin swings higher, leaning back until the sky is all she can see; just endless blue broken only occasionally by the flight of a bird or a plane on its path. Shouts in the distance make her sit up. Some older boys have arrived on the far side of the field, kicking a ball, using discarded T-shirts as goalposts. She watches them lazily until a scream rings through the air. Not from the boys. This is a girl, and it's not playful. Erin twists round to stare after Aidan and Bee but she can't see them. She leaps from the swing as Aidan had, but she's clumsier and jars her ankle as she lands. Wincing, she heads across the grass towards the gap in the wire fence.

A scrap of old carpet has been pulled over the jagged tears in the wire and some of the brambles. Carefully, she squeezes in, trampling over uneven concrete and thick weeds that spew from its cracks. She sidesteps a sagging sofa, nudging a rusting bicycle wheel with her foot. Everything is quiet and still. There's no sign of anyone. She thinks of the scream again and imagines things her parents have always warned her about: faceless strangers clapping their hands over children's mouths and dragging them away.

'Aidan?' she calls. 'Bee?' Her voice is shrill, her body poised to spring for the gap in the fence. Her ankle throbs.

The scream comes again. Piercing, and blood chilling… and right in her ear. Erin whips round and finds herself almost nose to nose with Bee. Behind her, Aidan has collapsed on the sofa, shaking with laughter.

'Got you,' Bee says.

'That's not funny.' Erin's voice is cold. 'I hurt my ankle coming to look for you.'

'Sorry.' Bee smirks, standing too close. Erin can feel the hiss of her breath. She doesn't like being this close to her.

It's the first time Erin has properly looked into Bee's eyes, and she finds that the smirk on her lips isn't mirrored in them. Nothing is. Erin is reminded of pond water: stale and murkily green, impossible to know what's going on underneath. At the same time she becomes aware of the smell of her. It's the odour of schools and doctors' surgeries. Sterile, clinical, chemical. It doesn't belong on a person. She thinks of the overwhelming reek of bleach when Daphne Webb opened the door. It's like the smell has got under Bee's skin.

Bee is looking at Erin, too. 'What's wrong with your eyes?'

There it is. The question Erin loathes. Her reply is automatic, the words spilling out in the exact same sentence her father taught her when she was old enough to answer for herself.

'Nothing. Eyes are for seeing, and I can see fine.'

It sounds so rehearsed, so pathetic. Bee likes that, Erin can tell.

'There's nothing wrong with her eyes,' Aidan repeats loyally.

It isn't strictly true. Erin's eyes are watering from the discomfort of the blazing sun and the effort it takes to keep looking at Bee. She's supposed to wear sunglasses for the sensitivity but she either loses them or sits on them.

'It's called a coloboma,' Aidan adds.

'The black bits in the middle—' Bee starts.

'My *pupils*,' Erin corrects coldly.

'They're strange shapes. Like goats' eyes.'

'I think they look like keyholes,' Aidan says softly. 'I like them.'

Bee's expression becomes bemused, as though she can't possibly understand why Aidan would say such a thing. It's the moment Erin decides she hates her.

'They're so weird,' Bee says.

'A bit like your scabby legs,' Erin replies. The comment has little effect on Bee, who simply leans down and tears at her calf, as if reminded it's there to be scratched. Rankled, Erin continues. 'Oh, and what was that sleeping bag outside your house? Do you wet the bed?'

Aidan blinks, uncomfortable, and Erin feels a hot prickle of shame. Aidan is never spiteful.

Bee shrugs and looks away, kicking at a broken doll. 'What is all this stuff, anyway?'

'Just crap people dump here.' Aidan delves a hand down the side of the sofa, feeling around. 'The council clears it out every now and then.'

Bee watches him rummaging with interest. 'What are you doing?'

'Seeing what's fallen down the sides. Last time there was an old armchair we found a tenner, didn't we, Erin?'

She nods. Actually, Aidan had found it, but he'd split it at the shops and shared it with her. They'd blown the lot on sweets and a *Smash Hits* magazine.

'Like a treasure hunt.' Bee flops down at the other end of the sofa and reaches between the cushions.

Aidan pats the middle cushion. 'Come on, Erin. See if you can find anything.'

Erin grimaces at the stained upholstery, shaking her head. 'People's dogs have probably peed on it.'

Aidan and Bee are undeterred. Aidan's hand emerges first clutching an empty cigarette box, then a receipt. Tossing them aside, he goes back in. Bee has yet to pull anything out, but she's elbow-deep and wears a look of intense concentration.

'There's something down here,' she says.

'Careful it's not an adder,' Erin replies, still sour from Bee's unkind words. 'They get in from the cornfield sometimes.' She's disappointed when, again, she fails to get a reaction.

'Got it,' Bee breathes, tugging hard. A mass of coloured paper, slightly tattered, emerges from the cushions and she drops it in her lap.

'Just a magazine,' Erin says scornfully.

At that moment Aidan yelps and leaps up.

'What?' Erin shrieks.

'There's something in there, something alive.' He flings the seat cushion away. 'I felt it move.'

'An adder?' she asks, suddenly fearful.

Beneath the cushion there's a hole in the lining. It looks like something has chewed its way in. Erin and Aidan peer into the hole, past the springs, and see a rat. Lined up beside it are half a dozen or so tiny forms, pink and hairless and unmoving.

'Rat babies,' Aidan whispers. He leans closer. 'They're all dead.'

'Are you sure?' Erin's fear gives way to pity.

He nods. 'She's half-dead herself, poor thing.'

'What do you think happened?'

Aidan shakes his head. 'Poison, maybe.'

Erin's eyes cloud with tears. 'Can't we help it – take it to a vet?'

'I don't think a vet would look at it. My mum says rats are vermin. It could spread disease to other animals. What do you think, Bee?'

Bee hasn't said anything for a couple of minutes, hasn't even moved, in fact. She's still staring at the magazine in her lap. So Erin and Aidan stare at it, too.

It isn't just a magazine after all.

It's a magazine for grown-ups, with lots of pictures, all skin-coloured. Men and women, and women and women together. Erin's cheeks surge with heat, yet she's unable to tear her eyes away. She knows how babies are made, of course – she is ten years old – but *this*… these pictures make her insides squirm as if she'd swallowed those little rat babies while they had still been alive.

She forces herself to look at something else, anything else. At Aidan, open-mouthed and equally red-faced. At the mother rat drawing feeble breaths, its front paws twitching. And at Bee, her face more mask-like than ever. Completely unreadable. Just staring, staring at the pictures.

'Stop looking at it, Bee,' Erin whispers.

Years later, she will think back to this moment and wonder if it would have felt different had it not been for Bee. If it had just been Erin and Aidan who'd found it, or if they'd been with other kids – Jamie and Jess, perhaps – who might have shrieked and pushed the pictures at each other until they'd all laughed it off. But with every second that passes and no change on Bee's milk pale face, Erin feels dirty. Seedy. Ashamed.

'Come on, Bee.' Aidan is uncomfortable.

Bee doesn't move. It's as if she hasn't heard. Then she asks, 'What are you doing about the rat?'

Aidan shoots Erin a troubled look. 'Don't know.'

'What if we take it with us?' Erin suggests. 'Put it in a box somewhere so our parents won't see it? Maybe it'll get better if we look after it.'

'It's dying,' says Aidan. 'It'll smell. We'll get found out.'

'You can't make it better.' Bee's voice sounds detached, and oddly grown up.

'So, we just leave it to die?' Erin snaps.

'The only other thing is to kill it,' says Aidan. His face flames. 'It's what vets do if an animal can't be helped. Better it dies quick than suffers. I'll... I'll do it, if you think I should.'

Both of them are looking at Erin, questioning.

'Do it,' she says. 'But I can't watch.'

Aidan nods and moves away, presumably looking for something to hit the rat with. Erin starts towards the gap in the fence. She doesn't want to see what he picks up.

His shout makes her spin round. 'What are you *doing*?'

Bee has pulled the rat from the innards of the sofa. Aidan

and Erin cry out in unison as she drops it to the ground and brings her heel down on it. But she's a small skinny girl in flimsy sandals, and she has to stamp again and again before it's done.

Aidan rushes forward, a brick in his hand. Erin stays where she is, too horrified to move.

'*Why'd you do that?*' he yells. 'I said *I'd* do it. I was looking for something to hit it with, something that'd kill it in one go.'

'It's done now.' Bee lifts her foot, peeling her heel away from the mess underneath.

'What the fuck are you lot up to?'

Erin spins round at the voice. The group of lads who were playing football on the other side of the field are now by the fence, watching them. There are four of them, and one is already ducking through the gap. She, Aidan and Bee have been so preoccupied with the magazine and the rat that none of them has noticed the group approach.

Instinctively she takes a couple of steps closer to Aidan. Even without the aggressive greeting it's clear these boys are trouble. They are older, fifteen or sixteen. Erin recognises the one first through the fence. His name is Donnie and he's always loitering round the shops, being intimidating. Usually, according to Erin's mum, when he should be in school.

Donnie eyes the mangled rat, then the brick in Aidan's hand. 'You do that?'

Aidan shakes his head.

'I did it,' says Bee. 'It was dying anyway.'

Donnie laughs and rubs a hand through his blond hair. It's buzzed short at the sides and longer on top. He's good looking, with a tanned face and light grey eyes, but there's a meanness about his features. Two of his friends sidle up to him. One is a dark-skinned boy with a shaved head and an earring. He has a softer face than Donnie. Erin doesn't recognise him or the pasty-faced one who looks like a potato and has hung back by the gap in the fence – and she's uneasy that he's stayed there, deliberately blocking the way out.

The fourth boy is familiar. His name is Nicky something. Erin remembers hearing her dad refer to him as 'slow' or 'backwards'. Erin's mum always hushes him and tells him not to be cruel, that the boy is harmless – unlike his father. He has a slightly crooked set to his jaw and large, wide eyes that frequently appear startled or curious, making him seem innocent and younger than he really is.

'Fuck me,' Donnie exclaims, noticing the magazine. He whistles and snatches it off the sofa. 'Oh, *yes.*' The brittle pages crackle as he flicks through them, his eyes roaming over the images. 'Get a load of that.' He flashes a page at Aidan, grinning. 'Does your mummy know you've got this?'

Aidan averts his eyes. 'It's not ours. We found it down the side of the sofa.'

'Nice.' Unexpectedly, Donnie takes a seat next to where Bee is standing and continues to look through the magazine. Bee watches, making no attempt move away. She has gone very still.

'What is it?' calls the lad by the fence.

'Porno,' Donnie tells him. 'Didn't your dad have a sofa like this, Spud?'

'Fuck off,' Spud replies, spitting into the grass.

Donnie and the boy with the earring laugh, and a second later Nicky joins in. He even glances at the younger children as though he expects them to laugh too, like they're in on the joke. There is a sweetness to his smile, at odds with those of the other boys and their canine flashes of teeth.

'Dunno what you're laughing at, mate,' Donnie says, giving him a sly look. He leans towards Aidan and Erin and does a loud, theatrical whisper. 'His mum's in here, you know. Randy Mandy.'

Nicky stops laughing. 'She's not. Show me!'

'That one there.' Donnie pushes the magazine at him,

smirking. 'The one with the massive bush.' He looks at Aidan and grins. 'Great tits though, eh?'

Aidan says nothing. He's bright red now and doesn't know where to look, but Erin can see the tension in him. He wants to get out of here as much as she does. She notices he's still holding the brick. Worry needles at her. Aidan is scared.

'That's not my mum.' Nicky grabs the magazine and stares at it, biting his lip.

'Yeah, I know. I'm joking.' Donnie reclines lazily, resting his head on the back of the sofa. 'Anyway, you don't even see your mum, do you? Everyone knows she done a runner and left you with your old man. Probably forgotten all about you by now.'

Nicky's eyes dart from side to side as he searches for an answer. 'I… no, my dad wanted me to stay with him.' His eyes look red suddenly, as if he's about to cry. Erin feels sorry for him. He doesn't belong in this group. He's out of his depth.

'Yeah,' Donnie says again. 'Needed a punchbag, didn't he? How long ago was it she pissed off?'

'F-five years.' Nicky begins to tug at his earlobe. His other hand is tightening around the magazine.

'Give that here, you're screwing it up.' Donnie holds out his hand and Nicky obediently passes the porno back. Donnie slaps it on his knees and jabs a finger at the woman in the picture, leering at Bee.

'Your fanny's gonna look like that soon. All hairy.'

The boy with the earring shakes his head. He's still smiling, but it's strained. He's uncomfortable.

'Mate. She's a kid.'

Donnie acts as though he hasn't heard. 'Is it hairy already?'

He laughs, looking to his friends. Nicky hesitates, then laughs uncertainly too. The one with the earring doesn't. 'Well?' Donnie continues, watching Bee with an expectant, wolfish look.

Erin feels sick. This has already gone too far, crossed a line. They're trapped and outnumbered, with no one around who can help. Is Donnie going to force Bee to answer him? Or worse – to strip? He and his friends could probably make them do whatever they want. She glances round for another escape route. There's a spot further up where the wire fence is damaged. It's smaller, tighter, choked with nettles. But they can get through it with a few scrapes, she's sure.

'Come on,' Donnie adds, nudging Bee. 'You got pubes yet?'

'*Mate.*' His friend tries again. His smile is gone. 'That's not funny. Kayla's her age.'

Erin wonders who Kayla is. The boy's younger sister, perhaps.

Bee looks up from the magazine. Donnie persists.

'Nicky wants to know. Don't you, Nick?'

Nicky hesitates. He starts to nod, then catches himself and stops, realising what he's agreeing to, but it's too late. Everyone has seen the slight nod.

'So, you like little girls?' Donnie says at once. 'What are you, a fucking nonce?' He stands, squaring up to Nicky like a boxer in a ring. 'You know what happens to nonces, right?'

'No.' Nicky steps back, his confusion deepening. He avoids Donnie's glare and begins speaking fast, stumbling over his words. 'I never said… you're the one who asked her—'

'Nicky the nonce,' Donnie chants. 'Paedo-Pemberton!'

Nicky shakes his head, stricken. He's tugging so hard on his earlobe that Erin's convinced when he lets it go it'll be hanging down to his shoulder. Donnie laughs and punches him in the arm. It looks hard enough to hurt, but light enough that Nicky won't complain about it.

'He's fucking with you, Nick,' says the boy with the earring, and he's smiling faintly now. It's a smile of relief, not amusement. He digs a cigarette box out of his back pocket and looks to Donnie. 'I'm nearly out of smokes.'

Donnie nods and claps Nicky on the back. 'Time for our mate Nicky to go and get us some more, then, eh? Your dad still got that stash off the docks?'

Nicky pauses, wary of another trick, then finally starts to relax. He nods. Donnie grins and gives a bow to Erin, Aidan and Bee. 'If you'll excuse us, boys and girls.' He picks up the porn magazine and rolls it up, tucking it under his arm. 'I'll take care of this.'

They exit through the fence to the field, laughing and jeering as Donnie shares more pages from the magazine. Nicky laughs louder than any of them, grateful his 'friends' haven't turned on him after all, and they walk off in the direction of the shops.

Erin's knees are shaking. The entire encounter took less than five minutes, but the day is ruined. She wants her mum, and she wants home.

'Arseholes,' Aidan says, now they're safely out of hearing distance. 'Are you all right, Bee?'

Bee looks up, and Erin wonders if the blank expression on her face is about to crumple. If she's holding in a flood of tears. But Bee simply nods.

'Shall we go back to the swings?' she asks.

Aidan glances at Erin uneasily.

'I want to go,' Erin says, and heads to the gap in the fence. Wire snags painfully in her hair as she squeezes through. Bee and Aidan follow, and they move towards the playground.

'I really thought he was going to make you,' Aidan mutters. He's gone a horrible colour, Erin thinks. His tanned face looks grey, his lips pinched and white.

'Make me what?' Bee asks.

'You know. *Show* him.'

Bee shrugs. 'So did I.'

Erin glances at her, disturbed. She can't stop thinking of the *what ifs*, and Bee's strange reaction is doing nothing to settle her unease. She doesn't sound shaken. She doesn't even seem bothered.

'We have to tell our parents,' Erin says. Her voice is dry and croaky.

'Why?' Bee asks. 'Nothing happened.'

'But it could have,' Erin argues. 'If that boy with the earring hadn't been there. If it'd just been us, on our own with Donnie.' She's trembling harder now, like her body is trying to exorcise the thought by jolting it out of her. There's a darkness in Donnie for even thinking those things, let alone saying them. The next ten-year-old girl might not be so lucky. But Bee carries a darkness, too. Her lack of reaction to Donnie's demands, the way she pulverised the rat without a moment's hesitation. The pleasure she takes in commenting on Erin's eyes. Something isn't right with her. She makes Erin's skin crawl.

'Well, it didn't.' Bee pouts. 'And we can't tell. I won't be allowed to play with you again.'

Erin and Aidan are silent. They don't *want* her to play with them again.

Bee narrows her eyes, missing nothing.

'I mean it,' she says. 'Don't say anything. If you do, I'll tell about the magazine. I'll say you knew it was there and you took me over to show me.'

Aidan blows out a breath, gobsmacked. He's gone even greyer now, and his eyes are starting to look swollen. Erin wonders if he's trying not to cry.

'You won't say anything,' Bee repeats. 'You won't tell *anyone*.'

'We'll see about that,' Aidan says, backing away. He begins to stride from the playground, towards the road. 'We're going.'

Erin hurries after him, her jarred ankle protesting with each step. She hears Aidan's breath coming in short gasps and thinks he must be crying. She looks back and sees Bee is by the swings. Then she starts running after them.

Let her, Erin thinks savagely. It will be the last time she does. She and Aidan are almost at the edge of the field when she becomes aware that Aidan is staggering, like he's just run a race. Erin catches up to him. There's something wrong with his face. It's puffy, bloated. His eyes are vanishing into his cheeks like currants in rising dough.

'Aidan?' Erin cries. 'What's wrong?'

'Erin,' he tries to say, but the word is shapeless in his mouth. His lips and tongue are swelling with every passing second. His eyes are slits, forced to close from the rapid ballooning of his face. 'Get… Mum…' he wheezes, sinking to the grass.

Erin takes off, not pausing to look back. She's scared to leave Aidan. Scared to leave him with Bee. But she's more scared of what'll happen if she doesn't get help. She runs, as hard as she can. All the way to Aidan's house with Bee's words chanting in her head like a curse.

I mean it.

You won't say anything.

You won't tell anyone.

5

SEPTEMBER 2016

Erin huddles on the floor, head back against the wall, knife clenched in her hand.

Only when grey light creeps in past the edges of the blind does she pull herself up off the kitchen floor. Everything aches. Her fingers are stiff as she puts the knife down by the sink. She glances at the time on the microwave: 06:30. There hasn't been another sound since she looked out before and saw the brown sleeve. The movement of the figure slipping away. Still, she hasn't dared to move until now.

Outside, car doors are slamming. Some of the neighbours are going to work. She locates her charger in the bedroom, brings it downstairs and plugs her phone in. As she waits for it to come to life she looks through the kitchen blind slats, half expecting to glimpse the man outside, waiting. All she sees is someone two doors down closing their gate and heading off for the day.

Her garden is neat aside from a small amount of gravel that's been kicked across the paving stones; the only sign someone was there. She glances at her bins out of habit, but there's no suggestion they've been disturbed. She doesn't put anything important in them now, anyway. Nothing that can identify her. Anything with Erin's name on gets shredded and driven to the tip, and has been since someone kept going down her bins several years ago. She wonders what the man wanted – confirmation that she is who he thinks she is? He's made no

39

attempt to speak to her directly, but she can't decide whether that's reassuring or alarming. Is he a journalist, or someone planning on attacking her?

When her phone is back on she unlocks it and calls the police non-emergency number. Her feet cramp with cold as she waits for the call to connect to a handler.

'Yeah, I want to report a… I was followed. Followed home.'

'Okay.' The woman on the other end is brisk, professional. 'Are you safely indoors now?'

'Yes.'

'And do you know if the person who followed you is still nearby, or have they gone?'

'He's gone.' Erin looks through the blind again. The day is growing lighter by the minute. 'I can't see him now. I… I think he left a while ago. I've only just been able to call.'

'Right. Let's start by taking some details from you. Your name?'

'Erin,' she whispers, closing her eyes. 'Erin Sinclair.'

She'd been Erin Morton once, before Bee. The courts had given the injunction against anyone ever reporting on who she and Bee were and where they lived, but they hadn't given the families new identities. That had been down to them. Sinclair was her grandmother's maiden name. They'd initially considered a subtle surname change, such as 'Morgan' to keep it similar in the event of slip-ups – but Erin had assured her parents she never would. She's always been too painfully, shamefully aware of why it had to change.

'What's your address, Erin?'

Erin hesitates. The police have a duty to protect her but she doesn't trust them. She thought they'd have had a duty to tell her they were releasing the new information about Bee, too, but nobody has. It's been sprung out of nowhere, as though Erin is not worth the bother of a warning. She doesn't trust them now and she learned not to back then, starting with the nice lady who asked her gentle questions about Nicky Pemberton all those years ago. The lady had assured her she wouldn't get into trouble as long as she told the truth. And then Erin *had* told the truth, and the shit that had already hit the fan went flying at turbo speed. The nice lady was not quite so nice after that.

The woman on the phone doesn't know who she is, but if the call continues Erin will have to tell her. Already she knows it's pointless. They'll not send a car or do anything now the man has gone. They'll take a statement and give her a crime reference number at most. And the woman's voice will change once she knows who she's dealing with. It doesn't matter how professional she thinks she is. Erin will hear the inflection, the unspoken accusation there. The disgust. *Child A.*

'Erin?' says the call handler. 'Are you there?'

'Yeah, I'm here.' Her phone bleeps in her hand, signalling that another call is coming through. She checks the display, feeling a stab of guilt. Mum again. 'You know what, never mind,' she says hastily. 'It was probably just some chancer. If he comes back I'll call nine-nine-nine.' She hangs up and stares at the phone screen as it continues to bleep. Her finger hovers over the display, then taps DECLINE. She can't speak to her mum yet. She needs to calm down first, to get a grip. Shake the night off herself. If she hears her mum's voice now she'll tell her about being followed, and her mum will freak.

God knows Erin's caused her enough grief already.

She leaves the phone plugged in then sets about charging the laptop, too. Her landline rings and she lets it go to messages. Her mum again. When she listens she finds an earlier message she has missed some days ago from the police, unable to reach her on her mobile. An attempt to alert her, after all, to the Child B link about to be released. WhatsApp messages ping through. Her mum is serious now if she's texting. Erin pictures her hunched over and frail, squinting at her basic phone and painstakingly typing out the messages.

Answer your phone.

Are you all right??

I'm okay, Erin types back. **I'll call you shortly.**

She feels cold. Clammy and disgusting. A hot bath will help. She runs it, then comes back downstairs to pull a clean towel from a pile of unfolded laundry. She can't help picking up her phone again and taking another look on Twitter, searching Belinda West's name. She can't stop trawling the replies, clicking links, reloading pages. There are mixed views, as always. Some calling for forgiveness or justice, but these are never the ones Erin homes in on. She has learned to look for the hate, perhaps as a form of penance. It's always there, even when it's targeted at women and girls in general – **liars, all of them** – rather than at her and Bee specifically. Before she knows it an hour has passed, then two. Her bath is tepid, forgotten.

The thud of something landing on her doormat snaps her out of it. She enters the hallway, shivering, to pick up the morning's post. Her stomach see-saws. It's a single item, a brown padded envelope that's been excessively stamped and redirected from her agent's two days ago.

For a moment she stares at it, faintly aware that the hairs on her arms are rising to stand on end. The telltale rows of stamps, stuck down by someone who has guessed at the postage, but wants to make sure the package gets to her. It will not have been opened by anyone at the agency; Erin stipulates that none of her 'fan' mail is screened. It is simply forwarded.

She picks it up, feeling the bulky weight of it, and brings it to the kitchen. It's so heavily taped she can't get into it without cutting it. She picks up the knife she'd not long put down. When she finally scores a slit in the end the smell is instant and overwhelming. A stench of meaty decay.

She gags and drops the parcel on the floor, sidestepping a splash of thin pink liquid that escapes from the opening. As she bends to look inside, the memory of Aidan flashes into her head. *Disco rice.* She could never understand his inclination to look at awful things.

Now Erin's the one who always looks. She doesn't know why. She looks every time.

Today it is an entire tongue, pierced with several pins and nails, and wrapped in greaseproof paper. Pale pink and cleanly sliced out, fresh from a butcher's some days ago.

It's not fresh now.

Erin runs to the sink and heaves.

6

AUGUST 1990

Erin is in the garden, waist-deep in a brand-new paddling pool her dad brought home yesterday. It's huge, almost half the size of the lawn, and she has taken care when getting in and out to prevent grass and dirt being transferred into it. It took hours to fill and, with the threat of a hosepipe ban looming, she's been warned that they may not be able to refill it if it's emptied. Later, the day will go on record as one of the year's hottest.

A half-read *Malory Towers* paperback is on the grass next to her. The kitchen radio is outside on the windowsill, and a song Erin likes by Suzanne Vega is playing. In the shade of a pear tree that rarely bears fruit, her mother sits on a deckchair, scraping new potatoes over a bowl of muddy water. Erin gazes up at the sky. It's cloudless, marked only by white trails left in the wake of planes. The sight of them reminds her of Aidan. Two days ago he left for a week in Zante with his mum, aunt and cousins. Erin's never seen him so excited for anything before. Aidan's mum saved for months to give them this holiday, and it's the first time he's been on a plane. He's also happy that his stepdad, Gavin, refuses to travel abroad and eat 'that foreign crap' and is therefore staying behind.

Aidan's okay now, following a trip to A & E. He didn't recall being stung and had no idea he was allergic. Neither he nor Erin remembered seeing or hearing a bee or wasp before his face swelled up, although the little black stinger found in his thumb told a different story. In the end, the doctor's explanation that Aidan's hand could have come in contact with a dead bee as he'd rummaged down the side of the old sofa last week was the only one that made sense.

Erin had not known that bees could still sting after they were dead.

They never told about the dirty magazine, or Donnie.

Erin hums along to 'Tom's Diner'. She and her friend Jess have been making up a dance to it. If Jess were here they'd be practising it on the grass, mucking about and splashing each other. But Jess is in Southend today with another friend from her horse-riding club. Erin wishes she were in Southend, or Zante. Sunshine and paddling pools aren't as fun when there's no one to share them with. The song ends and adverts come on, and above it a sharp rapping sound lances through the open windows of the house. Someone's at the front door.

'Probably Avon.' Her mum drops the paring knife into the bowl and goes to answer it. Erin slides under the water, counting how long she can hold her breath for. She makes it to forty-seven seconds before she bursts up, gasping. As she clears water from her eyes she's aware of someone standing close to the pool, blocking out the sun.

'Who was it?' she asks, reaching for the towel to wipe her face.

'It was me,' says Bee.

Erin's eyes snap open and sting as water and sun lotion run into them. 'What are you doing here?'

'Erin,' her mum chides. 'That's not polite.' She holds something out to Bee. It's one of Erin's swimming costumes. 'Go and put that on, love. Then you can cool down in the pool.'

Bee takes it silently and goes indoors to get changed.

'Why's she here?' Erin demands.

Her mother frowns. 'Her mum asked if I could watch her for a couple of hours. She had to go out.'

'Where?'

'I don't know, I didn't ask.' Her mother presses a finger to her lips and motions to the open windows. Erin doesn't care. She's fuming at the thought of Bee's scabby legs in her lovely new pool. She's still scowling when Bee emerges from the house. The swimming costume is slightly too big on her, and Erin's mum fusses and knots the straps to make it fit better.

'Have you got sun lotion on, sweetheart?' she asks.

Bee shakes her head, and Erin's mum diligently applies it. 'You're *very* good,' she tells her. 'Erin always wriggles away.' Bee giggles, standing perfectly still even as it's being rubbed into her scaly legs. 'Don't worry, it's for sensitive skin,' Erin's mum murmurs. She nods to a yellow bruise on Bee's arm. 'That's a whopper. And these.' She examines four purple dots above Bee's wrist. 'You've been in the wars! How did you get them?'

Bee shrugs, her smile fading. She slips her hand into Erin's mum's.

'Erin's a bit of a bruiser as well, aren't you?' her mum says lightly, but Erin can tell from the set of her mouth that something's not right.

'Not really,' Erin mutters, bristling at the sight of Bee holding her mum's hand. It gives way to reluctant sympathy. The purple dots on Bee's pasty skin look like they were made by fingertips pressing in, hard. Her sympathy vanishes as, without warning, Bee makes a run and leaps into the pool with a massive splash.

'God's sake!' Erin shrieks. 'You've brought a load of dirt and grass in now!'

'Erin!' her mum warns.

'*What?*'

'Sorry,' Bee says quietly. 'I didn't mean to.'

Erin huffs, dries her hands and leans over the rubbery side of the pool, picking up her book pointedly. For a few minutes she pretends to read but she's too wound up to take in the words. The radio is playing 'Killer' by Adamski. Her mum returns to the spuds and Bee leans back in the water, trying unsuccessfully to float. Erin ignores her for a few minutes more before relenting and putting the book down.

'It's easier if you lean your head right back in the water. That way your bum won't sink. Look, like this.' Within a few minutes Bee is doing much better and managing to stay up longer. Erin's mother gives her an approving nod.

'I like this pool,' Bee says. 'Was it a present?'

'Not really,' Erin replies. 'Dad just got it because it's so hot.'

Bee stares at her. 'Not a birthday present?'

'No, my birthday's next month.' Erin scoops up water and trickles it through her fingers. 'He just knew I'd like it.'

A dark look crosses Bee's face. Erin blinks, startled, but it's gone.

'My birthday's October the third,' says Bee. 'Are we the same star sign?'

Erin shrugs. She doesn't want to be the same anything as Bee.

'Let's see how long we can hold our breath,' says Bee. 'Like you were when I got here.'

They take it in turns to time each other, and Erin starts to enjoy it; mainly because she is better. Once or twice she comes up a few seconds early to give Bee a chance, but she is still unable to beat Erin. Erin senses Bee is getting frustrated.

'Let's do something else,' she says, breathless now. The phone has started ringing and her mum nips indoors to answer it.

'One more go,' Bee says obstinately. She glances at the window, and something about that glance makes Erin uneasy. 'You first.'

'Okay,' she says, edging further away. She takes a breath and submerges, suspecting that Bee's going to wait for her to begin to surface and then hold her under. *Let her try*, Erin thinks.

Erin is bigger, stronger, more confident in the water. She makes it to twenty, still going strong when a rush of warmth hits her face. Before she even surfaces, she knows.

Bee is standing right next to her. The water around her is tinged a cloudy yellow, and there's a sour little smile on her face.

'You filthy cow!' Erin leaps out of the pool and shoves Bee, hard. She vanishes under the water and comes up, spluttering, just as Erin's mum returns.

'Erin… pushed me,' she gasps, from under her hair which is plastered across her face.

'She peed in the pool!' Erin roars. She grabs the garden hose and starts rinsing herself off. 'She stood right by my face and did it when I was under!'

Dismay flashes over Erin's mum's face. 'Why did you do that, Bee? There's a downstairs loo just by the back door.'

Bee sniffles. 'I didn't think it mattered. It's only like weeing in the bath or sea, isn't it?'

'It's not very nice, love. Don't do that again, please.'

Bee eyeballs Erin, her face twisting. She appears oddly unsettled by the sight of Erin hosing herself down. Erin glowers back, dearly tempted to spray her, but not daring to.

There's no way she's getting back in the pool. When her mum suggests they go up to her bedroom, Erin shakes her head. She doesn't want Bee in her room, around her things. Her mum doesn't push it. Instead she sighs and fetches her purse, taking out a couple of pounds.

'Here. Get dried and dressed and you can go and get ice creams, I heard the van just now. Maybe go to the park for an hour?'

Erin takes the money, glad of the opportunity to get Bee out of her home.

They eat the ice creams on the swings, slurping them quickly as they start to drip in the heat. The park is quiet. It's too hot for ball games or dog walkers, and the grass is bleached yellow and scratchy. A couple with a pair of toddlers have set up a picnic blanket in some shade, but the toddlers are wailing and they're starting to pack up already. Sweat trickles down the back of Erin's neck, and Bee's pasty skin is starting to look blotchy, the only bit of colour about her save the purple and yellow bruises.

Aside from telling the ice-cream vendor which flavour they wanted, they've not spoken a word since leaving the house. Erin has her eye firmly on her purple Pop Swatch. There's an hour to kill. One hour, then Bee will go home. Erin's dad will have finished work by now, and he'll be in the pub having a cold pint or two. He's promised to do a barbecue this evening, and Erin's already looking forward to it.

Bee crams the last of her ice cream in her mouth, then gazes longingly at Erin's. Erin nibbles at her cone, deliberately making it last. She senses Bee's about to say something and wonders if it'll be an apology.

'Your mum's nice,' Bee says eventually. 'And your dad.'

Erin's confused. 'You never saw my dad.'

'He got you that pool.' A pause. 'Is Aidan's mum nice?'

'Yeah, she's all right,' Erin answers. 'His stepdad's a pig, though.' She regrets saying it instantly as Bee's face lights up with interest.

'Why?'

'You'll have to ask Aidan,' Erin mutters. Aidan hates Gavin and his drinking, but she isn't going to blab his business to Bee.

'Let's go in there again.' Bee points to the fenced-off corner of the field, where the old sofa was.

'No,' Erin says curtly, not wishing to repeat the experience they had last time. But Bee's already walking towards it.

'There might be new stuff. Treasure!'

Erin remains on the swing, watching stubbornly as Bee heads

over there. And because Bee's mother has left her with Erin and her family, Erin feels responsible for her. She swears under her breath and follows.

The sofa is still there, faded and baking in the sun. The bushes are more overgrown than ever, and once they're through the fence it's obvious there's nothing much that's new. Still, Bee insists on investigating, poking around under bushes with a stick. Erin suspects she's looking for the remains of the rat she killed, but it'll be long gone.

'Come on,' she says. She's uneasy being here alone with Bee, and the heat and insects are making her irritable. To her surprise, Bee drops the stick and returns to the fence. Erin's about to go through but the sound of feet pounding over the grass stops her. She catches sight of Nicky Pemberton, moving at speed across the field.

'Crap,' she whispers. For a moment it looks like he's heading straight for them. He's wearing ripped blue jeans and dirty white trainers, but his chest is bare and slicked with sweat. He's clutching a balled-up West Ham shirt as he runs.

Erin shrinks back. On his own, Nicky isn't a threat. But the thing about Nicky is that he's rarely alone. A couple of months ago he got beaten up by a gang of kids, and since then he's sought any protection he can get. That's how he's ended up with Donnie's crew.

Erin releases a held breath when he passes. They hear his ragged breathing and see him glancing over his shoulder, wide-eyed. Fearful. Erin surveys the field behind him but it's empty. Even the people with the toddlers have gone.

'Who's he running from?' Bee asks.

Erin doesn't answer. She's watching Nicky stoop to pick up something he's dropped, and hurriedly stash it back under the screwed-up shirt. 'He's got something,' she murmurs.

'Let's follow him.' Bee pushes past her.

'No,' Erin protests, but Bee climbs through to the field. Erin squeezes after her in time to see Nicky enter the neighbouring cornfield.

'He's up to something,' says Bee. 'Let's spy.'

'I'm not allowed past this field,' Erin says. 'I told you last time.'

'I won't tell if you won't.' Bee cranes her neck, trying to keep Nicky in sight. 'It'll take five minutes. We'll see what he's doing and come straight back.'

Erin shakes her head. If her parents find out she's gone beyond the playing field, she'll be grounded.

'Fine.' Bee shrugs. 'I'll go. You wait here.'

'Fine.' Erin stalks off to the swings, confident Bee won't have the nerve. But when she turns she's shocked to see Bee's almost at the cornfield. Then without a backwards glance she's gone.

'*Little cow,*' Erin exclaims. She jogs to the cornfield, tummy turning somersaults. A quick look over her shoulder confirms no one's around, but she's still afraid someone will see and tell her parents. But apart from warnings to stay out of the cornfield, Erin's always been told to stick with her friends. And a tiny part of her is curious about what Nicky Pemberton's up to. She steps into the swaying corn.

'Knew you'd come,' says Bee, emerging a couple of metres ahead.

'Had to, didn't I?' Erin answers hotly. There's no point trying to persuade Bee to turn round; she won't.

'He went that way.' Bee points to the woods. 'If we're quick we'll catch him up.'

They move left through a track in the corn. Soon they're at the edge of the woods and there's no sign of Nicky. Momentarily Erin is relieved. But then Bee spots a clearing signalling a path of sorts. They head for it and step into the woods. After the blistering heat of the sun the cool shade is welcome. Erin relaxes a fraction. The woods aren't vast, and the cornfield's easy to find again provided they don't stray far from the path.

'I think we've lost him,' she says.

Bee shakes her head and nods through the trees. 'He's there.'

Erin glimpses bare flesh between the foliage and feels a jolt of surprise. He's closer than she was expecting, and he's slowed down. The two girls creep nearer, trying to stay quiet, but Nicky's oblivious. He stops by a stained mattress, surrounded by charred trees. Last summer there was a fire in these woods, started deliberately, which damaged this part of it. It's one of the reasons – as well as stranger danger – that Erin's not supposed to come here.

Nicky turns in a slow circle, looking for something. Erin and Bee are as close as they can get without being seen. They crouch behind a tree and watch.

Nicky locates what he's looking for: a tree a few feet from the mattress. A thin rope hangs from its branches above an old tyre on the ground, the remnants of a swing. He takes out the item he dropped. It's a brown wallet. He opens it, thumbing a wad of cash, then tucks it into a hollow in the tree trunk. It's stolen, Erin realises. Why else would he stash it there?

When he withdraws his hand there's something else in it: crumpled pages. Even from where they sit hidden, Erin recognises it. It's the magazine from down the side of the dumped sofa. Nicky checks his watch, glancing around. Confident he's alone, he kneels on the mattress, opens the magazine and unzips his jeans.

Instantly Erin is uncomfortable. She doesn't know what Nicky is doing, but she knows it's linked to the pictures and that the way he's touching himself now must be something sexual and private.

'We need to go,' she whispers.

Bee's eyes are fixed on Nicky. She's got the same eerie, blank expression she had when they first found the magazine, and it further unnerves Erin, along with the strange moaning noises Nicky's starting to make. She wishes they hadn't followed. To her surprise Bee gets up without any resistance. Quietly they turn to leave – and freeze.

Donnie is leaning against a blackened tree a few feet away. He steps towards them.

'What's this, then?'

Neither of them answers. They're both rooted to the spot. Heavy footsteps sound behind them. Donnie's voice has alerted Nicky that he's not alone. He hurries towards them zipping his flies, red-faced, but the zip is caught on his boxer shorts. They have Bart Simpson on them and are faded and garish. The magazine is splayed open on the mattress.

'I said, what's this?' Donnie repeats, gesturing to the girls, then Nicky. 'Did you know you had company, Nick?'

Nicky shakes his head, staring at the ground.

'I remember you,' Donnie says, staring at Bee. 'The porno kids. Did you want your magazine back?' He laughs harshly, and a bird flaps from a nearby tree.

'It – it's not ours,' Erin says, hating how reedy her voice sounds. 'We were just going.' She takes a step but so does Donnie, blocking her path. Her instincts are kicking in, reminding her of the unease she felt in his presence last time. The wrongness of him.

'No, you weren't.' Donnie smirks. 'You were spying on Nicky. Having a good old bog at him having a wank. Did you like that?'

Again, neither girl answers.

Donnie stops smirking, and the transformation as his face hardens is instant and terrifying. 'See, my problem is what you saw before that.'

'We didn't see anything,' says Erin.

'We don't like liars, do we Nicky?' Donnie says softly. 'And we don't like nosy little cunts like you.'

Nicky shakes his head, watching Donnie with something halfway between respect and fear.

'We won't say anything,' Erin whispers. She risks a glimpse at Bee, who is still blank-faced. If Erin runs, can Bee keep up? Could they even run fast enough? 'We won't tell.'

'Good,' says Donnie. 'Because you know what happens to little bitches who don't keep their mouths shut? We can make them disappear.'

'Disappear,' Nicky repeats, happy to be part of this team with Donnie. To have him onside. 'Yeah.'

'So if anyone comes to us about that wallet,' Donnie goes on, 'we'll find you. Both of you. And no one will ever see you again.'

Erin's eyes sting with unshed tears at the horror of what she's hearing, but Donnie isn't finished.

'See, Nicky and me, we're mates. I do things for him, he does things for me. If I told him to chop the pair of you up he'd do it, no questions asked. Then we'd get rid of all the pieces, put them down fox holes and badger setts and you'd be eaten. Or I could just burn down the woods again, but this time with you in them.'

Erin reaches for Bee's hand and curls her fingers around it. Ever so slightly, Bee squeezes back. Though neither of them knows it, this moment is the closest they'll ever get to being friends. Erin is openly crying now. She faces Nicky, willing him to take a stand against Donnie, to reassure them he's only messing with them, but if anything Nicky seems buoyed up by all the talk of 'we' and 'mates'. He will never challenge Donnie, even if there is a trace of desperation about him now, beneath the camaraderie. Even if this friendship means terrorising a couple of kids. Erin wonders briefly whether on some level he is enjoying this sense of power, as someone who has been on the receiving end of other people's all his life. Suddenly she fears him for this as much as she does Donnie.

'Perhaps we should do that anyway.' Donnie's taken out a lighter. He starts flicking it repeatedly into life. *Flick.* 'So you never get the chance to grass.' *Flick.*

'We won't tell,' Erin repeats, her voice jerky between sobs. *Flick*. 'Will we, Bee?'

Bee says nothing, does nothing. Erin makes a decision: if she can't save them both maybe can save herself. In the end it comes down to survival.

She releases Bee's hand and runs.

'You're fucking dead!' Donnie yells.

Feet pound the earth behind her, but Erin doesn't stop. She thrashes through bone-dry leaf mulch, leaps over jutting roots, seeking out the path to the cornfield. There, at least, even if she can't outrun Donnie or Nicky, she has a chance to hide. She's half-wheezing, half-sobbing now, but the cornfield's in sight. She just needs one last push to speed up, to lose them—

'Erin!' Bee gasps behind her.

Erin whirls; shocked, guilty, relieved. She threw Bee to the wolves, but somehow they've both made it out of the woods and now they're stumbling through the cornfield, back to safety. 'Wait,' she pants, and they duck down between the golden eaves. They stay there for a minute, maybe two, getting their breath back and listening for Donnie and Nicky. There's nothing. Perhaps they're still in the woods or have made their way out by another route. Or perhaps they are quietly sneaking up on them.

A shout rings through the air, but this time it's the sound of children nearby.

'Come on.' Erin tugs Bee's arm and they scramble through to the playing field where a bunch of kids have turned up with water guns and are soaking each other. She and Bee sprint across the field, soon breathless once more with the heat. As they draw level with the kids on the other side Erin finally stops crying. There's no sign of Donnie or Nicky. Even if there was, there's nothing they could do in plain sight.

'You're not going to tell, are you, Bee?' she asks, as they head in the direction of home. 'Because we weren't supposed to be in the woods, and if we do, he said—'

'You *wanted* to tell before.'

'I know,' Erin whispers. 'But this time it's different. He'll hurt us if we do.'

'He'll hurt us if we don't next time.'

Next time. Bee has a point. In both encounters Donnie has crossed the line, but today was worse. They can probably avoid him to an extent, but they can't avoid him for ever.

'That's what happens when you don't tell.' Bee is speaking in a sing-song way that creeps Erin out. 'It gets worse.'

Erin stares at her. 'You're saying we *should*?'

'Do you want them to get away with it?'

'No. But if we tell, we can't prove they nicked that wallet. They've probably taken the money and dumped it by now. And all the other stuff he said about chopping us up and... and burning down the woods, they'll just say they didn't, or that they were messing around—'

'I know how we could get them back. We wouldn't get in trouble. And they'll be the ones who're scared to walk around because everyone will hate them. We don't need proof.'

'How?'

'Listen.' Bee's eyes gleam murkily, like a pond with unknowable things beneath the surface. 'This is what we can say.'

Erin stops walking. 'What we can *say*? You mean, make something up?'

'Most of it will be true.'

Erin doesn't get it. How can they be believed for something that isn't the truth, when they can't prove the things that are? But then Bee starts to talk, and the lie begins to take shape. And she sees what Bee means. Most of what they will say is already there, already true. It's just a couple of bits in the middle that they have to invent. The bits that will do the damage. The bits so horrible no one will imagine two little girls have made them up.

'But I don't want people thinking that happened to me,' says

Erin. She remembers hearing about a kid at school who was 'interfered with' by his uncle. Nothing was ever proven, but the uncle was shunned after that. Everyone talked about the poor kid, too.

'Say it happened to me, then,' Bee urges. 'We'll say they did it to me, but we got away before they could do it to you.'

Erin hesitates. 'It could just be you that says it. Say you followed Nicky, and I stayed on the swings—'

'No. You as well.' Bee's voice is flat. 'It has to be both of us.' Then, more softly she says, 'They'll believe you.'

When Erin thinks back, she's always scratching around for a recollection of her putting up a stronger fight. But the truth is, she hadn't. All she remembers is the terror and helplessness she'd been made to feel, and the burning desire for revenge. To make them pay.

So they go to Erin's, and they tell her mum about following Nicky to the woods. About the wallet, the dirty magazine, Nicky touching himself. The arrival of Donnie, his question – *You got pubes, yet? Nicky wants to know.* (A deviation to the sequence of events, but still true.) The promises of Nicky doing Donnie's bidding.

And the lie: Nicky *doing* Donnie's bidding. Making Bee do things from the magazine. Saying Erin will be next.

Donnie laughing. *Nicky the nonce. Paedo-Pemberton.*

The threats to chop them up and burn them in the woods if they breathe a word.

They even describe Nicky's faded Bart Simpson underwear.

By the time they finish Erin's mother is hysterical. When she rings the pub, asking the landlord to put Erin's dad on, she can barely get the words out. But somehow she does, and by then, Erin's hysterical, too. From the chaos and the enormity of it, and from the way her mum is tearing at her hair and pleading: *'Don't, Chris. Please! No, don't! Just come home now, and we'll... Chris? CHRIS?'*

'What's he going to do, Mum?'

Erin is wailing now, tugging her mum's arm as the phone receiver falls from her hand. *'What's Dad going to do?'*

Erin's mum doesn't answer.

7

SEPTEMBER 2016

THE TONGUE MOST LIKELY CAME from an ox. It's not always a tongue. In the past, Erin has been sent kidneys, liver, and a heart. All of them pierced, almost obsessively, with nails or pins or both. It's not always meat, either. Frequently it's dog shit, scraped up with blades of grass still stuck to it. There have been dead bees. Sometimes it is a handful of black feathers knotted into a length of cord – an old folk magic curse known as a witch's ladder.

The postmark is smudged, but it looks like the envelope was originally mailed in Bristol. She keeps a list of the places she's been able to discern – Cardiff, Stockport, Colchester, Margate. There seems to be no regularity, they arrive from all over. Despite this, Erin believes they are from the same person. Last year a live bee in a matchbox was posted from Gatwick airport. Erin had managed to release it while it was still alive.

It had started shortly after she signed with her agent and got her first book deal. A bunch of flowers from her publisher had arrived on the day the book came out. A week after, she received a padded envelope from her agent with a copy of her book and a compliment slip with a dubious note:

We weren't sure whether to forward this – it seems you have a mad fan?

The book had been defaced with a black marker pen. The author's name and title on the front had been scored through, leaving only Erin's name as the illustrator. The same on the inside. All the text was obliterated except for three letters in random words on random pages: *B,E,E*.

The sender wouldn't have known that the agency would screen Erin's mail. She hadn't known it herself. She'd gone back in an email and invented a fictitious, bitter ex, asking for all future correspondence to be forwarded without opening. Since then the sender has grown bolder, and the items worse.

Erin double bags the tongue and envelope in black bin liners and takes them outside to dispose of.

When she comes back indoors there's another text from her mum.

If I don't hear from you by lunchtime I'm getting on a train.

It's now twenty past nine. She doesn't have to call her mum yet. She could wait until she really must, but the thought of stringing it out is worse. She can't have her mother coming here. Can't look her in the eye. It's always been hard enough to talk to her about this. Harder to *not* talk about it. Trying to pretend they're a normal family when calling out things like, 'How many roast spuds do you want?' or '*Robin Hood*'s on later. Yep, the one with Alan Rickman,' when all the while there's this thing that's set in like rot. Erin's mother has always assured her she forgives her. Forgiveness she knows she doesn't deserve.

Best to get it over with. She makes the call. It's answered on the second ring.

'About bloody time.'

Erin hears a thin crackle. She pictures her mum in her high-backed armchair, folding her newspaper and putting it to one side. She can hear the TV blaring because her mum has it up so loud.

'Sorry.' It's all she says, but her voice sounds tinny, snagging on the second syllable.

'Erin?' She hears her mother's breath catch, imagines her sitting up straighter. The TV sound cuts out as the set is switched off. 'Are you… have you been drinking?'

'No.' Erin clears her throat. It's a fair question. It wouldn't be the first time her mum has caught her out, drunk before midday. It's not that she doesn't feel the lure of the bottle any more – she does – but it's rare she'll allow herself the luxury of drinking into oblivion. Erin's not an alcoholic but she could easily be, if fear didn't keep her anchored. Drink makes her lose control, and self-control is a tether she needs.

'I'm not drunk. Promise.'

'Oh.' Her mum hesitates. 'Well, good. I thought you might've… I mean with the news and everything. Are you eating? Have you had breakfast? Dinner last night?'

'Yeah,' Erin says, vaguely recalling two spoons of lemon curd straight from the jar. She closes her eyes. 'God, Mum. It's everywhere.'

'I know, love,' her mum says, her voice softening.

'What am I going to do?' Erin whispers. 'What if it leads back to me?'

'It won't.'

'How do you know?' Her voice rises, and she tries to bring it back down. She prays her mum's right. Mums are always right, aren't they? 'Now they've released it about Bee being Child B, everyone's going to start asking who Child A is. *Again*. And people *knew*, Mum. All the locals knew it was us.'

'No one's allowed to identify you,' her mum says. 'It makes sense for them to release the link to Bee, because it might crack the case. I'm surprised it took them this long, to be honest. But there's no reason for them to name you. And you can't be traced anyway. Different name, different area.'

They wouldn't need a name, Erin thinks. There are other ways to identify her.

The girl with the weird eyes.

'Half the people who lived on that estate are probably dead now, anyway,' her mum adds optimistically. 'Or senile.'

Erin knows that 'half' is pushing it. Her mother was in her forties when Nicky Pemberton was killed. She's in her early seventies now and her own memory is sharp as a blade. Erin pinches the bridge of her nose, feeling a dull ache coming on behind her eyes. God, she wants a drink. 'Maybe some of the older ones,' she says. 'But their kids will be my age, or thereabouts—'

'And they'll have their own worries,' her mum says. 'Elderly parents like me, kids of their own. Kids who tell lies, just like you did.'

Erin doesn't answer. There are lies, and then there are evil lies.

They change the subject for a few minutes, and chat about other things: Erin's illustration work, the picture book idea, when she'll next go to visit. Her mum asks, somewhat hopefully, if her ex, Amir, has been in touch. Erin answers truthfully that he hasn't, although she thinks he might contact her soon. Amir's one of the only people outside her family who knows the truth about her. Now her mum's mentioned him she has an overwhelming urge to hear his voice. She wants the comfort of someone that cares not because they have to, but because they want to.

She pictures him in the print studio. The whir of machines in the background, the click of his computer mouse as he designs graphics for packaging or posters. Maybe he's googling the news, catching up with how bad it really is. She could call him. He'd offer to come over, she knows this. If she says yes, he'll arrive in forty minutes flat. They'll talk for a bit and then end up having sex, right there in her dirty kitchen. Afterwards he'll make tea. While the kettle boils he'll wash the cups and plates that have sat in the sink since yesterday. They'll drink the tea, and she'll probably need to remind him that he's left his wedding ring on the shelf above the sink. She pushes the thought of him away. It's best for them both if she doesn't sleep with her married ex.

The conversation winds to a close with Erin promising to keep her 'head down' and her 'chin up'. Her mum assures her it'll all blow over, and life will go on. That, after all this time, it's unlikely anything new will be dug up, and Bee's murder will fade away once again. Erin tells her mum she loves her and her mum responds with, 'You, too,' because even though she does love her, she's from a generation that rarely says it.

They're on the verge of saying goodbye when her mother springs the question.

'Who do you think killed her, Erin?'

As always, Erin feels the back of her neck prickle as the tiny hairs there rise up.

As always, the question feels like a trap.

'I don't know, Mum. I only know the same as everyone else.'

There's a brief, unsettling silence at the other end before her mum speaks again.

'But you were there.'

Part Two

Thou shalt not suffer a witch to live
— Exodus 22:18

8

OCTOBER 1996

KITTY IS DRIVING LIKE A maniac. Not because someone's chasing them, or because they're late – which they are – but because it's apparently how she always drives. The Mini Cooper hares round another bend. Erin hears a sliding noise and a grunt from behind, and guesses that Mira is fending off Kitty's suitcase for the umpteenth time.

Kitty doesn't seem to notice. Instead she flicks a black corkscrew curl out of her eyes and points vaguely at Erin's lap.

'What's the cut-off time again?'

With one hand Erin lifts a rumpled sheaf of papers. Her other hand grips the side of the seat, slippery with sweat. Reluctantly she lets go, flicking past the road map to a list of tide times. She finds the date: 12 October. 'Ten twenty-seven,' she says. It's the third time Kitty's asked.

'Ten twenty-seven,' Kitty repeats. 'Precise, isn't it?' She glances at the clock on the dashboard. 'Twenty minutes. We'll make it.'

Erin stares out of the window, wondering how that can be true. Damp countryside whizzes past, and the car cuts through a carpet of leaves on the road, throwing them into the air like confetti. They don't appear to be anywhere near where they're supposed to be.

'It's a long wait if we miss it,' Erin says. 'The next low tide—'

'Is in eight hours,' Kitty interrupts. 'I know. Well, there's

67

nothing to do around here.' She grins. 'But we could be in Southend in an hour. London in two – there's this neat little boutique in Covent Garden.'

If anyone knows about boutiques, it's Kitty. Her mother has one in Brentwood, and Kitty is a walking advertisement for it. Even now, hunched over the steering wheel in the tiny car, she looks like she's stepped off a sixties catwalk. Drainpipe jeans, huge fluffy fake fur jacket, and beige boots up to her knees. Add this to her Californian accent, and it's easy to forget who and where you are with Kitty. Well, almost. Erin looks down at her own faded leggings and paint-speckled Doc Martens, and it feels like the sun has gone behind a cloud.

'Do you think the others are there yet?'

From the back seat, Mira's heavily accented voice is so soft that Erin barely hears it over the music. Kitty lowers the radio volume and Mira repeats the question.

'They must be,' Kitty says. 'They left early enough.' Erin hears the smugness in her voice and knows she's thinking of the extra hour in bed the three of them gained. Though, for Kitty, it was an hour and a half. Erin had been shivering on her doorstep for fifteen minutes with her backpack and a sense of dread both growing steadily heavier by the time Kitty arrived. Mira, too, wore the expression of a lost child when they finally reached her. Like Erin, she probably thought she'd been left behind. Like Erin, she got no apology, just a breezy, 'I overslept.' And both of them were too polite, too *grateful*, to say anything.

'Thanks again for the lift,' Erin says.

Kitty shrugs. 'Thanks for the company. Like I said, I get car sick if I'm not the driver.'

'Is anyone else taking their own car?' asks Mira.

'I heard Preston is. He was on some family ski trip over half term and it meant them getting back in the early hours. Everyone else is on the minibuses.' Kitty smirks. 'All squashed up and breathing in each other's farts.'

Even Mira sniggers at this.

'There are definitely other girls going though, right?' she asks, solemn again like she thinks the other two know something she doesn't.

'Yeah,' Erin tells her. 'Do you know any of them, Kitty?'

'Only that they're the boring ones.'

Her words send a little shiver of pleasure through Erin. Kitty thinks she isn't boring. Or at any rate, *less* boring than the others. It's a start. Erin has sat with Kitty in the canteen a few times over the past term and in class once or twice, but Kitty hangs round with another glamorous girl, Clair, who's missing the trip due to illness. Now Erin has a chance to prove to Kitty that she made the right choice in asking her along for the drive. A chance to make a real friend of her.

Mira relaxes. 'Good. I mean…'

Erin glances over her shoulder. Mira's dark eyes are apologetic. 'It's just, my parents wouldn't like it if…'

'Over-protective, huh?' Kitty's voice jolts as they go over a bump.

'Yes,' Mira replies. In the few conversations Erin has had with her in class, she's learned that she is originally from Romania and came to the UK when she was fourteen. She's a serious, intelligent girl who's always struck Erin as quiet – even quieter than she is. She's surprised Kitty asked either of them along for the ride.

'Well, your parents aren't here now,' Kitty says. 'And what they don't know can't hurt them.'

Mira looks confused. 'What do you mean?'

'Oh, come on. It's half the reason anyone comes on these trips.' When Mira still doesn't respond Kitty wiggles her eyebrows in the rear mirror. 'Hanky-panky.'

'Hanky-panky?' Mira echoes. The words sound strange coming from her and Erin wonders whether she's unfamiliar with the term or if the thought genuinely never occurred to her.

'Yeah. People always hook up on these things.'

Clearly Mira's starting to click on because she's looking really worried now. Erin wants to laugh.

'It's true,' Kitty goes on. 'I bet you both now that at least a quarter of us get laid. It's just a matter of who gets it on with who.'

The thought – the sheer *possibility* – of it brings a face to Erin's mind and heat rushing into her cheeks. The fact that there are so many boys on the trip in the first place is a happy coincidence, for the girls on the Psychology A level course outnumber them three to one. But some bright spark at the college came up with the idea of combining the trip with the History group, since what's on the island fits both modules. *Thank you, bright spark,* Erin thinks. She glances at the map again and tells Kitty to take the next left.

Kitty swerves out of the narrow lane. Erin wants to remind her that in England people drive on the left side of the road, but last time she said it Kitty got narked because apparently she took her lessons and her test here after moving from the States.

Kitty lifts her nose and sniffs. 'Smell that?'

Erin inhales dubiously. 'What?'

Kitty lowers the window and cold air blasts in. Erin smells it then, a salty sharp smell that makes her think of fish and chips and melting ice cream.

'The sea,' says Mira.

Kitty whoops. 'We're close.'

After a stretch of farmland another turn puts them on a dirt track, forcing her to slow down. It's like driving through a junk yard; surrounded by old tyres, scrap metal and a few dingy caravans either side of the road.

Kitty hums the theme tune from *Deliverance*. 'Creepy,' she mutters, and Erin agrees, although they're barely an hour from home. They haven't even left the county. Kitty zooms onward, pulling up before a wide wooden gate. An electronic key code box is fixed to a post.

'What's the number?'

Erin reads it out and Kitty punches it in. The gate swings open and they drive through, bumping over more uneven track. The salty smell grows stronger and gulls cry above. The track twists through untamed greenery, then inclines on to a narrow ridge. Kitty shoots up it, pausing on the brow. A thick sea wall trails away either side of them and ahead, a craggy road unfurls into the distance, stretching into low cloud. The only hint of what's at the other end is a faint smudge on the horizon.

'This is it.' Mira's breath tickles Erin's ear as she leans forward for a better look. 'The Devil's Path.'

Kitty laughs. 'Holy shit. This is *awesome*.'

Erin stays quiet. She doesn't think it's awesome. The road looks like something out of a horror film. And they're the idiots about to cross it.

A sign fixed to the sea wall says: DANGER! CAUSEWAY ACCESSIBLE AT LOW TIDE ONLY. Erin doesn't get to read the rest because Kitty nudges the car forward.

It's then that Erin is gripped by a sudden, irrational certainty that if they cross the causeway something terrible is going to happen.

'Wait,' she croaks.

Kitty barely pauses. 'What?'

Erin clutches the map and tide times too tightly, creasing them. Out of nowhere her skin is clammy. 'The causeway's nearly a mile long – it says we should allow ten or fifteen minutes to cross it.' She glances at the clock. 'We've got eight minutes. The water's going to start coming in.'

'Chill,' says Kitty. 'We'll make it.' The radio, which is playing 'Stupid Girl' by Garbage, starts to crackle and cut out. There's a tape sticking out of the car's cassette player and Kitty pushes it in, making a face as a seventies rock song starts playing.

'Ugh, sorry. It's my mom's tape.'

'Kitty, maybe we should—'

It's too late. She's off, and Erin resumes her death grip on the edge of the seat. Too soon, they are on the causeway. Within seconds it's obvious they've made a mistake. There are so many potholes the car is bouncing like a kangaroo on a trampoline. There's no way Kitty can keep up her usual breakneck speed – it'll be a slow crawl across to the island. A crawl they don't have time for.

'We should've waited,' Erin says, trying to keep the fear out of her voice. 'We're not going to make it.'

Kitty snorts. 'Will you relax? We're on it now. I can't turn around.'

Erin keeps quiet. The causeway is narrow but there are a handful of passing points where it's been widened to let cars wait while those coming in the other direction go by. There *has* to be space enough for her to turn, surely? Erin searches along the road, but it's too twisty to see properly. 'I can't believe this is seriously the only way on and off,' she mutters. She does not trust this thing, this *tentacle* of a road that emerges from water twice a day like some lopped-off part of Essex's answer to the Loch Ness monster. It appears, according to the info pack, at low tide for four hours in every twelve, giving visitors a short window to cross.

'There's a river taxi,' Mira volunteers. 'For the staff, I think, but even that has to be pre-booked and it's forty quid each way.' Her voice judders with the movement of the car. 'I read the causeway was built by the Romans.'

Kitty grits her teeth. 'No kidding. It doesn't seem to have had any maintenance since then, either.' She winces as gravel flicks up at the windows. 'My mom will go ape shit if I get any more scratches on this car.'

She doesn't sound *that* bothered. In the next breath she's singing along with the stereo, belting out 'Highway to Hell' at the top of her lungs. Erin wants to join in, just like she'd imagined she would all week, but she's too tense and the bumpiness is making her queasy. She stares out of the window, trying to focus on something stationary. Barnacle-crusted black rocks line either side of the road, seaweed perched on top like ugly wigs. Water gathers on the mudflats beyond the road. Then her heart leaps.

'There. Look!' She points. 'A passing point. We should turn round.'

'It's fine.' Kitty bumps past it. Her voice is even but Erin has the impression she's getting irritated.

Erin looks back to the mainland, and it's a shock to see how far they've already come. The gate they passed is doll-sized. She turns back around quickly. Ahead of them the road slopes down, and she realises they're approaching the lowest point – the middle – before the road rises again.

The causeway is becoming wetter by the second. Water leaks around the rocks, pooling in the crevices and potholes. Kitty stops singing and leans over the wheel, steering to avoid the larger areas.

'Kitty,' Erin whispers, eyes fixed on the creeping flood. 'We need to hurry—'

She's thrown forward as the car jerks to a halt.

'What the—?'

'Sorry.' Kitty lowers her window and yells into the salty air. *'Move, you little asshole!'*

A fat seagull sits directly in front of the car, pecking insolently at the road. Kitty blasts the horn and it squawks and flaps into the air, something stringy in its beak. There's a soft *phlat* and then red, glistening fish guts slide down the windscreen in front of Erin's face.

Mira's cry of disgust is drowned out by Kitty.

'Great!' she shouts, flicking on the wipers. The screen wash is empty, and all it does is smear the windscreen red. The car stalls. She turns the key and the engine coughs. She tries again. 'You've got to be shitting me.'

Erin looks at her sharply. 'Stop messing around. We need to get off this causeway.'

'I'm not messing around,' she snaps, her cool façade gone. 'It won't start.'

Erin looks out of the window, then wishes she hadn't. It's no longer just puddles surrounding them – the road is almost entirely underwater. It's being swallowed up.

'I don't understand. This car's never let me down. *Never.*' Kitty's voice is high, desperate. It sends chills over Erin's skin.

'Well, have you ever driven it through water this deep before?' she says sarcastically.

Kitty doesn't reply. In the back, Mira is utterly silent. Erin refuses to turn around. If she does she knows she'll see her panic mirrored in Mira's eyes, and she can't handle that. She needs to think, but it's impossible to look away from the rising water. Coupled with the entrails on the windscreen and the inexplicable foreboding she had as they got on the causeway, it's like an awful premonition.

'Keep trying,' she urges.

'I *am* trying!'

'Try harder!' Suddenly Erin doesn't care that it's Kitty she's shouting at. She wouldn't care if it was the Queen. All she cares about is that they're about to be swept on to the estuary. 'We wouldn't be in this mess if you'd listened—'

The engine roars into life, the stereo picking up where it left off. Kitty stays frozen, her fingers tight on the wheel like she's afraid the car will cut out again if she dares to move.

'*Go!*' Erin yells.

Kitty stamps on the pedal and the car jerks forward.

'Slowly… slowly,' Erin says. Water ripples away from the car. If they stepped out it'd be well above their ankles. If they can get through the flooding middle section and on to higher ground up ahead they'll make it. Kitty aims for it with steely determination on her face. This time there's no slowing for the birds. They rise into the air, their screeches like curses.

They near the second passing point but this time Erin barely looks. There's no turning back. When they make it to the incline it's all she can do not to hug Kitty for getting them there. Kitty manoeuvres the Mini through a final, wide expanse of water. Erin feels the *swish* as they pass through it, praying it isn't high enough to get into any parts of the car that matter. Then they're back on drier ground, still on the causeway but heading up and away from the flooded centre.

None of them speak. The island looms over them, shingle leading up into overgrown vegetation. Agonising minutes later they reach the end of the causeway. Kitty halts by a sign welcoming them to Blackwater Island. It feels somewhat insincere, given that it's rotting in the grass. The cassette suddenly goes into slow motion, stretching the word 'Satan' into a long, low growl. The timing of it is unsettling.

Kitty lets out a shaky breath then ejects the cassette, swearing as the tape unspools in a chewed-up mess. She turns off the engine and gets out of the car. Dumbly, Erin and Mira follow her to the slope leading down to the water.

The Devil's Path, indeed.

The centre of the causeway is submerged, no longer visible. Water slowly inches towards the land, claiming the rest of the road. A couple more minutes and it would have claimed them, too. Erin pushes the thought away and tells herself to stop being melodramatic. The feeling she'd had, the guts on the window – none of it meant anything. It wasn't an omen, just her being scared. As usual. They've made it. They're here, for two whole days.

Cut off from virtually everything.

Kitty throws her head back and cackles. Erin stares at her, bemused.

Kitty grins. 'That was close, wasn't it?'

Erin feels none of her excitement. Neither, apparently, does Mira, whose huge brown eyes are fearful, and slightly defiant.

'I can't swim.'

The smile is wiped off Kitty's face.

'God – Mira, I'm sorry. I'd never have crossed it if I'd known. Erin was right, we should've waited.' She reaches out and touches Mira's arm. 'Come on. Let's find out where we need to go. I've got hot chocolate in my case – I think we all deserve one.'

Mira's expression softens and they clamber back in the car. Kitty flicks the radio on, and before long she's singing to some bubbly song. Erin chews over Mira's admission, unable to help likening it to sailors and their superstition that it's bad luck to have someone aboard who can't swim, but with Kitty warbling next to her as they head inland, it's impossible to stay gloomy.

A white gate appears ahead. A pair of little brown rabbits skippity-hop in front of it. Beyond the gate there are a couple of whitewashed cabins, and opposite, something that looks like a row of brick stables.

They stop at the gate, seeing that the 'stables' are actually an office and a games room. A young woman a few years older than them comes out and opens the gate. She checks their names off a list and introduces herself as the island manager, then shows them where to park.

Erin studies an island map printout, eyeing the time on the dashboard.

'Everyone's meeting at ten forty-five at Stretch Neck Hill.'

'Is that where the gallows is?' asks Mira.

Erin nods, slightly queasy at the macabre name.

'We'd better not leave them hanging around then.' Kitty laughs at her own joke, swinging into the car park. There are only a handful of cars, and two minibuses bearing the Thameside College emblem. One of them has a flat tyre. Kitty slots the Mini neatly between one minibus and a battered blue

Peugeot. Erin's breath quickens. It's Preston's car. She clambers out and pings the seat forward for Mira, leaving Kitty in the driver's seat applying a fresh layer of lip gloss. A minute later she unfolds herself from the car, all legs beneath the fluffy jacket and a good three inches taller than Erin and Mira.

'Come on,' she says, slamming the door. 'Let's leave our stuff until we know where to take it.'

Once out of the car park they see that the island is signposted pretty well, and soon find where they're meant to go. Ahead of them half a dozen people are hurrying to join a larger cluster over on the corner. Beyond them, a tall wooden gallows squats like a guard dog, a long rope swinging down from it like a leash. The sight of it makes Erin's guts churn. She stares at the swaying noose, hoping it's a model just for show. That people haven't *actually* died on the end of that rope. Without warning a thought pushes into her head.

Legs dangling between branches. White trainers, flecked with red. The creak of rope.

She blinks the image away.

As they get nearer voices become clearer and faces familiar. Their tutors, Paul Callaghan and Charlotte Hewitt, are by the roadside. Hewitt is twirling her frizzy hair round a finger and smiling up at him. Is she *flirting*? Erin recalls Kitty's predictions about people getting laid, hoping they don't apply to teachers. *Gross.* She scans the rest of the group, smiling at some of those in her class, and trying to put names to faces from the other classes. She finds him towards the back: close-cropped sandy hair, laughing blue eyes, the most incredible dimples.

Patrick Preston. Her heart races. It's been a week since she last saw him, and he looks better than ever. He glances in their direction, and for a moment she thinks it might be at her. She's distracted by a movement behind him and realises someone else is watching her.

Aidan. Her insides tense. She meets his dark eyes and he nods at her, the way he always does when their paths cross around campus. She nods back, holding his gaze. She and Aidan drifted apart after what happened with Nicky Pemberton. Even their mothers don't speak any more. She's about to look away when she senses something unspoken in his eyes. A warning.

'Who's that?' says Kitty.

Erin is about to ask who, and then she doesn't need to because she sees her.

The girl is standing on the fringes of the group, alone. A face Erin recognises, but it doesn't belong.

What is she doing here?

Belinda Webb looks different to how Erin remembers. Her face is thinner, her hair no longer the mousy shade it once was. It's red. Not ginger or auburn, but scarlet.

But it's unmistakeable. It's her. *It's definitely her.*

Erin's innards are roiling. Just as they were on the causeway with the tide edging in and blood smeared across the windscreen; the inexplicable dread about what was waiting for her on the other side.

The same dread she'd felt that stifling summer afternoon all those years ago.

She never thought she'd see Bee again after they both moved away. And yet here she is… and so is Erin, and suddenly she's no longer seventeen and about to spread her wings and make something of herself. She burns with shame and guilt and fear, transported back to memories she's tried to forget.

And right here on the island is the absolute last place she wants to be.

9

SEPTEMBER 2016

AN EMAIL ARRIVES NOT LONG after Erin ends the call with her mum. She's forced herself to shower but afterwards she stays upstairs, alternating between slumping on her bed, obsessively checking her phone, and hovering by the windows to watch the street and her back garden. She sees no one except a neighbour mowing their grass and two cats having a stand-off. The butchered tongue remains strong in her mind. She feels sure she can still smell it.

She ignores another message from Sam as it loads into her inbox. One of her picture books has sold translation rights to France, but she's already clicking on to a new email that's arrived via her website, her stomach dipping as she sees the sender's name. Her first thought is that someone's playing a sick joke.

From: Kitty Dixon > kitty@kittydixon.com
To: Erin Sinclair > esillustration@gmail.com
Subject: hello stranger

Dear Erin,
I'm not sure how to start this. How do you begin to write
to someone you haven't seen in twenty years? Well,
first I want to congratulate you. I always knew you were
talented, so I'm real happy you made a career out of your

art. I suppose the next thing would be to ask how you are, but going by the current news I'm guessing it's not great.

I've never been much good with the writing stuff so I'll cut to the chase. I've been thinking a lot about Blackwater Island and the night Bee died. Not only since what's come out about who she was, but even before that. It's never really gone away, has it? Up till recently I'd accepted that's how it was and tried to make the best of it every time it's come back to bite me in the ass. I don't want to live under suspicion for the rest of my life. Do you?

If you've got this far, hear me out. We have to tell the truth. We aren't the only ones. We know others had things to hide, too. But if we work together on this it could benefit us all.

So I'm going back to the island. Not to be morbid or to make this any more traumatic, but because time plays tricks on the mind. If we're there it could jog memories that have been buried. Mira and a few others have agreed to join me. Yes, I know. You're the last one I'm asking. I very nearly didn't. I've been shitting myself about it.

I realise you've never spoken publicly about that weekend. I get it. You're scared. I am, too. But I need to know what happened. It's why I'm doing this with or without you. Please, at least consider it before you tell me to get lost. You trusted me once, twenty years ago. I'm asking you to trust me again.

Kitty

Erin reads it twice, incredulous. Infuriated. *Terrified.*

She turns her face into her pillow and screams until she can't breathe. When she lifts her head to gulp for air she's crying with rage.

Kitty fucking Dixon. The last person she expected to hear from.

Aside from the abusive messages, Erin's received many calls, letters and emails over the years regarding Bee's murder. Mostly from journalists hoping for the scoop that's going to make their career. Sometimes from do-gooders inviting – or demanding – a confession. The tone of these messages varies from honeyed to aggressive, aiming to wheedle or bully a response from her. The contact hasn't always come to her direct. There was even an open letter in the gutter press, laying the accusations bare.

She's never heard a peep from Kitty, until this. After Bee's death, Kitty was whisked back to America as soon as the police had finished with their questions, releasing them without charge. Erin had continued with her A levels, completing much of the work at home before returning to campus for exams.

But Kitty hadn't kept out of the limelight. As it happened, she'd been gifted at turning a bad situation to her advantage. Erin's lost count of the times Kitty's doe eyes have stared out at her from magazine covers over the past twenty years. It started with 'her story', proclamations of her innocence before it switched to become less about what occurred on the island and more about *her*. Erin remembers the exact moment it happened. Kitty had made it on to a talk show, stunning in this crazy dress made out of Polaroids. When the show's host had poured each of his guests a flute of champagne, an actor seated next to Kitty – a famous one – had side-eyed her and made a quip about the champagne bottle, and *not knowing where it might end up*. Kitty had looked him dead in the eye and told him if he didn't watch his mouth it'd end up shoved in his 'ass'. Two minutes later the guy asked her out, live on air. She accepted, and the media was all over the pair's whirlwind romance for the next six months. Before Erin knew it, Kitty was modelling for Urban Outfitters on both sides of the Atlantic, and then advertising a huge but now defunct vodka brand. In recent years she's branched out more in the UK for Kookai and Agent Provocateur, before launching her own brand of make-up and a range of sleepwear. There was even a stint on *Celebrity Big Brother*, followed by her turning up as a judge on some trashy Saturday night TV show. It's only now Erin realises Kitty's been uncharacteristically quiet for a while. She tries to remember the last time she caught sight of her in anything. A year ago? Two?

And now she's returning to Blackwater Island.

Erin was only just beginning to know Kitty back then, on the trip. It'd been clear right from the off that she was wild. It was partly what had drawn Erin to her. In the aftermath she'd thought Kitty was unhinged, the way she'd sought out attention when anyone normal would lie low. Now Erin wonders if she's cleverer than anyone gave her credit for. Clever, and always so sure of herself and her place in the world.

Mira and a few others have agreed to join me.

Erin's amazed Mira has agreed to this. She wants to know who these 'others' are. Charlotte Hewitt? Paul Callaghan – no. *Aidan?*

She can't seem to stop crying, to catch a breath.

Kitty claims she's scared, but Erin doesn't believe it. Scared people are those like her, people who hide. Kitty's never hidden, so maybe she's feeding Erin a line to get her onside.

Unless there's something else going on, something Erin's missing. It crosses her mind that Kitty's being blackmailed. That someone, somehow, knows something.

Her mum's voice echoes in her head. *You were there.*

Yes, Erin was there.

She deletes Kitty's email. Then she goes downstairs, finds a bottle of vodka at the back of her kitchen cabinet and slops a large measure into a mug. She knocks it back neat, pours another. Then another until the panic starts to blur. But it isn't gone.

It's never gone away.

She doesn't know what time it is when she retrieves the email from the deleted folder. All she knows is that she cannot allow this madness to go ahead – because Kitty will, unless Erin stops her. She *has* to stop her.

She hits reply and begins to type.

10

OCTOBER 1996

'I DON'T RECOGNISE HER,' SAYS Kitty. 'Maybe she switched courses?'

Erin can't speak. Her throat is tight, as though the noose from the gallows has snared her. Kitty watches the newcomer, assessing her in that way pretty girls size up other pretty girls.

'All right, listen up.' Hewitt claps her hands together for quiet. 'In a moment we're going to read out room allocations. When your hear your name, call "here" so we can check you off the register. Before that I want to introduce a new student.' She gestures to the flame-haired figure. 'For the benefit of those who weren't on the minibuses, this is Belinda West. She's just transferred to us and will be in Paul's group when we return next week. I hope you'll all make her welcome.'

Belinda West. Like Erin, she has changed her name. Erin knew she must have transferred, that she wasn't there when term began. Erin would have noticed her. She would have *known*.

Callaghan takes over, reeling off names and room numbers. Erin has already seen from the information pack they were sent that the cabins they're staying in all have quaint, chocolate-box names, like the Custard Pot or the Old Post Office.

'Kathryn Dixon?' Callaghan calls, looking up. He's softly spoken with a northern accent, from Leeds or somewhere in that region.

'Here,' Kitty answers.

'Erin Sinclair?'

'Here.' Erin's voice is so croaky she has to say it twice before she's heard. She looks up, feeling the sting of unwanted eyes. Bee watches her from beneath her long fringe, giving nothing away. Had she known Erin would be here, or is it as much of a shock to her? Unexpectedly, she smiles.

Erin looks away.

'Mira Vranceanu,' Callaghan continues. Then, 'And Belinda West. The four of you are in the Honeycomb.'

No, Erin thinks. *I cannot share a cabin with her.*

'Looks like we'll get to know Little Miss New Girl after all,' says Kitty.

Erin nods mutely. She feels ill, almost feverish.

'Leon Curtis?' Callaghan says.

'Here.'

'Aidan Lewis?'

'Here,' Aidan says, his eyes still on Erin. She senses Bee turn in his direction and wonders whether they were on the same minibus. Aidan is easily recognisable and hasn't changed much. He's taller and broader, but his dark eyes are the same. Brooding one moment and mischievous the next.

'Declan Murray,' Callaghan continues. 'And Patrick Preston. You four are in Land's End.'

Callaghan reads out the rest of the names and cabins, finishing by announcing that he'll be in the Burrow, and Hewitt's staying in the Sweet Shop.

'Yeah, ha ha,' Hewitt says affably as the snickers follow. At some point, Charlotte Hewitt has written her name down as 'C.Hewitt', and the nickname has stuck. 'Chewitt in the sweet shop, very funny.'

'Not sharing then, sir?' Curtis calls out. For some reason everyone calls him and Preston by their last names, Erin doesn't know why. It seems to lend them some authority like the teachers.

Hewitt crosses her arms and blushes at the inevitable whistles and a couple of comments that are just on the safe side of lewd. It's plain she has the hots for Callaghan. He's not bad looking: short brown hair, square-jawed and fairly muscular. Kind of average, but compared to other teachers who are either on the crusty side of old, or young and weird, he's a catch.

'Unlucky, Chewy,' Kitty murmurs. 'Bet she'd have loved that.'

Callaghan merely holds up a hand for silence. 'Any problems, that's where to find us.' He checks his watch. 'Right, the cabins are ready so grab your things, find where you need to go and unpack. We'll meet back here at midday, so you've got time for a snack or a drink before we make a start. Questions?'

There aren't. People break off into groups. Erin sees a flash of red coming their way and feels a sweeping dread. Hewitt and Callaghan are already heading for the car park. She ducks her head, hurrying after them.

'Erin, wait.' It's Kitty. 'Where are you going?'

'I'll just be a minute,' she calls over her shoulder, starting to jog.

Callaghan is kneeling by the minibus, assessing the flat tyre when Erin approaches. He is chuckling at something Hewitt's said when she reaches them. At the sound of her footsteps they turn, their eyes still crinkled from whatever joke they've just shared.

'Miss,' she says breathlessly.

'What's up, Erin? And you can call me Charlotte, you know. You're at sixth form now.'

Her second term into college and Erin still isn't used to calling teachers by their first names. It's too weird. 'It's the… the room arrangements,' she begins.

'What about them?'

'Can I switch?'

A crease forms between Hewitt's eyebrows, and it deepens as she stares into Erin's eyes. Erin lowers her gaze, fidgeting.

There's a tiny, crusty stain on Hewitt's jacket, like she's dropped porridge or something down herself and picked it off.

Hewitt checks the cabin list. 'Is there a problem?'

'It's Bee… the new girl.'

Callaghan looks up, concerned. 'Belinda?'

She nods. 'I know her. She lived on my street. We…' She searches for words, stricken. 'We had a falling out.'

Callaghan sighs and turns back to the puncture.

'A falling out?' Hewitt repeats. 'When? What happened?'

'We were ten.' Erin's stomach churns violently. 'She… something happened and it affected a lot of people. I'd… rather not say any more.'

Hewitt bites her lip. 'It was a long time ago, Erin. Children do silly, hurtful things sometimes. You're nearly adults now – can't you put it behind you? You'll probably find she's a very different person now. Have you even spoken to her yet?'

'No,' Erin mutters.

Hewitt gives a wry smile. 'Then give her a chance. I bet she feels just as awkward as you do. And besides, there's really nowhere else for you to go.'

'Can't I swap with someone?'

'Afraid not. The groups were largely by request. And even if you found someone willing to switch, people will ask why. Do you really think it's fair for Belinda to start on a sour note, all because of something that happened so long ago?'

Erin senses Hewitt's eyes on her, even though she isn't meeting them directly. She feels small, petty, mean.

'I won't say why.' Her cheeks flame. 'I'll make something up.'

Hewitt's next words are gentler. 'Look, see how it goes. If you have any problems with her then let me know. But I think you're worrying about nothing. Who knows, this time next week you could be the best of friends.'

She pats Erin's arm, then turns to assist Callaghan. Erin retreats, stung. When she heads back, looking for Kitty and

Mira she finds everyone else has gone. She's alone, save for the gallows. A chill breeze sends the noose into a spiral and a shower of sudden raindrops into her face. She pulls up her hood as the rain lashes down on her.

Soaked almost to the skin, Erin finds the cabin five minutes later. The Honeycomb stands between two other cabins a stone's throw either way. The front door has been left on the latch. Erin pushes it open and steps inside into a kitchenette. Her backpack is on the counter with the food bags. The others must have brought it from the car. Kitty's on the floor, hunkered over her suitcase. Clothes, shoes and cosmetics spill on to the tiles. A litre bottle of vodka peeks out from under a leopard-print top, alongside a brand-new copy of a book called *The Beach* by Alex Garland, which still has the receipt tucked inside. She stops rummaging and looks up, raising an eyebrow at Erin's dripping clothes.

'There you are. Where did you go?'

Erin squelches to the table, dropping the two halves of her disintegrated map on to it.

'I needed to ask Callaghan something about that essay he set.' Despite having time to rehearse the lie on the way to the cabin it sounds more defensive than she means it to, but Kitty shrugs it away.

'Look how cute this place is!' She grins, and some of Erin's tension eases. It *is* a sweet cabin. There's an old-fashioned electric hob and pots, pans and mismatched teacups in the kitchenette. A cosy living-room area has an old crate serving as a coffee table next to an ancient Chesterfield sofa. Everything is shabby and lived-in. Erin likes it.

'Where are the others?' she asks.

'Back there, unpacking.' Kitty jerks a thumb to the rear of the cabin, mouthing, 'She seems nice, the new girl.'

Erin forces a smile and collects her backpack, heading for the bedrooms. There are three doors ahead. Through the one straight on she glimpses a basin and shower cubicle. The door on the left is closed, but in the room on the right Mira's placing clothes into a drawer. There are two single beds with neat, white sheets and folded towels at the foot.

Mira glances up. 'You're drenched,' she says, handing Erin a towel. 'Here.'

Erin takes it and rubs at her wet hair ineffectually. 'Can I share with you?'

Mira smiles. 'Sure.'

Erin empties her bag on to the bed, picking out some dry clothes. She goes into the bathroom and changes, leaving her wet stuff on the radiator. When she returns the bedroom is empty and she can hear Mira and Kitty in the kitchen. From the other bedroom comes sounds of a case being unzipped. The door is still shut.

She edges towards it, hesitating. Before there's time to think it through, she knocks.

'Come in.'

It's a shock to hear her voice again. It's weirdly familiar, and yet… not. It's deeper, a reminder of the time that's passed. Erin twists the knob and goes in.

Bee's standing in front of the mirror, brushing her red hair. When she sees Erin her hand pauses midway, then continues slowly to the ends of her hair before she sets the brush down.

'Erin.' Her voice is quiet. She wasn't expecting this.

Erin doesn't bother with the niceties. She keeps her voice low and even. 'I can't see much point in pretending to the others that we don't already know each other, can you?'

'Probably not.' Bee looks down at her hands. 'What shall we tell them?' She sounds small. It chips away at some of the hardness in Erin. Perhaps Hewitt was right.

'Not the truth, obviously. We'll just say we lived on the same street and played together a few times. It's not a lie. I'm sure you're capable of making something up.'

Bee nods. 'Yeah. Okay. It wouldn't be great for either of us if it got out, would it?'

Erin stares, her pulse quickening. There's something about the way Bee is speaking, in a voice so soft it's almost menacing. Erin can't be sure whether it's a threat.

'No,' she says finally.

'Cool.' Bee smiles and mimes a *phew* action. 'It can be our little secret.'

And there it is: the familiar skin-crawling sensation she's never failed to provoke in Erin.

'It's not our little secret,' she hisses. 'And it's not "cool". Someone *died* because of us, for fuck's sake.'

Bee's eyes glisten. Even as a child Erin thought they were a strange colour, not quite brown nor green. Someone with kinder thoughts of her might have described them as hazel, but all Erin can think of is stagnant water. A scummy pond.

'It was a long time ago,' Bee says quietly.

'And I've thought about it every day since,' Erin answers. And she has. Regretted it every day. Felt dirty and ashamed every day.

'I only wish you knew how sorry I am. I didn't know what would happen, how far it'd go.'

'No,' Erin says, relenting just a little. 'We couldn't have known that.'

'I wish you could forgive me.'

'I can't forgive myself. So why should I forgive you?'

Bee bites her lip. Erin's emotions are fighting each other like the push-pull of a tide. A churned-up mix of disgust, shame, and sympathy.

'I heard about your dad,' Bee says. 'I'm sorry.'

'I'm not talking about my dad with you.'

'Okay.' A pause. 'You changed your name.'

'So did you. *West?*'

Bee's rosebud lips curve into a brief, tiny smile, filling Erin with revulsion. She can't help linking the name to wicked witches and wicked people, the horrors of 25 Cromwell Street still so recent. It's only when she's halfway out of the room that she realises she's still facing Bee, who watches her with a blank expression. Erin's been backing away the whole time. She forces herself to turn around. To walk, not run.

In the kitchen, Mira is unpacking tins of soup, cereal boxes and pasta.

'Nope. Can't find it anywhere.' Kitty stands up, abandoning her suitcase, its contents in a higgledy-piggledy heap. 'Maybe I forgot.'

Erin steps over her case to sit on the sofa. 'Forgot what?'

'The hot chocolate.'

'Let's have tea, instead.' Mira fetches a stripy teapot. 'I've always wanted to use one of these.'

'I'll make it.'

The voice comes from behind. Erin stiffens.

'Oh, thanks, Belinda.' Mira sets the teapot down and finds a carton of milk.

'Call me Bee.' The rosebud lips are smiling. 'I've always been called that, haven't I, Erin?' She gives a little laugh. 'And we're in the *Honeycomb*. Bzzz!' She skips barefoot into the kitchen and puts the kettle on to boil. Erin is thinking how her feet must be freezing on the tiled floor when she realises what Bee's said.

Kitty and Mira are glancing back and forth between them, waiting for one of them to elaborate.

Erin forces a smile. 'So, weird coincidence – Bee used to live across the road from me. I didn't recognise her straight away when they introduced her as Belinda.' She gestures half-heartedly. 'And her… your hair's different, now.'

'It's a gorgeous colour,' says Kitty. 'I love it.'

Bee twists a glossy tendril around her finger. 'Really? You know, it's funny because growing up, I was bullied horribly for having red hair. Wasn't I, Erin?'

What? Erin stares at her. She never had red hair. It was light brown. Mousy.

'I don't remember,' she says flatly, refusing to be drawn into the lie.

'So anyway, I tried going dark, and I was blonde for a while too, but neither was… well, *me*. And so I thought, you know what? If I'm a redhead then I'm going to embrace it. Go *really* red.' She grins, dropping teabags into the pot and pouring boiling water over them.

'Well, it looks great on you,' says Kitty.

Bee beams, bringing cups and saucers to the table, and then sugar and milk, and finally the teapot. She sits opposite Erin next to Kitty, leaving a space between for Mira.

'When did you two last see each other?' asks Kitty. She rips open a packet of cookies, cramming one in her mouth.

'Six years ago,' Erin says.

Bee nods. 'I got taken into care when I was ten.'

Erin stares at her, fuming. *Care?* She knew some parts of history would have to be rewritten but she'd expected a simple *moved away* story, something that wouldn't draw attention – or sympathy. But now Bee's said the words and Erin can't call her out on her fictitious past.

'Care?' Kitty repeats awkwardly. 'Oh. Sorry.'

Bee shrugs. 'It's okay. I mean, it hasn't been great but neither was home. My mum was…' She pauses, circling her index finger at her temple. 'Still is, for all I know. I'm with this foster family now. Haven't seen that loopy bitch for a couple of years.'

'That's rough.' Kitty watches her pityingly. 'What's the foster family like?'

'On my case. Like, constantly. I've just got to suck it up for another year and then I'm out of there. And it's still better than living with her. At least with them I've got a proper bed and they don't make me bath in bleach.'

There's a beat of shocked silence and Erin is pulled back into the memory of Daphne Webb opening her door, the sterile smell hitting Erin and Aidan like a wall on that airless summer day when they were ten. The clinical smell of Bee herself. She feels a creeping unease, as though maybe Bee isn't making this up after all.

'*Bleach?*' Mira says faintly. She's stopped what she's doing in the kitchen. Everything is still and silent.

'She said it was for my eczema.' Bee is staring blankly at the tea things. 'But I think… I'm sure the baths started before the eczema did.'

'Fuck,' Kitty murmurs.

'So, yeah. Everything was uprooted.' Bee shakes her head lightly and smiles. 'But things are better now. The foster parents are dicks but there's this other girl there that I'm kind of friends with. She makes it bearable. She's fun. Totally fucking feral, but fun.'

Kitty blows out a long breath. 'That's good – that you have someone, I mean, even if the rest sucks. And I can sort of relate to the uprooted part.'

Bee looks at her with a hungry interest. 'Yeah?'

Kitty shifts on the sofa, tucking her feet under herself. The movement breaks the spell of tension Bee has cast.

'I was fifteen when my parents split and my mom came back to England. It's tough leaving everything behind.'

'Which part of the States are you from?' Mira asks, still in the kitchen.

'Los Angeles.' Kitty glances at the window as another shower of rain hits the glass. 'I miss it.'

'LA to Essex,' says Bee. 'That's got to be depressing.'

'It was either here with my mom and asshole brother, or there with my dad's midlife crisis.' Kitty's mouth puckers in disgust. 'And step… *people*.' She pauses, tossing black curls away from her face. 'So, six years, huh? I guess you never stayed in touch because of the care thing?'

'I never knew she went into care,' Erin mutters. 'I thought they'd just… moved.' She tries to think back, but her mind is a blank on what happened to Bee after Nicky Pemberton. She only remembers the chaos in her own life. Police, questions. Her dad arrested, charged, imprisoned. *A killer.* The rush to pack up essentials and leave the house. A brick through the living-room window, her dad's van tyres slashed, the front door spray-painted with LIAR.

'Do you still live in the same place, Erin?' Bee asks.

Erin shakes her head and spins the version of the truth that's already been told elsewhere. 'We uh… had to move shortly after you. My dad lost his job and was out of work for a while, and Mum couldn't afford to keep things going on her own. We went to live with my aunt in Billericay. And then my dad died a couple of years ago – it was unexpected. We're still living with my aunt now.'

Kitty clicks her tongue sympathetically and pushes a cookie at her. Erin takes it but doesn't eat it.

'When did you move back?' Erin asks. This, at least, should be the truth.

'I didn't,' says Bee. 'I still live in Chelmsford. I was at college there but I've had to transfer.' She stirs the contents of the teapot. 'There was some trouble. I'm not really meant to talk about it.'

'Come on. Now you have to tell us!' Kitty rolls her eyes. 'What kind of trouble?'

The kind that follows Bee, thinks Erin.

'You have to keep it between us.' Bee's voice is small.

'Sure. Now, spill.'

'My tutor… he went weird on me.'

Kitty leans forward. 'What kind of weird?'

'Like, taking more than a professional interest kind of weird.'

'He came *on* to you?' Kitty exclaims.

Bee exhales shakily. 'I–I don't think I should say anything else.'

Kitty glances sideways at Erin in a *we'll get it out of her later* sort of way. Erin doesn't know where to look or what to believe.

Bee starts pouring the tea. 'Shit. One of the teabags split.' She pauses, staring into the cup. 'I know – I'll read our tea leaves.'

'You can do that?' asks Kitty.

'Not exactly.' Bee fills her cup, then pours for everyone else as Mira comes to join them. 'That's why it'll be a laugh.'

'What do we have to do?' Kitty asks.

'Nothing. You just drink it normally but leave a bit in the bottom.'

They drink, and talk about the subjects they're taking aside from Psychology. Erin's taking Art and English Literature. Her dream is to illustrate. Maybe write, too. Mira is taking English Language and Law.

'Pretty hefty,' Kitty comments.

Mira shrugs. 'My parents want me to be a barrister.'

'Is that what you want?' Erin asks.

Mira sips her tea. 'I'm not sure. I know I want to help people.'

Erin can't imagine Mira fighting her way out of a paper bag, let alone arguing in a courtroom. Kitty's other subjects are Fashion and Textiles, and Art. She's in a different art group to Erin, but Erin's seen her work. It's good.

'I'm going to be a fashion designer.' Kitty strokes one of the sofa cushions like she's assessing the quality of the fabric. Erin marvels at her confidence: Kitty doesn't *want* to be. Kitty is *going* to be. 'I figured if I chose Psychology I'd learn to influence people to buy my shit.' She snickers. 'But here I am, studying witches in the pissing rain.'

'Well, witches need fashion, too,' Erin quips, feeling a warm glow as Kitty hoots with amusement.

'So, why Psychology?' Kitty asks her. 'Doesn't really fit with illustration.'

Erin shrugs. 'Nor did anything else. I nearly went for Photography, but I thought it might get expensive with all the equipment. Psychology looked interesting. And me and my mum are into *Cracker* at the moment.'

Kitty laughs. 'That TV show? Cool.'

'How about you, Bee?' Mira asks.

'Biology, because I like cutting shit up, and Maths because people think you're smart,' Bee says. 'And Psychology because I like fucking with people's heads.' She grins. 'That's a joke, by the way.'

This elicits a snigger from Kitty. Erin stays silent, chilled.

'Right, I'll go first.' Bee drains her teacup, then demonstrates. 'You swill your cup three times, like this. Then you tip it upside down.' Tea dribbles into the saucer, along with a couple of stray leaves. When the pooling liquid stills, she turns the cup over. They all peer inside.

Most of the tea leaves have clustered together in a black blob but some have tapered into a thin line.

'Looks kind of like a… tadpole?' Mira ventures.

'Or a sperm.' Kitty grins wickedly.

Mira chokes on a sip of tea.

'Ha!' Bee shrieks. She tilts her head, thoughtful. 'I think it looks like a key.'

'It could be symbolic,' says Mira. 'A secret, perhaps?'

Erin shifts, uncomfortable. *Our little secret.*

Bee's eyes gleam. 'Who's next?'

'Me.' Mira upends her cup. When she turns it over the leaves have settled in a tall bell shape.

'A hill, or a mountain,' says Bee. 'Could mean an obstacle, or that you're about to go on a journey.'

'Journey my ass,' Kitty says. 'I know what it looks like to me, and I think you're about to get lucky.'

This sends Bee into another fit of giggles.

Kitty goes next. The shape is a very definite triangle, with a few stragglers around the three edges. Erin can't help thinking that it was just meant to be the three of them: herself, Kitty and

Mira in their own little triangle – until Bee showed up. Kitty, of course, has her own unique perspective.

'Maybe I'm getting lucky, too.'

Mira frowns. 'I don't understand.'

'Could be a sign the lady garden needs some attention.' Kitty points to the stray leaves around the edge of the triangle. 'Maybe time for a prune.'

Erin can't help laughing. 'You have a filthy mind, you know that?' When it's her turn she swirls the cold tea. Her first thought, when she turns over the cup is that the leaves have formed a similar shape to those in Bee's cup: a loop near the base which trails off in a tail.

'Is it me, or is that another sperm?' Kitty asks.

But even as she says it, Bee starts to frown. And as Erin stares at it, two possibilities occur to her. Neither is welcome.

'A noose,' Bee says. 'Like the one on Stretch Neck Hill.'

Erin doesn't like the way Kitty has stopped laughing, or the way Mira's eyes are rounder than usual.

The other resemblance, and one that, somehow, Erin likes even less than the first, is that it also looks very much like a 'b'.

Bee.

11

OCTOBER 2016

HER HANDS ARE CLENCHED SO tightly around the steering wheel that it takes Erin a few seconds to loosen her hold. She eases the car up the gravel slope and off the causeway, and the moment the vehicle is level her shoulders slowly unhunch by a fraction. There's a weathered sign pointing to the car park, but Erin puts the gear stick in neutral and pulls up the handbrake, leaning forward to rest her hot forehead on the steering wheel.

She breathes in and out slowly, like someone who's had too much to drink and is trying to delay being sick. She *feels* sick, and she's sweating. She opens the window to bring air in, but the briny tang of it conjures the memory of fish guts smearing down Kitty's windscreen. She rolls the window back up and wonders if she's having a panic attack.

Kitty had not engaged with her email. Erin's drunken, typo-ridden plea to think about what she's doing, what this could mean, was answered with a stoic response from Kitty's 'management team'.

Ms Dixon regrets that her current schedule prevents her from replying personally, but she would be happy to discuss this further in person.

There were a couple of attachments comprising the date and time of the meeting on Blackwater Island, and a causeway access timetable. Erin's later, sober request for a list of attendees went ignored. She'd even included her phone number, but never received so much as a text.

She lifts her head, forcing herself to look around. There's a black gate ahead, which she remembers being white before. This area looks different now. She doesn't recall the small, landscaped area which is badly overgrown. Beyond the gate is the building that looks like a row of stables. *The games room.* Still there. And why wouldn't it be? It's brick built, sturdy. Not a flimsy little pig's house made of sticks.

She closes her eyes, remembering the night in the games room twenty years ago. The party. Getting ready for it. Excited, with no idea of what lay ahead. Drinking, drinking. *So much to drink.* The long, long night, what she heard and saw. What she did.

Bee's corpse pulled from the water, pale and glistening.

I can't do this, she thinks. *I can't be on this island.* But she can. She is already here. She's sick of running and hiding. Of living her life hoping that if she stays quiet enough, small enough, it will all go away. It's not going away, and now she's had enough. She is not leaving her fate in Kitty's hands. She opens her eyes and reaches across the passenger seat to the sheet of tide information. She's already checked it so thoroughly that she knows there's time: time to speak to Kitty, to talk some sense into her, and then escape. To get back across the causeway before the water starts coming in.

She grabs her phone from its holder on the dash and refreshes the Sky News app. She's not checked it for a good couple of hours while she's been driving and now her anxiety is through the roof. A lot can happen in an hour or two.

Something *has* happened: Bee's grave has been vandalised. The write-up is short, with a banner declaring the story's just breaking and will be updated. The accompanying photo shows a basic headstone. The word 'LIAR' has been sprayed over it in black. More paint – red this time – has been thrown following that, dissecting the word and running down to puddle at the base. Judging by the thick weeds, it's the most attention anyone's paid to the grave in a while. Such hatred for someone twenty years dead leaves little doubt about what the feeling for the anonymous one, still alive, would be.

A movement in the rear-view mirror draws Erin's attention. A dark vehicle is on the causeway, making its way across to the island. Bright sunlight bounces off it. It's expensive, gleaming and sleek.

The panic clears from her mind momentarily. She puts her car in gear and turns, following the sign to the car park, a wide gravelled space with two areas, one for staff, the other for visitors.

As Erin pulls in a white catering van moves off and leaves. She parks on the visitors' side, counting three cars and a large black motorcycle. She wonders who these vehicles belong to, and who's in the one crossing the causeway right now. *At least six of us*, she thinks. It's unlikely any of the drivers will have brought a passenger. Few of them would have stayed in touch after that weekend – not the ones who were directly involved with Bee or what happened to her, at any rate.

Erin gets out of the car and locks it. Her feet crunch softly in the gravel as she heads round to where the games room is. Her phone chimes a push notification. An email has arrived. Her heart skitters as she sees it's come via the contact form on her website.

Sender: **Bee's Ghost.** Subject line: **EAT GLASS, BITCH.**

12

OCTOBER 1996

B y the time they're back at the gallows Erin has pushed the tea leaves to the back of her mind. The others have laughed it off, and she knows they're right to. Seeing shapes in teacups is like finding dragons in clouds. Look long enough and something will appear.

The rain has stopped but has turned everything underfoot to mush. Erin's Doc Martens are caked in mud. They follow Callaghan and Hewitt along the sodden trail. Kitty's fallen into step with Bee in front and, up ahead, Preston's talking to a girl named Tilly who's laughing and flicking her hair a lot. Erin watches resentfully, wondering why nothing ever happens the way you imagined it would.

She takes out the new map that she scrounged from Callaghan. The island is a mile and a half long, and around half that in width. Looking at their surroundings it's mostly open land and fields. She locates Stretch Neck Hill on the map and from there she tracks their path, heading east past Clover Field and the orchard towards the museum.

As they walk, Hewitt relays information about the island. As well as having remains of a Roman settlement and evidence of ancient burial grounds, it was used as a naval base in the second world war. 'More recently,' she adds, 'it was a rehabilitation retreat for people with drug or alcohol addictions, including the rich and famous. That explains the recording studio up at the

Beach House – which is the only bit out of bounds to you lot.' She gestures around her. 'You can see why it's perfect – we're cut off from the mainland for sixteen hours a day in total. But none of that is why we're here.' She rubs her hands together. 'We're here for the witches.'

They arrive at the ramshackle museum, stamping mud off their feet as they cram inside. Callaghan herds the psychology lot together, while Hewitt gathers the history students.

'You'll recall that we've been looking at anti-social behaviour – specifically, crowd behaviour and diminished responsibility,' says Callaghan. 'Before half term we covered football mobs, the Zimbardo prison experiment and authority figures. But now we're going to look at an example of human behaviour at its worst: the witch trials.

'Now, when we think of witches, Salem's what usually springs to mind, but the UK has its fair share. The Pendle Witch Trials are the best-known in England, but Essex has a rich history, too. Did any of you know there were four recorded witch trials in Chelmsford? The last one was in 1645, when fifteen people were hanged. And as you know, Blackwater Island has its own dark history. Four women were found guilty of witchcraft and sentenced to death here, in 1651.'

Erin's gaze finds its way to Bee. She's mesmerised, hanging on Callaghan's every word and Erin can't help but think back to the first time Bee ever spoke to her.

I'm a witch.

'The information you collect on the island will form the basis of your essay, so bear in mind how what happened here relates to modern day forms of crowd behaviour. Remember, the quality of your essay depends on the research you put in.'

'And this trip is a first.' Hewitt's finished briefing her students and is now addressing both groups. 'Your behaviour, and how well you do will impact forthcoming trips – not just for yourselves but for future students. Don't let us down.'

People break into smaller groups as Callaghan and Hewitt start handing out itineraries. By the time Erin and Mira receive theirs, Kitty and Bee have woven their way back to them. Kitty stuffs the papers in her bag and peers at Erin's. She smells like the Body Shop's cherry lip balm and coconut rolled into one, like they are ingredients that make up the magic of her.

'What else is on there?'

'A witch trial re-enactment,' Erin says, glancing down the list. 'That's tomorrow.'

Kitty groans. 'Re-enactment? I hope that's not one of those shitty role play things.'

Bee sidles closer. 'What's the witch hunt?'

Erin edges away from her, and reads it quickly. Callaghan and Hewitt have devised a list of various sites on the island that they're to visit. Each has extra information about the witch trials and a clue to be pieced together at the end. There's even an incentive – the first three groups to complete it win Pizza Hut vouchers.

Students are already spreading around the museum. Callaghan and Hewitt are speaking to the attendant, a severe-nosed woman who looks a bit like a stereotypical witch herself. Aside from the young woman who greeted them, she's the only person outside of the college staff and students that Erin has seen so far.

Kitty slips her bag off her shoulder and roots around in it for a pen and paper.

'Sooner we get this over with, the sooner we can party,' she mutters, heading towards a sign that reads 'Witchcraft on Blackwater Island'. The rest of them follow, stepping into a maze of glass cabinets, information boards and waxwork figures. Within seconds they become separated, each of them drawn to something different. Erin is alone for perhaps a minute before she realises Bee is shadowing her. She pauses before a painting of a naked woman drawing a protective circle around herself, and pretends to study it. Bee stands beside her, staring up at it, too.

'Was all that true?' Erin asks quietly. 'About your mum? The… the bleach?'

Bee stays silent, and for a moment Erin thinks she's not going to answer. She feels a jolt of shock as Bee's fingers rest against her own, very slightly, at their sides.

'Remember in the woods?' she says softly. 'You held my hand then.'

Erin remembers. She remembers it all. And now, she recalls that scruffy, piss-stained sleeping bag on show in the Webbs' front garden and marries it up with what Bee said earlier about the foster parents: *At least with them I've got a proper bed.*

'Bee,' she says, and at the same time she recoils, taking her hand away. It's like muscle memory, the revulsion of that summer. 'Did your mum really do that?'

'Does it matter?' Bee looks down at Erin's hand, at the distance she has put between them. Her gaze moves up over Erin and there's something reptilian about it. Like she is a snake working out whether she's big enough to swallow Erin whole.

'You told me to make something up, Erin. So I did.' Bee moves off, losing herself within the sea of cabinets, and Erin is left half-repulsed, half-relieved.

She takes out her notebook shakily, trying to concentrate. There are little carved wooden dolls believed to be fertility charms. Spells for beauty, riches, luck and love. She makes some notes and moves on. Some of the things in the next cabinet are truly horrible. Two black, congealed lumps – apparently a toad and a bull's heart – lie side by side, pierced with iron nails and pins. Both were found on the island, their intent to curse. Similarly, there's a 'witch's ladder' – a hex made from a mass of black chickens' feathers carefully knotted into thin cord. Its written description reveals it was found sewn inside the victim's mattress, the revenge of a dismissed servant. Engrossed, Erin forgets to make notes and instead begins to sketch it.

'Picked up any inspiration yet?'

She looks up. Aidan's close by, watching her intently.

'Inspiration for what?'

He smiles faintly. 'Self-defence? Now there's a witch in your camp, I mean.'

'Not yet.' Erin scans ahead to see where Bee is, but she's vanished. 'Let me know if you see a spell to turn someone into a toad.'

'Maybe you won't need to. It's been a long time.'

'Don't you think it's weird she's turned up here?'

He chews his lip, thoughtful. 'There's only so many colleges in the area. What've you told Kitty and Mira?'

'Only that she lived across the road. But I asked Chewitt to move me. Didn't say why, but she wouldn't.'

They both gaze into the cabinet. She tells him what Bee said about her mum, her skin crawling as she recounts it. 'And then she said just now she made it all up. Who *does* that?'

'Well, we always knew she was messed up,' Aidan says, his voice low. 'Want to hear something else that's weird? A couple of weeks ago I was at work on my break and I got stung by a bee. It's only the second time I've been stung. After the first I didn't take any chances, I got my manager to drive me straight to A & E. The whole time in the car I kept checking my face, waiting for it to swell up. But nothing happened.'

Erin looks up at him, confused. 'You didn't have a reaction?'

'No. It hurt like hell, but it was nothing compared to before.'

'That *is* weird,' she concedes. 'Maybe it was a different insect. A hornet, or something.'

'Or I outgrew the allergy. It happens.' He studies her. 'Remember how freaked out we were? How we thought Bee had hexed me so I couldn't talk?'

You won't say anything. You won't tell anyone.

Erin nods, moving along, her fingers trailing across the glass. 'Yeah.'

'Are you okay?' he asks. 'Must bring it all back, her turning up like this.'

Erin wants to say that it never really went away, that it's always there just under the surface. But she says nothing. Aidan knows what happened. They've spoken about it a few times, but never in depth. They never really had the chance to. His mother would have made sure of it even if Erin hadn't moved away. It was as though she was contaminated. Erin has always sensed his deep shock at what she and Bee did, but Aidan's never acted hateful towards her, or judgemental. Even so, there's an awkwardness between them that's existed since. Days before it happened, Aidan had confessed he liked her in a game of truth or dare and they'd kissed. Just once, a child's kiss on the lips. She had dared him to, and in that moment realised that while she'd always loved Aidan, she'd liked him – like that – too. But then everything had changed, and she and Aidan had lost touch completely until college.

Erin feels a sudden wave of grief for the life she might have lived, had none of it happened. Right now she'd be enjoying this trip, making the most of her first taste of freedom. Instead, she's mired in the past and the evil thing she did. And it's easy to dwell on evil in this place. It's everywhere, all around her.

'Some of this stuff's crazy.' Aidan rests a hand on the glass cabinet. Erin is distracted by its largeness, by the dark hairs on the back of it. As children they were so familiar, but the years that have passed have turned his hand into that of a stranger's.

'Yeah,' she agrees, glad the subject has moved on. 'It's horrible to think of people making this crap. Stewing and cursing. It's creepy.'

Tilly's laugh tinkles on the other side of a partition. She's with Preston and Curtis, who've ignored the witch section and gone straight for the naval history bit. Predictably, Tilly has followed and is trying to look enthusiastic as they stand around a scaled-down model of a ship. Erin snaps her notebook shut, irritated.

'Guess you'll be wanting that toad spell for someone else,' Aidan says.

'I don't know what you mean.'

'Don't read too much into it. She flirts with everyone. So does he.'

Erin glares at him, expecting to find amusement in his eyes, but they're curiously empty, and his expression is closed.

'See you later,' he says, moving away.

Preston's shaken Tilly off and is getting closer. Erin reopens her notes, trying to look busy. Surprisingly, what she's written is coherent even though she barely recalls writing it.

Throughout the world the element associated with witchcraft is water, whose tides are ruled by the moon. Blackwater Island, surrounded by water and accessible only when the tide permits, was once believed to be a powerful hive for witches.

Suddenly he's beside her, all sandy hair and seawater eyes and smelling incredible.

'Hi, Erin.'

'Hi, prick.'

There's a stunned silence in which they both gape at each other. She is mortified. And then she's babbling.

'I mean, *Patrick*. Sorry – I started saying Preston and then it… well, it came out wrong.' She laughs nervously. His eyes crinkle, and then he's laughing, too. Those *dimples*.

'So, are you having fun?' he asks.

'I wouldn't call it fun. This place is pretty creepy.'

'Better than being stuck in a classroom though, right?'

'Yeah, when you put it like that.'

'Listen, everyone's getting together later in the games room. Coming?'

'Yeah! I mean, I'll check with the others, but I reckon they'll be up for it.' She hears her own eagerness and cringes.

He winks. 'See you later, then. And no more name-calling, or that's the last time I rescue you.'

The wink makes her bold. 'Maybe next time I'll rescue you,' she tells him, enjoying the way his eyebrows lift in response, and even more that they have an 'in' joke.

They'd met on the second day of college. Erin was queuing for a bus home when a man pushed past, knocking into her. A second later when she reached for her purse it was gone, and that was when she knew.

'He took my purse!'

Her shout spurred him into a sprint. But it had also alerted others, and ahead, someone lunged for him. She saw a flash of blond hair as the two figures tussled. Both took a punch before the thief tossed the purse and ran. By the time Erin got there he was gone, leaving her purse in the clutches of a bloody-nosed stranger.

'Are you all right?' she asked, breathless from the adrenaline rush.

'I'll live.' He coughed, handing her the purse. 'Not sure if he took anything.'

A quick inspection confirmed he hadn't. 'Everything's here… my door key, bank card.' She pulled out a tissue and handed it to him, watching as he touched it to his nose. The white paper quickly turned red. 'Thanks. Sorry about your face.'

He smiled through the blood, and she saw that it was a good face.

'I'm Erin.'

'Preston.'

She gestured to the college gates. 'Do you go here?'

His answer was snatched away by people surging forward

with the arrival of the bus and she'd had to get on, noticing only when she sat down that a trace of him was still with her. A smear of blood on her thumb. Later that night she'd thought of him, making silent bargains with anything that might be listening to let her see him again. When he turned up in the canteen the next day she knew something had heard.

Now, as Preston heads off he glances back at her. Maybe she won't need a toad spell after all. She carries the moment with her like a charm, moving through the museum. She finds Kitty in front of a wooden chair, with a waxwork of a woman in a brown smock sitting in it. Her glassy eyes are wide and her mouth is open in a scream. Her arms and legs are fastened to the chair with thick leather straps. The whole thing is fixed to a frame that has some kind of lever.

'Sick, huh?' Kitty says.

'What is it? Some sort of torture device?'

'A ducking chair.' Kitty nods to a series of old-fashioned woodcut illustrations alongside it. They depict a sobbing woman in a similar chair being lowered into water.

'If they drowned it meant they were innocent. If they lived, it was taken as proof of their guilt – that the devil was protecting them. So then they'd be burnt at the stake or hanged.' Kitty presses a button, and sounds of splashing water, coughing, and a woman's frantic voice come through a nearby speaker.

'No… please! I don't know anything about the sickness, I didn't curse them. Please, I can't swim…'

A chanting crowd drowns her out.

'Float the witch! Will she sink or swim?'

The recording stops and Erin stares at the chair, repulsed. 'And they say the witches were the evil ones.'

The next item on display is a manacle, attached to a heavy iron block by a short chain. An enlarged sepia photograph shows that it was once positioned by the shore.

'You've got to be joking,' Erin murmurs.

'The accused were chained to an iron weight,' Kitty reads. 'The terror at the sight of the incoming tide was found to be more effective in drawing out "confessions" than the relentless ducking chair, whose victims were often unable to speak with their lungs full of water. Depending on the severity of their witchcraft, those who confessed were either spared or put to death. Those who refused were left to the mercy of the water.' She shakes her head. 'That's seriously screwed up.'

They continue around the museum, seeing torture implements including thumbscrews and iron boots into which boiling water or oil was poured, written 'evidence' and confessions.

It transpires that seven women died on the island after being tried as witches. Of the seven, three were deemed innocent after drowning. The other four were found guilty and sentenced to death. Three were in the care of a woman known as Mother Blackwater, a local midwife and healer who often took in orphans and foundlings. The fourth was Mother Blackwater herself. Erin and Kitty note the so-called evidence against the witches. None of it amounts to any more than feeble gossip and personal grievances. *He said, she said.* The more they read, the more they see that those targeted were easy to blame. Vulnerable, or 'problematic' in some way. The outcasts, the spinsters, the wayward. Those who made others uncomfortable, perhaps in appearance or by way of disabilities that had no names back then. And so instead of being helped they were shunned, vilified, eliminated.

When they catch up to Mira and Bee, Mira looks haunted, plainly finding the museum as unpleasant as Erin does. In contrast, Bee is peering into the cases so eagerly that it looks as though she'd climb into them if she could.

'Shall we get out of here?' Kitty drawls, leaning heavily against a glass case. A fluttering movement catches their attention. A key is dangling from its lock. Someone's left it there by mistake: there's a spray bottle of glass cleaner and a cloth on top of the case, forgotten.

'Ooh,' Kitty murmurs, glancing into the cabinet.

It contains a rounded glass bottle finished with a silver lacquer that, in places, is speckled with age. The cork stopper is tightly sealed with black wax. A yellowed label is tied around its neck with string.

Erin reads the sign next to the cabinet.

Silver bottle, found on Blackwater Island in 1917 near the site of Mother Blackwater's cottage.

'I've read about these,' Kitty exclaims. 'Is it a witch bottle? People would put piss and needles and stuff in them and hide them in chimneys to keep evil out of the house. Like as protection?'

'That's fucked-up,' says Bee, clearly entranced. Again, she's edged closer to Erin.

'This is different. It's not protection, more like a curse.' Erin shifts away and continues to read about the bottle. 'It says there's a witch inside it. And "if she's released, it will bring great misfortune".'

'A witch inside?' Bee asks. 'Like, a witch's *soul*, or something?'

Kitty glances over her shoulder, then reaches past them to open the cabinet. It isn't even locked. She takes out the bottle and holds it. Erin feels a terrible thrill, partly admiration, partly dread of getting caught. But the museum is busy and loud, its only attendant is engaged in conversation with Hewitt. There is a single security camera, currently pointing halfway between them and the till.

'You shouldn't touch it,' Mira says edgily.

Kitty ignores her. A mouldering smell reaches Erin's nose as she unfurls the label. She flashes her Hollywood grin. 'Let's smash it and see what happens.'

'Don't,' Mira begs. 'Put it back.'

'It's only a bottle.' Kitty laughs scornfully. 'An old superstition from years ago.' She replaces the bottle and sniffs her fingers dubiously before locking the cabinet and removing the key. 'It can't hurt us.'

13

OCTOBER 2016

Erin deletes the email without opening it then puts her phone away, narrowly avoiding a rotting, eyeless hare carcass that's been dragged across the path and is now being hollowed out by a crow. She pauses briefly, unsettled beyond the fact it's dead. She thinks she recalls a link between hares and witches, something about shapeshifting. Averting her eyes, she moves on.

Upon arrival everyone is to meet for coffee and an informal 'icebreaker' session at eleven o'clock in the tea room. Erin spots it, set back a little beyond the games room. There was no tea room twenty years ago. This building looks new. There are a few empty tables and chairs outside. The awning is stained, grubby cream and brown stripes; once the colours of milky coffee. The sign above reads 'Witches' Brews', and has a small silhouette of a sexy-looking witch perched on a broomstick, cup in hand. If she weren't so nervous, Erin would grimace.

Her crunching footsteps don't sound soft at all now. As Erin approaches the door she's aware of figures shifting within. The sunlight is bouncing off the glass front of the shop, making it impossible to see who's in there. She wishes she'd remembered her sunglasses, but they're in the car. Instead she averts her gaze to the gravel, where she realises that a large proportion of it is actually rabbits' shit.

She pushes the door open and its creak is like a shriek to

her; like everything on the island, living and inanimate, is intent on announcing her arrival. She steps inside to warm, coffee-scented air and expects to see four pairs of accusing eyes staring back at her. But to her surprise there are only two people seated at one of the tables and there's no hostility, only curiosity and recognition. A dark-headed barista has his back to them, frothing milk at a hissing coffee machine.

Erin's eyes sweep back to the table. Her knees are trembling. She sees Mira first, seated closest to the door, her large brown eyes fixed on Erin. Erin almost smiles in relief. Mira's eyes are how she remembered: warm and kind, though there's a wariness to them now.

'Erin,' she says faintly.

Next to her is a short, stoutish woman with light-brown hair smoothed back in a bun. It takes Erin a couple of seconds for recognition to hit, as her face is thinner now, but it's Charlotte Hewitt, one of the teachers from the trip. *Chewitt*. A bigger surprise is that she's younger than Erin realised. When Erin was seventeen anyone over the age of twenty-five seemed ancient to her, but she now estimates Hewitt to be only around ten years older than her; mid to late forties. She looks better now than she did back then, like she's grown into herself and shed a layer of dowdiness. She gives Erin a small smile and Erin nods at her.

She has mixed feelings about them recognising her so readily. On one hand she's glad because it means she hasn't changed much. On the other it means strangers can probably recognise her, too. Erin has no photographs of herself on her website. Instead she has a colourful self-portrait sketch, as many children's illustrators do. She avoids events where there's likely to be much publicity and, when she visits schools – as she sometimes must to keep her publishers happy – she wears tinted glasses which help obscure her eyes in the event that any photographs of her end up online. Not that there's much photography allowed in schools these days, with the safeguarding laws.

'Refreshments are over there,' Hewitt says awkwardly, nodding to two catering urns on a table to one side along with trays of mugs and sachets of teabags and instant coffee. There's fruit, cereal, artisan breakfast pastries and other snacks and brunch bits, but it all appears untouched. Erin wonders how much all this is costing. All expenses are being covered by Kitty, including whatever the fee is for the private hire of the island, which won't come cheap.

'There are no staff,' Hewitt adds. 'But a catering team just left. So, it's a help yourself set-up.'

'Then who—?' Erin begins. She's starting to sway on her feet – perhaps it's the shock of being back on the island. When the 'barista' turns to look at her she feels her knees give way.

It's Aidan.

'Steady.' Suddenly, Mira's at her side, guiding Erin to a chair. She sinks into it, trembling and embarrassed.

'It's okay.' Mira's hand is gentle on her shoulder. 'I'll get you some tea.'

Erin nods, her eyes still locked on Aidan's. He moves out from the counter towards the table, placing a frothy latte before Hewitt and keeping another for himself.

'Hello, you,' he says quietly, taking a seat beside her. 'Long time.'

'Yeah,' she croaks, taking in his expensive jeans, his crisp shirt. He wears his dark hair a little longer now, just skimming his collar. It's as thick as ever, with a sprinkle of grey at the temples. His chocolate-brown eyes search hers, and she feels the pull of their familiarity, their shared childhood. *Minstrels*, she used to call them, after the sweets. There are a few fine lines around their corners now, and while his face is smooth and clean-shaven, it won't be for long, for his jawline and upper lip are dark, ready to bristle in the coming hours. She feels a pang of something, a sadness for those shared memories and how their friendship was cut short. Not once, but twice.

She throws a bewildered glance at the shop counter. 'Why—?'

'Oh.' He shrugs. 'The coffee in the urn wasn't great, so I said I'd have a go at making the good stuff.' He pauses, seeing she's still confused. 'I worked as a barista for a while when I was at uni. Still got the knack, and now I can't stomach bad coffee.'

She nods. 'Just blood and guts, right?'

He smiles. 'Want me to get you something?'

'Mira's bringing me some tea.' She glances at the door. 'No Kitty yet?'

'Fashionably late.' Aidan's eyes roam over her face. 'I didn't think you'd come.'

'Neither did I.'

'Drink this,' says Mira, returning with a steaming cup. She sets it down, touching Erin's shoulder lightly again, but doesn't stay. Erin's grateful when she returns to her seat. Mira has done well, she thinks. Shown concern, but not too much. Too much, and it looks like they're in cahoots. Too little, and it looks like they've got something to hide.

Another figure emerges from the back of the cafe, through a doorway with a sign for the toilets above. Erin's breath hitches.

The woman is in her late forties with short blond hair. She's heavily made-up, attractive, average height but fit-looking, slightly muscular. Though they've never met, Erin knows who she is. Paul Callaghan's wife has had her share of headlines as a result of Bee's murder. From the look on her face, she knows exactly who Erin is, too. It's a look of unconcealed contempt.

The tea room has gone deathly silent.

'Hi,' Erin says feebly. Tori Callaghan doesn't answer. Instead, she turns her gaze, like a withering beam, to include Mira a moment before settling again on Erin. But Erin has gathered herself a little. She sits up straighter and levelly returns the icy glare. She's well-practised at this. But so, it seems, is Tori.

They remain locked in this stare like cats about to fight. *This isn't an icebreaker*, Erin realises. *It's an arena.* Tori looks away first as the door to the tea room opens.

Erin is last to turn round.

Kitty stands in the doorway. A few red-brown leaves swirl round her ankles in a breeze, as though she's been blown in by the wind.

'Well, goddamn,' she says. 'Here we are again.'

For a second, her presence commands Erin's attention in the same way it always did – though not for the same reasons. Kitty looks terrible, but the thought barely touches Erin as a man appears behind her. She stares into his face with a sickening recognition.

He's thick-set. Broken nose, greying hair. Pocked skin.

Today he wears a padded black military style coat instead of a brown corduroy jacket.

14

OCTOBER 1996

Later, Erin's reading through her notes on the so-called witches. Edith Bywell, a loner with a twisted face who gave the 'evil eye' to the parson's daughter, causing her to have bad dreams. Ivy Bramble, who cast a spell to disease her neighbour's hens, stopping them from laying. Sarah Lovett, who bewitched her master into falling in love with her and bore his child, bringing shame to his wife and family. And all of them learned this witchery from Mother Blackwater, who was said to have the power to shapeshift into the form of a hare.

Modern day translation, Erin thinks: *a disfigured girl who made someone uncomfortable by looking at them, a couple of sick chickens, and a young girl most likely raped by her employer and shunned by everyone. All outcasts taken in by a well-meaning, but kooky old woman.*

She puts down her pen and goes to the mirror, brooding. She hates her eyes. *Weird. Creepy. Animal eyes.* All things that other people have told her about herself. She wonders what cruel things would have been said to – or about – Edith Bywell. If Erin had been on this island three hundred years ago, she'd have been accused of giving the evil eye, too. She'd have been the 'freak'. It might have been her neck stretched up at the gallows.

'Shower's free!' Kitty sticks her head around the bedroom door and spots the open notebook. 'Are you working?' Her hair's in a towel and her face scrubbed clean of make-up, yet she still looks like a model. 'I thought you were having a *nap*?' She says the word disapprovingly, like naps are something only babies or old people are allowed.

'I tried, but ended up giving my notes another once over.'

'Come to the kitchen,' Kitty says bossily. 'Mira's fixing something to eat.'

She scoots off through the cabin and Erin rubs her tired, gritty eyes. Even if she could sleep during the day, she wouldn't have done. Not with Bee around. It had been an excuse to escape, to try to clear her head a little. She approaches the kitchen, not sure she can face eating. Mira's poking through cupboards and pulling out utensils.

'Want some help?' Erin asks, aware that Mira's been left to it while Bee and Kitty are sprawled on the sofa giggling. Kitty's vodka is on the crate, and two empty glasses stand next to it. They've been doing shots. Bee, too, has showered. Her hair is in a towel, exposing her pale doll face. Erin shudders. Devoid of make-up and with the red hair hidden, there's virtually no difference to how she looked as a child.

'You can pass me the eggs,' says Mira. 'I'll do omelettes. It's something quick.'

'We've got eggs?' Erin thought they'd only brought things like baked beans and Super Noodles, which are pretty much the extent of her own culinary skills.

'They're in the fridge.' Mira starts washing her hands. 'Part of a care package thingy.'

Erin takes out the egg box and puts cutlery on the table.

Kitty approaches her, splashing an inch of vodka into a clean glass. 'Down it.'

'Now?'

Kitty snickers. 'No, next week.'

Erin lifts the glass to her lips and knocks it back, retching embarrassingly as the liquid burns her throat. Kitty and Bee clutch each other, shrill with laughter. Erin wonders how many they've had and feels a crest of resentment. She hates that Bee is here.

Kitty shoves the cutlery aside and lines up the three glasses, reaching for a fourth.

'Mira, you want one?'

Mira doesn't answer. Erin looks up, realising the kitchen has gone quiet. Mira's standing at the counter with her back to them. 'Mira?' Erin repeats.

Something's wrong. Erin remembers how Mira was fretting in the car about other girls being on the trip. If her parents are strict, she's probably reluctant to drink – and worried the rest of them will get out of hand. Erin heads over, ready to assure her that *she* at least, doesn't plan on getting wasted. There's no way she's getting out of control around Bee.

But when she arrives at Mira's side she sees that Mira is staring into a bowl, where she's cracked all but one of the eggs. The bowl's contents makes Erin gag.

Every single yolk is red, thick with lumps of blood. The jelly-like whites are tinged pink. A few of the blood clots are so dark they appear black.

'What the *hell*?' Erin whispers.

'They're all like it.' Mira cracks the last egg and its contents slither out, every bit as grim as the others. Erin studies the broken shells which Mira has put back in the box. None of them has the little stamp that's found on supermarket eggs. They're probably from chickens kept somewhere on the island. *Ivy Bramble. Diseased hens.* Erin doesn't recall seeing any evidence of chickens here, but they've only explored a small portion of the place.

'Rank,' says Kitty, who's come to see what they're looking at. 'Whatever laid those needs putting to sleep.'

'I'll do pasta,' Mira mutters, taking the bowl off to be emptied down the toilet.

'Good thing it's not 1645, eh?' says Kitty. 'Or we'd all be hunting the witch.'

She lines up the four glasses and pours more vodka.

Erin's last to shower. When she emerges, Bee's face has been painted back on and Kitty's worked makeover magic on Mira, whose long black hair is blow-dried sleek. Tawny eyes and red lips complement her perfect olive skin. They've pooled make-up and accessories. Erin's embarrassed by her dried-up mascara and crumbled eyeshadow when Kitty and Bee's contributions are endless, expensive and glitzy.

'This is good shit,' Kitty says approvingly, smearing on Clarins' Beauty Flash Balm.

'Yeah,' Bee agrees. 'That girl I live with, she's always on the rob. Gives me loads of stuff.'

'Just her?' Kitty has a glint in her eye. 'Or have you got sticky fingers as well?'

'Maybe.' Bee adds more vodka to her glass. And there is something in that *maybe* that makes Erin question whether this other girl even exists. *That girl I live with.* Yeah, right.

'She's full of ideas,' Bee goes on. 'At weekends she goes to this casino and does this whole routine where she says she's lost her bag and cons blokes into buying her drinks. Sometimes she fucks them down the alley next to it and takes their wallets.'

Kitty laughs. 'That's grim, but kinda badass.'

'How old is she?' Erin asks disbelievingly. 'Don't you need ID to get in those places?'

'Not if you suck off the doormen.' Bee grins, but it fades as she reads the disgust on the other girls' faces. 'Told you she was wild.'

'No kidding.' Kitty hands Erin a glass of something pink and perches in front of her. 'I'm doing your make-up. What kind of look do you want?'

'Something different,' Erin says, tasting the drink. Vodka and cranberry. It's strong, but good after the shots. 'Completely different.' She wants to look like someone else.

'Okay.' Kitty studies her. 'Well, you're kind of girl next door. So, I'm thinking *sultry*.'

Erin chews her lip. 'I don't know if I can pull off sultry.'

'Sure, you can.' Kitty lunges at Erin's eyebrows with a pair of tweezers, plucking in earnest. Erin glugs her drink. It's helping numb the pain.

Kitty sets to work sweeping, blending, dabbing. 'Who's this for?'

Erin hesitates. 'Just me, I suppose.'

'There's no one you want to impress tonight?'

A flush creeps into Erin's cheeks. She wants Preston to notice her, properly notice her, and not just because she's having her purse snatched. But she can't admit that to Kitty or the others. Maybe one of them likes him, too. 'Not really,' she murmurs. 'You?'

Kitty smiles faintly. 'I've got my eye on someone. Not sure I'm their type, though.'

'Who's *your* type?' Erin asks. It's hard to think of anyone turning Kitty down. She's beautiful, fun, witty. It's impossible not to look at her.

'Don't really have one,' Kitty says vaguely. 'I just like who I like. You?'

'Er… Jordan Catalano,' Erin says. 'From that TV show?'

When Mira's asked the same question she swerves it, as though the thought hadn't occurred to her. 'I just want to get good grades,' she mutters, studying her drink.

'How about you, Bee?' Kitty presses. 'Seen anyone you like yet?'

Bee continues tonging her hair. 'I'm sort of with someone already. He's… older.'

'How much older?' asks Mira.

'Not enough to be my granddad or anything. I just like men. Not boys.'

'He's not married, is he?' Kitty asks. 'Oh, *god*, it's not that teacher guy, is it?'

'Course not.' Bee smiles as though the thought amuses her. 'It was nothing at the start, just a bit of fun. I was using him, to be honest. And then I don't know how, but it changed.'

Erin gives her a scathing look. She doesn't believe in the creep teacher or the older boyfriend. She wishes Bee would shut up. Mercifully, Kitty blasts the hairdryer, followed by hairspray. Erin's feeling distinctly woozy from the drink, despite her vow to watch herself around Bee.

'Done.' Kitty hands Erin the mirror. She peers into it, afraid she's going to hate it, and even more afraid she won't be able to wipe it off for fear of offending Kitty.

The first thing she notices is her eyes. They've never looked so blue, and smoulder under a smoky shadow. Her eyebrows are sleek, straight from the pages of a magazine. A soft peach blush highlights her cheek bones. Her lips are nude, velvety. Her hair tousled and effortlessly sexy. She doesn't look like someone else, and now she doesn't want to. She looks like a new version of herself. One born under a different star sign, perhaps. One who has always made the right choices.

'Like it?' Kitty asks.

Erin nods. 'You have to teach me how to do this.'

Kitty waves her hand dismissively. 'You have great bone structure, so there's not much to it. And your eyes are *so* cool. I always thought they were lenses, or something?'

Loosened up by the drink, Erin explains what a coloboma is.

'Huh,' says Kitty, with interest. 'So it's a defect? They look kinda like cats' eyes.'

Goats' eyes. Erin glances at Bee, the cruel jibe from all those years ago still fresh. Bee stares back, a small smile on her lips.

'Right, clothes,' Kitty says, looking at Erin expectantly.

'I've got this dress,' she begins, but Kitty's raking through her case, tossing out black cropped jeans and a pewter corset top. Erin eyes them doubtfully.

'Trust me,' Kitty says without looking up.

Ten minutes later, Mira wears Erin's dress and Erin's in the pewter corset. It complements her eyes and clings to curves that have sprung from nowhere. Bee has nabbed a silk scarf of Mira's and fashioned it into a necktie. She's in a short black dress with white polka dots. Her bare legs are eczema free.

'Yeah,' she says softly as she sees Erin looking. 'It cleared up.'

Kitty's wearing white capri pants and a leopard print top, and she's slicked on some eyeliner and peach lip gloss. She looks like a young Whitney Houston. 'Whose are these?' she demands, squeezing her foot into a red kitten heel. Erin wonders if she's always been this confident, this pushy, or whether it's an American thing.

'Mine,' says Bee.

'My stupid hoofs are too big.' Kitty kicks off the shoe in defeat. 'Bollocks.'

Erin chokes with laughter, spraying Mira with vodka and cranberry.

'What?' Kitty asks, bemused.

'You, saying *bollocks*,' Erin splutters. 'With your accent.'

She grins. 'Well, you Brits have the best cuss words. Like *cunt*.'

Mira goes into peals of shocked laughter, setting Erin off again. They're both tipsy.

Kitty spies a red bangle on Bee's wrist. 'You got another one of those?'

'No, but you can wear this one.' Bee hands it over despite Kitty's protests. 'Hey. I've just realised: we're all wearing something of each other's.'

'Well, duh,' says Kitty.

'There are superstitions about wearing other people's stuff,' Bee says. 'Like, you're not supposed to wear something of someone else's before they do. Or wear the clothes of someone who died – it's bad luck.'

Kitty shrugs. 'Half my clothes are vintage. I guess some might have come from people who've snuffed it.' She snickers at Mira's spooked expression.

Erin is chilled. The dress she lent Mira is unworn. She's had it for weeks since buying it on sale, and only removed the tags today. She stays quiet, refusing to let Bee's witchy talk freak her out. In Kitty's clothes, she feels invincible.

And then they're ready. Getting shoes and jackets on, stuffing make-up into bags, and slopping the last of the vodka neat into pink-tinged glasses.

'In one,' Kitty commands, and the four of them knock it back with hacks and hoots.

It's only just past seven, but it's been dark for a couple of hours. When they step out into the chilly night, Erin's struck by just *how* dark it is on the island. There are no street lights, but small solar lamps pick out the main pathways. The sky is beetle black, dotted with stars. They teeter away from the cabin. A fox ambles boldly across their path and vanishes into undergrowth. The office is locked up and dark, but there's light and strains of music coming from the games room. A few people are outside, cigarette tips glowing in the velvety blackness. The girls approach arm in arm, catching sight of themselves reflected in a window. They remind Erin of something: four girls she's seen on TV, walking in slow motion.

'You know who we look like?' she says dreamily, as if she is in slow motion, too.

'The Spice Girls?' Mira asks hopefully.

Kitty snorts. 'Christ, I hope not.'

'No, that film that's coming out,' Erin says. 'The one about the witches.'

'Ooh, yeah,' Kitty agrees. '*The Craft*. We should go see it.' She flings open the games room door, and they walk in.

15

OCTOBER 2016

'*You*,' Erin whispers, locking eyes with the stranger beside Kitty.

He steps through the door into the tea room, but it's a step too close. Erin jerks backwards in her chair. She forgets that her fingers are through the handle of the mug of tea Mira placed in front of her moments ago and doesn't extricate them quickly enough. The mug comes with her and scalding liquid hits her right thigh, soaking through her leggings. She cries out as the pain registers and the mug shatters on the floor.

'*Fuck*.' Tears spring to her eyes, blinding her. Her skin is on fire. And then just as quickly it's like ice, and the pain eases momentarily. She blinks and Aidan's next to her, an empty water jug in his hand. He's thrown the lot of it on her leg and is calling for Hewitt to grab the other jug from her end of the table, but Erin takes off.

'You stay the fuck away from me,' she yells, edging round the table towards the door. The man in the military jacket stands motionless, saying nothing.

'What the hell's going on?' Aidan demands. 'Erin, for god's sake, you're burnt, you need—'

She isn't listening. She's terrified, bolting for the door past Hewitt and Mira who are frozen in confusion.

'Erin,' Kitty begins. '*Wait*.'

Erin pushes past her, throws open the door and tears across

the gravel towards the car park. Kitty has lured her here, but that man – the blackmailer? – is the one pulling the strings. She's breathless, half-sobbing, and already the pain is back. Her leg is searing like a piece of cooking meat, but she pushes herself to get to her car and across that causeway. She scrabbles for her key as the pain throbs with each heartbeat. There's a bottle of water in the car, she can douse it with that.

'*Erin!*' Kitty yells after her. 'It's not what you think. Stop running, dammit. He's with me. I know why you're scared, but *he's with me!*'

Still she doesn't stop, not till she registers the footfall pounding behind her and she turns, wild, ready to smash the heel of her hand into his already broken nose—

The eyes, nose and throat are sensitive spots. Punch, bite, gouge, jab and elbow your attacker if you can.

Her arm is flung out and narrowly misses Aidan's face. He jumps back.

'Jesus, Erin, it's me! What's going on? Who *is* that guy?'

'I don't know, I don't *know*,' she sobs. The burning is so overpowering she can barely think straight. 'He followed me, through the town where I live and to my house—'

'What? Are you sure?'

'Yes, I'm bloody sure!'

Aidan glances back at the tea room. Kitty has come outside and is making her way towards them. The man is in the doorway, making no attempt to approach.

'Listen.' Aidan takes her arm. 'I won't let him near you. But we've got to get that leg sorted—'

'I don't care about my leg! I'm going, I—'

'*Erin.*' Kitty catches up to them, slightly out of breath. 'He's not here to hurt you. He's my bodyguard. Look, give me a chance to explain.'

Erin shakes her head, trying to clear it. To make sense of what Kitty is saying.

'Your body— *no*,' she mumbles. 'He followed me. He—'

'I told him to,' Kitty says.

Erin stares at her stonily. 'You did *what*?'

'I'm sorry.' Kitty swallows. 'I knew you'd be on edge because the anniversary was coming up, and I thought if you realised you were being followed it'd push you to come back when I asked.'

There's silence as Erin takes this in. The bright sunshine from earlier has been swallowed by billowing grey cloud, and it's starting to spit. She is furious with herself – as well as Kitty – for being taken in, manipulated in such a rudimentary way. Perhaps without everything else – the Child B leak, the tongue in the post – she would have rightly told Kitty to get lost or not replied at all.

'Come back?' she chokes finally. '*Here?*'

Kitty nods, holding her gaze. 'I knew it'd scare you and I thought—'

'Scare me?' Erin prickles with rage. She raises her hands and shoves Kitty hard, but she's surprised when Kitty staggers under the force of it. There's nothing of her. Erin feels her ribs in that one brief touch. At once the door behind opens and the bodyguard – if that's who he really is – is striding towards them.

Kitty holds a hand up without looking back. 'Leave it, Bomber. It's fine.'

Bomber halts but doesn't back off. He stands, arms folded, watching.

'I deserved that,' Kitty says quietly. 'But if you do it again he'll flatten you.'

Erin has already decided not to do it again, even without the threat. She's still fuming but something in her regrets pushing Kitty. She doesn't look well, and Erin wonders if she's been on another of her well-documented drink and drugs binges.

'Yeah,' says Erin. 'You did deserve it, you manipulative bitch. As for scaring me, I'm scared every bloody day. I didn't come here because of him.' She jerks her head at Bomber. 'I came to stop *you*. But it doesn't matter what I say, does it? You'll do what you want and to hell with everyone else. I don't know what you're playing at, and I don't care. It should all be left alone.'

'Wait.' Aidan says. 'Stop her from what?'

Erin stays quiet, wondering what, exactly, Kitty has said to Aidan. Whether there was any mention of *telling the truth*.

'You don't want it left alone,' Kitty says. 'You want it to go away.'

'It's been twenty years. It's never gone away.'

Kitty gives her a long look. 'So then let's try a new approach.'

Erin grimaces, her burnt leg driving her to distraction. She glances at Bomber, wondering again where all this has come from, and why now. 'What do you need a bodyguard for, Kitty? To show off how rich you are, or something else?'

Kitty starts walking back to the tea room. 'I just think you can't be too careful,' she says over her shoulder.

Erin stares after her. 'What's she said to you?' she asks Aidan. 'Why did she ask you to come here?'

'Reckons she's got new information,' he replies. 'Why, what's she said to you? What did you come here to stop?'

Erin wavers, avoiding his gaze. 'I think she should stop meddling with it altogether. Nothing good will come of it.'

'Maybe you should give her a chance. Hear what she's got to say.' Aidan glances at her wet legs. 'You can't leave like that, anyway. Come on, there'll be a first-aid kit somewhere.' He takes her arm, steering her back to the door. The pain in her leg is now so unbearable that she has no choice but to go with him.

Inside, she sits down and Aidan lays tea towels soaked in cold water on her thigh.

'You'll have to change out of these leggings,' he tells her. 'It might be blistering. Give me your car key, I'll get you a change of clothes.'

'I haven't got a change of clothes.' The icy water seeps further into her leggings. She's starting to shiver. 'I didn't bring an overnight bag because I'm not staying.'

He sighs heavily.

'I've got something you can wear.' Mira stands up, reaching into her bag for keys. 'I'll get it from the car.'

Five minutes later Erin is in the tea room's only lavatory, peeling off her sodden leggings. She stands for ten minutes with her leg raised as she runs cold water in the sink and sluices it on the angry pink skin. Aidan stands outside and passes her a dressing from a medical kit that is, he says, remarkably thoroughly equipped. Erin's not surprised. Given what happened here she imagines that further nasty incidents are the last thing the owner wants.

She applies the dressing, wincing. Aidan's quick actions with the water jug appear to have gone some way to help. There's no sign of blistering for now.

The dress she puts on is from a bag of clothes destined for a charity shop, which has been forgotten in Mira's car boot for several days. It's a size too small, Mira says. Something she bought to slim into, but never managed and so never wore. Erin removes the price tag and slips it on. It's loose and comfortable.

Kitty's persuaded the rest of them to stay the night – all expenses covered by her – the idea being that they don't have to rush off before the causeway is inaccessible. The second, more formal email sent by Kitty's team had advised Erin to bring an overnight bag too, but Erin wasn't having any of that.

'Thanks,' she tells Aidan as she comes out of the loo. He's putting things back in the medical box and sealing it up. 'Suppose you've had a bit of practice in patching up playground war wounds.' Her mum sometimes mentions Aidan, even though Erin's not seen him in years. The last she heard he was working in a school in Wanstead.

'I patch people up for a living now,' he says. 'Left teaching four years ago and became a paramedic. Got Gavin to thank for that.'

'Gavin? Your stepdad Gavin? Christ, is your mum still putting up with him?'

'Not any more. He tried to stop drinking about five years ago, went cold turkey. Ended up having a massive seizure from the withdrawal and died right in front of Mum and me on Christmas Day.' He rubs a hand over his head. 'That feeling, of being so helpless, not knowing what to do… I didn't ever want to be in that position again. So I quit my job and retrained.'

'Shit. Sorry, I didn't know.'

'No,' he says, nudging her lightly with his elbow. 'Well, staying in touch was never your strong point, was it?'

She shakes her head guiltily. And then there are raised voices from the main area. They glance at each other, then towards the shouting.

Something is kicking off.

16

OCTOBER 1996

Inside, the games room is dimly lit and the music is loud. People cluster in the small space, and heads turn as Erin, Kitty, Mira and Bee go in. Aidan and another history student, Declan, are looking through a stack of vinyl records, pulling them out and choosing what to play next on an ancient record player.

When he catches sight of Erin, Aidan stares as though he almost doesn't recognise her. Her eyes sweep the room, checking out what's there, and who is where. Halfway across there's a wall partition. On one side there are a couple of beat-up sofas and low tables with board games, puzzles and magazines. Above one of the sofas there are shelves of books. Framed art prints line the other walls. Erin imagines it being similar to a boarding school common room. It's shabby but there's something cool about it. A trendy vibe.

On the other side of the partition there's an open door leading to a room with pool tables, and above the thrum of music Erin can just about hear the *chink* of the balls being hit. It's by this door she locates Preston and Curtis. Preston looks their way and smiles lazily. Her heart flips. She smiles back, touching her hair self-consciously.

'Oh, Jesus, what're *they* doing here?' Kitty sighs. Callaghan and Hewitt are at the side of the room. 'Way to ruin a party.'

Erin shrugs, but she's gutted they're there, too. 'I guess they have to be here to make sure we're not off our faces or getting our drinks spiked.'

'Huh.' Kitty scoffs. 'I reckon pretty much everyone here's been boozing.'

Erin doubts this is true. Aidan doesn't seem drunk, and neither does strait-laced Declan. If it were not for Kitty, there's no way Mira would have been drinking, either.

'They don't look like they want to be here.' Mira's swaying lightly, her eyes glazed.

'No,' Kitty agrees. 'Callaghan looks fed up and Chewitt can't wait to get out of here.' She grins wickedly. 'God, that's tragic – has she tried to do something with her hair? Probably hoping he's going to rock her socks off later.'

'As if,' Bee sneers. 'What the hell is that dress she's wearing? The state of her.'

Kitty cackles.

'Maybe she's a really nice person,' Mira says, a little defensively. 'Not everything is about looks. She might be funny, or interesting.'

'Trust me, she's not,' Kitty says, with authority. 'She came in my mom's shop last month and kept her talking for like, an hour. I was in the back pricing stuff up, so she didn't see me but I heard everything. My mom couldn't get rid of her. She's fucking weird.'

'Why?' asks Erin. 'What was she talking about?'

'Ugh – something about her family. Having to look after her mother, who'd had a breakdown. How she'd almost had a breakdown herself. And then her mom died. She tried on so much stuff and didn't buy any of it because she ignored what my mom knew would look good on her and kept pulling out things that were all wrong. Like she was trying to be someone else. And then she wondered why she looked hideous in everything. My mom was *pissed.*' Kitty rolls her eyes. 'And she had all this dodgy fake tan as well, and everything she'd put on had to be washed and re-tagged afterwards. Honestly – nightmare.'

Mira has gone very still. Something Kitty's said has touched a nerve. Despite the pleasant fuzziness of the alcohol Erin feels a nudge of anxiety, like one wrong word could bring this fledgling friendship to a swift end.

'Having a breakdown doesn't mean someone is weird,' Mira says at last.

'Not because of that,' Kitty says easily, reaching out to touch Mira's arm. 'Hey, relax. I didn't mean that. I meant how she was sharing all this stuff with a total stranger. It was too personal, too much. That's all.'

Mira blinks and gives a faint nod, and Kitty lowers her hand.

'Let's mingle,' she says.

They skirt round the room, skimming faces. Erin is fixed only on one: Preston's. He's grinning, animated in conversation with Curtis.

'So,' says Kitty, her breath warm in Erin's ear above the music. 'It's him, right? The one you like?'

Erin meets her knowing gaze, and for a split second she swears she sees something a little sad in it. Perhaps Kitty knows Erin doesn't stand a chance. But already she's taking Erin by the hand, making a beeline for Preston. People move for them, parting to let them in.

'Ladies!' Preston says as they arrive, cutting across Tilly who has thrown her head back to laugh at something. 'Looking good this evening.' Hazy-eyed, his gaze roams over the four of them, lingering on Erin. He's been drinking, too.

Curtis leans over Erin. 'Looking good,' he says, parroting Preston as though he has no words of his own. 'You scrub up all right.'

'Thanks,' Erin answers. He's not out of control but he's drunker than Preston, reeking of lager. She glances over at Callaghan and Hewitt, but they're not taking any notice. Hewitt's putting her coat on to leave. Callaghan sits down when she's gone, and his face has changed. It's lost the bored look. *Poor Chewitt*. It's easy to imagine her in Kitty's mum's boutique, waffling on and spilling her secrets.

'So, what other subjects are you taking?' Curtis asks, saliva spraying her cheek.

She tells him, and he edges in even closer. Preston's talking to Kitty and Bee, but his gaze darts to her. She begins to move away from Curtis, but stops herself, remembering the look in Kitty's eyes. It's probably good for Preston to see he's got a bit of competition. She zones out as Curtis drones on about himself. He puts his hand on her arm, trailing sweaty fingers over her skin. She squirms away, her back against the wall. The music changes to something punchier. A couple of people start to dance.

Curtis persists in talking at her, asking questions without listening to the answers. She realises it's not worth enduring this, being pawed in the hope of making Preston jealous. She's unsure if it's deliberate but as Curtis gesticulates his hand brushes against her left breast. He doesn't apologise or acknowledge it, and she decides she's had enough.

It's now he leans in, his face coming towards hers. Horrified, she realises he means to kiss her, and ducks out of his way at the same moment Kitty pulls her to safety. Erin staggers sideways, looking up gratefully.

'Thought you needed rescuing,' Kitty says, not particularly quietly. Erin allows Kitty to lead her away. She grabs Mira's hand, too, and they head to the dance floor. Kitty's good, of course. She's good at everything. Mira is as well, her shyness melting away into the music, although her timing is off. The booze has hit her hard. Erin suddenly registers that Bee isn't with them. It's not that she cares, particularly, but it's like being aware there's a spider in the room and wanting to know exactly where it is. She spots a flash of red hair. Bee is talking to Callaghan, and he looks vaguely annoyed. He gestures in their direction, and Erin has a horrible feeling he's called Bee over to ask her about them drinking. Bee shakes her head, her glossy hair bobbing. Callaghan pulls on his jacket and takes out a pack of cigarettes, then gets up and heads for the door alone. He's leaving.

Erin turns away. Someone has put on a song called 'Candy', and there seems to be a dance to it that she doesn't know about but it's okay because Kitty does, and by the time the song ends Erin's sort of got the hang of it. They dance, get it right, then get it wrong and laugh, and occasionally Erin sees Preston looking.

'We'll make him come to you,' Kitty says.

Erin carries on dancing even when Kitty disappears for a few minutes and returns with a bottle of Coke from a vending machine which she shares round the three of them, then uses as a microphone to rap along to 'I Got 5 On It'. The song bleeds into another, then another, and everything's speeding up and Erin forgets about Preston because she's enjoying herself, properly enjoying herself and if this is what friendship feels like then she wants all of it, and more than that she's starting to believe she is someone who might be worth liking. She's drunk and having fun and maybe even starting to like herself, a little. And then this song comes on and everyone's going nuts singing about *lager* and something about *Romford*—

Erin catches sight of Bee alone by the wall. She's staring at the dancers, mouth moving soundlessly, and at first Erin thinks she's singing, but the words on her lips don't match and it's like she's muttering a curse. Her eyes are narrowed in a scowl. Erin feels a dull stab of horror at the familiarity of it.

Listen, she hears ten-year-old Bee say, with that same look on her pinched little face. *This is what we can say.*

Erin squeezes her eyes shut. *Don't think of it, don't think of it.*

They finish the Coke and Kitty goes to put the bottle on a ledge but it topples to the floor. Someone's foot catches it and sends it into a spin. It slows to a halt, pointing at Kitty.

'Spin the bottle!' she yells above the music. 'Who's up for it?'

There are cheers. Everyone is up for it. Kitty reaches down to spin again and Erin watches it circle. The bottle stops, pointing straight at her.

She laughs, suddenly unsteady on her high heels. 'You'd better spin again,' she shouts. Someone boos.

Kitty stares at her. 'I'm game if you are.'

Fear and excitement zigzag through her. *She's serious.* Erin feels eyes on her and, along with the look on Kitty's face, it makes her daring. *Why not?*

'How long for?' she asks.

Preston steps forward, holding a coin. 'Heads to the count of five, and tails to…?'

'Thirty seconds.' Bee's appeared on the sidelines. Her scowl is gone.

'Twenty,' says Kitty, and it's final.

Preston flips the coin. 'Heads. Five seconds.'

Erin's heart races. She's terrified, but she can't back out now, not with everyone watching. She can count on one hand the number of people she's kissed in her life. She's never had any experience with girls before.

'Ready?' Kitty asks.

She isn't, but she nods jerkily as Kitty leans in. A strand of Erin's hair has caught in her lipstick. Kitty gently pulls it free, and the gesture is so intimate that Erin shivers. People whistle and catcall as Kitty touches her lips to Erin's. Their audience starts to count, voices swelling above the music. Erin gulps, realising she's the envy of many in the room. Fleetingly she wonders whether *she* fancies Kitty; she's so stunning, so self-assured. Whenever she's around Erin can't stop looking at her. But as the count hits five Erin's the first to pull away.

The room erupts into cheers. Erin find Preston's eyes, and they share a look that's heavy with desire. It makes her feel powerful. She can't believe what she's just done.

'Erin's turn to spin,' Kitty announces, kicking the bottle towards her.

Dizzy, Erin bends down and spins. There's only one person she wants it to land on. It circles and slows, passing Tilly, Curtis, Preston. Erin's eyes travel up.

Aidan stares back at her, his face unreadable. When did *he* come over? He was on the other side of the room a minute ago, messing about with the vinyl. She waits for him to shake his head, turn away. This isn't his thing at all. But he pulls out a coin. Tosses it, catches it.

Heads, Erin begs silently. *Five seconds.*

'Tails,' he announces, shoving the coin in his pocket and moving towards her.

She can't meet his gaze. Instead she stares at the dip in his throat, just above the neckline of his shirt. She's known Aidan for ever. She can't move. She can't do this.

But he does. He steps in close and puts a hand on her face, tilting her chin up. She's forced to meet his eyes. Their dark brown depths appear black and impenetrable in the dim room. Her breathing is shaky, and she knows he feels it. He brings his lips to hers, closing his eyes.

The counting begins, and so do the whoops and cheers. She closes her eyes too. The kiss is light at first. The smell of him washes over her, familiar and different all at once. When they were kids Aidan always smelled of Imperial Leather soap and cola bottle sweets. Now he's musky with aftershave or shower gel or something. She feels a rush of the old affection for him. And something new, an unexpected excitement.

They're up to five when he opens his mouth slightly, and when he kisses again it's more urgent, dampening her lips. His hand is still warm on her cheek, the other one on the small of her back. Hers are on his waist and she feels the warmth of his skin through his shirt. *This is so, so weird*, she thinks. *But not unpleasant.* The chanting gets louder. Someone yells, 'Get a room!' It's only then Erin hears the counting, 'Twenty-two, twenty-three—'

She breaks away, breathing hard. *Twenty-three?*

Aidan looks away, red-faced. Someone slaps him on the shoulder, and he brings his hand up to his mouth, touching his lips. Erin makes her way back to Kitty, Mira and Bee, but her eyes seek out Preston. She searches his face, hoping to see jealousy there but he's leaning towards Curtis, laughing.

Someone shouts for Aidan to spin again. This time it lands on Mira, and Erin feels a tug of something – she's not sure what – within her. Mira's nervous, but the drink has dulled her inhibitions. If she was sober Erin thinks she'd probably refuse. Someone else flips a coin, and it's heads. Five seconds. Erin is glad, which confuses her.

'Aidan's cute,' Kitty murmurs.

'You think?'

'Yeah. God, yeah. And he's into you.'

'Is he?' Erin shrugs it off, embarrassed. She and Aidan haven't been close for years. Yet now she's looking at him with Mira, Erin is seeing him properly for the first time in a long time. Aidan is good, decent. He always has been. And she realises now, he is, as Kitty puts it, cute. His dark-lashed eyes are gentle and he says something to Mira. It looks like, 'Okay?'

Mira nods, and they kiss with closed mouths. It's over exactly on the count of five. Mira stands stiffly throughout but her face breaks out into a smile afterwards. Erin wonders if she's ever been kissed before. Her emotions are even more confused, because she thinks, out of everyone here, Aidan was the best person it could have been. He smiles at Mira before stepping away. She spins the bottle again, braver now.

It stops on Bee, who steps forward with a curtsey.

'Mira's getting an education tonight,' Kitty quips. 'Not the kind her folks had in mind, though.'

Mira looks uneasy about kissing another girl. Bee, on the

other hand, saunters towards Mira like she's a film star on the red carpet, working her audience. A coin is flipped. *Tails*. Mira is rigid as Bee leans in. Straight away it's clear this is nothing like Aidan's innocent kiss. Bee latches on to Mira like a lion going in for a kill. People cheer. Curtis shouts, 'Yeah, baby!' and there's an eruption of laughter. Bee's tongue pushes against Mira's lips. Mira shoves her away. They're only on the count of three.

Someone jeers. 'Frigid!'

Mira lurches towards Erin and Kitty. Bee stays put, eyes darting around as though she's searching for something. Someone kicks the bottle and the game starts over. The circle of people closes, sealing Bee inside.

Mira's lipstick is a red slash across her face. Kitty thumbs some of it away like a mother cleaning up a child. 'Let's get you some air.'

They head outside, the door banging as they exit. The night has turned colder, and there's no one there but them. Just the scent of lingering cigarette smoke and a pile of discarded butts in the dirt. Kitty produces a tissue from her bag and dabs at Mira's face, trying to redo her lipstick.

'Hold still,' she murmurs.

'I'm so drunk.' Mira sways lightly, eyes unfocused. 'I drank too much. I don't like it.'

'You're fine,' says Kitty. 'Fresh air helps. Come on, it's still early. It's gonna be fun.'

Mira nods, shivering. Erin feels drunk, too, especially now the cold autumn air is on her. Its sharpness is only making her head feel fuzzier. She reapplies her own lipstick, thinking of the traces it has left on Aidan. The kiss is still strong in her mind.

The door bursts open and Bee appears.

Erin rounds on her, old resentment bubbling. 'What was that about?'

Bee tilts her head. 'What was what about?'

'You took it too far. You could see Mira wasn't up for that.'

'You and Kitty kissed. What's the difference?'

'Kitty didn't try to stick her tongue down my throat.'

Bee holds her hands up. 'Look, sorry, okay?'

'It's fine,' Mira mutters. 'I was just… surprised.'

Bee shrugs. 'It was meant to be fun, a bit of a turn-on.'

'A turn-on? For who?' Erin's angrier now, and a small part of her knows it's because Bee has backed down. She wants her to resist, to argue, to storm off. But Bee is clinging on like she always did.

'I don't know.' Bee throws her hands up again, in exasperation. 'You're telling me you didn't do it for that too? That you didn't get a kick out of being watched?'

Erin squirms. She can't deny seeking out – and enjoying – Preston's reaction.

'Chill.' Kitty's fingertips brush Erin's arm. 'Mira said it's fine. No harm done.'

'I didn't mean it, Mira,' Bee adds, but her eyes are on Erin. 'Let's go in. We'll play some pool.'

Mira hiccups, blinking hard. The fresh air has only exacerbated the drink.

'Come on.' Bee props an arm round Mira and they go back in, releasing a blast of music as the door swings open. Before Erin and Kitty can follow, someone steps out. Erin's heart skips. It's Preston.

He lights a cigarette, and offers them out. 'Everyone's talking about you two.'

'Are they?' Kitty says casually. She takes a cigarette and inhales coolly. Erin didn't know she smoked. Perhaps it's a social thing.

'Yeah.' Preston mimes fanning himself. His blond hair is pushed back off his face. Erin can smell aftershave. She thinks it's *Joop!* She's seen him take a bottle of it from his locker at college and spray himself. 'So, what do you think of the trip?'

Kitty shrugs, looking in her bag. Erin wonders if she's deliberately acting uninterested. 'It's okay, I guess.'

They chat for a few minutes about the messed-up stuff in the museum. Erin tries to follow Kitty's lead and not appear too keen. She checks a pocket, fiddles with the zip on her jacket, but always her eyes are pulled back to him like a tide.

'It's nice out,' Preston says expectantly. 'We should go for a walk.'

'Where?' Erin asks. She glances up at the black, black sky. Tiny stars wink back at her. Does he mean all three of them? She feels dizzy, excited. Something is about to happen.

'It's fucking freezing,' says Kitty. 'I should've brought my big jacket. I'm gonna go get it.'

'On your own?' asks Erin.

'Yeah.' Kitty waves an impatient hand. 'I'll see you back here in a minute.'

'We'll come with you.' Preston crushes the cigarette butt under his heel. From the inside pocket of his jacket he takes out an open bottle of lemon Hooch and downs a mouthful. 'Don't want you ending up in a ditch somewhere.'

They start walking, with a shivering Kitty in the lead. Erin hopes she's going the right way. Her own sense of direction is normally spot on, but the drink has left it scrambled and Preston's an extra distraction. She can't tell whether it's her or Kitty he's interested in. Seconds later she gets her answer when he slips his hand around hers. Patrick Preston is *holding her hand*. They walk in silence, following Kitty down the dark track. He offers Erin the Hooch and she drinks, her lips where his have been. The liquid is warm from the heat of his body. They pass it back and forth until it's gone and he tosses the bottle into the long grass. Soon they reach the cabin and Kitty is rootling in her bag for the key.

She lets herself in and thumps through the cabin. Erin prepares to wait outside, Kitty is only going to be a few seconds. But Preston strides into the cabin, tugging her hand. She follows, heart colliding with her ribs, head swaying from the drink. Kitty has not turned on any of the lights bar one: the bathroom. She's shut herself in there, rattling around. A tap is running. Erin is standing in the dark with Preston by the upturned crate, where pink vodka cranberry glasses gleam stickily in the moonlight.

'You're beautiful,' he says quietly. 'I never noticed how beautiful until tonight.' He releases her fingers and his hands move to her waist. Erin's whole body is pulsing. If she wasn't drunk she'd be trembling. She's wanted this so long. She stares up at him, and his pupils are huge in the dim light. She tries to think of something witty to say but her mind is blank and now it doesn't matter anyway because he's kissing her. Soft at first, and then harder, his arms encircling her, pulling her to him. He tastes sour, of cigarettes and booze, but it's okay because it's Preston and she wants this. She lifts her hands on to his shoulders, tentatively touching his hair where it's buzzed short at his nape. It's nice. He grabs her hips, grinding against her. She feels him, hard through his jeans, and a little, '*Oh*,' of shock escapes her.

'Sorry,' he whispers, between kisses, picking up on her discomfort. 'Got carried away. That's what you've done to me. Sorry.'

She relaxes into the kiss again. He touches her hair and she becomes bolder, moving her mouth on to his neck, breathing in the scent of him. He groans softly. Her mind is adrift, bobbing drunkenly to the thought of the tea leaves, and Kitty's talk of *getting laid*. She could, she thinks. She and Preston could sink into the couch right there and have sex. He could be her first. Something twists in her at the thought of it, a niggle, but she pushes it away. His insistence starts to build. When he slides a hand to her breast and says, 'Is this okay?' she nods. She doesn't want to be called *frigid* like Mira.

He moves his other hand up now, both cupping her through the thin material. Rubbing, squeezing. She starts to feel weird, like she's on a driving lesson and she's put the car in too high a gear. The niggle is pricking at her like a splinter. She doesn't want to get called *slapper*, either. The kisses aren't as nice now. They're harsh and too wet, and she makes her own softer, trying to show him what she wants, what she likes, but he's not picking up on her cues. The kiss with Aidan flashes into her mind and she realises, with regret, that it was better than this.

'You're so fit,' he murmurs. 'So fucking fit it's unbelievable.' His voice has changed, become rough. It had been different when he'd told her she was beautiful. She'd preferred that. He takes her hand and she thinks he's going to kiss it but instead he guides it lower and in one practised movement his zip is down – *and how did he even do that so fast?* – and her hand is *around* it. She freezes, stunned. His fist is clamped over hers, moving back and forth.

'*No.*' She jerks her hand away. 'I don't want to do that.'

'Okay, okay.' He laughs softly, rearranging himself. He moves his hands to her shoulders, bending his head to trail his lips over her skin. 'You're just so sexy. I can't control myself. You know what really turned me on?'

'What?' Her voice is deflated. The opposite of what she can feel prodding against her insistently. She wants to smack it away but the thought of touching it again is unbearable. She'd wanted the gentle kisses and the tender compliments. Not this.

'You and Kitty,' he whispers into her hair. 'I want to see that again. Or better still, you, *me* and Kitty.' He lets the suggestion hang, still stroking her shoulders but now it feels all wrong, like she's being mauled. The splinter inside her becomes a shard of glass. She feels grubby. Cheap. *Used.* He doesn't really like her, she realises. He just wants to fuck her *and* Kitty, together. She's suddenly aware of his saliva drying on her face, her neck. She's disgusted by it. She recalls the hungry look in his eyes as he watched her and Kitty after they'd played spin the bottle, and something her dad used to say pops into her head: *play stupid games, win stupid prizes.*

She registers now how curiously silent the cabin is. The running tap has stopped. Where the hell even *is* Kitty, and how long have they been standing there?

'What d'you think?' he asks when she doesn't respond.

Erin swallows. 'I think we should go back to the games room.'

The bathroom door opens, flooding the little area with light. Erin blinks in relief and risks a glance down. Thankfully Preston has put himself away, but he hasn't given up.

'How about it, Kitty cat?' he offers.

Kitty gives him a blank stare as she grabs her fluffy jacket from the sofa and shrugs it on. Her eyes are glassy. Erin wonders what she was doing in the bathroom for so long. She seems sharper, more with it. Erin's guess is that she made herself throw up.

'How about what?'

'You, me and Erin.' Preston touches his lips to Erin's cheek, and her skin crawls. 'And a bottle, if you like. I can think of stuff we could do with it.'

Kitty's lip curls. 'Don't be gross.'

He is gross, Erin realises bitterly. He's made *her* feel gross.

'Erin said she didn't want to,' Kitty reminds him, coolly.

He looks genuinely confused. 'No, she didn't.'

'She wants to go back,' Kitty says slowly, as though she's explaining it to a very young child. 'Read between the lines. Let's go.'

'Won't be a sec,' says Erin. She peels herself away from Preston and dives into the bathroom, shutting herself in. She pumps soap into her hands, lathers and rinses. Repeats, desperate to scrub him off her. After that she scoops up handfuls of water and swills her mouth out. She will not cry, she tells herself. Not yet.

Once she's out Kitty shoos them from the cabin and locks up. Erin stays by her side, out of Preston's reach, and then they march back in the direction of the games room. He's somewhere behind, calling after them.

'What was all that before, then?' he demands. 'You like teasing, is that it?'

They ignore him. Kitty slips her hand into Erin's and squeezes. 'I'm sorry I left you alone with him.'

'It's not your fault.' Erin's voice is thick, on the verge of tears. 'I wanted to be alone with him at first.' She knows now that Kitty set the whole thing up, lingered in the bathroom. Probably overheard most of it.

'You're still doing it.' He's stomping after them angrily, and the change in him is frightening. 'Holding hands! You winding me up, or what?'

'Fuck off, Preston,' Kitty snaps, tossing him a look of contempt. 'And do your fucking flies up.'

He trails after them, shouting insults. *Prick-teases. Pair of tarts.* They speed up, but his tirade continues. *Sluts. Slappers. Dykes.* Erin is trying to stop the tears she knows are coming, but they spill on to her cheeks anyway. She swipes them away. An hour ago she'd felt so grown up, so sexy. Now she feels like a stupid little girl. She wants to go home and she wants her mum. She wants her dad, too, but her dad is gone and it's all her fault.

The games room comes into view. Weak with relief, she glances over her shoulder. Preston's hanging back, silently glowering at them. The sight of him turns her stomach and she wants to wash her hand again.

Kitty releases her hand and throws open the door. Aidan's on the other side, about to come out, and just seeing him makes Erin feel safer. She looks back again. Preston is stalking in the other direction, away into the night. Aidan watches him, eyes narrowed, then begins speaking urgently.

'I've been looking for you.'

'What's up?' Kitty asks, but for once Erin's one step ahead. She knows instantly from Aidan's face that something's wrong.

'It's Mira,' he says.

17

OCTOBER 2016

Aidan heads back through to the main area of the tea room and Erin follows, catching the tail end of a rant from Tori Callaghan, who is jabbing a finger in Charlotte Hewitt's direction.

'Paul used to laugh at you, you know.' Tori's face twists, and her tone changes to become girlish and mocking. 'Baking him cakes, working late whenever he did… the anonymous Valentine's cards and cringey little Post-it notes.'

Hewitt is frozen in her seat like a deer in headlights as Tori continues to lay into her. Mira and Kitty watch helplessly, and even Bomber isn't bothering to pretend he's not listening.

'He'd tell me how you were always hanging round him, confiding in him every time you had a row with your boyfriend or a bad date. Making it so *obvious* you were available to him. Even the students who were after him never acted that desperate.'

'I wasn't desperate.' Hewitt's cheeks are alight with humiliation. 'I just… liked him.'

'*Liked* him? You were obsessed.' Tori looks Hewitt over spitefully.

'Well, you didn't need to worry, I didn't make the cut.' Hewitt looks like she wants to cry, but there is now an underlying current to her voice. As though she's barely managing to contain an explosive anger. 'His hands were clearly full enough, not that you or I knew that at the time.'

'*You or I?*' Tori laughs incredulously. 'I was his *wife*. Make no mistake, I always knew when Paul was up to something. You? You didn't know shit about him.' She throws up her hands and Hewitt flinches at the sudden movement. 'Why are you even here? Are you actually still obsessed with him after all these years? Trying to find a little nugget of truth somewhere that makes him less culpable?'

'Stop saying I'm obsessed with him!' Hewitt snaps, banging the table with her fists. 'I was… infatuated with him back then, I'll admit that. I let myself get… distracted by him. I wasn't doing my job properly, turned a blind eye to the drinking that was going on that night, Paul and I both did. Just kids having fun, we thought. So I didn't come out of it blameless, either. What happened on that trip was the end of my career in education, as I'm sure you're well aware.'

'Hardly surprising,' says Tori, unperturbed by Hewitt's display of temper. 'How it was signed off in the first place I'll never know. You must have pulled some serious strings there. It was a fucking recipe for *Lord of the Flies* even without what happened to that girl.'

'Bee.' Aidan walks behind the shop counter and puts the first-aid kit away.

Tori narrows her eyes. 'What?'

'*That girl* had a name,' Aidan says shortly. 'It was Belinda.'

'I know her bloody name, all right? She's the reason he killed himself. My kids – *Paul's* kids – have had to grow up in the shadow of all this. So I'm here for them. I want answers.'

'What about justice?' Aidan asks.

Tori scoffs. 'Oh, I'd say justice was done.'

'Really? You think a seventeen-year-old girl being half-drowned, forced to swallow broken glass and having her throat slit is justice?'

'I take it you've not seen the news for a couple of weeks? Or that *Crimewatch* special?'

Aidan folds his arms and leans against the counter. 'Of course I have.'

'You know she was Child B, then.'

Erin, who has taken a seat next to Mira, stiffens. Tori's expression is venomous, and the pale blond hair and heavy make-up make her face look harder still. She's never been particularly soft – not if the newspapers are to be believed.

'Doesn't make what happened to her okay,' says Aidan. 'That's not justice.'

'Some might see it as justice for that Nicky kid.' Tori taps a manicured nail on the side of her coffee cup. 'He died because of her and the other one.'

'She was a *child*,' Aidan retorts. His dark eyes are suddenly tortured. 'She was still basically a child when someone—'

'What kind of child makes up a lie like that?' Tori interjects. 'Not a nice one.'

'Plenty of people aren't nice. Doesn't mean they deserve what she got.'

'Can everyone please calm down?' says Mira. 'This isn't helping anyone.'

'Good idea,' says Kitty. 'Right. Now everyone's here, let's move on.' Having helped herself to a cookie, a Snickers bar and a black coffee from the snack table, she's taken a seat next to Hewitt who seems to have shrunk in her chair during the outburst. Bomber has also got a mug of something and taken himself off from them to a small table over in the corner. Erin watches as he dunks a flimsy teabag on a string into the cup. He's not looking their way but she knows he's listening to every word.

'We're not expecting anyone else, then?' Hewitt asks.

Kitty gestures around them in a *this is it* motion. 'There *is* no one else – no one who had a question mark over them that night, I mean.' She pauses. 'No one still alive, anyway. I take it you all heard about Preston and Curtis?'

There are sombre nods. Eighteen months after the island trip Leon Curtis drove home from a party three times over the limit and crashed into a tree. Patrick Preston, in the passenger seat, and a girl in the back had both been killed instantly. Curtis died a week later in hospital. Erin's mother had sent the write-up from the local news to her at uni. *Such great guys*, the tributes had said.

'So, I guess the first thing you're all wondering is, why now?' says Kitty. She breaks off a chunk of cookie and crams it in her mouth, chewing slowly and with a total lack of self-regard. Now Erin's calmed down and established that Bomber is not here to murder her, she finds she can't quite tear her eyes away from Kitty – but it's for completely different reasons to twenty years ago. Kitty's dressed as glamorously as ever, in orange crocheted flared trousers and a matching bell-sleeve top. On anyone else the outfit would be ridiculous. On Kitty it's nothing less than Erin would expect. Yet her face is haggard, and she's rake thin. She looks closer to sixty than forty, which Erin finds strange, given Kitty's heritage. The feeling of her bony chest under Erin's fingers is vivid in her mind. *Cocaine Kitty*. Erin remembers that headline. The many, many drugs binges and rehab check-ins caught on camera. More scandals even when she was well; caught shoplifting in Hollywood, busted cheating on her film mogul fiancé with his sister. The press had loved that. She recalls, too, interviews in which Kitty has spoken about letters and other things from cranks obsessed with Bee's murder: silver glass bottles, film scripts about what happened on the island. Not quite the offal and shit that's sent to Erin, but unnerving enough to warrant employing private security, now she thinks of it. It's not like Kitty can't afford it. And who's to say she doesn't receive worse things? Perhaps she does, and refuses to give the sender the satisfaction of talking about them.

Erin tries and fails again to remember the last time she saw

Kitty online or in a magazine. Whenever it was, she didn't look like this. Airbrushing has a lot to answer for, although Erin feels as though she, too, has aged a decade in the past couple of weeks.

'It's pretty obvious why now,' Tori says snippily, pausing as Kitty gives her an expectant look. 'To kickstart your comeback. Money running low, is it?'

Kitty chuckles. 'Honey, I got problems but money ain't one of them.'

'Yeah, you've certainly done all right out of all this. Takes a special kind of nasty to capitalise on someone's death.'

'Well, you know what they say.' Kitty sucks chocolate off her thumb. Her American drawl is far stronger than Erin remembers. 'When life gives you lemons, shit gets sour. I made the best of the cards I was dealt.' She puts the cookie down on a paper napkin. 'But life changes. Which kinda brings me to the second thing you're all thinking.'

'What *are* we all thinking?' Hewitt prompts. She still looks shellshocked from the row with Tori. Erin can't help feeling sorry for her. Her hands shake as she lifts her cup to her lips.

'Oh, come on,' Kitty scoffs. 'You're not all wondering why I look like shit? Thinking the party girl lifestyle finally caught up with me?'

There is an awkward stillness.

'You look… fine,' Mira begins weakly. 'Everyone ages—'

'Cancer,' says Kitty, zipping the Snickers into her bag. 'Stage four. Started in my bowel, then went to my liver. Docs don't really like giving estimates, but I've not got long.'

Erin is reeling. For a minute she can't speak. Can barely think of anything except the violent shove she delivered to Kitty earlier. She feels wretched, wishes she could take it back.

'How long?' she manages at last.

'Six months, give or take. I'm leaning more towards take.'

'Oh, Kitty.' Mira looks stricken. 'I'm so sorry. But… why are you here, on this miserable island? You should be spending the time you have left—'

'With my *loved ones*, making *memories*?' Kitty interrupts in a sing-song voice. 'Yeah, did a lot of that last year when I got the diagnosis.' She laughs wryly. 'Nothing like your own mortality knocking to make you start living. Bucket list, yada-yada. I'm at the point now where I've just got enough juice left for the unfinished business. So *voilà*.'

'It really means that much to you?' Aidan asks. 'Finding out who killed Bee?'

'I'm *dying* to get to the bottom of it,' Kitty quips. 'Hell, maybe I could even die here on the island, that'd be something, wouldn't it? A kind of symmetry to round off my life story. I can see the headlines now: MURDER ISLAND CLAIMS THIRD LIFE.'

'Fourth.' Hewitt's voice is quiet, but it drains the oxygen out of the air. 'It'd be the fourth life, not the third.'

Kitty's face slackens. 'Oh,' she says, horrified. 'Yeah.'

Yeah. A small word for a small thing carrying such enormous weight: a tiny cluster of cells, a missed period. Because it hadn't just been Bee's murder, and Callaghan's suicide.

Bee had been pregnant.

18

OCTOBER 1996

'WHERE WERE YOU?' AIDAN ASKS as they enter the games room. Kitty goes ahead, scanning the room. After the chilly freshness of outside it's warm and stale indoors, and Erin experiences a wave of nausea. They've been gone only about twenty minutes but it feels longer. A few people are crammed on the sofas, playing Jenga. Declan and Tilly are pressed into a corner, kissing. A pairing, perhaps, that's come about from spin the bottle. No one's playing it now, but the empty bottle is still being kicked around by those who are dancing.

'Just went back to get Kitty's jacket,' Erin mumbles, folding her arms around herself.

Aidan is watching her closely. 'With Patrick Preston?'

She looks away. 'Yes.'

'Did something happen?'

'No.'

'Then why was he skulking off like that a minute ago?' His voice is sharp. 'And why are you crying?'

'I'm not.' Erin pushes past him. She can do without Aidan policing where she's been, and with whom. 'What's up with Mira? Where is she?'

'I saw her playing pool with Bee,' Aidan replies tersely. 'If you can call it that – she can barely stand up. She's pissed out of her head.'

Though he doesn't say it, Erin can hear his unspoken thought:

and you're not far behind. She tries to walk more steadily, but it's impossible when her head is so fuzzy. Aidan's stepdad is an alcoholic – or at least, he was when they were kids. She can't imagine much has changed, including Aidan's loathing for drink and what it does to people. No wonder he's concerned. She looks over to where the pool tables are, seeing that, now, the door to the room is closed. Her muddied mind sharpens a fraction, with *something*, an inkling that all is not well.

'That door wasn't shut a minute ago,' Aidan says.

Kitty is there now, pushing at it. 'I think someone's holding it closed.'

Erin checks for a lock. There isn't one. Her unease deepens at the thought of Mira, drunk and out of control, shut in a room alone with Bee.

'Move,' says Aidan, and he shoulders the door. It gives, just an inch or so and he barges it again. Something scrapes on the other side. The gap widens enough to reach through now and Aidan does so, pushing at a table that's been butted up against the door. Then they're in, squeezing past it, Aidan followed by Kitty, then Erin.

Her initial feeling is one of relief. Mira isn't trapped in there with Bee – Bee's nowhere to be seen. Mira is sitting, just about, on the side of the pool table with Curtis standing between her legs, one arm round her waist. His other hand is on her thigh, high up, where the dress she's wearing – Erin's dress – has ridden up. Mira's arms are loose by her sides, but it's clear they've been kissing. Their mouths look red, like a rash, though perhaps it's from the wine-coloured lipstick she's wearing.

Erin feels a barb of disgust. Curtis was pawing drunkenly at her not an hour ago. Mira can do so much better.

Mira's head flops backwards, then jerks up. She looks like a marionette, or someone who's falling asleep on a train. She raises a hand to push at him, but it lands limp on the pool table, sending a red ball rolling slowly across it.

'What are you doing?' Aidan says. His voice is dangerous, incredulous. It's not a question. It's obvious what Curtis has been doing – or was about to do.

Mira sways, eyes rolling in her head.

Kitty marches up to the table. 'Get away from her.'

He steps back, hands raised, eyes wide. Trying to look innocent. Without his arm round her, Mira slumps backwards on to the pool table. Kitty tugs at the dress, trying to pull it down.

'You're in deep shit,' Aidan says.

'Calm down, mate,' says Curtis. He's half-smiling, taking a step towards Aidan.

Aidan stands his ground. 'I'm not your mate.'

'No one's in deep shit,' Curtis continues. He is edging closer to the door. 'Mira's had a few too many and didn't know where her friends were.' He turns to Kitty. 'We were just coming to get you.'

'The hell you were,' Kitty snarls. 'That why the goddamn door was barred?'

'Where's Bee?' Erin asks faintly. She hasn't moved since entering the room, has barely taken her eyes off Mira. Mira, who is wearing Erin's dress. Erin thinks back to earlier, their talk of superstitions and how it's bad luck to put on an unworn garment of someone else's. 'We left her with Bee.'

Aidan shakes his head. 'She was here when I looked in a few minutes ago.'

'So where did she go?' Erin is struggling to catch up, to understand why – and when – Bee left.

'Maybe she went looking for you two,' says Aidan.

'She shouldn't have gone,' says Kitty, a note of worry in her voice. Bee *shouldn't* have left, but it's Kitty who supplied the vodka, Kitty who urged them all to do shots. Kitty is a big part of the reason why Mira is out of her head. 'Come on.' She puts her arm round Mira. 'Let's get you some air, and some water. Erin, help me.'

Erin tries to assist but she's unsteady. She wonders again how Kitty's holding it together so well when she's drunk as much as the rest of them. Aidan walks past her, helping Mira up.

She has started to cry softly, and Kitty is *shh-shhing* her but it's not working. She's mumbling something incoherent, one hand is flailing outwards, fingers splayed.

'Erin,' she manages, as Kitty and Aidan get her to her feet.

'I'm here,' Erin says, feeling useless. 'It's okay.'

'My… my—' Mira cuts off abruptly as vomit gushes out of her and hits the wooden floor, spattering Kitty's white trousers and Aidan's jeans. Kitty recoils, grimacing, but somehow manages to keep hold of Mira. Aidan doesn't flinch. The smell hits Erin's nose and she clamps a hand over her own mouth, in danger of puking herself. Another wave of it comes, hitting Aidan's trainers and adding to the puddle on the floor. And then Erin sees something white and crumpled next to it, just under the pool table. She makes the connection between Mira's hand movements – not flailing but trying to point. *Erin, my… my—*

Her underwear.

Erin looks up in time to see the back of Curtis exiting the pool room. Erin, Aidan and Kitty stare at each other, breathing hard. Aidan's eyes are dark with fury, Kitty's are panicked and round. The knowledge of what has been happening in this room is as inescapable and potent as the smell of vomit. Mira groans, and it's a sound Erin knows will haunt her: a sound of pain that's both physical and emotional.

'Pick them up,' Kitty says faintly, and Erin stoops to collect the white knickers, speckled with pink vomit. She balls them up and stuffs them in her bag. Aidan and Kitty manoeuvre Mira out of the pool area and through the games room to the door. Erin follows, having collected Mira's bag – miraculously unscathed from sick – from the pool table. Curtis is nowhere to be seen. She's aware of eyes upon them. Not everyone has noticed, some are too busy dancing or kissing, but of those who are watching, a couple look concerned and a few are sniggering. *There's always one*, their faces seem to say, and Erin wants to scream at them. She wants to lash out and tell them that a girl was just being assaulted right under their noses. She wants to scratch their stupid, smirking faces.

They manage to make it outside before Mira heaves again, this time into the dirt.

'Sorry,' she mumbles, more lucid now. 'I really want… to lie down.'

'I know, honey,' Kitty soothes. 'That's where we're taking you – back to the cabin, so you can rest. And we're going to get some help. I think maybe Bee went already.'

'No, she…' Mira's face crumples and she starts to cry again, streaking her face with mascara. 'I told her… told her…' Strands of her hair stick to her cheeks, soaked in sick. 'I said don't leave me, don't… with *him*, and she went anyway. Said she had to go.'

'To get help?' Kitty repeats. 'Unless she got sick, too.'

Erin wonders if that's true. Did Bee start feeling rough and go back? Perhaps she's at the cabin, but surely they'd have crossed paths returning to the games room. Has she gone the wrong way, got lost? Throwing up in a bush somewhere? Something isn't right.

It takes an age to get Mira back to the cabin, stopping several times on the way so she can continue to throw up. The cabin's empty, with no sign Bee's been back. Of course she hasn't, Erin realises then. There's only one key, and Kitty has it.

'Need to be sick,' Mira mumbles, bumping into the couch.

'You can't have anything left in you,' says Kitty. She helps take off Mira's shoes, guiding her to the bathroom. Moments later Mira is retching into the toilet. Erin stares at the detritus of the evening. Sticky, pink-tinged glasses, an empty cranberry juice carton on its side. Kitty's open suitcase, contents everywhere. Pesto pasta congealing on plates that Kitty had dumped in the sink, declaring she'd do them later. Erin is standing right where she and Preston kissed, where he made her touch him. She wants to cry. The memory of it makes her feel disgusting. But it's not the same as what just happened to Mira, is it? Erin was able to say no, to stop it. She wishes they could go back to before they went out that evening, perhaps not even go out at all. A considerable chunk of the night has been a disaster.

Aidan finds a glass in the kitchen cabinet and fills it with water. He taps lightly on the bathroom door, handing it to Kitty. She vanishes inside as another gurgle sounds behind her.

Aidan stares at the closed bathroom door. 'Something needs to be done about those two.'

'Kitty and Mira?' Erin asks. She blinks and the room sways.

'No. Preston and Curtis.'

'Preston wasn't there.' She's silenced as Aidan looks at her. Anger is coming off him in waves. For a second she is convinced he knows what happened but she can't work out how. Did Kitty say something? And if so, when did she have the chance to? Aidan turns away, fills another glass with water and passes it to Erin. She takes it wordlessly, lifting it to her lips.

'There was a rumour about a party a couple of months ago,' Aidan continues. 'The parents were away, a load of people gatecrashed and it all got out of hand. Someone walked in on the two of them upstairs with a girl who'd passed out on the coats. Seems that's their style, taking advantage of girls who've had too much to drink.' He stares at her. 'Or just girls who like them.'

She takes a mouthful of water and swallows noisily.

'Did something happen with Preston tonight?'

'No,' she whispers. She doesn't want to talk about it, or think about it. Doesn't want other people knowing. 'Why do you even care?'

'We grew up together, Erin.' His voice is quiet. 'I care. But maybe—' He hesitates, then shakes his head. 'Maybe I'm not much better.'

'Why would you even say that?' She sets the glass on the upturned crate and turns to him, incredulous. Even in her drunken haze there's not a lifetime in which she could ever imagine Aidan trying anything like what Preston tried, or doing what Curtis did. 'You're *nothing* like them.'

'I lied earlier,' he says, and something in his voice cuts off a further protestation from her. Erin's mind is blank. She's barely spoken to Aidan since they've been on the island, so what could he have lied about?

'The coin.' He can't look at her. 'Before we kissed. I said it was tails, but it was heads.'

Her mind whirs, recalling how intently they'd kissed – so intently Erin lost track of time. And now Aidan's admitting he lied to make that happen. She's not sure how she feels about it.

'It's not the same.'

'Isn't it?'

'It was a game. A stupid game.'

'It was still a lie, to get what I wanted. Taking advantage.' Finally he looks at her. 'I'm sorry I did that.'

She shakes her head, trying to clear it but she only feels more muddled. And it's not really about what he did, she knows that much. Because even if on some level it wasn't right, it's not comparable to the others. It's nowhere near. Aidan, questioning himself, beating himself up over it, is nowhere near. She's tried so hard for so long to push away her feelings for him. She pushed *him* away after what happened with her and Bee when they were ten, because she couldn't bear him being around her knowing what she'd done. And now she can't understand why Aidan wants to kiss her, or says he cares about her, when he knows this awful thing about her. Aidan is good, and Erin is not.

They stare at each other silently. Not knowing what to say or how to be. She wishes everything had happened differently tonight, wishes she was someone else, wishes that Aidan would kiss her now – and not just as part of a game with a time limit.

But these are pointless wishes. She feels suddenly empty and tired, too drunk. She wants the night to be over.

Kitty emerges from the bathroom. The sour smell of vomit follows. Mira is visible kneeling by the toilet, head propped in her hands.

'We need to report this.' Kitty's voice is low. 'Mira's saying she doesn't want to, but I think we have to.'

'Perhaps we should wait till morning.' Erin doesn't like the idea of going against Mira's wishes. It feels like another violation on top of what she's already suffered. 'She might change her mind once she's sobered up.'

Kitty hesitates. It's the first time Erin's seen her unsure about anything. She glances back at Mira, deliberating. 'I don't know. It might be worse to wait. More questions about why we didn't report it straight away. It's already going to be our word against his. But even if Mira doesn't want to pursue it I think it needs to go on record.'

Reluctantly Erin concedes. It's up to Mira what she wants to do, but an adult – a teacher – will be better placed to advise her and help her decide.

'Let's get Hewitt,' she says. If it were her she knows she'd prefer to speak to a woman, and she's heard Hewitt mention the college counselling service a few times. She's softer than Callaghan, more serious.

'Okay,' Kitty says. 'But Mira can't be left alone.'

'You stay, then.' For once Erin is decisive. If she sits in that puke-filled bathroom she knows she'll puke herself, and besides, Kitty's better at knowing what to say. 'I'll go.'

'I'll come with you.' Aidan glances down at Erin's feet. 'You might want to put on some better shoes.'

She changes into her Doc Martens and Kitty calls after them as they near the door.

'Keep an eye out for Bee, as well. I want a word with her when she's back.'

They head into the night, neither of them speaking. The cold air livens Erin up. Once more she's struck by the silence and darkness of the island, the clear sky so inky above, but if she looks across the water the mainland is lit up like a switchboard. The path they're on takes them close to the shore and the briny smell of the water. Aidan is leading the way, taking them in the opposite direction to the games room. They pass a cluster of cabins on their right. A few windows are lit up, and there's movement in one. Some of the students have returned, or perhaps haven't been out in the first place.

'It's up here,' Aidan says shortly, the first thing he's said since they left. They go through a copse of trees and two more cabins appear, roughly twenty metres apart. As they walk up the path, solar lights pick out the way as well as the names of the cabins: the left is the Sweet Shop and the right, the Burrow.

Hewitt is in the Sweet Shop, Erin recalls. They go up the path and knock lightly at the door, then harder when no one comes. The cabin is wreathed in silence. Aidan moves to the round window beside the door and peers through. It's small but curtainless and offers a narrow, but clear view through to the living area.

'She's in,' he says. 'I can see her.'

Erin peers through. There's a flickering bluish light coming from a TV screen, and a bulky huddle of blankets on the sofa. A wine bottle and a half-filled glass sit nearby on the floor. There's something forlorn about them, and if circumstances were different Erin might have pitied Hewitt then, as she sometimes does. She remembers her puppy dog eyes at Callaghan earlier, the girlish laughter, the abrupt exit from the games room. Kitty's account of her in her mother's shop. All Erin feels now is irritation that she can't be reached when she's needed. She knocks again, but Hewitt's either a deep sleeper or she's passed out drunk.

'We'll have to go to Callaghan,' she says, and as she does a bizarre thought comes to her that perhaps the shape on the sofa *isn't* Hewitt, and that perhaps she's got herself some Dutch courage and is shacked up next door with Callaghan. She voices the thought to Aidan but he dismisses it. They arrive at Callaghan's cabin and Aidan reaches out to knock.

A noise stops him. It's faint, but distinctive. Something inside has smashed. There's another sound, high-pitched. A female voice, muffled, like a cry. Dread unfurls in the pit of Erin's belly. She can see the same dread on Aidan's face, the same knowing that they've stumbled on something they shouldn't have.

He looks through the round window next to the door and shakes his head. Nothing. Quietly they edge round the cabin, checking the other windows. All are obscured by blinds. Erin slips her hand into Aidan's.

'Let's go,' she whispers, suddenly convinced she knows what's going on inside and having no desire to witness it. In her mind she can clearly imagine Hewitt, drunk and dishevelled, confessing her feelings for Callaghan and tearfully smashing things when he's not reciprocating.

But Aidan's gaze is on the bottom corner of the last window. The blind has caught on a bottle of washing-up liquid on the sill, creating a triangular chink. He leans down, bringing his eye to it. She waits, impatient to go, then hears his intake of breath.

'What?'

He draws away sharply, shock etching his features. Before she can think it through she's at the gap, looking into the kitchen. Straight away she sees movement, quick and rhythmic, something pale in the thin light coming from the cooker hood.

Oh, god.

She closes her eyes instinctively, but she can't erase what she's just seen: Callaghan, his back to the window, leaning over the kitchen counter. T-shirt hem skimming his bare buttocks, thrusting hard into someone pinned beneath him. She opens her eyes again. He's still pumping, faster now. One hand grips the edge of the worktop next to a mug and a glass – she knows now that something has been knocked off and smashed. She can't see his other hand but guesses it's in front of him, twisted into a knot of hair or gripped onto a slick shoulder.

'*Shit*,' Aidan whispers. 'I think that *is* Hewitt.' He's shell-shocked, like he's just walked in on his parents going at it. Erin blinks, appalled as Callaghan stops pumping, his arse clenched. The horror keeps her there, frozen as he yanks up his pants and shifts away. Black and white spotted fabric falls down over slim legs.

A polka dot dress.

'Oh, my god.' Erin sinks to her knees, clamping a hand over her mouth. She sits in the dirt, revolted. 'It's… it's…'

She can't say the words, can't process it.

Bee and Paul Callaghan.

'That's not Hewitt.' She tries again. 'It's…'

The sound of a door opening silences her. A low voice comes from the front of the cabin.

'So, that's it then? A two-minute fuck and we're done?'

Aidan's horrified eyes lock on to Erin's. '*Bee?*' he mouths.

'We were already done,' Callaghan replies. He sounds tense, strained. Unsurprising, given that he's just had sex with a seventeen-year-old student. 'Weeks ago, you knew that. You shouldn't have come. I can't believe you fucking followed me, *transferred*—'

'Didn't stop you though, did it?' Bee laughs harshly. 'You're all the fucking same. Can't say no when it's in front of you.'

'Keep your voice down,' Callaghan hisses. 'And yeah, it shouldn't have happened. But you came here asking for it.'

'It doesn't have to end.' Her voice changes, becomes small, pleading. 'We were having fun, weren't we? You said so. There's no reason—'

'My job! Wife, kids!' Callaghan fumes. 'Three reasons! What's not to fucking understand? Now, fuck off or I'll put in a complaint against you once we're back.'

Erin feels displaced, like she's woken up somewhere unfamiliar and recognises nothing and no one. *Bee and Callaghan?* Bee and Callaghan. And not just once.

'*You*?' Bee spits the word. '*You* will put in a complaint against *me*? I really, *really* don't think so.'

'Try me,' he says. 'No one will believe you. One teacher coming on to you, that's unlucky. But two? Everyone will see it's you, and what a little slag you are.'

'Do you want to know something funny? He never even did anything.'

'*What?* What are you saying?'

'It was practice. I wanted to see how easy it was – to show *you* how easy it was. He got suspended because I said he tried to kiss me. Imagine what'll happen to you.'

'You've got no proof.'

'I've got condoms from that hotel we went to. *Used.*'

Erin hears her own breathing, startlingly loud in the silence. Aidan's hand tightens around hers.

'That… that was months ago.' Panic has crept into Callaghan's voice. 'Before you went on the pill. You twisted… you're *sick*.'

'Maybe,' she says, in a weird, chanting voice, 'I'll hold on to them for a while. Perhaps I'll call your wife first. I wonder what she'll say. What she'll tell your kids when they're old enough.'

'You wouldn't dare. She'd kill you.'

'I'll tell everyone,' Bee says quietly. 'I'll ruin you.'

There's a gasp from Callaghan, then a grunt – Bee, followed by the sound of a scuffle.

'Don't touch me!' she growls.

'Don't *touch you*? At least we're on the same page, finally. Now for the last time, fuck off.'

'I'm going.' She sniffles, resigned. 'But there *is* something I came to tell you. I'm pregnant.'

'No, you're not. You're just a nasty little liar.'

'Yeah. But here's the thing, Paul. Even liars don't lie about everything.'

There's silence, then a click as Callaghan closes the door on her. Erin and Aidan remain pressed up against the side of the cabin, not daring to make a sound.

Bee's quiet footsteps recede away from them and into the night.

19

OCTOBER 2016

'I DIDN'T BELIEVE SHE WAS pregnant, not then,' Erin says wretchedly. 'I thought it was all a lie.'

Aidan says nothing, but his eyes are haunted.

'Do you think Paul believed her?' asks Hewitt. 'I know he *said* he didn't.'

Erin and Aidan remain silent. It's something Erin's asked herself many times, but only Paul Callaghan knew the answer to that, and now he's dead.

'I mean, he told the police he didn't know she was pregnant, either,' Hewitt adds. She's shredded a paper napkin into tiny pieces and is moving them around on the table as though trying to fit them together again in a different order. 'I guess he panicked, but it was pretty stupid to lie, given that they'd… you know.' She grimaces. 'That his DNA was… *in* her the night she died.'

Tori makes a disgusted noise and gets up, swearing under her breath. She walks out of the tea room without a backwards glance.

'Oh,' says Hewitt, stricken as Tori strides away through the drizzle.

'It must've come as a shock to you, too,' Mira says to her gently. 'Finding out about him and Bee.'

'I felt sick.' A raw, anguished look crosses Hewitt's face. 'Physically ill. Right under my nose and I couldn't see it.' Erin is suddenly on edge at the change in her and that her reaction is still so forceful after all these years. Almost as though she were the one Paul Callaghan betrayed. And then the grief leaves her, or perhaps she remembers herself. She glances after Tori once more.

'I didn't mean to upset her.' She gets up hurriedly and slips on her jacket. 'I'll go after her.'

'Perhaps it's best to leave—' Mira begins, but Hewitt's already through the door.

'Fuck's sake.' Kitty pinches the bridge of her nose, irritated. 'It's like trying to round up squirrels.'

'That was good of you,' Aidan says to Mira.

For a moment Erin doesn't understand what he means. But then Mira replies, and she gets it.

'Unrequited feelings are still feelings. Sometimes people need them acknowledged. Validated.'

'What is it you do now?' Aidan asks. 'Counsellor?'

'Social worker,' she replies. 'Not quite the barrister my parents hoped for, but still making a difference, I think.'

Erin watches Hewitt lumbering away across the gravel. *Charlotte*, she corrects herself, but the old nickname surfaces in her mind. *Chewitt*. Her former teacher's cheeks are still red from the altercation with Callaghan's wife.

Obsessed.

They'd all known it back then. Hewitt's crush had been painful to watch, even for them; teenagers who'd barely cared enough to notice in the first place. But like Hewitt said, she'd never been a threat to Tori. Paul hadn't been interested in her.

Erin read most of the details of his affair with Bee after they came out during the inquest into his suicide. The pair had met six months before Bee's death, in April of that year, at a casino where Callaghan had been out on a friend's stag night. He'd seen Bee alone at the bar when he'd gone to buy a round of drinks. She told him she'd lost her housemate, who'd had Bee's purse and cloakroom ticket in her bag, meaning she had no coat and no money to get home.

Callaghan bought her drinks and offered to keep her company until she found her housemate, or pay for her taxi home if she didn't. She told him she was a trainee beautician living in Leigh-on-Sea. He'd told her he taught at a local sixth form college, and that he stayed in a loveless marriage for his children. In reality, Bee was in foster care in Chelmsford, and Callaghan a serial cheat who'd no intention of leaving his wife. Both lied about their ages. Bee, then only sixteen, said she was two years older. Callaghan, who was thirty-six, told her he was twenty-nine. When Bee's housemate didn't return, Callaghan ordered her a taxi and while waiting for it to arrive, the two had sex in an alley beside the casino.

According to a friend of Callaghan's the affair went from there and the pair started to engage in rough sex, something Callaghan's wife wouldn't give him. He only discovered the truth about Bee's age – and that she was in foster care – when she transferred to his college. He broke it off instantly and initially denied any involvement with her after he was arrested for her murder. Crucially, he failed to admit that she told him she was pregnant at all, unaware that Erin's and Aidan's statements said otherwise. Hours after his arrest, Paul Callaghan took his own life in his cell using a piece of the broken glass bottle from the island's museum. Though he'd been treated for a cut to his foot when taken into custody, the medical staff had dressed the wound without realising the glass was still in his skin.

'I always thought it was him,' Aidan says now. 'Still do, if I'm honest. He had more reason than anyone else to shut her up.' He looks at Kitty expectantly.

'Maybe.' She drums her fingers on the table but doesn't elaborate. A glance at the windows confirms that she's waiting until Tori and Hewitt are back.

Erin's leg is throbbing. She goes through her bag, finding a blister pack of painkillers but it's empty.

'Wait there, I've got something,' Aidan says. He leaves the tea room and she sees him jog towards the car park, vanishing from view.

It is just Erin, Kitty and Mira remaining, with Bomber further off in the corner.

'What are you doing, Kitty?' Erin murmurs. 'Why are you messing with this? Why can't you just leave it be?'

'Because I don't want to,' Kitty says simply. 'I want answers.'

'It's always what you want, isn't it? Don't we get a say?' Erin looks to Mira for support, but Mira is staring at the table.

Kitty levels a stare at her. 'I hope you both make it to eighty, maybe ninety. Grandkids, whatever. That's a lot of years to get through, and I wish you both well. I really do. If you live that long you might feel differently at the end. Maybe, in a really fucked-up way, you'll thank me for this one day.'

Erin cannot imagine she will ever thank Kitty, not in two lifetimes. Her own life, her pathetic little existence, could be over if Kitty has her way.

'Well, that's it, then,' she says quietly. 'You've made up your mind. You don't need me here for this.'

'I thought it was only right and fair that you were,' Kitty says. 'Both of you.'

There is no time to say more. Aidan returns with a packet of ibuprofen and hands it to her. Erin pops two out and swallows them with a mouthful of water, half-wishing it was Valium or anything that would calm her down. The fear of what Kitty is waiting to say, and the race of her own pulse is making her feel ill.

Aidan nods to the coffee mug Kitty has just put down. 'You must be shattered. How long was your flight?'

'Eleven hours, but I flew over a few days ago. Been holed up in London at the Savoy, stuffing my face, using the spa and watching trash TV. *Living the life.*' She emphasises the last three words and chuckles wryly.

'The Savoy?' Aidan repeats. 'Nice.'

Kitty breaks off another piece of her cookie, and Erin wonders what qualifies as 'stuffing her face'. She hasn't stopped picking since she sat down but it's all sugary junk, nothing nourishing. If Kitty hadn't told them of her illness Erin would have been convinced she'd just finished another stint in rehab.

'Are you seeing your family while you're here?' Mira asks. In contrast to Kitty, her Romanian accent has worn away to a trace. If she's afraid, there's no hint of it in her voice. If anything, she sounds resigned. She's still attractive, her black hair silky with no hint of grey. She's curvier now and rounder in the face. It suits her. Yet her dark eyes are dull and there are deep creases around them, like lines of a ghost story that's scripted on her skin.

'You mean my mom?' Kitty doesn't miss a beat. It's been well documented that in the aftermath of Bee's death, Kitty and her mother became estranged, with Kitty moving back to the States to be with her dad while things died down. Only they never really did. 'No. I reached out to her a few times. Once or twice I thought it seemed promising, but then…' Kitty shakes her head, and her corkscrew curls move softly over the shoulders. Aside from her dress sense her hair is the only part of her, physically, that appears unchanged. 'She never really got over the fingerprints-on-the-bottle thing. It always came up eventually.'

In her dreams sometimes, Erin sees Kitty reaching for the bottle. That awful, silver bottle.

'The CCTV in the museum showed you picking it up,' Aidan cuts in, reiterating what's common knowledge. 'And putting it back.'

'Uh-huh,' Kitty says. 'But it wasn't as simple as that, was it?'

'I'll never understand why you touched it in the first place.' Aidan's not looking at any of them now. He's collecting the used mugs and placing them on the counter, although Erin doesn't know why. Maybe he's on autopilot from his barista days.

'Well, not everyone's squeaky clean like you,' Kitty says lightly. 'I never gave it much thought at the time. I was young, dumb. Showing off, I guess. How was I to know bits of it would end up in a dead girl's throat?'

There's a terrible silence. Erin grips the edge of the table as the room blurs around her. *Throat. Mouth.* A fragment of glass had even been found embedded under one of Bee's nails. Erin's vision settles and she reaches for the water jug, topping up her glass.

'Then again,' Kitty adds, 'there's the question of where *you* went after you saw Bee and Callaghan.'

Aidan's expression darkens. 'Like I said at the time, I didn't go back to my cabin. It would've kicked off with Leon Curtis so I crashed on one of the sofas in the games room.'

'Yeah, I get that,' Kitty says. 'But you didn't go straight there, either.'

'No. I was pissed off, needed to let off some steam. I walked round for a bit, kicked a few things. Ended up on the beach on the other side of the island. Got back to the games room around eleven. I didn't see Bee again, if that's what you mean.'

'Someone's calling me,' Mira mutters, getting her phone out. 'My daughter.' She pulls on her camel-coloured coat and goes outside to take the call. Erin wonders if it's genuine, or an excuse to get away from the strained atmosphere. More specifically, the mention of Leon Curtis. She hadn't heard a ringtone or any buzzing from Mira's bag.

Kitty stares after her. 'I bet she's a great mom.'

Erin nods. She imagines Mira is. She thinks of Kitty's mother, turning her back on her, and her own mum, who believed Erin even when her daughter had been shown, publicly, to be a liar once already. She wonders which kind of parent she would have been. Probably better not to know.

'You never had kids?' Kitty asks now, as if reading her mind. Erin shakes her head tersely. 'But kids' books, though? You've done well for yourself. I'm happy for you.'

Don't be, Erin thinks. *I can't even be happy for myself.*

'I thought about getting in touch once,' Kitty adds. 'When I saw your first book had been published. But I didn't want to rain on your parade.'

Erin frowns. 'How did you know about it?' Aside from a trade acquisitions announcement there had only been little pieces on Erin's own website and her agent's. Her first book had been with a small press with a tiny marketing budget, back in the days before internet sensations were a thing. The book had done well in libraries but sold poorly, and eventually gone out of print.

'I tried looking you up a few times,' Kitty says. 'We all have a little stalk now and then, right?'

'Do we?' Erin mutters, unsettled by the use of the word *stalk*. She's always kept an eye on Kitty, although there's never been any need to stalk her. She's offered up enough of herself to the press without much encouragement.

'You know what I mean,' Kitty says. 'Curiosity and all that.'

'You've done well for yourself, too,' Erin says without warmth, although she feels herself soften a fraction. There is something about Kitty, and not just because she's ill, that makes it hard to stay entirely mad at her. She's always had it, that indefinable *something*. 'You're a success.'

'Define success. I'd rather have your talent.' Kitty turns to Aidan. 'How about you, Squeaky? Wife, kids?'

'One ex-wife, one kid,' he replies, a little irritably. 'A son, Nathan. He's eleven next month.' His eyes find Erin's. 'We've got all your books.'

'Really?' she asks, surprised. A tiny ember of warmth glows somewhere inside her.

'Didn't have much choice,' he says. 'Your mum sent copies.'

The ember is instantly snuffed out.

Mira comes back in then, her phone away and her arms wrapped around herself. Tori Callaghan arrives next, granite-faced and composed. Before she's even taken her seat Charlotte Hewitt is there too, slightly breathless, eyes downcast like a scolded dog.

It's Tori who speaks first, addressing Kitty.

'Are you going to tell us what this is all about?'

'Yeah.' Kitty sits up a little straighter. 'It's, uh… it's about the bottle. How it got out of the museum.' Her voice flickers before righting itself once more, like a needle on a scratched record. 'And the fingerprints on it.'

Erin's heart claps like thunder. She wills Kitty to stop talking, silently begging with her eyes and the faintest shake of her head.

'The camera showed you putting it back.' Aidan glances at Erin, then Mira. 'And that's what you told everyone. All three of you said it, that you'd passed it to each other in the museum and then put it back.'

'We lied,' Kitty says. 'And not just about that.'

'Kitty, please,' Erin whispers, even though the damage has already been done. '*Please* shut up…'

'We lied about the last time we saw her, too.'

20

OCTOBER 1996

After Bee walks off alone from Callaghan's cabin Erin and Aidan wait several minutes, making sure she's gone before creeping away from the window. They don't dare to pass by the door in case Callaghan's watching, and instead trample alongside a hedgerow until they're hidden by the copse of trees bordering the cabin. There, they stop, trying to work out what to do.

'We could. try Hewitt again,' says Erin. Her teeth are chattering, though with shock rather than cold. 'Bang louder on the door until she hears us.'

'I don't know,' Aidan says hoarsely. 'What do we tell her about Callaghan? About… *that*? I don't think she'll have a clue how to handle it.'

The thought of telling brings a hard lump of fear into Erin's throat. The idea of repeating what they've seen, what they heard, makes her feel ill, desperate. She knows what it's like to tell people something awful. To have all eyes on you, to have questions coming from every angle. She doesn't think she can cope with that again, even if this time, it's true. And part of her thinks, why *should* she? Why should she get involved in this disgusting thing? It's not her business, or Aidan's. It's no one else's business but Bee's and Callaghan's, and they deserve each other.

'Do we… I mean, why do we have to say anything about that? This is about Mira.'

Aidan stares back at her. 'Are you serious?'

'It's our word against theirs. What proof have we got? None, that's what. And I—' She breaks off, clenching her teeth. 'I can't get involved in something like this again, Aidan. Something sordid. And it's her. It's *her.*' She feels like she's been living a half-life for the past six years, trying to put what happened behind her. And just as she'd almost started to feel normal, started to believe she could actually be happy, Bee has come back. 'And you're right about Hewitt. I don't think she'd be able to deal with this. She won't *want* to believe it.'

'So you're saying we should do nothing? Say nothing?'

Erin doesn't answer.

'She said she's pregnant,' Aidan says quietly.

'And you believe that? She lies about everything.'

'What if she isn't lying? Whatever you think of her – actually, forget her for a minute – do you think he should be allowed to carry on teaching? One day you might have kids, Erin. Would you want someone like that around them?'

'I'm never having kids.'

Aidan's dark eyes glint with fury. 'He can't get away with this.'

Erin falls silent, knowing, deep down, that he's right. 'Look,' she says eventually. 'We've got enough on our plates with what's happened to Mira. For god's sake, let's wait till we're off this island and home, and then we can think about Callaghan. We don't know how he'll react if we blow this open.'

They start to move off again but almost immediately Aidan freezes, grabbing Erin's arm to still her.

'What?'

'I heard something,' he whispers, eyes darting. 'Leaves crackling, like someone creeping around.'

They wait, breath held, squinting into curtains of shadows but seeing nothing. When they finally set off they convince each other that the sound must have been a badger or a fox.

They try Hewitt's cabin once more, knocking insistently, but she doesn't answer. The TV is off now and it's too dark to see anything inside. They give up and Aidan walks her back. All the way, Erin imagines Bee lurking in the shadows, listening to every word they've said.

When Erin arrives back at the cabin she's shaken and sweaty. The night no longer feels real. She staggers in alone and is surprised to see Kitty and Mira on the couch. From the state of Mira when Erin left, she'd expected her to still have her head down the toilet, but while she's looking rough as hell she's stopped being sick and her eyes are no longer rolling in her head.

'Are you… okay?' Erin asks, feeling stupid immediately. Mira *isn't* okay. Her eyes are red-rimmed, haunted. But she gives a slight nod.

'Where's Aidan?' Kitty asks. 'Did you walk back by yourself?'

'No.' Erin slumps into a chair, using her foot to push away a pile of rumpled clothing spilling from Kitty's suitcase. For someone who loves her clothes, Kitty doesn't look after them very well. 'He walked me back but thought Mira would want some… privacy.'

'Is Chewy coming?' Kitty glances at Mira, and they both seem edgy. It's making Erin feel even more sluggish. 'Did you find her?'

Erin shakes her head, sitting up straighter. 'We tried twice. She didn't come to the door.' She tells them about the shapeless bulk on the sofa, the half-empty wine bottle. 'She must've properly crashed out.'

'Bee never went for help, then,' says Kitty.

'Help?' A bitter laugh escapes. 'That was the last thing on her mind.'

Kitty frowns. 'What do you mean? Where is she?'

'I don't know.' Erin closes her eyes, wishing she could wipe clean everything she's seen this evening. She knows none of it's going away, and she doesn't know what to do about any of it. 'Forget it. I don't know where she is. I'll try Hewitt again in the morning.'

'No.' There's a hardness to Mira's voice. She's sitting with her legs drawn up to her. Her hair is scraped back off her face and Kitty has placed a blanket round her shoulders. 'Just leave it. I don't want to tell Hewitt.'

'Honey, think about this,' says Kitty. 'You don't have to decide right now.'

'I'm not telling her,' Mira repeats. She wipes her nose, staring stonily ahead. 'Or anyone else.'

'Okay.' Kitty shoots an anxious glance at Erin. 'We don't have to do anything you don't want to. But I think it's really important that—'

'I don't care what you think. It wasn't you it happened to, was it?'

'No, but—'

'I don't want to be the girl everyone whispers about,' Mira hisses, glassy-eyed and sharp. '"*Oh, look, there's the girl who got fingered on the pool table!*" I don't want my parents, my *father*, knowing that happened to me. They didn't want me coming on this trip to begin with.'

'Curtis took advantage,' says Erin. 'Doesn't matter if you were drunk or not. No one's going to blame you. And maybe Kitty can take you back early tomorrow, if you want to go. Once the causeway's open and she's okay to drive.'

'You don't understand,' says Mira. 'My father had a breakdown last year. He'd already had a heart attack from stress at work, and then it got worse from there.' Her lips press into a thin line. 'He will not cope with this, too. So, I'm not going home early, I'm staying. He's not going to know. I'm not bringing him any more worry or shame.'

'There's nothing to be ashamed of,' Kitty insists. 'It wasn't your fault. It was that asshole's.'

'And Bee's.' It slips out of Erin like a draught through a keyhole. She's slurring slightly now, a combination of drowsiness and drink. She can't bear that Curtis is going to get away with what he's done. She needs someone to blame. 'She shouldn't have left Mira.'

'Well, yeah.' Kitty's fidgety, agitated. 'But we don't know why she did. For all we know she got sick herself. It's a bit weird we haven't seen her – don't forget that creep Preston's out there.' She pauses. 'Wait. Isn't Aidan sharing a cabin with him and Curtis?'

'Yeah, he is.' Erin glances at the cabin door, uneasy. She'd completely forgotten about that, and now she wonders where Aidan will go because she knows he won't return there after what's happened. 'He'll probably crash in the games room, I reckon.'

'And what about Bee?' Kitty presses. 'Should we go look for her?'

'I know where she was.' Erin blurts it out, unable to disguise the bitterness in her voice. It's rising up in her, too far gone to temper. 'Trust me. She didn't go for help and she's not sick. Not in the way you mean, anyway.'

'What the hell are you talking about?' Kitty is wide-eyed, expectant. 'Where is she?'

'She…'

It hangs in the air like a thread, and Erin is close, *so* close to telling them. And why should she keep it hidden? If Callaghan needs to be outed, then Bee will be exposed anyway. It's just one more brick in the wall of loathing Erin has built. And she does loathe Bee, with every cell of her being. She detests her for this, and for her ruined childhood, and for what she's allowed to happen to Mira.

So, in a few stumbling, jerky sentences, Erin tells them what she and Aidan saw. What they heard. When she's finished, Kitty's mouth is slightly open. Mira's face is curiously blank, and she still has that eerie, glassy-eyed look. Erin is starting to wonder if she's gone into shock.

'*Fuck,*' Kitty says faintly. 'Bee and Callaghan… what in the *hell*?'

'It's disgusting,' Mira whispers.

'I know.' Erin's exhilarated, dizzy. Unsure if she's done the right thing by telling, but it's too late now. It would've come out soon enough, anyway, wouldn't it? The silence is jarring and she feels the need to break it. 'God, I need coffee. I'm too drunk to think straight.' She gets up, stumbling to the kitchenette.

'Coffee won't do shit,' Kitty says. 'If you need to sober up I've got something.' The quietness of her voice makes Erin stop what she's doing. Kitty's watching her. A questioning sort of look.

'*Something?*' Erin asks.

Kitty glances at Mira, then back at Erin. Then she reaches down her top and pulls out a tiny, clear plastic bag containing a small amount of white powder. Erin's heart quickens. Despite all the warnings from her parents, posters up in school, police coming to do assemblies about the dangers of drugs, she's never once been offered them. She's never even smoked a joint. 'Is that…?'

'Coke.' Kitty gives the bag a little shake.

'Cocaine?' Erin asks stupidly.

'Well, it ain't fucking Diet Coke.' Kitty laughs. 'Yeah. *Cocaine,*' she repeats, in a posh English accent.

Erin dithers. She's scared, for two reasons. First, it's been well-publicised that last year a sixteen-year-old local boy died after taking Ecstasy on New Year's Eve. The family released pictures of him on life support before the machine was switched off, in the hope of deterring other teenagers from experimenting with drugs. Erin's mother had shoved the paper under her nose while she'd been eating breakfast and made her swear she'd never do anything so stupid. Second, for the past six years Erin has stuck to rules, avoiding anything that could get her into trouble or cause her mother any more strife than she already has.

'You don't need much,' says Kitty, sensing her trepidation. 'Just a tiny dab. It sharpens you right up, promise.'

A dab. It sounds playful, like a kitten swiping at something.

'Where did you get it?' Erin asks. Things are fitting into place; Kitty taking her time in the bathroom earlier. It explains why she's handled her drink better than the rest of them. 'Do you always take it?'

'Hell, no.' Kitty snorts. 'Too expensive. I've done it a couple of times when other people had it at parties. I got this from my brother. The shitbag wouldn't give me back money I'd lent him, so when he was out I raided his room and found this. So, do you want it?'

'I don't know.'

'Mira's had some. Look, it's sorted her out.'

Erin is stunned. *Mira?* Taking drugs?

'It worked,' Mira says flatly. 'I don't feel as out of control now.' Erin had put the strange staring down to shock but clearly it's more than that. Given the choice of being paralytic after what's happened to her or doing this, Mira has chosen self-preservation.

So Erin hears herself saying, 'Okay, then. Just a tiny bit.'

'Sure.' Kitty leans over and takes out a bank card from her purse.

Erin watches with apprehension. 'Is that to cut the lines?'

'Nah.' Kitty carefully taps out a small amount of white powder on to the corner of the card. 'No lines. Just a dab, like I said. Look.' She lifts the card to her nose and, holding one nostril closed, sniffs the white powder into the other. 'Like that.'

She adds more coke to the card and carefully hands it over. Erin hesitates. It's such a small amount. What harm can it do? She sniffs. Within seconds she feels a vaguely unpleasant sensation as it drips down the back of her throat.

'Oh.' She passes the card back and touches her nose self-consciously. 'My nostril's gone numb.'

'Yeah, it does that.' Kitty adds another pinch to the card and offers it to Mira, but Mira shakes her head, so Kitty does it herself. 'You want another one?' she asks Erin. 'We may as well finish it.'

'I suppose so.' Erin takes the card. Apart from the gross dripping and numbness she feels no other effect. After the build-up the whole thing is, so far, anti-climactic. She says this to Kitty, who laughs.

'You won't feel anything for a few minutes.'

'Are we going to get the munchies?' asks Erin.

'That's with weed. You won't want to eat anything with this.'

A loud click makes their heads swivel in unison to the door, but it's only the fridge clicking on.

'I thought that was Bee coming in,' says Erin, relaxing back into the sofa.

'Wonder when the little tramp will turn up?' Kitty muses. '*If* she shows up. Maybe she's trying to make it up with Callaghan.'

'She'd be wasting her time.' Erin rubs her nose, paranoid about powdery residue. 'He told her to fuck off. She has to come back here, there's nowhere else for her to go.'

'I hope she does,' Mira says. 'I've got a few things I want to say to her.'

The cocaine is all gone now. Erin suggests getting rid of the bag but Kitty says no. She tucks it into a pair of balled-up socks, declaring her plans to put it back in her brother's room, empty. 'What's he going to do?' she says. 'Tell Mom?' She leans past Erin to grab a handful of the clothes that are strewn about, but as she lifts them something silvery rolls out, landing with a soft thud at Erin's feet.

It's the globe-shaped bottle from the museum, the one which supposedly contains a witch.

'Oops,' says Kitty, lazily. 'Forgot I'd put that there.'

'Frigging hell, Kitty!' Erin gapes at the bottle in disbelief. 'You took it? When? *Why?*'

'When I went to hand the key in. The attendant was talking to Chewy and I got bored waiting. It was a spur of the moment thing. I thought it'd make a good souvenir.'

'You can't steal stuff from museums. Even crappy ones!'

'Yeah.' Kitty picks at one of her nails thoughtfully. 'It seemed like a good idea at the time.'

'What about the camera?' asks Mira. She's staring at the bottle warily, as though it's something not to be trusted. 'There was CCTV in there.'

'It was facing the other way, on the till.' Kitty picks up the bottle, turning it in her hands. 'I made sure.' She brings the bottle up to her face, trying to look through the speckled silvery glass. 'I wonder what's actually in this thing?' She shakes it and there's a faint rattling, a sound like broken glass. 'Probably fuck all.'

'Well, I doubt it's a witch,' Erin says. Maybe it's a placebo effect, but her head's already less groggy.

'Mm.' Kitty lowers the bottle away from her face. 'I'll return it tomorrow. I doubt they even know it's missing. You know what, though? We should make the most of it while we have it.'

'You mean like hiding it under Bee's pillow?' Erin suggests.

'Yeah.' Kitty smiles wickedly. 'Sweet dreams, bitch! Or we could stash it in her stuff. Make it look like she took it.'

'Or we could just throw it at her, so it breaks,' Mira says, and there is no trace of the Mira who freaked out in the museum earlier when Kitty suggested breaking the bottle. Now she's the one talking about smashing it.

'She'd probably enjoy it if we did any of those things,' Erin says savagely. 'She's always been weird. The first time I met her she said she was a witch. She was a horrible kid.'

'And now she's a horrible teenager.' Kitty narrows her eyes. 'But I thought you two were friends?'

'That's the last thing we were.' Erin's heart is beginning to pound again, with anger or nerves or both. 'I hated her. She's a liar. She lies about everything. All that stuff she said about her mum, that was lies, too.' The words are pouring out now, and it feels unbelievably cathartic. 'I even asked Chewy to move me but she wouldn't. Said I should give Bee a chance.'

'Why didn't you tell us what she was like?' Mira asks. Her voice is gentle, but it feels to Erin that she's being pushed to a precipice. She's clinging on, doubt and fear nudging her back from the edge. Back to safety. Still something compels her to take the leap. She *needs* them to understand why she hates Bee so much.

She needs them to hate her as well.

'Because I lied, too,' she says finally. Her voice gives and she's horrified to realise that she's crying, but now she's begun she has to see it through. 'Bee and I… when we were kids, we did something terrible.'

21

OCTOBER 2016

'I took it.' Kitty holds her hands up. 'I stole the bottle from the museum. Brought it back to the cabin, stashed it in my stuff. I'd… kind of forgotten it was there, what with the party and everything that night, but then later we, uh… we found it.'

Everyone is looking at her, and there's not a single sound from any of them. The only evidence that the island is still breathing is a scatter of leaves thrown up against the window outside. Erin starts to feel as though she is detaching from the room, like she's having an out-of-body experience. It doesn't feel real, that these secrets kept for twenty years have been blurted out in an instant, even though it's exactly what Kitty said she'd come here to do.

'Don't ask me why I took it.' Kitty shakes her head. 'I know it was stupid—'

'Where did you last see Bee?' Aidan interrupts. He looks suddenly drawn, and there is something in his voice that Erin can't quite read.

Kitty pauses, gaze going to Mira briefly before resting on Erin.

'She came back to the cabin,' Kitty says.

'But… but you told us she didn't.' Hewitt's voice wavers and her eyes dart between the three of them. 'Why would you lie?' She focuses on Erin. 'You and Aidan said you were the last ones to see her after she left Paul…'

'As far as I knew, we were,' Aidan says, his voice snagging, as though he's holding on to some tiny hope that the story he's believed for two decades can still be true and the lie Kitty referred to had been hers and Mira's, and not included Erin. 'So… when? When did she come to the cabin?'

'After,' Mira says unexpectedly. She is still staring at the table, but her hands reach for her bag and she takes out an asthma pump. She sucks in two lungfuls but does not return it to her bag. It remains in her hand, which is trembling slightly. 'After Erin got back.'

Aidan goes very still, then gives a barely perceptible nod.

'Go on, then.' Tori folds her arms. 'What happened?'

Kitty licks her lips. 'She arrived around fifteen minutes or so after Erin got back—'

'Kitty, wait.' Erin cuts in. 'I-I'll…' For one mad moment she almost takes over, desperate to tell it her way, in her words. But she can't, and so she falls silent.

'My god,' Aidan murmurs. 'Don't let this be what I think it is.'

'Just let me say it,' Kitty says tiredly. Doggedly.

And so she tells him, and Charlotte Hewitt and Tori Callaghan, what happened. About the cocaine they snorted on top of so much to drink, and how Erin told them that she and Aidan had just witnessed Bee and Paul Callaghan having sex and arguing at his cabin. She does not speak about Mira's assault, or that Erin had confessed to Mira and Kitty about Nicky Pemberton, because those things are not hers to admit. But Aidan already knows about both and Erin wonders, from the way he is looking at her, whether he has worked out for himself that those elements factored.

Kitty tells them how they left the cabin with Bee for the final time. How the bottle got smashed. How they left Bee on the shore when they'd finished her. When she reaches the end Erin waits for some miraculous weight to lift from her, but all she feels is the ache of her throat closing in. She waits, willing someone to say something.

Their quiet stillness wraps around her like a noose.

22

OCTOBER 1996

'Nicky and Donnie were still in the woods when they caught up with them.' Erin's voice is a whisper. She can't bring herself to look at Kitty or Mira, so she's focusing on a patch on the sofa where the brown leather is starting to split. So far, the two other girls have listened without interruption – although she heard Kitty's breath catch when it came to the lie.

'There were three of them. My dad, his mate Kieran, and Mick Pemberton. Nicky's dad.'

'His *dad?*' Kitty repeats.

'Yeah.' Erin still can't look at her. 'Everyone knew he was trouble. He used to knock Nicky and his mum about. Then one day she took off, without Nicky.'

'She left him with a man who beat him?' asks Mira, aghast.

Erin nods. 'She took her other kid though, the one that wasn't Mick's. No one knew where they went, but Nicky used to say she was coming back for him. She never did.'

Kitty shakes her head. 'Poor kid.'

'When Mum called my dad at the pub and told him what had happened, he just lost it.' Erin was never there at the pub of course, but she's heard about it so many times that she's always been able to picture it in her head as though it were one of her own memories. 'Mum begged him to come home. She wanted the police to deal with it, but she said it was like something switched in him.' She gulps, trying to keep her voice under

189

control. 'She couldn't get him to listen. He pointed straight at Mick Pemberton and told him what Nicky and his friend had done, in front of everyone. And then he said he was going to kill them, because… because… sorry—' She fights to get herself under control. 'Because no one touches his little girl. And Mick Pemberton started raging, saying he wasn't having a nonce for a son, and that he'd kill Nicky himself. So when my dad took off to look for Nicky and Donnie, Mick was the first one behind him.

'They found them easy enough. Donnie and Nicky didn't even try to run at first. They thought it was about the stolen wallet, and Donnie had told Nicky to brazen it out and deny it all. By the time they realised it wasn't about that it was too late. They broke Donnie's nose and some of his teeth, but he managed to get away. He ran and left Nicky to face it alone.

'They… they beat the shit out of him. Literally. Beat him unrecognisable. Stripped him down to his Bart Simpson underwear and hung him from a tree with an old rope swing.' Erin wipes her face. 'Mick was the one who'd strung him up. Dad said that haunted him after, the memory of Nicky just dangling there, covered in his own crap and blood.

'The police weren't far behind. Someone in the pub made an anonymous call. Dad was at home washing off the blood when they came for him. By some miracle Nicky was still alive when they cut him down, but he died on the way to hospital.'

'Fuck,' Kitty says shakily. Mira says nothing, but she's gone even greyer in the face.

The cocaine is taking hold. Even without it, at this point Erin would have told Kitty and Mira the rest anyway, but she finds she's unable to stop talking. For the first time all night her mind is clear and focused, and the words spill out of her. She tells them how Donnie went into hiding, too afraid to show his face despite his attackers being in custody, for fear others would finish what they'd started. She tells them how she and Bee were questioned by specially trained police officers who asked the exact details of what had happened. Again, and again, and again. She tells them how she was the one to crack and admit the truth after a couple of days. That however awful Donnie and Nicky had been and the threats they'd made, they had not done the deplorable thing she and Bee had accused them of. Only then did Donnie come out of hiding to give his statement to the police.

'Dad got eight years for manslaughter,' says Erin. 'Reduced from murder on the grounds that he'd lost control. Kieran was given fifteen, I think, but he appealed and got it reduced. Turned out he'd been abused as a kid and it set him off. Mick Pemberton had already been in and out of prison. They gave him life without parole.'

'So your father is still in prison?' Mira asks.

'No.' Erin speaks quickly, perfunctorily. Trying to detach herself from the worst part of it all. 'I wasn't lying when I said my dad was dead. Three years into his sentence, he tried to break up a fight and got stabbed in the neck. Died almost instantly.'

'Oh, Erin,' Mira murmurs.

'I can't remember which paper it was that first called us the "Two Little Liars". I think it might have been the *News of the World*. We'd been called everything by then. Demons, disturbed, wicked. All they could throw at us. Child A and Child B. There were even petitions to get us named. Most of the tabloids said we walked free, which we did, but we both got convicted of wasting police time.' She takes a steadying breath. 'They decided not to punish us any further, so we got absolute discharges. I never saw Bee again until she turned up here. So, now you know,' she mumbles. 'Now you can see why I hate her – and myself. She's rotten. Always has been. And it's like I can't escape her no matter what. Maybe I don't deserve to.'

'Don't hate yourself.' Mira gently touches Erin's arm, and Erin gets a waft of vomit. Despite this she is grateful, *so* grateful for that touch that it brings fresh tears to her eyes. 'What you did was wrong, yes, but—'

'You were a kid,' Kitty interjects. 'And you were the one who came clean. It was her idea to lie. I mean, who the *fuck*… what kid makes up something like that?' Her dark eyes blaze with disgust.

'I should've said no,' Erin insists tearfully. 'I knew it was wrong. If I hadn't done it Nicky would still be alive and my dad would never have gone to prison. He wouldn't have died.'

'Listen,' Kitty says fiercely. 'You didn't know what would happen. And she—' Kitty breaks off at a sound from the front of the cabin. The door is opening.

Bee walks in, throwing her coat on the sofa before heading for the bathroom. Erin watches her, expecting her face to be tear-stained and puffy, but it isn't. Her expression is eerily blank. She doesn't say a word or seem to notice that Erin and Mira have both been crying.

'Well, well,' Kitty drawls. 'Look what the cat dragged in.'

The bathroom door closes swiftly.

Kitty sits up a little straighter, eyes narrowed. 'Let me handle this,' she says in a low voice as the toilet flushes. The door unlocks and Bee comes out. 'Where'd you get to, Bee?'

'Nowhere,' Bee says. Her eyes are downcast, and Erin is glad she's not looking at them. Kitty is doing a good job of being casual, but Erin can see the loathing simmering in Mira's eyes. What would Bee see if she looked at Erin properly? Would she know Erin has just spilled her darkest secrets?

'You must have been *some*where,' Kitty adds conversationally. 'You've been gone ages. We were starting to think you'd hooked up with someone.'

Bee fidgets, tugging at the hem of her dress. 'I wasn't feeling great, so I went for a walk. I couldn't find you back at the games room so I came here.'

'You went off by yourself?' Kitty's eyes are wide, mocking.

'After having so much to drink? Kinda dangerous, young girl alone, don't you think?'

Mira's face hardens.

'I was fine.' Bee's voice is flat. Repulsed, Erin takes in her tousled hair, her crumpled dress. The image of it gathered at Bee's waist, Callaghan behind her, forces itself into her head.

'Wait, is that…?' Bee is gazing at the silver bottle on the crate. She picks it up, turning it over in her hands.

'Yeah.' Kitty takes it from her. 'I snuck it out the museum. Thought we could have some fun with it.'

'What have you got in mind?' There's still a dull, flat quality to Bee's voice but there's a spark of interest there, too. The bottle has her attention, although it's plain she's preoccupied. Erin wonders what Kitty's plan is – or if she even *has* a plan.

'I don't know.' Kitty looks thoughtful. 'What if we have, like, a séance, or something? See if there really is a witch inside?'

'You mean open it?' Bee asks.

'Maybe.' Kitty taps her nails on the silver glass, making sharp *ting-tings*. 'We shouldn't do it here, though. You know, just in case. But I know the perfect spot.' She scoots to her feet and pulls on her fluffy jacket, then tosses Bee her coat from the sofa. Erin and Mira stand too. Erin's still wearing her jacket and Doc Martens from when she walked in.

Bee hesitates for just a second or two. Then she puts on the coat.

None of them checked the tide times, but it looks as though it's going out. The mudflats are partially visible in the faint moonlight, and they have a pitted appearance, like acne-scarred skin. Broken branches, stones and chunks of brick are submerged in the gritty sludge of the shoreline. In the distance, dots of yellow light are visible, picking out a trail across the mainland.

'It's along here someplace,' Kitty mutters, traipsing across the shingle bordering the low water. She's had the sense to put boots on, and a crafty nod to Mira ensured she did the same. It's Bee alone who's in wholly unsuitable footwear, which she's only now realising as she squelches through the gunge in the strappy red shoes she's had on all night.

'How much further?' she grumbles, shivering. 'These shoes are wrecked.'

'Nearly there,' says Kitty, searching for something across the water. 'Yeah, this is it.'

They stop level with a wooden signpost mired in the mudflats, shallow water lapping around its base. If the tide was fully out they'd be able to reach it in under a minute. There's a wooden jetty of sorts leading out to it. Though it's too dark and too far away to read the post, Erin remembers a photo in the museum which she thinks is of this spot: it's where the so-called witches were tethered to an iron manacle and left to float or flounder as the tide came in. She's surprised Kitty was interested enough to remember this detail. But then, she'd been interested enough to steal the bottle, too.

Kitty takes it out of her bag. The silvery surface glints in the moonlight, mimicking the water glistening in the dips of the shingle. It's cold, but a calm, still night. Inside, Erin is anything but calm. She's jittery with a greedy anticipation. It's unclear what Kitty's about to do, but it's certain she's concocted something.

'So, what do you guys think?' Kitty says, with a slow smile. 'Are we really in the presence of a witch?'

Bee swears under her breath, examining her ruined shoes. Her feet are caked and she's looking behind at the way they've just come, evidently contemplating going back.

'Yeah,' says Erin, getting the gist of where Kitty is leading. 'I reckon we are.'

Mira remains silent. Bee's oblivious, trying to scrape sludge off her heels with a stick.

Kitty buffs the silver glass with her sleeve and snickers. 'Hey

– maybe if I rub it she'll come out and give us three wishes? Wait, no – that's a genie.'

Erin feels a hysterical laugh bubbling up, and fights to hold it in. Kitty's either mad as a box of frogs or high as a kite. Possibly both.

'What would you ask a witch, if you could?' Kitty angles the bottle as though it's a microphone. 'Bee?'

'Huh?' Bee flings the stick away, irritated. 'I don't know. If it's meant to be a séance, then does she have a message for us, I suppose. Can we go back to the cabin to do this?'

'No, we stay here,' Kitty says evenly. 'I don't know about you guys, but I can feel this negative sort of *energy*. I wouldn't want to bring that back with us.' Perhaps it's the dismissal or her abrupt tone, but she has Bee's full attention now. 'Hey, Erin – catch.' She tosses the silver bottle. Erin's heart skips, but somehow she catches it. 'What would you ask?'

The glass is ice-cold. 'I'd want to know if the witch felt bad about what she'd done,' Erin says softly. Her pulse is racing. Normally she hates confrontation and avoids it at any cost, but this is different. This is six years' worth of shame and resentment waiting to be purged. 'Especially if she'd caused someone else's death.' She pushes the silver glass globe at Mira. Touching it is making her skin crawl.

Mira's fingers wrap around the bottle. She never takes her eyes off Bee.

'I would ask why bad things happen when she's around.' She speaks slowly, her accent stronger than usual. 'Because surely these things can't be a coincidence.'

Bee frowns. 'I think you missed the point of the museum. Those women, the *witches*, weren't guilty of anything – it *was* all coincidence and superstition.'

'Right.' Kitty laughs easily. 'Thing is, we're not talking about them. We're talking about you. What's it like, knowing you've fucked up so many lives?'

There's an icy silence. Bee blinks. 'Oh,' she says finally. 'I get it. Erin's opened her trap, has she? Well, everything I did, she did as well. We both lied. And it was her dad who led that little mob. She tell you that?'

'Yes.' Mira's gripping the bottle so tightly her fingertips are turning white. 'She told us everything.'

'Didn't waste any time, did you, Erin? Busy girl.'

'I could say the same about you,' Erin retorts. 'Where did you say you went on your little walk earlier?'

Bee ignores her, turning to Kitty. 'Tell me why, exactly, Erin's any better than me?'

'She told the truth in the end, didn't she?' Kitty folds her arms. 'And she's sorry. That's one reason.'

Bee scoffs. 'Only because her dad got banged up. She's not sorry that kid's dead.'

'Yes, I am!'

'Liar.' Bee jabs a finger at Erin, her face half in shadow. The other half is contorted with spite. 'Nicky Pemberton was a weak little follower who did what he was told. If that Donnie kid *had* told him to touch us, he'd have done it. Are you so stupid you can't see that's where it was heading? The threats, the questions about pubes. That's how it starts. If you're sorry about anything else, it's that Donnie didn't get killed as well.'

'Fuck you,' Erin says, furious.

'No. Fuck *you*. Fuck the lot of you. I'm out of here.' Bee turns towards the road, and the sand sucks wetly at her foot. It's now apparent that the tide is coming in, not going out, for even in the few minutes they've been there it's inched further up the shore.

Kitty is faster. In a couple of steps she's in front of Bee, blocking her path. 'Hold on. You didn't hear the other reasons.'

'Like I give a shit!'

'And you didn't answer Erin's question,' says Mira, moving to stand beside Kitty. 'Where did you go after you left me by the pool table?'

'Yeah,' Kitty adds. 'What was so important you had to ditch Mira when she was that out of it she could barely stand? With that asshole feeling her up?'

For the first time a look of worry flits across Bee's features. It's quickly replaced by defiance. 'There was a room full of people right next to the pool table. Anyone could've looked through.'

'Not when he closed the goddamn door,' says Kitty.

'I *asked* you not to go!' Mira hisses. 'I was afraid! And when you left, I froze. If Kitty and Erin and Aidan had not come in when they did…'

'He'd have raped her,' says Erin. 'But you probably don't give a shit about that, either.'

'So that's reason number two,' says Kitty. 'Don't leave drunk friends alone with sleazy guys. It's a shitty thing to do.'

Bee shrugs. 'She looked like she was enjoying herself to me.'

Glass shatters. Mira has hurled the bottle at Bee.

'Well, that was fucking stupid,' Bee remarks. All four of them stare at the shingle. The bottle lies at Bee's feet in jagged, lethal pieces. At the centre of the shards is a small bundle, tightly bound with rotted string or hair, but it is so decayed that it's impossible to discern what is there, or what it ever was. There is something deeply, incredibly malevolent about it. Erin takes a step back.

'Say that again,' Mira whispers. 'I dare you.'

'That was stupid.'

'No.' Mira is quivering with rage. 'The other part. About me enjoying it.'

Bee straightens up, cocky. 'Well, you were—'

She is cut off by a sharp, stinging slap that rings through the night. Her hand flies to her face. Mira has struck her.

'Look.' Bee's eyes are watering. 'Maybe I shouldn't have left you.'

Kitty hoots, incredulous. '*Maybe?*'

'I didn't know Curtis was going to touch her up.' Bee's cheek is darkening, blood rushing to the surface. 'Why don't you fucking go after him?'

'You gave him the green light when you walked off,' Erin says, relishing the sight of Mira's fingerprints appearing on Bee's pale skin. 'Mira's right. Bad things always happen around you. Why is that?'

Bee glowers, saying nothing. Water swirls around their feet. Erin's boots are starting to leak.

'Don't ask her any more questions, she still hasn't answered the first one.' Kitty raises her voice. 'Why did you really leave Mira?'

Bee gives a tight, vicious smile. 'None of your damn business.'

Erin's anger spikes. 'You made it our business, you fucking skank.'

'Reason number three,' says Kitty. 'Don't leave drunk friends alone with sleazy guys while you go off to fuck a married teacher.'

Bee's smile becomes a grimace. Erin drinks it in, triumphant.

'Yeah. We saw you, Aidan and me. We heard you.'

'You and Aidan?' Aside from the angry handprint on her cheek, Bee has gone deathly pale. 'And you couldn't wait to get back here and blab that to your new friends, too.'

Kitty tuts mockingly. 'Sisters before misters, Bee. And Callaghan? *Really?* So gross.'

'You should've kept your mouth shut, Erin.' Bee's face is a mask. That same eerie mask Erin knows and detests. 'One day someone might shut it for you.'

'Yeah? Try it.'

Bee shakes her head, almost imperceptibly. 'You know,' she says quietly. 'All I ever wanted was to be your friend.'

Erin cannot help it; a disgusted noise bursts out of her.

'Girls like you,' Kitty sneers, 'don't get to be friends with girls like *us*. You're a skank, with skank friends who fuck strangers in alleyways for money and give blowjobs to doormen.'

'Only there is no *friend*, is there?' Erin guesses. 'All that stuff you said – it was you. It's all *you*.'

Bee holds Erin's gaze, her eyes burning with a terrible darkness. Then, feet sloshing through the shallow water, she shoves her way past. 'Out of my way, bitch.'

Erin staggers but stays on her feet. She doesn't really mean for her hand to go out, she's not really thinking. Her fingers twist into Bee's hair, and she yanks it, hard as she can, jerking her off balance. Bee lands on her back in the shin-deep water. She gasps with shock and cold. One of her shoes has come off. The sight of her should sate Erin's anger, but instead it only fuels it. She kicks water in Bee's face, once, twice. She feels good, strong. *Justified*. Bee splutters, trying to catch a breath. When she does she lunges for Erin's legs, trying to drag her down but then Kitty is there straddling her and the water is rising and her hand is on Bee's face, pushing her under. Polka-dot fabric rises and falls with the water.

'Float the witch!' Kitty chants as Bee surfaces, choking. Kitty allows her to take a single breath before plunging her down again, laughing. '*Float the witch!* Will she sink or swim?'

A jet of bubbles shoots up as Bee thrashes and screams. Erin is on her knees, soaked up to her waist. Things bob and cling in the water. Tendrils of weed or hair wrap round her fingers as she clamps on to Bee's wrists. It is bone-chillingly, breathtakingly cold.

Bee comes up, gurgling, eyes wild. Dark water gushes from her nose, mouth. Erin watches, transfixed, horrified, gratified. It's like an unholy baptism, or an exorcism, or something between the two.

'Are you sorry, yet?' Kitty hisses. 'Say you're sorry!'

Bee doesn't – or can't – say anything. This time it's Erin who pushes her under.

Bad things always happen around you... why is that?

Bee didn't murder Nicky but she set it in motion. She didn't hurt Mira but she left her to it. She may be the student, and Callaghan the teacher, but she knows right from wrong. Her presence is always the cause. The root. The poison.

'Enough!' Mira's voice cuts through the darkness, breaking the spell. Erin blinks, looks down at her hands, submerged in the chilled water. They're in Bee's hair, and Kitty is sitting on her chest, breathless from laughing and the effort of keeping her under. Mira is knee-deep beside them, frozen, panicked.

Bee is no longer struggling.

'*Shit.*' Erin is on her feet, reaching for Bee's arms. 'Fuck! We need to get her out.'

All three of them lift and drag her up shore, far enough to where the shingle is only just starting to glisten damply. *We killed her*, Erin thinks numbly. *We killed her, we killed her. The wicked witch, West. Slain by water.* The thought loops in her head. She wonders if she has lost her mind as well as her conscience.

But as they roll Bee on to her side she retches, and brown water gushes from her lips. Her hand grips Erin's weakly. Erin recoils and extricates herself. Kitty is tapping Bee's face repeatedly, hard enough that it's verging on slapping, but Bee is conscious. Moaning, gasping, shaking. She shoves Kitty off and twists away, on all fours as she throws her guts up. One of her hands lands near to a slice of silver jutting from the grit. Unwittingly – and even though Erin could swear it was further along the shore – they have dragged her to the exact spot where Mira broke the bottle.

Silver glass lies scattered, the bottle now in three large, jagged pieces. What was a fourth lies crushed into irreparable shards. There is no sign of its grisly contents; they have either been swallowed up by the estuary or driven down into the silt. Bee sinks slowly on to the shingle, sobbing, water lapping at her bare feet.

It is the first time Erin has ever seen her cry.

'You'll pay for this,' she says between sobs. 'You'll fucking pay.'

She is still crying as they walk away and return to the cabin, numb and silent from what they have done. From what they have almost become.

23

OCTOBER 2016

THE SILENCE STRETCHES, BECOMING UNBEARABLE.

'She was alive when we left her,' Kitty insists at last. 'I swear.'

Mira sucks on the asthma pump again. All Erin can do is nod. She feels sick with horror at what's been confessed, even though she and Mira share a look of silent acknowledgement that Kitty has told a pared back, somewhat sanitised version of what they did. Perhaps that's how she chooses to remember it, or can't bring herself to recount the level of cruelty, but she's omitted the worst parts. The chanting, the laughing. How many times Bee went under. Still, it sounds awful, even with some of the uglier details spared.

Are you sorry, yet? Say you're sorry.

When Aidan finally speaks Erin almost flinches at the disgust in his voice.

'I can't believe the three of you could do something like that. *Jesus.* Now it makes sense why you'd lie about seeing her again. It's no fucking wonder, is it?'

Aidan has always known the worst thing about Erin up till now, and he's never judged her. But maybe she's misjudged him and his capacity to forgive. She cannot bear the look on his face, and so she glances at Hewitt and finds the same horror there. A deep, haunted revulsion.

'She was breathing, speaking,' Kitty says forcefully. 'We got carried away, but we did *not* kill her.'

'You sure about that?' Tori asks. 'You lured her away from the cabin, broke the bottle. Pushed her in the water. What's to say you didn't do the rest?'

'We… we pulled her out,' Erin whispers. 'We didn't do anything else. We didn't… cut her.'

Tori shakes her head. 'I always knew it was dodgy, how you explained the fingerprints away by saying you'd passed the bottle round in the museum.' She points a talon at Kitty. 'Because from the camera angle it always looked like you were the only one who touched it.'

'The camera was shit,' Kitty counters. 'And that's irrelevant now. You've heard the truth.'

'The truth?' Tori scoffs. 'From three people who covered for each other for twenty years?'

'Yes,' Mira says. 'We covered for each other. Of *course* we did, we knew how it'd look. We behaved unforgivably… and *god*. I'm more ashamed of it than anything I've ever done. Is it any surprise we hid it? Kitty's right, though. Someone else killed her, not us.' She counters a scathing look from Tori. 'We were seventeen, not stupid. There's no way we'd have done that, knowing our fingerprints were all over that bottle.'

'Right,' says Kitty. 'Because if it was us then I wouldn't be here right now. I'd just be damn grateful we'd got away with it.'

Erin finds she is observing them all in the reflection of the window. Just watching them in the glass like they're characters on television, like it's something she'd seen a long time ago and is revisiting to find that nothing is as she remembered. She feels strangely removed from these people, these strangers. Part memories, part figments of her imagination. Or at least, they have been for so long that now they hardly feel real to her. Sometimes Bee doesn't feel real, although she was once. Now she is a story, a figure from a nightmare, a phantom. For ever seventeen.

'Did you know who she was?' Hewitt's voice brings her back. She is watching Erin guardedly. 'That she was one of the liars? That first day, you said you knew her.'

Erin's heart thuds faster. 'I— yeah, I knew. It was local hearsay that she was one of those kids.' Sometimes she's wondered if any of it would have happened if Hewitt had let her switch cabins when she asked. Erin might never have opened her mouth about Bee to Kitty and Mira, and they'd never have lured her to the water or smashed the bottle. One word from Hewitt might have altered the entire course of the night.

'What about the other one?' Tori adds. 'Child A?'

Erin shakes her head weakly. 'There were a couple of names bandied around.'

'Did you know the boy who was killed?' Hewitt probes, softening a fraction.

'Not really. He was older, hung around with a rough crowd. That's all I knew.' Erin averts her eyes, desperate to end this line of questioning. 'So… what now?' she asks, glancing at her watch. She has been on the island for fifty-six minutes. There's less than an hour left before the causeway is underwater and the island will be cut off for the next eight. 'We've told the truth, Kitty, just like you wanted. So, what now? What do you *expect* to happen?'

'I thought we'd do a tour of the island,' says Kitty. She doesn't rise to Erin's hostility, not outwardly, at least. 'Work our way round it, remind ourselves of the geography and whatnot. Say at… one-thirty, starting back here? The rain's meant to clear up by then. Gives everyone a chance to decompress, take a breather, maybe bring their overnight bags up to the Beach House. After that, well… I was hoping that what we've admitted might encourage anyone else who's been hiding things to come clean. There has to be another part of the puzzle we're missing, somewhere.' She glances round expectantly but is met with a bleak silence as Aidan, Tori and Hewitt continue to process the awful confession. 'Maybe later, then. I've arranged for dinner where we'll get to talk it all over. Ask each other questions. Iron out any creases for good.'

'I'm not staying,' Erin says. 'I need to go before the causeway floods.'

'Why?' Kitty tilts her head, studying her. '*Why* do you need to go now? The road opens again just after nine this evening.'

Erin is fully aware of this. She doesn't want to be on that causeway in the dark. *The Devil's Path*. She doesn't want to be on the island at all, and she has to remind herself that while it's a place with a bad history, it is still only a place and not a malignant, living thing out to hurt her.

'Because,' she reaches desperately. 'I can't… I only came to… to—'

To stop Kitty. But Kitty was never going to be stopped, and the part they played that night is now out, for good. There's no taking it back.

'You're here now,' Kitty says. 'And I know you're pissed at me, and I deserve it. But this guilt… it's got too much. Sometimes I've even felt like this place, and what we did, left us cursed, somehow. And now it's my last shot at finding out what happened. Can you indulge me, for old times' sake? Don't *you* want to know?'

'Well, yeah, but—' She cuts off, aware that everyone is watching her. She asks herself why she feels the need to escape so badly when all she'll be going back to is more of the same. Hiding, fear, isolation. A prisoner in her own home. And yes, everyone here now knows what the three of them did to Bee that night, their appalling treatment of her. But for now at least, it is contained. The moment Erin leaves, she will be cut off, and there are three people here who know her bigger secret. If she stays she has a better chance of containing that, too. Securing their silence.

'It's one day, Erin,' Kitty says. 'A few hours. Stay. Have

dinner.' She smiles wryly and mimes playing a violin. 'And hey, I'm dying, so you can't say no.'

Erin hesitates, then finds herself nodding stiffly. 'Okay.'

'Okay,' Kitty repeats. 'In that case, I'm going for a smoke and then taking my things up to the house. There's another car park up there. See you back here in a bit.'

The group dissipates, the scraping of chairs fracturing the quietness. Before Erin's even outside she's shivering, and the freshness of the air as she leaves makes her gritty eyes water. Her feet are cold and wet, her Converse trainers soaked from where Aidan dumped the water jug over her. She thinks she has a pair of walking boots in her car. She checks her watch again. It's just coming up to midday, yet already she's exhausted, having barely slept last night for worrying.

She passes Kitty and Bomber who are sparking up cigarettes just beyond the awning of the tea room. Ahead, Mira and Hewitt are going to their cars, with Tori a little way in front. Aidan is striding after them, but as he nears the car park he halts, hanging back as Erin approaches. He does not look at her until she is virtually level with him. She can barely meet his eyes.

'So, now you know,' she says quietly.

'Yeah.' He tilts his face up to the sky. The rain is turning to a fine mist. 'You could have told me.'

'No. I couldn't.'

He says nothing, but she senses a silent acknowledgment that what she says is true.

'You know,' he adds, 'I always sensed you were holding something back about that night. And it wasn't just the fingerprints on the bottle.'

'What, then?'

'The morning Bee was found. You knew exactly where to look for her.'

She stares at him, hearing the blood pulsing through her ears.

The disgust she had seen on him earlier has faded to sadness and disappointment. Without another word he walks away and mounts the black motorbike. When he roars off on it, it is like he is roaring at her.

24

OCTOBER 1996

'**S**HE DIDN'T COME BACK LAST night.'

Erin wakes to Kitty shaking her by the shoulder in a way that is none too gentle. She opens her eyes with difficulty; they're gummed shut and the room is stark with light.

'What?' she murmurs. She feels awful. She's been hungover before, where she's stayed in bed with a thumping head, vomiting into a bowl until three in the afternoon. But this is nothing like that. She feels indescribably ill, in a way that she cannot think of anything that would make her feel better apart from the sweet oblivion of sleep. Her nose is simultaneously running and bunged up. With a hot flush of shame, she remembers the cocaine. The rush of invincibility.

She wants to crawl up the walls.

'Bee,' Kitty says. She's looking surprisingly groomed, standing at the end of the bed in jeans and a T-shirt, tugging a wide-tooth comb through her hair. The only signs of anything amiss are the dark shadows under her eyes and a snappish edge to her voice. 'She never came back.'

Erin drags herself into a sitting position. The room sways, then rights itself. Something smells sour. She grimaces. Mira is in the other bed, submerged under the covers. There's a bucket by the side of her, but it's empty.

'Maybe she went back to Callaghan's.' Erin reaches for a glass of water on the bedside table and sips with difficulty. She is never drinking again. 'Or Hewitt's.' The night flashes back. Her kiss with Preston, and the one with Aidan. Mira and Curtis in the pool room. Erin and Aidan at Callaghan's window. Bee, coughing up brown water. Broken silver glass. Her conscience stirs with the first prickling of guilt and unease, but for now it's too heavily blanketed in self-pity.

'Or she just stayed out.' Kitty dabs on concealer, then lip gloss. 'Perhaps she's waiting for us to leave so she can come back.'

Erin glances at the damp clothes strewn around the room. The black trousers of Kitty's that she wore are bunched on the radiator, drying out. The pewter top is next to them. Erin's dress is discarded on a chair, no doubt soiled with estuary water and Mira's vomit. Erin closes her eyes and sees Bee, thrashing under the freezing surface. Could she really have stayed out all night, in October? Even if she hadn't been soaked through, surely it's not possible.

Kitty chucks the lip gloss into her make-up bag. 'We've got about a half hour before we need to be at the gallows for registration. Chop, chop.'

Erin checks her watch on the bedside table. It's ten twenty. 'What if she doesn't show?'

'Why wouldn't she?'

'What if… I mean, what if she's not okay? That water was freezing.'

'If she was that cold she'd have come back. The door was unlocked all night. I reckon she went crying to Callaghan.'

'Yeah,' Erin says uncertainly. 'He was pretty clear about telling her to get lost, but I guess she could've gone there. She probably wanted to warn him.' She imagines Bee crawling up the shore, dripping and shaking all the way to Callaghan's cabin. Tearfully begging to be let in, telling him what Erin, Kitty and Mira had done. What they know.

'Good. I hope she did,' says Kitty. 'I bet the pair of them are shitting bricks right now.'

*

Bee is not at registration. They get there a few minutes late, but they're not the only ones. Curtis arrives after them, bloodshot-eyed and rumpled. Preston is close behind. He stands at the back and is wearing a baseball cap, pulled down so his face is in shadow. Erin and Kitty flank Mira protectively, but Curtis never looks their way even though Kitty is glaring daggers in his direction. Mira stares at the ground. Initially she'd refused to get out of bed but at the last minute she'd dragged herself up. On the way to Stretch Neck Hill she stopped twice to retch in the hedgerows, but only white foam came up.

Erin is watching Callaghan as Hewitt calls the register. He stands with his arms folded, in a way that deliberately pushes out his biceps. *What a twat.* He's neat and groomed but slightly flushed in the face, like he's not long stepped out of a hot shower. He looks the same as he always does, and rocks back and forth on his heels, his eyes fixed somewhere in the distance. He doesn't appear to be searching the rows of faces for Bee. Perhaps he knows where she is. In his bed, or on the sofa? He seems too relaxed for that; his isn't the face of a man who has a student holed up in his cabin. But nor does he look like a man who was having sex with one of his students a few hours ago. Either he's a good actor or Bee never went back to him last night. Erin feels another ripple of apprehension. She glances at Aidan. He's watching Callaghan, too, but a couple of times his eyes meet hers, and memories of last night surface. Their kiss, and his admission that he'd engineered it to be longer.

'Belinda West?' Hewitt calls. No one answers. 'Bee? Anyone seen her?'

Again no one replies. This time there are a few shaken heads and blank faces.

'She didn't come back to the cabin last night,' Kitty says coolly.

'What?' A crease appears in Hewitt's forehead. 'Why wasn't this reported?'

Kitty shrugs. 'We figured she'd gone back with someone else.'

Callaghan now looks mildly perturbed. 'When did you last see her?'

'Outside the games room last night, at around…' Kitty blows out a long breath. 'Eight-thirty, I guess?'

'She came with you three?' Callaghan asks.

'Sure,' Kitty says easily. She explains how she and Erin returned to the cabin for her jacket, leaving Bee and Mira to play pool. She doesn't mention Preston. 'Then she told Mira she had to go somewhere.' She gives Callaghan an innocent look. 'It was after you left, sir.'

Erin sees Aidan shift in her peripheral vision and resists the urge to look at him. To anyone else Kitty must sound innocuous but, to those who know the truth, she's said just enough to raise the level of discomfort. Callaghan clears his throat lightly.

'Perhaps she came back after you and left before you got up?' he suggests, but Kitty shakes her head.

'Her bed wasn't slept in, and the study bag she had yesterday was still by the door when we left.'

Callaghan rubs a hand over his chin and sighs. Something is stirring beneath the calm façade. He must be wondering what Bee is playing at, and guessing it's aimed at him.

'Should we go look for her?' Kitty asks.

Hewitt and Callaghan don't answer right away. They're speaking quietly among themselves, but Erin catches something about delaying the witch trial re-enactment. There are murmurs now within the group, some jokey, others concerned. Erin, Kitty and Mira stand silently. Kitty is examining her nails, doing a good job of appearing casual, but Mira is peaky, chewing her lip. Hewitt addresses the group.

'Everyone listen up,' she says. 'Paul and I are off to have a quick word about the itinerary for today, so rather than you lot waiting around here twiddling your thumbs, I suggest you take a walk back to your cabins and check Bee didn't wander back to the wrong one last night.' She gives a knowing look. 'That way, if she's crashed out on someone's sofa she can be given a polite nudge to get her skates on.' She leans into to Callaghan, closer than necessary, to check his watch. 'We'll meet back here in thirty minutes. Oh, and we've only had two teams hand in the witch hunt task so far, which means there's still one Pizza Hut voucher up for grabs for the next team to get that to me. Okay? Right, see you all in half an hour.'

'So you don't want us to look for Bee?' asks Tilly. She has been whispering and making dramatic faces since Kitty said Bee never returned to the cabin last night.

Hewitt shakes her head. 'Just a quick check of cabins, that's all. This isn't a search party.'

'She won't have gone far,' Callaghan adds. He gives one of his matey smiles as the group disperses. Erin is unnerved by the normalcy of it. She wonders what else he's hiding behind that pally exterior, this man who has casual flings with students. And despite what Hewitt said, the words 'search party' only heighten her anxiety, even though it's plain Hewitt thinks Bee's hungover and that someone's covering for her.

'Well, this worked out pretty good,' says Kitty, as they turn back in the direction of the cabin.

'What did?' Erin asks distractedly. She has caught sight of Preston moving away and, though it might just be the light, she thinks he's trying to hide a black eye. Aidan watches her, making no attempt to leave. She can see immediately that he's concerned, and her insides twist unpleasantly. She thinks of herself and Kitty, breathless and exhilarated, holding Bee under the freezing, dirty water. She imagines seeing it as if she were Aidan, and the thought disgusts her. She cannot bear Bee, but even worse, she can't bear the thought of people finding out what they did to her. She tears her gaze from him and glances at Kitty, who is grimacing a little.

'Going back to the cabin,' Kitty mutters. 'I think I need a dump.'

On another day Erin would have laughed, but nothing seems funny now. There is a gnawing worry burgeoning inside her, which is not just that Bee might not be all right, but that if she isn't, then it could well be because of them. Before she thinks through what she's doing she turns and starts to head in another direction.

'Erin?' Kitty calls, bewildered. 'Cabin's this way.'

'I'm not going to the cabin.'

Kitty jogs over to her, linking her arm through Erin's.

'Sure you are.' Her voice is pleasant, but there's an edge to it that wasn't there before, and she keeps it low as she steers Erin back the other way. 'We're going to check the cabin, like Chewy told us to.'

'We know she's not there.'

'She might've snuck in after we left.'

'Erin's right,' says Mira. 'We should go back… back to where we were last night.'

'And we will,' Kitty says. 'Right after we go to the cabin.' She unhooks her arm and gives Erin a sharp look. 'Use your head, honey. We go chasing off over there and someone's gonna see.' She inclines her head slightly, motioning to Aidan, who is still watching from a distance.

Erin swallows. 'You think something *has* happened to her.'

'No,' says Kitty. 'I think she's fine. She's either licking her wounds somewhere or being a little bitch and hiding away to make lover-boy worry. But *if* she's still over there – which I don't think she is – it won't look good for us if we head straight over when I told the group we last saw her at the games room. I'm just thinking ahead here, covering our asses. Okay?'

'Okay,' Erin mutters. She trudges after Kitty, and Mira follows. Though Erin doesn't turn back again, she's pretty sure Aidan is still there.

The cabin is empty, all as they left it. Bee's bag by the door and her things in the room are untouched. While Kitty uses the bathroom, Mira sits on the sofa, massaging her temples. Erin paces in the small kitchen area, in her Doc Martens that are still damp despite her blasting them with a hairdryer before they left. The walk to the gallows and back has cleared her head a bit and she's feeling marginally better. She is starting to wish, to *will* Bee to walk through the door with a cocky smile. Although she is not sure that even Bee could manage being cocky in the face of how they treated her. When they left her sobbing on the shore last night, it was the most emotion Erin has ever seen from her. It was as though something stoppered up had been unleashed.

She thinks of the corked silver bottle, smashed.

It will bring great misfortune.

Kitty emerges from the bathroom and searches through her bag, pulling out the island map and list of places to visit for clues to the witch hunt task. 'Right, we still have just over fifteen minutes. We can swing by the shore now,' she says breezily. 'If anyone asks, we're just searching for these clues.'

They set off through the lanes towards the island's edge. The route is shorter and easier during the day, without the pitfalls and uncertainty of darkness. The morning is brightening, and though it's chilly there's a promise of sun waiting to break through the cloud. Some of the dread Erin feels is shaken away. There's no way Bee stayed out. She must be at Callaghan's, and Callaghan must be lying. That's the only explanation.

The tide is in when they reach the shore. It almost looks like a different place, but there, out in the impossibly calm water, is the post marking the site where the iron manacle was once mired.

Float the witch.

'See?' Kitty indicates the thin strip of gravel above the waterline. 'No sign of her.'

'What's that?' Mira stiffens. 'In the water. There's something out there, by the jetty.'

They see the hair first, floating on the surface like amber seaweed, maybe fifteen or twenty metres from where they stand. The colour is duller than Erin remembers. Later she will imagine that it faded as the life seeped out of its owner. In reality, it's probably more to do with the mud and silt caked in it. There's a wet billow of polka-dot fabric, almost camouflaged in the shadow of the jetty. The next thing they see is a rounded shape bobbing. The back of a head.

Bee is face down in the scummy estuary water, like she is nothing more than a thrown away crisp packet. Erin stares at her. At *it*. Bee is no longer really a person. She is a body. The part that made her *her*, gone for ever. Detached. Erin is detached, too. She is unspooling. Nothing feels real.

You'll pay for this, Bee had said. And now Erin will. She will be locked up, just like her dad. Her life is over.

'Fuck,' Kitty says softly. 'Oh, my *god*. We've got to get her out.'

Somehow Erin recalls that those were almost her own exact words last night, as they were holding Bee under. When they knew they'd gone too far.

Kitty takes a step into the water.

'Don't,' says Erin.

'But what if she's—?'

'She's dead.' Erin knows this in her bones. The water is so flat that there's no way Bee can be alive. Even in warm, dry clothes, Erin is shivering, but Bee, there in the cold of the water, is utterly motionless. Erin cannot face Kitty dragging her out. She doesn't want to be here when that happens, even though it must. 'Don't touch her. We need to get someone.'

'I'll go.' Mira's voice is a whisper. Erin had almost forgotten she was there. Her dark eyes are bloodshot and terrified, her black hair a wild tangle. There's something crusty in it by her ear; a thread of dried vomit. She turns and runs, the pounding of her feet like a drum counting down. Erin stares after her. In the distance the roof of the museum is just visible. She wonders if anyone knows about the missing witch bottle yet.

Kitty's foot makes a horrible sucking sound as she pulls it from the water and steps back on to the shingle. She tugs at a handful of her tight curls. Her nails are chipped. 'What the hell happened?' Her voice is chipped too. She gives a little sob. 'I don't get it. We… we…'

Erin doesn't get it, either. Her mind see-saws between accepting blame and deflecting it. She tries to remember how long Bee was underwater, how long it was that she'd stopped struggling.

'I don't think we did that. Maybe she tripped, hit her head or something. She was fine when we left her.'

'Fine, my ass!' Kitty croaks.

Okay, so she hadn't been fine, exactly, Erin thinks. And Kitty's American-ness, which she'd found endearing the night before, is starting to grate on her. *It's arse*, she wants to tell her. *You're in England now.*

'You know what I mean,' she says. 'She was *alive*.'

'And now she isn't. What the fuck do we say? It was an accident. We didn't *mean* it!'

'We held her under. We did mean it.'

'Not to fucking *kill* her.' Another sob escapes Kitty's lips. 'I just wanted to scare her, to get her back. But now we've already lied about where we last saw her, and…' Her face crumples. 'I can't go to jail.'

'It wouldn't be jail.' Erin's thinking out loud, her brain running away with itself. 'It'd be a young offenders' place.' Over the years – since Nicky Pemberton's death – she has read things about minors who are incarcerated for crimes and consoled herself that what she and Bee did never landed them in one of those places.

'Same difference.' Kitty is openly crying now. 'You know what goes on in them? My cousin worked in one. They shit in the food and everything.' She cuffs tears off her face, sniffing. 'We have to stick together on this, Erin. No one can know we were involved. Like you said, she was alive when we left. Whatever happened after wasn't us. We can't say we were here with her.' She glances out at the body and back again. 'And we can't help her now, but we can help ourselves.'

Bee seems to have drifted closer, as though, somehow, she's eavesdropping. *You'll pay for this*, she whispers again in Erin's mind. Erin's already paid dearly for one mistake with Bee. Must she now pay for another? She thinks of her mum and the pain she's already suffered. Even if Erin deserves punishment, her mother doesn't. This will kill her.

'What if someone saw us?' she says hoarsely.

'No one saw us,' Kitty insists. 'If they had, they'd have said so at registration. Or they'd have… stopped us.'

'What about Mira? What if she says something? We shouldn't have let her go.'

They both fall silent. Mira is a risk, possibly the biggest risk they face. It was Mira who threw the bottle at Bee, and Mira who slapped her, but Erin was the one who pulled her down into the water and made sure she stayed there, along with Kitty. Not only did Mira not partake in holding her under, she's the one who stopped it. And now, neither Kitty nor Erin knows what she's going to admit, to implicate them in.

'Surely she'll have the sense to keep quiet.' Kitty's eyes are darting from side to side, trying to figure out her next move. Or if there even is a next move. '*Surely*—'

She shuts up. Two figures are speeding towards them: Callaghan in the lead and Hewitt a short way behind. Then Mira appears, every step dragging as though she's wading through muddy water. Erin wonders whether she chose to go for help because it was the right thing to do, or because she wanted to be as far away from the body as possible. Maybe it was both.

'Shit!' Callaghan's face is contorted in panic. He starts untying the laces of his grey trainers, all fumbling fingers. Hewitt crashes straight past him into the water.

'What are you doing?' she yells back at him. 'There's no time for that!'

Callaghan straightens up and follows her, wading out to Bee, shoes still on. Erin experiences a jolt of shock when they reach her – the water is only up to Hewitt's thighs and barely skimming Callaghan's knees. Shallower than Erin remembers.

Mira comes to stand beside Erin and Kitty, hugging herself, trembling uncontrollably.

'What did you tell them?' Kitty asks, her voice low and urgent.

'Nothing.' Mira speaks so faintly that her words are almost swallowed up by the sounds of the sea birds calling above.

'*Nothing?*'

'I said we'd found her. That's all.'

Kitty releases a *hiss* of breath. Erin's chest is heavy, like something's pressing on her and has crushed all the air out already.

Hewitt and Callaghan turn Bee face up and for a moment Erin's heart jumps up her throat as Bee's marble-white hand reaches for Callaghan.

She's alive..?

No. The hand slaps the surface of the water as Bee's arm flops across her body, lifeless. Her red hair is plastered over her face and, as they start to pull her through the water, it becomes clear that one of her dress straps or something is snagged on some part of the jetty. Hewitt wrenches, and the dress comes down to expose her left breast. Callaghan looks at it, looks away, then looks again, horrified. Hewitt pulls the dress up, trying valiantly, and pointlessly, to preserve the last of Bee's dignity. By the time they lay her on the shore it's come down again. This time Erin, Kitty and Mira all see the love bite, just above the nipple.

'Jesus,' Kitty whispers, her hand going to her mouth.

Hewitt takes charge, barking orders. 'Paul, help me get her on her side. You girls stand back.'

They do as they're told, and so does Callaghan. Hewitt grunts as they roll her. Dirty water leaks from Bee's mouth. Erin half expects a bout of coughs and splutters from her, the way it happens in films. *The way it did last night.* She waits for her to sit up, gurgling. But there's none of that. Bee really *is* dead. As her sodden hair falls away from her face Kitty muffles a scream. One of Bee's eye sockets is black and empty. But then a clump of mud dislodges to reveal that the eye is still there, grit-covered and staring at nothing.

Hewitt lifts her into a sitting position, tapping her face sharply. 'Belinda?'

Bee's head tilts back like it's on a hinge. Through the strands of hair her throat gapes red and open, slit from one side to the other.

Hewitt lets out a cry and drops her. Bee falls back and hits the shingle with a sickening *flump*. Callaghan scrambles away, gagging. Kitty whimpers, covering her face with her hands. Erin is suddenly aware that Mira's fingers are clamped on her arm. She's hyperventilating, the stink of alcohol coming off her every breath. It curdles Erin's stomach.

She can't look away from that gaping throat. The horror of it.

The terrible, guilty relief of it.

She wraps her fingers around Mira's cold hand and squeezes back.

'It's all right,' she murmurs. 'It's all right, it's all right.'

Bee's throat grins at them, as if offering friendly reassurance. *It's all right.*

Because it means they are innocent. Of killing her, at least.

Part Three

It is always the best policy to speak the truth, unless, of course,
you are an exceptionally good liar
– Jerome K Jerome

25

OCTOBER 2016

Erin heads up to the Beach House alone.

It's a short drive from the main car park, along a hedge-rowed lane that takes Erin past Stretch Neck Hill and a designated nature trail area. She is struck again by how so little of the island looks familiar, even though she has been here before. She leaves her car on the gravelled drive next to the others and approaches the front of the building.

It's a large, white manor house which feels a little at odds with the wilderness that makes up most of the rest of the island. The grounds are well-maintained with walled gardens and, somewhere to the rear, the recording studio. Erin enters a foyer with plush sofas and silk flower arrangements. Pinned to a noticeboard is information for private hire of the house – business conferences, wellness retreats and weddings. According to what she's read in the few days prior to coming, all this is how the island makes the bulk of its income. A touch of glamour in a rough landscape.

She approaches the empty reception. On the desk is a list of names and a corresponding handful of room keys, including one for her. Though Erin had arrived with no intention of spending the night, a room has already been made up for her anyway.

Her room is number three of twelve which are spread over the first and second floors. She heads up two flights, finds the room and lets herself in. The decor is a tasteful duck-egg blue and white, with matching towels and a bathrobe. There's even a selection of swanky mini toiletries in the shower cubicle. She throws her handbag on the bed. A few hours and she's out of here. She just has to get through the rest of the afternoon, until the causeway reopens. Dinner, refuel and a strong coffee and she'll be good to go – or at the very worst spend the night at a bed and breakfast she saw near the motorway. She'd rather stay there than on this island with its haunting memories. Already, she cannot imagine that anything else that might come out will be as significant as the confession Kitty has forced, and she feels a flash of despair.

The sound of a splash draws her to the window, left open a crack to air the room. She moves to it and gazes out. The room is at the rear of the house, overlooking the River Tithe on the opposite side to the causeway. Below her window there's a sun terrace and, beyond that, a stretch of man-made beach that is nothing like the muddy shingle shoreline near the causeway. Between the sun terrace and the beach is an outdoor pool. A dark shape streaks across it under the surface. Someone is swimming. She watches the figure glide seamlessly, before doing a graceful tumble turn and arcing back on itself. Only when it nears the centre of the pool does it surface, moving in lean, professional strokes.

A chilly breeze whistles through the window. Erin wonders how cold the water must be – though she doesn't need to question who it is down there. There's only one person she knows of who's good enough to swim in such conditions.

The trill of a phone carries to Erin's window. Within seconds the figure is out of the pool and reaching for a towel next to a bag on a sun lounger. Tori Callaghan removes her swim cap and shakes out her short, peroxide hair before taking the call.

Erin closes the window quietly, takes out her own phone and searches *Tori Callaghan* in the browser. Years' worth of articles about Bee's murder and the affair with her teacher fill the screen. She selects 'images' and scrolls past split-screen pictures of Paul and Bee, the guilty couple, and Tori and Bee – wife versus lover. Many show a radiant Tori on her wedding day, her hair a darker, more natural blond worn in long ringlets, next to a grinning Paul as they cut their cake.

Erin finds the picture she's searching for: a grainy newspaper image from 1988 in which a nineteen-year-old Tori, then going by her maiden name of Wakefield, is pictured holding an oversize cheque. It's for just over ten thousand pounds, an amount she raised for Great Ormond Street Hospital after swimming the English Channel. Yet the photograph does not accompany the original article about the charity donation. Instead, it's been unearthed in the wake of the murder by a journalist keen to present suspects other than Paul Callaghan.

As the wronged wife, Victoria 'Tori' Callaghan had as much reason to want her husband's lover out of the way as he did. Belinda West may have been the last infidelity in the six-year marriage, but she wasn't the first. A source claims Tori Callaghan had already discovered her husband had been unfaithful more than once, including a fling when she was five months pregnant. Allegedly, Tori followed one rival for weeks before creating flyers falsely advertising her services as a sex worker. These were distributed in local call boxes and posted to the woman's family, neighbours, and place of work.

The article reminds that, on the night Bee died, Tori claimed to have been at home with her twin sons. According to her she'd put the boys to bed at around seven, showered, and then watched a rented film. A neighbour's CCTV showed the Callaghans' car remained in the drive all night (Paul had driven a college minibus to the island) and their Blockbuster account confirmed the rental of a VHS copy of *The Usual Suspects*, which was returned early the next morning. The article then outlines an exchange between Tori and the staff member on duty when she returned the video.

'I always chatted to her when she came in,' he recalls. 'It was a running joke that she never rewound the VHS tapes. I'd tell her off about it in a jokey kind of way. But this time the tape was rewound, which I commented on. She just laughed. But then I started asking her about the film and whether she'd guessed who Keyser Söze was, and at that point she said she'd fallen asleep and hadn't watched it.'

The piece goes on to detail Tori's sporting achievements. Prior to the Channel crossing she'd swum for a Maidstone club and won various regional awards and championships. By the time the article was published in March 1997 Tori was a widow, and mother to twin boys who were just fifteen months old. Though her competitive swimming days were behind her, she'd returned to work part-time as a personal trainer when the twins were nine months old, and still swam a couple of times a week. Her family may have been her first priority but her fitness was a close second.

Most would argue that the timing – both of Belinda West's death and the tide limiting access to Blackwater Island – made it impossible for the killing to have been committed by anyone other than those on the island that night. But let us examine what is impossible and what is merely unlikely.

If Tori Callaghan HAD discovered the affair between her husband and his student, it is unlikely that the car left in her drive and the rented movie she never watched were a cover intended to place her at home that night. It's unlikely that she left the house unseen and travelled approximately an hour to the River Tithe by taxi or public transport. It is even more unlikely that she swam a mile across to the island in mid-October, in dangerously cold water, to murder Belinda West, before swimming the mile back and returning home to her sleeping children.

All of this is highly unlikely and, for the average person, impossible. But Tori Callaghan is not the average person. She is a woman persistently cheated on, lied to, determined, obsessive and, crucially, a fearless former champion swimmer who'd braved the cold English Channel — a distance of twenty-one miles.

For Tori Callaghan, it is entirely possible.

When Erin looks up a second time, Tori has ended the call and is staring directly at her window.

26

OCTOBER 2016

Disturbed, Erin steps away from the window and sits on the bed. Aside from the article on Tori, she is thinking about what she, Kitty and Mira did on the night of Bee's death. Perhaps Kitty was right about being here dredging up memories. Things Erin has tried to bury are surfacing, things Bee said to Paul Callaghan on her final night.

Even liars don't lie about everything.

What she said to Erin, Kitty and Mira after they almost drowned her. Her and the unborn child everyone thought was a lie.

You'll pay for this.

And yet. The things troubling Erin most are the small ones, things which had seemed insignificant at the time. Utterances Erin only recalls because they either irritated her – *Your mum's nice… is Aidan's mum nice?* – or repulsed her.

All I ever wanted was to be your friend.

It was one of the last things Bee ever said to Erin. Possibly one of the last things she said at all. An uneasy guilt has crept up from nowhere and is like a physical thing that lurks, unseen, in the room with her. For the first time, she is starting to look back on her childhood through the eyes of an adult. At the privileges she took for granted. Back then she'd resented Bee's intrusion, her oddness, and had seen only an antagonising, unlikeable girl. Now she wonders whether Bee knew any other way to be, and if some of it had come about from sensing Erin's own instinctive rejection of her. She thinks of the witches in that terrible museum. The outcasts, the misfits, the disturbed. The ones people didn't want or know how to help. It was simpler to get rid of them. Harder to help or look for the good. But sometimes there are those who do.

She goes into her phone's call log, tapping the screen. Her mum doesn't pick up, but the moment Erin ends the call it rings.

'Hello, Mum.'

'Sorry, love. I was in the loo, couldn't get to the phone in time. Where are you?'

'Oh.' Erin is not going to tell her mum where she is. She'll only worry. 'I've just come out… into town. Going for a coffee in a minute.'

'Okay, love.' There is relief in her mum's voice. 'I was thinking I might come to stay for a few days.'

'Yeah,' Erin says. 'I'll come to you, though. We'll go round the market, then get lunch, and you can show me how to make Victoria sponge again. I don't know why mine always goes wrong.' There are tears in her eyes, and they have crept into her voice too, and her mum hears them because she says, 'Erin, why are you talking about Victoria sponge? What's the matter?'

Your mum's nice. Erin's mother *is* nice. The kind who bakes, and calls, and visits, and gives money for ice cream and believes her daughter.

'I wanted to ask you some things,' she whispers. 'About Bee.'

Her mum wavers. 'You never wanted to talk about her. Not properly. You always—'

'I know.' Erin always changes the subject, clams up. Whenever Bee's discussed it's only in relation to Erin and the effect on her family, and the mentions of her are as scant as possible. 'You said her mum died a few years ago.'

Another pause, another conversation Erin had shut down at the time.

'She did. Your aunt heard about it. Her cleaner worked in the care home where Daphne ended up. It was about four years ago she died, I think.'

'What did she die of?'

'I don't know, but she was there because she had early onset dementia. She wasn't even that old. Early sixties, but she was in a bad way. Incontinent and all that. Apparently, she was always difficult, and a bit of a mystery to them there.' Erin's mum is speaking slowly, cautiously, as though she is waiting for Erin to cut her off, but gradually she picks up her pace.

'The carers knew who she was – knew her daughter had been murdered. But Daphne always spoke about Bee as if she was alive, sometimes even as though she'd just visited her. She never had any visitors though, no other family she mentioned. The only time she said any different was on her last birthday when one of the other residents asked if her daughter was coming to see her. Daphne went for them with a cake knife and started screaming that her daughter was a little witch, and she was glad that she was dead.'

Erin's guts are twisting. *I'm a witch.*

'Those bruises on her, that day in the paddling pool.' She can call them to mind at will, the yellow blotches on Bee's scabby legs. Four purple dots on a skinny wrist.

'Well, it was her, obviously.' Her mum clears her throat, uncomfortable. 'I know children do get bruises anyway. But short of charging over there and accusing someone of beating up their kid there's only so much you can do. That's not the way to deal with people like that, it just pushes them further inward. I thought it'd do Bee good to be friends with you, to get her out of there now and then…' She hesitates. 'She wanted so much to be like you, I think. To have what you had. Nice things, parents who cared. She could've been a completely different child. I just wanted to include her, show her a little kindness.' When she speaks next she sounds old. Quavery. 'Sometimes I wonder if

I could have done more. Mostly I wish I'd never involved us at all.'

Raindrops are gathering on the window.

'*Did* anyone ever… do anything?' Erin asks. 'Say anything?'

Again, her mum pauses. 'Jermaine,' she says at last. 'Next door to them. He came to speak to me about Daphne and Bee a couple of times.'

Erin remembers Jermaine, or Mr Baxter, as she'd known him when she was a child. A gentle widower always pottering in his garden, bringing her mother tomatoes from his greenhouse and giving Erin and Aidan sticks of tart rhubarb to dip in sugar. She'd been fascinated by his long dreadlocks and bright clothes that always looked like summer, no matter the season. 'What did he say?'

'That she wasn't right in the head.'

'Bee?'

'No. Daphne. She never told anyone a thing about where they'd lived before, or who Bee's dad was.'

Erin thinks of her own reclusive life. She never tells anyone anything either. Is she the town weirdo now, the focus of the local gossips? The opposite of what she has tried to be?

'And it'd been noticed that Daphne had different men over,' her mum adds.

'How many men?'

'At least three that he mentioned to me. Remember they'd only been there a few months before… before all the trouble.'

Before Nicky Pemberton.

'Jermaine thought it was wrong, all these men coming and going with a little girl in the house. I tried not to judge, but I agreed with him. So did your dad.'

'Are you sure they were boyfriends? That she wasn't… you know.'

'Yes. They were boyfriends, or flings, whatever you want to call them. There was never any suggestion she was on the game. But sometimes she'd go out and leave Bee alone with them.'

'Do you think they did anything to her?'

'I… I don't know.' Her mum's voice is strained. 'But Jermaine saw other things.'

The slow, creeping unease Erin feels is building. Circling her like flies.

'What? What did he see?'

'He used to smoke. Out the back, never in the house. Said it was early one morning, sometime in February. He was just about to light up when he heard the Webbs' back door go and Daphne saying, "Get over there!" She sounded livid. So he crept to the fence and looked through a gap and saw Bee standing on the grass in just a thin little nightie, nothing on her feet. She was shaking with the cold and saying, "Sorry, Mummy. I'm sorry." Daphne was hanging bedsheets on the line, and a pair of kid's knickers. Pulled the line as high up as it'd go and said, "That's what happens to dirty little girls who piss the bed. Their drawers go on the line for the neighbours to see." Then she whacked her one, right across the legs.'

'*Christ*, Mum,' Erin whispers, but her mum isn't finished.

'After that she got the hose and started spraying her down, right there on the grass. Ice-cold water. In February.'

'Why didn't he *do* something? Why didn't he—'

'He banged on the fence and told her to pack it in, and to get Bee inside. He thought she'd drop that hose like a hot potato once she knew she'd been seen, but she didn't. She aimed it over the fence at him and told him he'd best mind his own business or she'd tell the police he liked looking at little girls. Then she told Bee to get upstairs and in the bath, and Bee was pleading with her. Saying she didn't want to, that it hurt her legs.'

Erin has gone cold from head to foot. Things are shifting in her mind. Lies rearrange themselves into truths. She thinks of Bee slipping her hand into Erin's mum's, and a stained sleeping bag drying in the sun. Of scabby legs and bleach baths. *Even liars don't lie about everything.*

'He reported her,' her mum says softly. 'Social services were aware of Bee before what happened with Nicky Pemberton. But they were too slow to act.'

'Did Daphne know it was Jermaine?'

'He did it anonymously. He was scared, see, after Daphne said that about him liking little girls. Not straight away, but soon after. Because Bee started leaving him things.'

'What… what things?'

'Just kid's stuff she'd push through his letter box. Pictures she'd drawn for him, or daisy chains when it got a bit warmer. That sort of thing. He got worried people might think there was more to it. That he was… what's that word they use now… *grooming* her, or something. When really, she was just an angry, damaged little girl trying to show she was grateful someone had taken any notice of her.'

27

OCTOBER 2016

The tour begins at the main car park. Kitty leads in a motorised wheelchair, managing to steer it successfully and light a cigarette at the same time. She eyeballs Hewitt, who is watching her with bald sympathy.

'It's a wheelchair, honey. Not the end of the world.'

'Sorry.' Hewitt reddens. 'I didn't mean to stare.'

'I don't use it all the time.' Kitty waves a dismissive hand, streaking the air with smoke. 'But I get tired real quick now, and if I'm going to haul my ass round this island this'll make things easier.' She taps the arm of the wheelchair, deadpan. 'Vroom, vroom.'

They set off, and it quickly becomes obvious that she's not having a particularly easy time of it in places where the lanes are rough. Still, she rebuffs Bomber's attempts to assist, telling him to 'bugger off'. Following the confession, the atmosphere is strained.

When they stop outside the museum they find it's closed for refurbishment, the exhibits now in storage. There's an air of gloom around the place, as though the essence of its grisly contents has permeated the very bricks and mortar that hold it together. Several windows are boarded up, the frames damp and rotted. Erin wonders if the others are as relieved as she is that they do not have to go in.

They go to the cabin next. It's not called the Honeycomb now.

Instead there's a simple number 4 on the door. Erin gazes at the darkened window, half-imagining a flicker of movement from within; a red-headed spectre. There's nothing except a dead insect inside the pane. Whatever is left of Bee on the island isn't a ghost, not in the true sense of the word. It's a feeling, a history, a stain.

They move on to the games room. No one speaks, but as it comes into view Mira takes out her inhaler.

'You okay?' Aidan asks her softly.

She nods tightly, shoving the inhaler away. 'Fine. I think it's just the damp air.' But her hand trembles as it rests on the door, which Erin catches and holds open for Aidan. Their eyes meet briefly, but he's first to look away. She feels the sting of his dismissal. He'd been glad to see her at first, she'd known it. Felt it. And now he's learned what she did to Bee he doesn't know what to do with it.

She feels eyes on her and realises Kitty is watching. She's watching them all, every exchange, every reaction. Erin's throat tightens. This is not just about jogging memories. It's a rat trap, designed to catch them out.

Inside, the games room has barely changed. The decor is freshened up, and there's an updated sound system but the layout is the same. There's a poster for a music festival which took place in the summer. Erin has read that it was a wash-out. On the wall is a framed print of a film that was partially shot here, a comedy which had flopped into obscurity. It's as though the place cannot drag itself out of the mire, like whatever attempts are made to change its fortunes are doomed.

Through an open door is what was once the pool room. There are no pool tables now, just a sofa and a coffee table. Kitty outlines the fragments of that night – the drinking, dancing, spin the bottle – and the brief walk back to the cabin taken by herself, Erin and Patrick Preston. The only sign as to what's going on in Mira's head is the slight movement of her hand twitching on her bag. She wants to reach for the inhaler again.

'At some point during that party Bee left alone to meet Paul Callaghan,' says Kitty. They leave, eventually arriving at a pair of cabins several metres apart. The wooded area from which Erin and Aidan had watched Bee is desperately overgrown, like it is intent on consuming the cabin. Erin waits for some illuminating thought to hit her, a glimmer of something she hadn't known at the time, but all she gets is the emergence of existing memories: Aidan's insistence he'd heard someone within the trees. Her mind returns to the indiscernible shape on Hewitt's sofa that night, and their initial assumption that it was her who'd been with Callaghan. Had she really been asleep? If the simmering, barely concealed rage at the affair exists even now, what would Hewitt have felt back then?

Tori starts to cry softly. At first she tries to hold it in with the heels of her hands, but she quickly succumbs, staring at the door where her dead, unfaithful husband stood twenty years ago. Despite everything, how acerbic she's been, Erin pities her.

She is no longer crying when they reach the final stop. Dense clouds gather as they near the edge of the island. A slice of gravel shore hems in the rising water. The wooden post jutting from it marks the spot, both where the witches were submerged as the tide came in and the site of Bee's death.

Float the witch.

How could we have been so cruel? Erin thinks. *How could I have not only held someone under that water, but enjoyed doing it?*

Ahead, the shoreline thins into nothing, replaced by a rugged outcrop of rocks.

Tori steps down on to the damp shingle. Hewitt is next, followed by Aidan and Mira. Reluctantly, Erin joins them. Only Kitty and Bomber remain on the road, though it's not steep it's still inaccessible to the wheelchair. Even though thousands of tides have washed in and out since that night and it's no longer a crime scene, taped off, it still feels wrong to walk here.

I was here when Bee went into the water, Erin thinks. *And here when she came out.*

Hewitt is grey-faced, her hand clutching the neck of her top. Erin feels a stirring of sympathy. Selfishly, she never gave much thought to Hewitt over the years. Never considered what it had cost her, or how pulling Bee's body from the water must have affected her. She'd charged straight in while Callaghan dithered with his shoelaces.

'We thought she'd drowned,' Mira says softly. 'Until—'

'Who's that?' Tori cuts in. A figure is unfolding itself from the rocky outcrop further along. They wear dark clothes, and though too far away to make out any features properly, Erin thinks it's a man. He's holding something.

He starts to raise it, and she sees something long, black and sleek. Erin can't move, can't run. Someone – Mira, she thinks – emits a horrified gasp. There's a low grunt and Erin feels herself barrelling to the ground as someone knocks into her, taking her down with them.

She crashes to the shingle. Aidan lands with her, shielding her from the thing being pointed their way.

'Keep down.'

There's a scream – Tori – and then chaos as the group panics. And then Bomber is shouting. Furious. Running towards the figure, not away like everyone else.

'Get the fuck out of here!' he yells, pounding up the shore.

'What's going on?' Erin cries. 'What's happening?'

The next thing she hears is the roar of an engine as a boat speeds away. Aidan is close enough that they're almost nose to nose, his hand tight on Erin's shoulder. His dark eyes are wide, afraid.

He blinks, releasing her, then gets to his feet and pulls her up. Her entire left side feels bruised and covered in grit. It's in her hair, in her mouth.

'Sorry,' he mutters. 'For a second, I thought he had—'

'Journalist,' Bomber returns, grim-faced. 'One of us must have been followed.'

'Great.' Tori throws up her hands. 'Just *brilliant*.'

Erin stares at Aidan, his unfinished sentence hanging between them.

She'd thought the man had been holding a gun, too.

28

OCTOBER 2016

'A GUN,' KITTY SNORTS. 'GIVE ME a break. I knew it was a camera right away, and I'm an American.' She places her fork on her plate of barely touched food.

The evening meal has taken place at the Beach House, in a conference room overlooking the pool. It's after eight and has been dark for a while. The drapes at the French doors are drawn, shutting out any chance of another opportunistic photographer. Erin has said little during the meal and is counting down the minutes until the causeway reopens.

'But let's talk about Aidan dive-bombing Erin to save her from the big bad camera,' Kitty adds. 'That was some real action-man stuff there, Squeaky.'

'So, why Erin?' Tori asks, a little miffed.

Aidan wipes his mouth with a napkin and sits back. 'She was the nearest.'

'Maybe I should hire *you* as my security,' says Kitty.

'I'm sure you'll survive with the Terminator over there,' he replies drily.

Kitty snickers, her gaze flickering to Bomber who's eating alone at the edge of the room. She lowers her voice. 'He might look like a thug, but can you believe he collects Paddington stuff? I'm serious – fucking Paddington Bear! You name it: figurines, clocks, coins, he's got it. It's brilliant.'

Bomber glances up, aware and unimpressed that he's being

spoken about. The subject returns once more to the photographer.

'He could've got lucky,' Hewitt suggests, attacking a messy wedge of quiche. 'There's been a lot of publicity these past few weeks. The Child B link, the anniversary. Maybe he came to get a shot of the island and struck gold.'

'Someone who works here probably leaked it,' says Tori, topping up her glass. 'Trying to make a quick buck.' She's back to her usual caustic self, all traces of her brief vulnerability gone.

'Could be,' Kitty replies. After the photographer ran off, she'd made a furious call to the island's management, demanding to know whether they'd spoken to any press. 'All publicity's good publicity, right? Anyway, shall we cut the bullshit? Let's talk about that night. Who was where, and when, and if anyone can back them up.'

Tori scoffs. 'Just because your story changed, doesn't mean everyone else's will.'

'Maybe it does.' Kitty eyes her meaningfully. 'There's still question marks over a few of us.'

'You expect us to pull alibis out of our arses when we couldn't twenty years ago?' says Tori. 'I can't fucking prove I was indoors because the only people with me were the twins, who weren't even a year old at the time. My neighbour's CCTV showed my car didn't move all night. What else *is* there?'

'The phone calls,' Kitty says. 'The voicemails from Paul.'

'They didn't prove anything.'

But this isn't exactly true. The landline calls Paul had made to Tori on the night of Bee's death had placed him at his cabin for a good portion of the evening, and nowhere near where she'd died. He'd made nine calls in total between nine thirty and one in the morning, the last four with voicemails begging Tori to pick up, that there was something he needed to tell her. Tori hadn't listened to any of them until six o'clock the following morning. The intent behind Callaghan's calls was never proven. During questioning, it was put to him that he'd called to confess to the killing. Callaghan denied this, saying he'd planned to come clean about the affair.

'They suggested you weren't home to take them.'

'I *was* home. Asleep, obviously.'

'All night?' Mira questions. 'With babies under a year old?'

'Of course not, but when they woke up I wasn't exactly monitoring the phone, was I? And it was on silent so it didn't wake them.'

'Fair enough,' says Kitty. 'But look, now we've got the ball rolling, let's carry on. This is the last opportunity we'll get – well, *I'll* get – to try and find out the truth.'

'What if there's stuff we're not comfortable asking?' says Hewitt.

Kitty is undeterred. 'Then we do it anonymously.' She takes out a block of Post-it notes and a pen from her bag. There's a collective shift of uneasy looks, but no one objects.

The Post-its are passed round in silence as each of them writes something down.

When they're all done Kitty shuffles the folded paper slips and then plucks one out.

'Okay, first one's for Charlotte.'

Hewitt looks up. There is an eggy quiche crumb in her hair. 'Me?'

'It says, "Why were students who'd gone to you for help unable to find you? Had you left your cabin at any point after going back from the games room?"'

'I've said this before,' Hewitt mutters. 'I didn't go anywhere after I got back. I… I *thought* about it.' Her eyes dart guiltily in Tori's direction. 'I thought – *hoped* – something might happen with Paul.'

'Yeah.' Tori settles back, swilling wine around her glass. 'Even some of the students noticed you'd tried to tart yourself up. Done up like a dog's dinner, wasn't that how one of them put it?'

Hewitt says nothing, but each word visibly chips away at her.

'So, you *thought* what? You'd mosey on over and seduce him? What stopped you?'

'I didn't go because I knew it was pointless. I had a drink, trying to get my confidence up. I thought if I let him know how I felt… But the drink – I don't know. It was like it held up a mirror showing me what a fool I was.'

Erin wonders who asked that question. She suspects it was Aidan.

'Okay.' Kitty reaches for the next note, her expression sombre. 'Tori. "After Paul's arrest you drove to the station, leaving the twins with a friend. Both babies had severe nappy rash. Why was this?"'

'They never had nappy rash.'

'What's the point of that question?' Erin asks. 'Sorry, I've never been around babies so I don't get the relevance.'

'Come off it,' Tori fumes. 'You must've seen things suggesting I'd swum out to the island, killed Bee and swum back again. It's implying I left my kids alone for ages in dirty nappies while I did it. How can anyone seriously believe I swam across? In the dark?'

'Well, I guess you could've flown over on a broomstick,' Kitty says. Tori bristles. 'Next question. Erin.'

Erin waits, her stomach dropping. But Kitty's mouth snaps shut and she's scrunching up the paper and tucking it in her bag. 'Never mind.'

'Wait,' says Erin. 'What's the question?'

'Nothing,' Kitty replies. 'It wasn't a question.'

'What is it, then? Show me.'

'I thought the idea of this was that anything could be asked?' Tori gripes.

'It was someone being spiteful.' Kitty zips her bag with finality. 'Like I said, not a question.'

Erin's head is spinning. Not a question – *spiteful*? Her first reaction is that it's something about her eyes, but she dismisses it before the thought is even properly formed. They are not children and this is not a playground and it's not about her, so why is someone *making* it about her and taking the opportunity to be spiteful? She lapses back into the conversation, missing the next question. It's Tori who responds, irritable.

'Christ, *again*? No, I never knew about Bee until she was dead. I guessed he was at it with someone, just not who. He'd done it so many times by then. You get to know – this gut feeling of something being off. I thought maybe it was someone he worked with. Not you.' She smiles contemptuously at Hewitt. 'Never dreamed it was a student, either. Didn't think he'd be so bloody stupid.'

There are two scraps of paper left.

'Okay, Aidan.' Kitty throws him a curious look. '"After Bee's body was found, Patrick Preston had a black eye. He said you hit him, you denied it. What's the truth?"'

Aidan sighs resolutely. 'Fine, yeah. It was me.'

'I thought he'd fallen into a signpost, drunk,' says Mira. 'Wasn't that what he told everyone?'

'Yeah, at first. Trying to save face, I suppose. And when the police got involved, that's when he said I hit him.' Aidan looks down at his hands, flexing and unflexing them slowly. 'I told them my knuckles bled after I'd punched a wall, that I had no reason to hit him.'

'What *was* the reason?' asks Erin, even though she knows the answer. He will never say it, not here, in front of everyone. She hears his voice, asking her if something happened between her and Preston. Remembers his face darkening as he took in her tear-stained cheeks.

'I thought he was a wanker. Sorry, I know you're not supposed to speak ill of the dead, but he was. Him and Leon Curtis, coming on to girls, being too… pushy. And after seeing Paul and Bee I was in shock, I think. Went for a walk to clear my head and that's when I saw him. I was already wound up, and seeing *him*… the mood I was in, I snapped. Walked up and punched him straight in the face. He was so stunned he didn't even hit back. I lied to the police because I didn't want to get kicked out of college.'

'Would they have kicked you out for that?' asks Kitty.

'They might have. Preston's dad was on the council, he had sway. *My* dad… I don't even know where he was, but my *stepdad* was a drunk. Whose side do you think the college would've taken? Especially with all the uproar about Bee. They'd have made an example of me.'

'What did you tell the police?' asks Mira. 'What was the reason you gave for hitting the wall?'

'I told them I was pissed off about Callaghan. It wasn't a lie.'

'Is that the only reason you lied?' asks Erin. She senses a flash of anger beneath the calm exterior.

'What other reason would there be?'

'You said you didn't like him. Did you want him to take the fall for killing Bee? Hope it'd look like she'd hit out at him before he killed her?'

'That's ridiculous. I didn't like him, but I never thought he killed her and I didn't think the police would either – whether they knew it was me who'd hit him or not. I thought Callaghan killed her. Still do, if I'm honest. I lied to protect myself, simple as that.'

'And you're only admitting this now?' says Tori. 'Doesn't seem that big a deal.'

'It was a big deal to me. And that's what we're here for, isn't it? To get to the truth. It wasn't relevant to Bee. If I'd said I lied, it would've made a fuss and drawn the focus away from whoever really was guilty.'

'Not so squeaky after all,' says Kitty.

He shrugs. 'Is anyone?'

'Good point,' she concedes. 'Nice to have a little more of the truth, finally. Because, honestly? I'm getting mighty pissed with people who aren't who they say they are.'

Erin goes rigid. Is Kitty hinting at who Erin really is?

Child A.

'Care to elaborate?' Tori asks.

Kitty smiles cryptically. 'Let's just say I've already started doing a little digging.'

'What kind of digging?' Erin's gaze passes between Kitty and Bomber. Kitty said she sent him to rattle her, but was there more to it? Her mind jumps to the night she saw him outside her house, and how she'd wondered, then, if this was the faceless, shadowy creeper who'd gone through her bins before. But that had happened a long time before Kitty ever got in touch.

'The kind that's called a private investigator,' Kitty replies, quashing Erin's suspicions. 'There's been a couple of hold-ups, but I'm expecting news any day.'

Tori looks furious. Mira and Hewitt appear shocked, and Aidan is rolling his eyes.

'Good luck with that,' he says. 'Might be a couple of parking tickets, but let me know, yeah?'

Erin remains silent. There's nothing a private investigator could unearth on her that Kitty doesn't already know, apart from the occasional meeting with her married ex. Besides that she's never so much as returned a library book late since that college trip.

Kitty stares at the final Post-it for a long time before speaking. So long that Erin convinces herself it's another barbed comment aimed at her.

'There's no name,' Kitty says at last. 'So I guess it's for everyone. "Is anyone else glad that bitch is dead?"'

A faint, incredulous shake of the head from Aidan is followed by a small breath of disgust from Mira. Hewitt is motionless, like something about to be roadkill.

Tori is watching them all. Her question, then.

'No,' Erin says at last. She allows herself to wonder what kind of adult Bee would have grown into. Whether she would have done something good. *Meant* something good, to anyone. She feels guilt for everything she missed. For having the kind of childhood Bee didn't. And now there's some part of her that feels a fierce, unfamiliar urge to protect Bee. 'She was seventeen. She was barely even alive for long.'

'I have this thought sometimes,' Mira starts hesitantly. 'This awful thought that… that after what we did, and what happened with Callaghan… could it have been suicide?'

'She'd swallowed glass and had her throat cut,' says Tori, incredulous. 'Who'd do that to themselves?'

'It does seem extreme,' says Hewitt.

'Isn't suicide always extreme?' Mira asks. 'Someone in their final, most desperate moments? And maybe it wasn't just about ending things, for her. Maybe she saw a way to get revenge on Callaghan, and us.'

Erin thinks of Bee, her vindictive little face in the playing field all those years ago as she outlined her idea to get Donnie and Nicky back. Can Mira be right? Momentarily, the energy within the group shifts, becoming charged. They want this to be it, the truth. Erin allows herself to imagine that there *was* no murder, that the whole thing was a scheme. A final lie concocted by Bee, who must have hated the world and everyone in it. Not one person had loved her enough, cared for her enough, or even liked her.

'She told him she was going to ruin him,' Aidan says uneasily. 'And cutthroat suicides aren't as uncommon as you'd think.'

'For real?' says Tori. 'Shit.'

'But I'm pretty sure the coroner would've ruled it out,' he adds. 'There are usually what are called "hesitation cuts". Where the person's tried a few times to get up the courage to do it. If there'd been any wounds like that then it would have been noted. Saying that, it's not *impossible* for someone to do it straight off. But it's rare.'

'Okay, let's shelve that and circle back,' Kitty interjects. '*How* she died. Aside from anything else, it never made sense if it was Callaghan. Plenty of people said so.'

'No,' Hewitt agrees. 'You're right. Murders of women by men who are spouses, or former partners, tend to be by beating, strangling or stabbing. But the glass… it doesn't fit. Whoever did that wanted her to suffer.'

Tori regards her icily. 'And what makes you an expert?'

'Working for a domestic violence charity,' Hewitt says, the most confident she's been since she arrived. 'Lots of statistics about abusers.'

'Tori?' Aidan says tentatively. 'This is a bit personal, but was Paul ever violent towards you?'

'Never.' Tori sniffs. 'He was a lying, cheating bastard but he never laid a finger on me. He always thought he could sweet-talk his way out of problems. *I* was the one with the temper.' She smiles thinly. 'He never hit back.'

'He shoved Bee that night,' says Erin, remembering the scuffle outside Callaghan's cabin. '"Don't touch me." That's what she said.' Erin meets Tori's cold stare, thinking of the things that came out about Callaghan in the aftermath. The rough sex with Bee that his wife wasn't interested in. 'He did things with her that he never did with you.'

The conversations around the table divide and quieten. Kitty and Tori are going in heavy on the wine. The five slips of paper sit on the table before Kitty. The sixth, with Erin's name on, is in Kitty's bag yet Erin feels its presence as keenly as if it were another person in the room.

Kitty digs in her bag now, washing down a couple of tablets with wine.

Somewhere in the building a phone rings, the shrill tone of a landline.

'I think that's coming from reception.' Kitty stuffs her medication back in her bag and stands unsteadily. She heads out of the conference room, each movement dictated by fatigue and discomfort. Some of Erin's bad feeling towards her dissipates. Kitty may still be wise-cracking and downing wine like she once downed shots, but the girl who'd tirelessly danced and sang and rapped the night away is gone.

The ringing stops. Perhaps it is the island's management, calling back with an update on the photographer. But then Kitty appears at the door and there's something unreadable about her that immediately puts Erin on edge.

'It's for you,' she tells Erin. 'Your mom.'

Alarmed, Erin pulls out her phone, checking for missed calls. There's nothing. In the same instant, she registers it cannot be her mum. She never told a soul she was coming to the island.

Aside from those who are with her, there is no one else who should know she is here.

29

OCTOBER 2016

Erin follows Kitty out into the empty foyer, her stomach churning in a way that is now maddeningly, sickeningly familiar.

An expensive looking retro telephone sits on the desk, its receiver off the hook. Erin picks it up, hearing a dialling tone. She feels as though she's just walked into a trap of some kind.

'There's no call.' Kitty shuts the door quietly. 'I rang it from my cell while I was going through my bag.'

'What, then?' Shakily, Erin replaces the receiver on the handset. There can be no good reason for Kitty to separate her from the rest of the group.

Kitty opens her bag and takes out the slip of paper. The question, or *not*-question, she refused to read out.

A dozen horrible phrases jostle in Erin's mind. *Murdering scum. Fucking liar. EAT GLASS, BITCH.*

'What… what does it say?'

Kitty goes to hand it to her, then pauses. 'Erin, it *is* a question. But it wasn't one I could ask you in front of everyone.'

'Just give it to me,' Erin says hoarsely.

Kitty hands it over, and Erin unfolds it and reads the neat print:

FUCK YOU, ERIN. WHEN YOU'RE DEAD, WILL
YOU BE OUTED AS CHILD A?

The words bleed across the paper as her vision blurs.

'Who wrote this?' she whispers.

'I don't know. That was the point of doing it anonymously.'

Erin screws the paper into a tiny ball and pushes it into her own bag. She is hot and cold all at once.

'Who else knows?' Kitty asks, her voice low.

'Of us here? You, Mira and Aidan.' Erin only has herself to blame for telling Kitty and Mira, but Aidan's always known.

Kitty holds her hands up. 'It wasn't me.'

'Wasn't it?' Erin's temper flares, getting ahead of the fear. 'What was all that about someone not being who they said they were, then?'

'That?' Kitty's eyes widen. 'That wasn't… *Shit*. That wasn't about you. I was talking about people hiding stuff. Tori, Aidan, us. I never meant *that*, and I never wrote that thing, honest to god. And Mira – I can't think why she would, either.'

'Nor would Aidan.'

'Sure about that?'

Erin wavers. She trusts him more than she trusts anyone else here, but she cannot trust anyone fully, not now. Not after that slip of paper.

'He lied about hitting Preston,' Kitty adds. 'I mean, how well do you really know him? How well did you think you knew him back then?'

'You can't think Aidan had anything to do with Bee's death.'

'I don't know what I think any more.' Kitty exhales, her breath sour with wine and illness. 'I thought it was Callaghan for the longest time. But it never properly added up.'

'Aidan would *not* have hurt Bee. It was more likely to be Preston than him. You even said what a creep he was, about him being out there somewhere when we didn't know where Bee was, before we… *before*.'

'They both said they were alone when Bee died, neither of them had an alibi. Now Aidan's finally admitted that he ran into Preston. What if he ran into Bee, too? And yeah, Preston *was* a creep, but I'm pretty sure attacking girls for sex wasn't his style. He'd want to think he was seducing them. Whereas *Aidan…*' Kitty throws a cautious look at the door. 'He was besotted with you, anyone could see that. If he knew how much you hated her, hated what the two of you had *done…* what if he came across her while he was still riled up about her and Callaghan? He could've lost his temper, like when he punched Preston.'

'No.' Erin shakes her head fervently. '*No.* How she died – that was more than someone losing their temper. It was nasty. Vengeful.'

'Yeah.' Kitty's shoulders slump. She is so frail now, so thin. 'I just… can't shake the feeling Tori's lying. And the island's not as inaccessible as everyone thought. That fucking journalist on the boat today proved that. And that question about Child A. It's weird.' She gives Erin a long, searching look. 'Watch your back. Someone here either doesn't like you or doesn't mind throwing you under the bus.'

When they return to the conference room only Mira and Hewitt remain at the table, and there's a bracing draught whistling through the French doors. Tori and Aidan are outside by the pool, too far away to hear but for once, Tori's smiling as she reaches over to brush something off Aidan's jacket. Erin wonders which one of them wrote the note.

Kitty heads for the wine chiller. There, Bomber intercepts her, showing her something on his phone.

'*Shit,*' she spits, then confers quietly with him before returning to the table.

'The photo.' Erin sees it in her face, feels the mounting dread. 'It's up, isn't it?'

Kitty nods. 'Twitter. Some gutter press reporter, already got thousands of likes and retweets.'

'I… I didn't tell my daughters I was coming here,' Mira says.

'Only my husband. They think I'm away with work. They'll know I lied.'

'My people are on it, trying to get an injunction to get it taken down.'

'They can do that?' asks Mira.

'The island's private land, so yeah. He trespassed to get it. Ignorant little fuck should've known that.' Kitty's livid. 'Too late now, it's out there. But I'll have his ass fired, you watch.'

Erin had no one to tell except her mum, who isn't on social media. It doesn't matter. It will be everywhere soon and she will know, too. *More lies.*

It's still early, but Hewitt rises from the table. She's dishevelled and shaky as she bids everyone goodnight and leaves.

'Okay,' says Kitty once Hewitt's gone. She sits, massaging her temples, contemplating her next move. 'It's okay. We can still spin this. We came here for the truth, and that's what we'll give them.'

'Like we've got a choice?' says Erin. 'Everyone knows we're here, like sitting ducks. And now it's out, what we did, it'll only grow. It'll snowball.' She doubts Aidan will publicise what they did, but she's not naive enough to hope for the same with Tori or Hewitt.

Kitty pops another wine cork. 'So, we get in first,' she says. 'We go straight out with it. We go *big.*'

Erin watches her with a quiet despair. 'I never wanted this. All this time we've managed to keep it hidden. We've been damn lucky it never got out, and now…'

'*Lucky?*' says Mira. 'Have we? Sometimes I've felt like the secrets from that night would kill me. I never even told my husband what we did to Bee, because then I'd have to admit why. What happened to me. Maybe we should've told the truth from the start. All we did was create more suspicion. Kitty's right. I'm sick of carrying this around.'

Erin takes in Kitty's ravaged face, wondering how long she

has left. By doing this she gets to absolve herself. It's Erin and Mira who'll live with the consequences, come what may. 'Are you sure it's not just about easing our consciences? You want the world knowing what we did, and that we lied?'

'Better than thinking those fingerprints meant we're murderers. We could well take some shit for it, but now the public knows she was Child B, some might even think we were justified. You heard what Tori said, about Bee getting what she deserved.'

They are still blaming Bee. As though she isn't hated enough already. Erin tells herself that Bee is one person, and she is gone. There is no one left to care about her or her memory, not that anyone ever did. Years of looking over her shoulder have made Erin selfish. She is still alive, and she wants a life without fear or more blame than is necessary.

'What about me?' She cannot hold back any more. She reaches for the wine and fills her glass, taking two hefty swallows. Anything to stop the tremor in her voice and movements. To obliterate the thought of that note. One of them here hates her. One of them is taunting her. Is it the same person who sends the emails? 'What if it comes out, who *I* am? We're all guilty, but I'd be the guiltiest, the most unforgivable.'

'Why would anyone release that information? You were given lifelong anonymity, right? I never told a soul what you confided that night. Did you, Mira?'

'No,' Mira shakes her head earnestly. 'I promise.'

'I have to do this.' Kitty's eyes are suddenly damp, and it's as though a shroud has been pulled back, exposing how ill she really is. 'I can't… *die* with this hanging over me. With my *mom*—' Her voice breaks. '—with her thinking there's even a chance I killed Bee.' She sniffles, blinking furiously. 'She knows I'm not perfect, but I can't go with her thinking that of me. I won't.' She wipes her eyes, fierce once more. 'We *need* to do this.' And it's like they're seventeen again and Kitty's taking charge, leading them down a path that binds them, for ever, to each other, and Erin can't help thinking that the last time they were here they had no idea what lay ahead. That, before the weekend was out, someone would be dead. But she finds herself nodding, because the damage is already done. So what other choice is there?

'Okay.' Kitty blows out a long breath. 'That's that, then. We're doing this.' She nods resignedly to herself. 'I've got this media guy. I've already arranged for him to be here in the morning. He's good with this stuff.'

The thought of this has Erin knocking back the rest of the wine. It burns the back of her throat.

'When that bottle smashed,' she says. 'What we did was so vicious, so out of control. Have you ever wondered if there was something inside – something noxious, I mean, that made us act like that?'

'There wasn't,' Kitty says softly. 'We'd been drinking, we were coked up and pissed off. We *wanted* to hurt her. We wanted to humiliate her. If that bottle had any effect it was the idea of it, the whole thing about there being trouble if it smashed. Like it gave us permission to do something awful.'

'We went too far.' Mira's eyes are haunted. 'Whatever happened after we left her, we'd already made her last night on this earth hell.'

'Do either of you…' Erin begins, hesitant. 'Have you been sent stuff, to do with Bee? Usually around this time of year. When she died.'

'You mean like letters?' Kitty asks. 'About the fingerprints? Because sure, I've had that kind of thing. There's a lot of weirdos—'

'No. I know you've had letters and glass bottles. I don't mean those.' Erin describes the tongue, and hearts pierced with nails. The feather witch's ladder like the one in the museum. The dog shit and dead bees.

'Fucking hell,' says Kitty. 'No. Nothing like that.' They're both staring at her. Mira is shaking her head, looking like she's just opened one of the packages herself.

So it is only Erin. She contemplates this, fear and the aftertaste of wine coalescing, acidic in her throat. *MURDERER. LIAR.* Many of the objects have pointed towards the island, reminding her of what she did *to* Bee, but she's always felt the emails could just as easily be about what she did *with* her. And if Erin's the only one getting them then it suggests the sender knew about both.

The slam of a door ends the conversation. Erin huddles into herself, replaying the messages in her head. *Only her.* Tori is weaving her way to the table, cheeks ruddy with cold. Aidan follows her in, pausing to pull the drapes back across the glass.

'Fuck me.' Tori pauses, eyeballing the three of them. '*When shall we three meet again?* That's what you lot look like.'

'Potion?' Kitty offers the wine. 'Sit. Join the coven.' She traces the rim of her glass with her finger, suddenly wistful and slurring a little. 'That weekend might've been good, you know? Before it all went to hell. I guess we'll never know. But whatever happens after tonight, this'll probably be the last time we'll all see each other, together like this. So why do I feel sort of… sad about it?'

'Something to do with time passing us by, perhaps,' says Mira. 'The memory of us so young and naive. Full of hope, not knowing what was ahead.'

'That's how I felt earlier.' Tori sits heavily between Mira and Kitty. 'Seeing Paul's cabin. It wasn't even so much about the betrayal. It brought it home to me, how I could have lived a different life, if only I'd chosen one without him.'

Erin watches Kitty, a question on her lips. She decides to ask it, if only to distract herself from thoughts of the vile packages. 'Why did you ask Mira and me to ride with you to the island back then? We barely knew each other.'

'Oh.' Kitty groans softly. 'What the hell, I'm dying anyway. I thought you were cute. And I'd seen you looking at me around campus and in class, and… I don't know. I figured maybe I had a shot.'

Erin is at a loss for what to say. All those months she'd spent admiring Kitty, wishing to be like her, never dreaming Kitty had a crush on her. The thought of it is alien to her.

'You asked,' says Kitty. 'And I'm a little drunk. Anyway, that spin the bottle kiss? That was the best five seconds of the weekend for me, even though I knew from that kiss you didn't feel the same. That you admired me and liked me, but not the way I liked you.' She shrugs. 'I didn't have to lick my wounds for long before everything went tits up with Bee.'

'And me?' Mira asks. 'Did you like me, too?'

'Truthfully?' A sheepish look crosses Kitty's face. 'I knew you worked hard. I figured I'd spend the weekend boozing and having fun, and then catch up using your notes.'

'*Seriously?* You asked me because you thought I was a nerd?'

'Yeah,' Kitty confesses. 'That's really shit, but it's the truth. Sorry.'

Mira laughs incredulously, and the tension breaks. 'You cow!'

'I was, wasn't I?' Kitty grins.

Even Tori smirks. Aidan smiles faintly, but it's strained.

'I'm turning in,' he says. 'Been a long day. Night, all.'

Kitty's face falls. 'Ah, come on, Squeaky. You won't stay for a drink?'

'I don't drink.' He softens a little. 'Have one for me.'

He nods vaguely at them, holding Erin's gaze for a second, no longer, before he strides to the door.

'I'll stay.' Tori raises her glass, with a glum glance after him. 'Might as well drown my sorrows.'

'Why not,' Mira agrees. 'Erin?'

Erin is staring after Aidan. If she leaves in the next few

minutes when the causeway opens she won't see him again. Not for years, or possibly ever and she cannot bear it, not with things the way they are between them. The glass of wine she's necked has gone straight to her head and she knows she can't drive away from here just yet. Even if she could, she doesn't want to – not without speaking to him first. She gets up from the table, snatching her bag, and without a word, runs after him.

By the time she's out of the conference room he's almost up the stairs to the first floor. 'Aidan,' she says urgently, starting up the first flight of steps.

He continues, giving no sign he's heard.

'*Aidan,*' she says again, closing on him in the corridor outside her room. 'I'm talking to you.'

He stops and turns resolutely.

'What's left to say? Why not put it in an anonymous note and have Kitty read it out?'

'I'm sorry. I'd always wondered whether you *did* hit Preston.' She risks looking into his eyes, finding unbridled hurt there. 'And why you never told me.'

'Why I never told you? Because you were so honest with me about that night?'

'Can you blame me? You said yourself it's no wonder we lied. And that morning when we found her, I didn't know she was there. I didn't know she was *dead*. All I knew was it was the last place we'd seen her.'

'You should go,' he says, quietly. 'Leave while the causeway's open.'

Hot tears prick at her eyes. She turns away, taking out her key to open the door. 'Yeah, I get it. You can't stand the sight of me. Don't worry, I'm going.'

'That's not what I meant.'

She takes a breath, getting herself under control enough to detect a new note of discord in his voice. 'Are you talking about that photographer?'

'Yes,' he says shortly. Then, 'No. I don't know. Just… I don't think it's safe here.'

'Safe?' She almost laughs. 'You want to know what that note said, the one Kitty wouldn't read? It outed me as Child A. Someone wants me exposed.' She pauses, seeing the flicker of alarm on him. They stare at each other for a long, loaded moment. Perhaps he is right and there's nothing more to say. She is about to turn away, for good. His voice stops her.

'You must know why I punched Preston. I was jealous. Jealous and angry, because I was bloody well in *love* with you! I saw you go off with him. I knew you liked him, and I knew he didn't deserve it. When you came back I could see something had happened, and that you were upset. It pissed me off even more.' His jaw clenches. 'So, that's the truth. And my reasons for lying were true as well. I cared then, and I still do. If you want me to stop caring, just say the word. I can't promise I will, but I'll promise not to show it.'

A light flickers above them in the starkly lit corridor. Erin knows she *should* tell him to stop caring, because she isn't worth caring about. At the same time she knows she never will, because Aidan's one of the few people who's ever made her feel she's worth something. And so instead, she steps towards him and pushes her mouth on his. She feels the warmth and softness of his lips, the rough scratch of his chin against hers. He swallows in surprise then kisses her back. Softly at first and then more intensely. She moves her hands on to his shoulders, threads her fingers into his hair. He grips her waist, her hips, and then together they move back into the room. Aidan kicks the door shut behind them.

30

OCTOBER 2016

THE LIGHT IS STILL OFF and the room is threaded silver with moonlight and outdoor lamps from Erin's window overlooking the pool. They make it as far as the chest of drawers when Aidan lifts her on to the edge of it, then kisses her deeply, his hands tangling in her hair. Erin pulls him to her, pressing him between her thighs. He slides up her dress, pausing to look at her, taking her in as his warm hands connect with her skin. He gently skims the dressing covering her burn, eyes never leaving hers. Fingertips rising, teasing, sending her into shivers of anticipation. And then neither of them is prepared to wait a second longer, for he is rushing to unbuckle his belt. She reaches down, pulls her underwear to one side, and he pushes into her. Already she's overcome with it and with him, every sensation heightened through the combined familiarity of him and the unfamiliarity of what they're doing. She comes quickly, burying her face into his neck as she does, which in turn spurs him to climax. They cling to each other, breathing hard, neither wanting to let go. Eventually, she releases him and slides down off the chest.

They stand there wordlessly, watching each other. She waits for him to button up, to leave, but he makes no move to. Silently she slips off her clothes, standing naked before him as she watches him undress. She drinks in the outline of him, the broad chest and defined shoulders, and her breath catches. She takes his hand and leads him to the bed.

They lie there, skin on skin. Erin's cheek is against his chest. His chin rests on top of her head. She listens to his breath, feels his heartbeat. His fingers explore the shape of her. Minutes slip away. She doesn't know how many and doesn't care. For the first time since she stepped back on the island she feels safe, and fully at ease. Aidan has always made her feel that way. The knowledge of it makes her ache. Aidan. *Her Aidan.* She lifts her head, trails kisses along his collarbone, his jaw, his mouth. This time she takes the lead, pushing him back, and it's unhurried, deliberate, tender.

Afterwards they hold each other and she touches his face, pushing a strand of damp hair away from his forehead.

'I haven't even shaved my legs,' she mumbles.

'I didn't notice.'

'Liar.'

They both laugh and she sinks on to the sheets beside him.

'I'm definitely not going back down there again now. Tori's been trying to get her hooks into you all evening. I think she'd throttle me if she knew about this.'

The laughter lines leave his face. She wonders if she's said something wrong.

'What's the matter?'

'Tori.' He rubs a hand over his face. 'I don't think she's after me. She just wanted someone to talk to.'

Erin snorts lightly, but he doesn't respond.

'What was she talking about?'

'Where she really was the night Bee died,' he says eventually. 'She wasn't indoors like she said. She told me she left the house through the back, on foot. Got a bus from a couple of streets away to this woman's flat, someone Paul was messing around with before Bee.'

'But he was here, on the trip. Why would she think he was with someone?'

'She said she knew he was cheating but couldn't prove

it. She'd taken a copy of the tide times from his work stuff, thinking he might come back across the causeway to pay a visit to this woman.'

'That's crazy.'

'I told her that, but she said she pretty much *was* crazy at the time. Hardly getting any sleep because of the twins and being gaslit and lied to by him. She'd covered her tracks about leaving the babies alone, but when Bee died she had to keep lying because she knew what it'd look like.'

'So, why tell you and not the rest of us when it came up earlier about the nappy rash?'

He sighs. 'I don't know. People tend to open up to me with stuff – it's the job, I think. Or perhaps because she'd got a couple of drinks in her by then… all that wine at the table. She said she was going to tell Kitty when she went back in, that she hadn't wanted to admit any of that in front of Hewitt. She really detests her, so I suppose she can't deal with the idea of Hewitt gloating or seeing a weakness.'

'I get that. It's a big thing to admit.' Erin pushes her face further into the comforting crook of his neck.

The conversation moves on and they talk in low voices. About the small stuff, and the big stuff, steering away from the island. She almost tells him how she wishes she could have a cat; how she *did* have one, once, a little black cat called Nero, and that it had broken her heart when she'd had to rehome him after the pieces of dead things began to arrive in the post. She wasn't willing to risk that whoever was watching her might track her down properly and make him one of them. But she doesn't say any of this, because she doesn't want to talk about the island and everything that followed. They go back in time, before Bee.

'Remember when we pierced my ear?' he asks.

'As if I'd forget – and how pleased you were when it got infected, you grot.' She feels for the small nub in his lobe. 'Is that… is it still there? It *is*, I can feel it!'

'Yeah.' He laughs softly. 'I wouldn't have suffered all that to let it close up.'

'What was it we used to numb it… peas?'

'Frozen Yorkshire puds, the ones in the little foil trays. God, the stuff we did – you even made me learn all the words to that bloody song you liked off *Neighbours*.'

'I forgot about that!' she exclaims delightedly. 'The one from Scott and Charlene's wedding… and then you swore me to secrecy.' She feels him grin in the darkness.

'I miss those days.'

'Me too.' Her face aches from smiling; she can't remember when she last smiled this much. She tells him about the children's story she's just written, he tells her about his son.

'I read all your books to Nathan,' he says. 'So many times.'

'The books my mum sent?' she teases. 'The ones you didn't buy?'

'I might've bought a couple,' he says, nudging her with his hip.

'Oh, thanks.' She nudges him back. 'A *couple*?'

He exhales heavily. 'I had a wife. A very watchful wife who I loved, but who noticed everything. It was easier to let your mum send them. I've still got them, you know. Maybe I should get you to sign them for me.'

'Maybe you should.'

He slides his hand across her navel, then kisses her slowly. 'How about next week?'

She plays along. 'I don't have any book signings next week.'

'You never have any book signings,' he says quietly.

'No,' she says, recognising what this means, that Aidan is one of the faceless people who looks at her website, monitoring her movements – or lack of. And because it's Aidan, the thought doesn't bother her in the same way it does when she thinks of strangers, but nevertheless it brings her back to why she doesn't do public events in the first place. The island, and Bee. The unknown sender of awful things, reminding her that to advertise her whereabouts would be putting a target on her back.

'I nearly agreed to a bookshop event last year,' she says. 'With two other illustrators. I was mulling it over, feeling a bit braver about things. And then that girl got attacked – the singer who won that music reality show. She had a book out, and a guy queued up to get a copy signed and punched her in the face.'

'Yeah,' Aidan says. 'I think I remember that.'

'That was the same store that invited me to do the event. And I realised that if a TV star with private security wasn't safe then neither am I.'

'I saw you were down for a kids' literary festival a few years ago,' he says. 'Some draw-along thing. I was going to bring Nathan, but then it got cancelled.'

'I pulled out,' she says hoarsely. 'My publisher pushed me to do it, and I thought I could, but the closer it got I just… I couldn't. I still can't. I visit schools now and then,' she adds. 'It's good for book sales. Without those I'd probably sink. But nothing public, no shop signings.'

'You think someone might recognise you?'

Erin thinks of the packages. The ox tongue, the emails.

'Well, yeah. Our faces were all over the news.'

They lapse into silence. Aidan's the one to break it.

'I'm serious, Erin. After this is over and we leave here I don't want that to be it. I want to see you.'

'After this is over,' she repeats. Her body feels suddenly freezing under his warm touch. It will be over soon enough, once she, Kitty and Mira go public with what happened the night Bee died. After whatever media storm Kitty is cooking up. Self-loathing curdles with a surge of disbelief that it's out.

'Even if you can't do that, then stay here tonight.' He kisses her, turning into her, sliding his thigh between her legs. 'Stay here, in this bed with me. Just us, like this.'

'You told me to go,' she mumbles. 'It's not safe.'

'You're safe with me. I won't let anything happen to you.'

She feels her body responding to his hands, his lips. It would be so easy to let go, but she can't. Not this time. It's not fair on him.

'No, *no…*' She breaks away from the kiss. 'I can't. I'm sorry.'

His hand pauses on her breast. 'Can't what? Stay, or…?'

She takes his hand, presses it hard to her lips for a long moment, then rests it on the sheets, moving off the bed. She grabs the bathrove draped on the end of the bedpost and slips it on, hands shaking as she ties it and goes to stand by the window. She's surprised to see someone out there, seated near to the pool on one of the sun loungers. It's Kitty, wine glass in one hand, cigarette in the other. A short distance from her stands the dark, bulky figure of Bomber, partially obscured by shrubbery.

Erin grips the windowsill and closes her eyes.

'I can't stay with you tonight, and I can't see you again after this.'

She hears the rumple of sheets as he shifts, sitting up.

'Why… why not? What was that, then?'

She stares out over the pool, searching the water as though she can find the right words in its murkily green depths. She knows what it was: a lifetime of love for him. The best time she has had for as long as she can remember. But she can't tell him that.

'I suppose it was goodbye.'

He doesn't move. 'I don't understand. I thought you felt the same. I… thought you cared.'

'I care,' she says, sadly. 'Too much. That's why I can't mess your life up.' She turns to him, trying to smile, but the look on his face almost destroys her. 'What happened between us tonight, it was—'

'Don't say a mistake.' His dark eyes blaze in the dim light.

'No. Not a mistake. It was perfect.' She pauses. 'But I don't want you watching your back, or mine. You've got a son, and he's your responsibility, not me. I've lived it, Aidan. The bricks through the window, spray paint on the car. Dog shit in the post. You don't want Nathan growing up around that. And once Kitty puts it out there, what we did, I've got no control over what happens next. Whether it'll be better or worse.'

He is so silent and still that the moment teeters on a knife's edge, and if he tries to convince her otherwise, if he *fights* for her she might just give in and believe him. But the moment passes and he swallows, and nods. And then he's out of bed, crossing the room to retrieve his clothes. Pulling them on, half-dazed. 'For what it's worth I think *that's* a mistake. Letting Kitty do this. Once it's out to the public there's no going back.'

'It's too late now,' she croaks. 'If we don't do it perhaps there's no moving forward.' She wonders if that's the best she can hope for – a stagnant, watchful life spent looking over her shoulder. Perhaps that's exactly what she deserves.

'*Fuck*, Erin.' His eyes glisten in the darkness. 'We could've at least had tonight.'

'I'm sorry.' She takes a step towards him, but he shakes his head and moves to the door. Though he closes it quietly as he leaves, she feels it like a punch that leaves her winded.

She turns back to the window, too distraught even to cry. She feels wrung out, wishes she had been selfish. Aidan was right. They could have had tonight.

She checks her phone and registers with a jolt that it's now past midnight. Outside the window, the poolside is empty with no sign of Kitty, but Erin glimpses a shadowy figure slip out of sight close to where Bomber had been standing. As her gaze settles she realises the pool's surface is disturbed, rippling out towards the edges, lapping at its rim. She frowns. A dark shape floats into the centre, picked out in the up-lit murky green.

There is a body in the water, unmoving.

Kitty.

31

OCTOBER 2016

'No!' Erin grapples with the window but it's on a safety catch and only opens a couple of inches. She screams through the gap, fists pounding the glass. 'Is anyone there? Help!'

The pool remains silent, the water smoothing with each second.

Erin flees the room, shoeless, wearing only her robe. Aidan stands at the end of the corridor, frozen by her shouts. He takes one look at her and follows as she sprints for the stairs.

'What's the matter?' he demands. 'What the hell's happening?'

'Kitty.' Panic steals her breath as they descend to the ground floor. 'Pool!'

She bursts into the conference room with Aidan on her heels. The air is warm and thick with the smell of what's been eaten, and the tang of red wine. Erin races past the tables towards the French doors. There are only two people left in the room: Tori, drunk and tearful, and Mira, who appears to be comforting her. Their heads snap up in unison, and then all hell breaks loose as they both stand and start gabbling questions at once.

'The pool!' Aidan yells. He and Erin arrive at the doors, left ajar. The cold air hits Erin like a bucket of water in the face as she plunges into the night, bare feet pounding over damp decking and dodging sun loungers until they reach the pool. She's willing what she saw to be wrong; willing Kitty's face to suddenly appear, illuminated in the darkness by a lit cigarette while she calmly drawls something pithy about Erin being underdressed, but as they arrive at the pool Aidan's shout of, 'FUCK!' tells her all she needs to know.

He leaps in, and Erin follows him to the edge. She's already shivering, her feet ice cold. Freezing water splashes back at her, drenching her hair and the bathrobe.

Aidan surfaces, gasping. He reaches Kitty and turns her over. She's motionless, her black hair fanning around her head and her clothes billowing in the water. Her mouth is open, and so are her eyes. They stare at nothing.

'Is she breathing?' Erin cries. She follows Aidan to the far side of the pool as he pulls Kitty to the edge.

Bomber arrives at the side of the pool, his face a mask of dread. Tori and Mira watch from behind him, seemingly paralysed with shock.

'What the fuck happened?' he yells. 'Kitty! *Kit!*' He leans over, grabbing the sodden mass of clothes that have swallowed her up, and hauls her out as though she weighs nothing.

Aidan clambers from the pool, his face contorted with cold and panic.

'Get her indoors,' he tells Bomber. Then to Mira, 'Call an ambulance.'

Erin's shaking uncontrollably, the thin robe plastered to her skin. Her bare feet are becoming numb. Somehow she gets herself inside, following a sopping trail on the floor to where Aidan is leaning over Kitty. Mira shouts that she has no signal, and runs for the phone in the foyer. Erin, Bomber and Tori watch helplessly as Aidan performs chest compressions.

It's already clear that it's useless. Kitty's eyes are fixed vacantly on the ceiling, her mouth open, lips grey. Water pools on the floor, from her and from Aidan who's shaking with cold or adrenaline. Kitty's voluminous clothes stick to her body, as flat as if they've been punctured. Every twig-thin limb is visible, along with the clear outline of a colostomy bag.

Bomber paces beside them, raking his hands back and forth over his shaved head.

'Is she gonna make it?' he pleads. 'Will she be okay?'

Aidan doesn't answer. He pauses the compressions to deliver two breaths, then returns to pumping her chest. His movements are even and professional, but his eyes have a blank, hopeless look. Kitty is not okay. She's already dead, and Aidan can't bring her back.

'What's going on?' Hewitt bursts into the conference room, blinking. Her hair is loose and messy, and she's wearing fleecy pyjamas with little white sheep on. 'I heard shouting—?' Her hands fly to her mouth as she takes in the scene. 'Oh, my god.'

Aidan perseveres. Over and over, time and again. Minutes tick by, but Kitty doesn't respond.

'Keep trying,' Erin begs. 'Don't give up. Don't stop.'

'Wouldn't she have a DNR in place?' Tori asks.

Aidan glances at Bomber, who nods.

'Yeah, but...'

'It'd be for the cancer.' Aidan's words jolt with his movements. He pauses, delivers two more breaths. 'Not something like this.'

'A DNR?' Erin asks.

'Do not resuscitate,' Hewitt replies.

'I'm sorry.' Aidan leans back on his heels, hair dripping in his eyes as he checks for Kitty's pulse once more. 'There's nothing else I can do. She's gone.'

'She can't be.' Bomber stops pacing and slowly sinks to his knees. 'Not like this.'

Aidan gently closes Kitty's eyes. 'She was dead before I even got to her.'

'But she was only gone a couple of minutes,' Tori whispers. 'How'd she end up in the pool?'

No one answers. Erin is numb, chilled to the core. Like she will never be warm again. She can't take her eyes off Kitty.

Poor, dead Kitty, her body ravaged by disease, meeting such a terrible end.

Maybe I could even die here on the island, she'd said. *That'd be something, wouldn't it? A kind of symmetry to round off my life story.*

And now she has. Kitty's life is rounded off, over. Erin reaches out and touches her lifeless hand, and she thinks of Kitty twenty years ago. Though her illness has chewed her down to the bone, it hadn't broken her. Kitty had still been vibrant, witty, sharp. She'd still had life in her.

Mira enters the room and sees at once that Kitty is gone. She collapses into one of the nearby chairs, staring at the body. 'Oh, god. Oh, *my god…*' she says, over and over, rocking back and forth. 'They're sending an ambulance,' she says at last.

'Call them back,' Aidan says sombrely. 'Tell them we need the police instead. Until there's a post-mortem, they'll treat it as unexplained.'

Mira continues to rock, not attempting to get up.

'I'll go,' says Hewitt.

'How can she have drowned so fast?' Mira asks. 'It doesn't make sense.'

'She didn't necessarily drown,' says Aidan. 'Someone that ill, in water that cold… the shock alone probably killed her. It's likely her heart gave out.'

'But how did she fall in?' asks Tori. 'It's well-lit out there.'

'Maybe she misjudged,' Mira says. '*God!* She's been drinking all evening.'

'Where were you?' Erin interrupts, directing the question at Bomber. 'I saw you from my window just before it happened. You were both out there. Kitty was smoking.'

Bomber nods, glassy-eyed. 'Yeah. I was with her, but I needed a piss. She told me to go in, said she'd be back in in just a minute. So I went.'

Erin feels a prickle of unease, remembering the dark shape moving away from the pool as the ripples were still spreading.

'Went where? Which toilet? Did you hear a splash as you walked away?'

'A splash? No. If I had I'd have turned around.' He frowns, pointing to the foyer. 'I used the one through there. Why?'

Erin swallows. 'You didn't walk through the grounds?'

'No, lady.' Bomber jabs his thumb at the foyer to emphasise his point. 'I went through there. You accusing me of something?'

'No,' Erin whispers, through chattering teeth. 'But I saw someone, or some*thing*, going the other way. It was so quick I couldn't be certain…' She pauses, questioning her memory of it. She'd been convinced it had been Bomber, but now she's no longer sure it was even a person. It'd happened so fast, and she'd been upset, preoccupied with Aidan. 'You didn't see anyone else?'

He shakes his head, bewildered.

'Bomber did walk through,' Mira says hoarsely. 'A couple of minutes before you and Aidan came running past.'

Bomber goes to the French doors that are now exposed, the curtains thrown back. They all stare out, and the black, blank night stares back.

'So, if it wasn't him then who was it?' asks Tori, rattled.

In the brightly lit room they are now like fish in a barrel, on show to anyone who might be outside, looking in. Terrible thoughts flood Erin's mind. Did Kitty spot an intruder — another photographer, or a reporter, even — and slip into the pool as she went to investigate? But then, who's to say it *was* someone from the press? It could have been anyone. Someone obsessed with Kitty, or some true crime nut who's followed one of them here. The island might be cut off by road, but it's not inaccessible altogether.

She finds herself walking to the French doors to join Bomber, squinting out across the sun loungers and through tall potted planters.

'It was over there somewhere.' She points to the right of the pool to a shrubby, shadowed area.

He pushes the door open and steps out, heading off to the area she gestured to. She waits and watches at the door, tugging the thin robe tightly around her. It makes little difference. The air is icy on her wet skin.

He returns a couple of minutes later, ashen-faced. 'No sign of anyone. But there's a path leading down to the beach.' He secures the doors. 'Someone could've been here.'

'Who?' says Tori. 'That photographer again?'

'I don't know. I should never have left her.' He glances at Kitty, then away, trying to gather himself. 'The causeway's still open for about forty-five minutes,' he says, checking his watch. 'Should be enough time for the police to get here.'

Aidan nods. 'Yeah. They'll want to question everyone.'

Erin fights a rising panic. 'We can't leave?'

'Officially, no. But that's only what I can advise people. I can't stop anyone from going.'

How long will it take for help to arrive? Erin can't properly remember what the process had been when Bee died, only that it had taken hours and hours. After the body was found the students had all been ordered to return to their cabins. Time to get their stories straight before the questions. Time to rehearse the lies, and frantically dry damp clothes with hairdryers. And once again they've been here only a matter of hours, and someone's dead. The same as the college trip all those years ago.

'I need to uh, go and make some calls,' says Bomber. His eyes are red-rimmed. He's fighting back tears. 'Inform next of kin.'

'I'm think I'm going to be sick,' says Tori. 'All the wine, and…' She's grey and woozy, unsteady on her feet. As she weaves towards the doors she overtakes Bomber, already starting to heave.

Hewitt mutters that she's going to get changed out of her nightclothes before the police arrive, and leaves the room. Mira stays where she is, silently staring at the body.

Erin can't take any more, can't be in this room with Kitty's corpse any longer. She kneels by Kitty's side, strokes her cold cheek. Then she gets up, heading to the foyer.

'Erin, wait.'

She halts, shivering. Aidan has followed her. He goes to say something, then stops awkwardly, as if the words have got lost. She feels an indescribable sadness.

'I swear this place is cursed,' he mutters.

'You could be right.'

He hesitates, then closes the space between them in two strides, pulling her to him. She sinks into his arms. Even though he's soaking and freezing, she holds him tight.

'What if someone pushed her? She's the one who brought us back here, digging up the past. Hiring private investigators. What if she rattled someone?' Her voice is muffled against his chest. 'I'm sure I saw…' She stops. *Is* she sure? Perhaps she's finally losing it to fear and paranoia. She would see shapes in tea leaves if she looked. Demons in clouds. 'I know I sound crazy, I just really thought I saw someone…'

'Don't jump to conclusions. She was drunk, probably slipped. The police will figure it out.' His lips brush the top of her head, and too soon he releases her. 'Go and dry off. Warm up.'

She steps back, her eyes fixed on his face. Then she turns and leaves.

It's only as Erin is approaching her room that she realises she ran out of it without the key or any thought of it. She tries the door, worried she's shut herself out but to her surprise it opens, and she enters the room cautiously, snapping on the light and half-expecting to see a shadowy figure lunging towards her. She's confronted only by the rumpled bed, and her discarded clothes by the chest of drawers.

The room smells of sex. She locks herself in then snaps the curtains shut, blocking out the view of the pool before peeling off the wet bathrobe.

She puts the clothes she wore earlier back on, and as she

dresses, she begins to cry. For Kitty and the loss of her life. For Mira, having to relive her assault. She cries for herself and the friendships she might have had with these two women, and what might have been with Aidan.

Once dressed she reaches for her phone on the windowsill, wincing at a sharp prick in her finger. She stares at the screen. It's not only blank, but cracked into a kaleidoscope of black glass.

'*Shit.*' When had that happened? She's further unnerved to realise that her handbag, which she'd thought had been dropped somewhere behind the door when she came in with Aidan, is not there.

An awful, helpless alarm descends as she mentally rifles through her bag: door keys, car key, bank cards – and then it's gone, replaced with weak relief as she spots the bag in the en suite, lying on the shower mat. The relief does not last, for as she's stepping into the little bathroom she cannot fathom how it has ended up there. She reaches for it with the unshakeable sense something is wrong.

Before she's even looked inside she knows by its familiar weight that nothing's missing, but it does nothing to ease her foreboding. And then she sees it.

The shower curtain is pulled across. Erin could swear that following the shower she took before dinner, she'd left it open. Her hand goes out and sweeps the curtain back. The expensive mini toiletries gleam in a beautiful little row.

Below them, the eyeless, mangled hare she'd seen on arrival is splayed in the shower tray.

Erin shoves her broken phone in her bag and runs.

32

OCTOBER 2016

Her feet drum like her heart as she descends the empty stairs, two, three at a time, almost tripping down them.

She is not spooked, or paranoid or imagining things. Someone was there by the pool. Someone was there in her room. Just like the someone who dictates the way she lives and her every thought whenever she leaves her home. The someone who is here for her, right now. And Erin is not staying on this island for another minute, let alone the night.

The foyer is eerily quiet, ominous and heavy with Kitty's death as Erin races past the reception desk. There will be no goodbyes. When she bursts through the exit into the night, Aidan's on the steps staring down the drive. He startles at the sight of her, and she almost knocks him over as he intercepts her.

'Erin, *whoa* – for god's sake! What—?'

'Someone was there, in my room… they put the hare there – that dead hare that was on the path in the car park, and they broke my phone…' She's babbling, wild with fear. 'I'm not imagining it, *any* of it. There's either someone else on this island or it's one of us – they pushed Kitty and now they're after me!'

'Okay – slow down.' He grips her by the shoulders, looking past her into the foyer with fear in his eyes. 'The police are coming. Nothing's going to happen now, you're safe—'

'No. Screw the police,' she sobs. 'I'm *not* safe, they can't help me. They've *never* helped me. I can't stay here, I'm getting across that causeway while there's still time.' She wipes her face, checking her watch. There are thirty-nine minutes until cut off.

'Okay,' he repeats, following her as she twists out of his grasp and starts jogging over to the car park. Charlotte Hewitt is by the car next to Erin's, slamming the driver's side door. She has a phone charger in her hand and has changed out of her sheepy pyjamas into a dark tracksuit. Her face and eyes are puffy, as though she's been crying. She stops and stares, her bottom lip trembling as Erin and Aidan rush towards Erin's car. Erin is scrabbling in her bag for the car key.

'Is everything okay?' Hewitt asks uncertainly, stepping towards them.

Neither of them answers.

'Erin,' says Aidan. 'You've got to calm down. You can't drive like this.'

'I… I thought we all had to stay,' Hewitt says. 'For the police?'

'I'm not staying here.' Erin unlocks the car, managing to steady her voice a fraction. 'I'll go to that bed and breakfast, the one near the motorway. The police can find me there.'

She's about to open the door when she hears Aidan's breath catch.

He points to her wheel. 'You won't be going anywhere with that.'

'What?' Erin's heart judders as she sees her front driver's side tyre is completely flat. She looks about wildly, almost cowering. 'Someone's done that. They don't want me leaving, they don't—'

'*Erin.*' Aidan cuts in, firm. 'It's a puncture. You saw the state of the causeway, all those potholes. You got a spare?'

She shakes her head despairingly. 'Only one of those stupid inflation kits. I'll have to call the breakdown, but by the time they get here…' Her voice cracks. 'You can take me,' she begs. 'Just drive me across and I'll get a taxi back tomorrow when it's fixed. Please, Aidan, I can't be here. You said yourself it's not safe…'

She sees him hesitate.

'I need to stay, for Kitty.' He jerks his head to the sleek black motorcycle behind him. 'Plus I only have one helmet.'

'I'll take the risk.'

'I won't.'

'I'll take you, if you want me to,' Hewitt interjects timidly. 'I think I remember seeing the bed and breakfast on the way. It's not that far, is it? I can make it back in time?'

'Yeah,' Erin says in a rush, her knees loosening with relief. 'It's not far. Are you sure you don't mind?'

'Of course not.' Hewitt wipes her nose, attempting to smile, but she looks so miserable that Erin wonders if she merely wants off the island too. If, on some level she is hoping to get stuck on the other side so that she doesn't have to return to this wretched place.

'Leave the key with me,' Aidan tells her. 'They'll need it for the wheel nut.' He holds out his hand and Erin passes it to him. He takes her entire hand in his and pulls her to him.

She takes a breath to say something but finds she has no words, and so she holds that breath of him in her lungs until it burns. Her eyes sting, and she releases the breath and kisses him hard, just once.

He opens the passenger door of Hewitt's little red car and Erin clambers in, blinking back tears. Hewitt's already in the driver's seat, setting up the maps on her phone. She clips it on the dashboard and starts the engine, lowering the volume on the radio which comes on blaring.

Erin shuts the door and straps herself in.

'Lock the doors,' she urges. Her eyes are on Aidan as Hewitt hits the central locking and reverses out of the space. She watches him as the car slowly pulls away and until he's lost from view.

'Did something happen?' Hewitt ventures, shooting her a curious look.

'Yes.' Erin whispers the word but a bump in the road turns it into a hiss, making her sound like a creature about to attack. She is thankful when Hewitt does not push for a further explanation.

Erin settles back in the seat. Something crackles underneath her. She pulls out a receipt and discreetly drops it in the footwell, next to a carrier bag full of papers. There are empty takeaway coffee cups in every holder. Hewitt's car is a tip.

'He always was decent,' Hewitt says thoughtfully. She hunches over the wheel, intent on the dark road which is hemmed in by hedges and the occasional signpost.

'Aidan?'

Hewitt nods. 'A much better choice than Patrick Preston.'

'Oh.' Erin's fingers tighten involuntarily on her handbag at the mention of Preston. Aside from her memory of him the night Bee died and the news of his death, she hasn't thought of him properly in years. The horrid, sloppy, groping kiss is one she's consigned to bad experiences that she no longer allows herself to dwell on, and she finds it odd that Hewitt has mentioned him – or was even aware of the dalliance – at all.

'Thanks for this,' Erin mutters, keen to change the subject. 'It's good of you.'

'It's okay,' Hewitt replies, seeming to sense Erin's discomfort. When they reach the causeway the road stretches ahead with only a few metres of wet grit picked out in the beam of the headlights. If it was unnerving in the daylight, it's terrifying in the dark. The track is marked only by green-furred debris at its edges, with the thick sludge of the estuary bed on either side. Any vehicle that deviates from its precarious path will quickly and easily become stuck.

Erin pushes the thought away as the car rolls down the slope and on to the tidal road. It's a mile long. Just one mile, or thereabouts, and then they'll be on the mainland.

Hewitt leans further over the steering wheel to better see

the road. She looks agitated, her hairline shimmering with perspiration. Perhaps she is regretting her offer to help and is already dreading the way back across, alone. Erin can't blame her. The causeway is daunting at the best of times, let alone in the pitch dark. She glances at the clock on the dash. 00:40.

Erin huddles further into her coat, wishing the heater would kick in. Her leg brushes the paperwork-stuffed bag in the footwell again. She's starting to feel claustrophobic with the clutter and rubbish everywhere.

'Okay if I stick this in the back?' she asks.

'Sure.' Hewitt's voice is clipped, and she wipes her hands quickly on her tracksuit bottoms: one then the other. She suddenly seems to be pouring with sweat, even though the car is freezing. 'Sorry. Just work stuff.'

Erin heaves the bag on to her lap, trying to keep the loose papers in it. Most are stamped with a charity letterhead and there are a couple of neater files at the back. She turns with difficulty and manoeuvres it into the back of the car, catching a glimpse of a newspaper cutting within the papers. In the dark, with only the lights from the dash, Erin can't read the print, but she can see Bee's face in grainy black and white.

She wonders why Hewitt kept the cutting. Perhaps the guilt she spoke of compels her; makes her obsessive about the case and her part in it. Erin understands the compulsion to read any mention of Bee's murder – she does it herself – but she doesn't cut things out and keep them. She dumps the bag on to the back seat on top of a black puffer jacket and turns back to face the causeway. They've been on it perhaps a minute now, with the pitted surface and low visibility forcing them to a crawl. At this rate, Erin calculates it's going to take around another ten minutes to reach the mainland.

Hewitt turns the radio up a little, filling the car with the inane burble of a late-night DJ that grates on Erin's nerves.

She is trying to focus on her breathing instead of the rattle of the car, when Hewitt's phone starts to ring. The display shows *Unknown Caller.*

Hewitt accepts the call and Aidan's voice comes through on loudspeaker.

'It's me.'

Erin leans forward in her seat. 'Aidan?'

'Bomber got Charlotte's number from Kitty's iPad.'

Her skin prickles at the sound of his voice. He's trying to stay calm but she senses something underlying. Something not good. 'What's wrong?'

'How long till you're at the B&B?'

'I'm not sure. We're barely a third of the way across. What's up?'

'I took a closer look at your tyre to see if the inflation kit might work,' he says. 'I don't think it was a pothole. I think you were right. It looks like it's been deliberately slashed.'

'Oh, god,' she whispers, her mind cartwheeling.

Hewitt's head swivels sharply towards her, then snaps back to the causeway as they hit a dip.

'Just get to the hotel,' Aidan says, in a low voice that sends dread crawling down her spine. 'Call me when you're there and be careful. Get Charlotte to walk in with you, and don't open the door to anyone.'

'Okay,' Erin says faintly.

Hewitt ends the call and swipes at the phone. For a second she mistakenly closes the maps application and Erin glimpses her home screen. There's a photo of a small child of around four years old with wide eyes and a sweetly crooked smile, who's eating an ice lolly and making a mess of it. It's there for fraction of a second before Hewitt fumbles and reopens the map.

'Do you really think someone slashed your tyre?' she asks softly.

'Yes. And someone pushed Kitty. I know it.' A sob forces its way up Erin's throat. 'She was dying anyway. Who could *do* that? What kind of coward would you have to be? She was skin and bone.'

'Awful.' Hewitt's eyes glisten with tears.

Erin glances out of the window fearfully, checking the locks are down. She knows it's crazy but she can't help imagining a figure materialising on the road next to the car, smashing through the window and dragging her on to the causeway. They must be almost halfway now. The lights on the mainland seem a touch closer, but there's no sign of any police vehicle approaching on the other side.

Her eyes return to Hewitt's phone. Something about it is already bothering her, but then she notes the estimated arrival time on the display. She sits up a little straighter, wondering if Hewitt has somehow put in the wrong bed and breakfast, for the map is showing a journey time of two hours and twelve minutes. Her mind flashes back to her own drive time to the island yesterday morning. A sick recognition swirls in her stomach.

The bouncing of the car disguises her breathing, suddenly shallow. It's there again: that familiar, nagging sensation of wrongness in her core that she has learned, too late, to trust. Charlotte Hewitt has always been a sad, creepy bitch. But perhaps she is more, much more than that.

'Charlotte?' Erin says firmly, trying to mask the tremor in her voice. 'Do you mind telling me why you've put in my address? And how the fuck you know it in the first place?'

'Oh.' Hewitt swallows visibly. 'Oh, I see.' She doesn't take her eyes off the causeway, and when she readjusts her hands on the steering wheel, wet streaks of sweat follow them.

'How do you know where I live?' Erin repeats faintly.

Hewitt blinks several times, saying nothing. The car speeds up.

'Let me out.' Erin fumbles for the door release. 'Stop the car. I want to get out!'

'You're not getting out.' Hewitt's voice is quiet. 'You're not going anywhere.'

33

OCTOBER 2016

Erin stares at Charlotte in horror. She tries to recall the dark, bulky figure she'd seen out by the pool and glances over her shoulder into the back seat, at the black puffer jacket under the carrier bag.

'*You*,' she whispers. 'You killed Kitty?'

'I had no choice.' Hewitt wipes sweat from her upper lip. 'After what she said about the private investigator I knew I had to shut her up. Buy some time. The fact she was dying made it easier.' She presses her lips together tightly.

Erin's head swirls, shock and fear keeping her prisoner. There's only one reason why Charlotte Hewitt would need to shut Kitty up. In those rare moments when Erin has suspected Hewitt might not have been in her cabin the night Bee died, whenever she has considered any slim possibility that Hewitt could have been Bee's killer, there has only been one motive that made sense to Erin. But she is starting to understand that it cannot be as simple as Paul Callaghan's affair with her. She is starting to understand that there is far more to it.

The hare. The slashed tyre. The note. *Child A.*

This. Erin closes her eyes, nauseous. It has all come back to this thing, the terrible thing she can never get away from.

'That photo,' she murmurs, with sick clarity. 'On your phone.'

The child with the crooked smile, eating an ice lolly. *Nicky.*

'How exactly did you think Kitty was going to find you out?' she whispers. 'Who *are* you?'

'I don't suppose you remember a woman called Amanda Lane, do you?'

Erin is momentarily thrown, unable to place the name.

'Most people called her Mandy,' Hewitt adds. 'She was my mother. But I guess a lot of people knew her as Mandy Pemberton.'

It hits with a horrifying jolt of recognition.

'Your *mother*? And Nicky Pemberton's mother. Who… she left him.'

Hewitt's face contorts into a snarl and Erin is jolted to one side as the car hits a dip in the road. Hewitt has sped up.

'She *escaped*. And Nicky should've been with us but it all went wrong. It nearly killed her to leave him! Don't talk about what you don't understand.' Her voice softens. 'Nicky was my half-brother. Mum wasn't married to Mick Pemberton, but when Nicky was born he took Mick's surname. Same as I did, with my dad. Mum was traditional like that, and Mick – well. He wouldn't have had it any other way. Nicky was his property as far as Mick was concerned. That's probably why he thought he had the right to beat him to death, along with your dad and the other one. All because of you and Bee. The two little liars.'

'I'm sorry,' Erin whispers. 'I'm so, so sorry for what we did and I have been every day. I'll never stop being sorry.'

Hewitt doesn't react.

Erin is silent with terror now. She tries to imagine how much Charlotte Hewitt hates her. Thinks of how much she has hated herself, and the extent to which she detested Bee. She imagines how she would feel if Nicky had been someone she loved. The loathing Erin feels cannot come close. Perhaps hatred, like guilt, only worsens with time. At what point does it become a madness, a willingness to kill?

Erin is trapped in a car with a killer.

If an assailant takes you to a second location, chances of escape or rescue are significantly reduced.

With every passing second her window of escape grows smaller. She has to get out of this car, and if it's between here on the causeway and at high speed on a motorway, then the choice is already made. Her eyes roam the passenger door in the dark, locating the handle. If she can get out and make a run for it she stands a chance. As it is, she wonders how much of a chance she stands at all. Erin is reasonably healthy when she takes care of herself but her periods of self-loathing and self-neglect have left her thin and not especially fit. Hewitt is roughly the same height but looks a good three or four stones heavier.

Slowly, Erin slides her hand towards the seat-belt clip. She'll have to be quick: unfasten herself, release the door and jump—

'Don't.' Hewitt slams on the brakes, propelling Erin forward.

Adrenaline kicks in. She raises her arm and smashes her elbow into Hewitt's face. There's a sickening crunch as it connects with her nose, and Hewitt howls. Erin pulls back, rushing to unclip her seat belt, twisting away as Hewitt gropes for her. Erin jabs her a second time, finding soft flesh as her other hand locates the door pull. She opens it and launches herself out, staggering across the pocked causeway. In the car, Hewitt wheezes for breath.

After a few steps Erin's feet get used to the rough surface, but she has underestimated the darkness and she must make a decision: back to the island, or forward to the mainland. She chooses. The island is closer. And there at least, she knows where to head. On the mainland there are several miles of farmland and Erin has no idea where to go. Most importantly, Hewitt's car is facing the mainland, and she'll have to find somewhere to turn if she intends to chase Erin down, which will buy time. *Where the fuck are the police?*

With the car behind her, Erin fixes her sights on the dark mass of the island. Her feet pound the causeway, jarring on its uneven surface. She hears the car rev and realises it's getting closer – she's wrongly predicted what Hewitt would do. Erin casts a horrified glance back. Red tail-lights are soaring towards her.

Hewitt didn't need to turn the car around. She's reversing straight for her.

Oh, my god…

Erin swerves, trying to deviate from the car's path, weaving as it gains on her. Her foot dips into a rut and her ankle twists. Somehow she stays on her feet. She risks another glance back, seeing a red glow. Her only chance now is to leave the causeway and lure Hewitt into following her, where her car will surely end up mired in the mud. Years of slime-encrusted rubble lines the edges of the road. She starts picking her way over it, ankle twinging. She's almost cleared it when the car grinds across it and rams her, knocking her off her feet.

Erin lands painfully on the debris at the causeway's edge. Jagged stones scrape into her legs, gravel embeds itself in her palms. She knows she's cut and bleeding, but she forces herself to roll, to keep going until she clears the rubble and hits the soft, stinking estuary bed. She grunts but it's lost under the roar of the car which grates to a halt. The engine cuts out, a car door creaks. Gritty footsteps approach. She claws herself up and out of the mud.

A blow to the back of the head sends her straight back down.

34

OCTOBER 2016

The impact of the blow shoots daggers along Erin's spine. Whatever Hewitt has used to strike her – a lump of wood, she thinks – rolls away. Before she can react, strong hands twist into her hair and she's being dragged over sand and stone, Hewitt grunting with each step back to the car.

'You've made this hard, Erin.'

Erin tears at Hewitt's hands, her eyes streaming with the pain. Hewitt yanks her up, forcing her to her knees. Erin feels some of her hairs breaking, others are ripped out at the root.

'It doesn't need to be hard. It's all down to how much you struggle.'

Erin goes rigid. One hand grasps at Hewitt's hands, the other blindly reaches around her in the hope of finding a weapon. Hewitt has her so tightly that her fingertips don't even reach the ground. Her head throbs dizzyingly, and white spots dance before her when she blinks. *Like polka dots.* Bee was wearing polka dots when she died. She remembers how she'd admired Hewitt springing into action, straight into the water while Callaghan dawdled over his laces. She'd taken that as a sign of his guilt – but she sees now it was simply shock. Whereas if Hewitt already knew Bee was dead then she'd have known how to act. She'd had time to plan for it.

'Charlotte,' she gasps, stalling. 'You sent me all those things? The messages? The *tongue*?'

'I kept it mainly to the anniversaries of Bee's death.' Hewitt smiles thinly. 'But there were other times, in gloomy moments, when I just couldn't help myself. Sometimes I thought about sending things on Nicky's days. His birthday, or the day he died. But I couldn't risk you linking it to Nicky for sure, in case it led back to me if you ever got it looked into. So I made it about her, and not letting you forget her.'

As if Erin ever could. 'You still haven't told me how you knew my address.'

'When you work for charities there are ways to get that kind of information,' Hewitt says softly. 'Mailing lists. So, yeah, I know where you live. That was just the start. I know who your agent is. The name of your editor. Where your lovely little mum lives. Where you do your shopping, the kind of things you buy. I even know what brand of tampons you use.'

'If you knew where I live, why send everything via my agent? Why not send it direct?'

'I didn't want you to run.' Hewitt eyes her mutinously. 'I didn't want you *too* scared. Just enough.'

'*You sick fuck.*' Erin's knees give out and Hewitt, sensing she can no longer hold herself up, releases her grip on Erin's hair. She drops, shins digging painfully into the rough debris and wet sand. Hewitt hunkers over her. When Erin looks up into her face she expects to find a gloating madness there, but Hewitt is calm despite a gash on the bridge of her nose which is leaking blood. In the dim light it looks black.

'I didn't want to kill Kitty,' she says. 'If only she'd left it alone. I mean, now the police have released the new angle on Bee I can't see it all holding together much longer, anyway. If they start looking properly, I've a feeling they'll be a lot more thorough than they were twenty years ago. I was so sure they'd find me out, that Nicky was my brother. But they never did. I got away with it then because of their mistakes, their tunnel vision. They were so desperate to pin it on Paul.' She leans closer to Erin's face. '*He* was the sick fuck, sleeping with teenagers. Not me.'

Erin sways, unsure if it's shock or the blow to her head. Slowly she lifts her hand to her scalp, and perhaps because she's caught up in her memories, Hewitt allows it. Erin's fingers come away smeared with blood and her own hair.

'I suppose I should be grateful to him, really,' Hewitt muses. 'Anyone looking at a motive for me would think it was because of him and Bee.' She shakes her head, scornful. 'Like I'd kill for a man who wasn't even mine. Though if I'm honest, the affair didn't help. It shocked me. Disgusted me, in fact. Disgusted me so much it did me a favour. I've never become so disillusioned with someone so quickly as I did when I found out.'

Erin's shaking now, compelled to listen to the madness of this woman whom she'd thought harmless but is anything but. At the same time, she tentatively feels around her for something she might use as a weapon. She has to hold her off, or keep her talking. The police can surely be only minutes away. She glimpses a fist-sized rock by Hewitt's foot but can't get it unless she lunges – and Hewitt will undoubtedly prevent her.

'Tell me about Nicky,' she says softly. 'Why didn't he go with you and your mum?'

For a moment Hewitt doesn't respond, and Erin cowers, expecting to be struck again. But then Hewitt speaks.

'He was supposed to,' she says quietly. 'But Mick wrecked everything. Mum tried again later but he threatened her, and when Mick made threats he meant them. She didn't dare after that. And somehow five years went by without Nicky. I still hoped, and *believed* we'd get him back – until you and Bee told your lies. And Nicky died, in the most horrible way. Mum had a complete breakdown after that. Sometimes I almost wished for a breakdown myself. Wished someone would step in and look after me. But life carried on and so did I. I thought of you and Bee often. Wondered what your lives were like and whether you had any idea of the ripple effect your actions had. I memorised the hearsay that someone Mum secretly stayed in touch with had passed on to us, about who you were. What you looked like.'

'So that's how you found us?'

'I didn't find you, Erin.' Hewitt's eyes turn hazy, but her gaze flickers back to the island. 'In a way, it was you who found me. I was just doing my job, trying to get on with my life. Then the academic year ended and the new one began. And there you were: the girl with the distinctive eyes that I'd heard about. But I'm digressing, and we can't stay here. How's your head?'

The blood on Erin's hand is sticky, drying out in the night air. She is light-headed, unsure she has any strength left in her to fight. 'Woozy,' she says.

'Good.' Hewitt's fingers dig into Erin's shoulder. 'I'd rather not hit you again. Now get in the car.'

Erin sways, moving deliberately slowly.

Secondary location. The words loop in her head. Erin cannot let herself get driven away from here. It comes to her then that Hewitt's biggest obstacle is moving her. Erin has to make herself unmovable.

'I feel sick,' she mumbles, hunching over.

'Do it in the car,' Hewitt says, impatient. 'I've got bags.'

'I can't…' Erin feigns pushing herself up, then collapses on her side.

'Get up.' Hewitt wrenches her arm. Erin turns her face away, gritting her teeth. The pressure on her arm makes her eyes water all over again. It feels dangerously close to coming out of its socket. Hewitt takes her other arm and pulls, but Erin doesn't move. She is a deadweight. Her plan is working. If Hewitt can't budge her, then she'll either be forced to leave or commit a messy murder right here.

'*Move*,' Hewitt rages. 'I know you can move!' When she gets no response she stamps on Erin's thigh, right where the burn is. Erin doubles up in agony.

'Get up.' Hewitt leans over her. 'Unless you want me to kick the living shit out of you like they did to my little brother.'

Unable to take any more, Erin rolls on to her knees. Her fingers close over something: the rock she'd seen near Hewitt's foot. She musters up every bit of strength she can, and swings.

Her aim is poor and she misses, but it's enough to momentarily throw Hewitt off-guard and Erin uses it. She barges past her and leaps back on to the causeway. Her vision sways. There's no way she can beat Hewitt to the island on foot. Even without the injuries she doesn't have the stamina. She sprints for the car, hearing Hewitt grunt behind her. She leaps into the open driver's door, trying to pull it shut but Hewitt is already there. Erin fights to pull it closed, realises she's not strong enough and pushes instead.

Hewitt is taken by surprise, releasing her hold on the door and flying backwards. Erin slams it closed and hits the central locking, breath ragged and hands fumbling for the ignition, praying Hewitt got out in too much of a rush to take the key. It's there.

Almost crying with relief she pushes it in the ignition, but the car won't start. She tries again, but it's as though the key is jammed. She jiggles the wheel, then screams as Hewitt slams against the driver's side window, raging and pulling the handle.

'Open the door!' she roars. 'Open that bloody door!'

Erin grapples with the gear stick, seeing then that it's an automatic. She panics. Her own car is a manual, and for a moment she's flummoxed. A mighty crack scatters her thoughts. Hewitt has smashed a rock into the windscreen, splintering it. She hits a second time, and the entire thing gives way and rains broken glass in on Erin. Hewitt is screeching, clambering on the bonnet, reaching in for her, glass crunching under her weight.

Automatic. Something clicks in Erin's head. She puts her foot on the brake and tries the key again.

The car starts and she slams the stick into *Drive*, flooring it blindly. Hewitt is thrown into her, her weight almost crushing Erin, forcing pinpricks of tiny squares of glass into her face and neck. She brakes hard and Hewitt's crushing weight is released as she rolls off the car bonnet to land on the causeway.

Erin hesitates for a fragment of a second. She thinks of Bee, and of Kitty. Of cruel words and envelopes with seeping contents. She removes her foot from the brake and eases the car forward. There's a sickening bump and the front of the car lifts as Hewitt goes under the wheels. The screaming starts.

Only then does Erin stop. She puts on the handbrake, cuts the engine, and gets out. Her feet rasp on glass as she walks to the front of the car. She feels more working its way down the neck of her dress, down the back of her coat. Some is in her hair.

Hewitt is pinned beneath the front passenger side wheel, somewhere between the pelvis and the tops of her thighs. She is howling, trying to twist and drag herself out, but the car is going nowhere. In the garbled cries that come out of her, Erin catches her own name. She bends down, keeping sure to stay out of reach. She waits in silence as the howling subsides to pained gasps.

'That's better,' Erin says finally. 'I can hear you now.'

'*Get this car off me, you bitch!*'

Erin shakes glass from her hair. It sparkles as it falls through the beam of the headlights to land on the road. 'Why would I do that?'

'*Please*,' Hewitt's teeth are gritted. 'It's… crushing me.'

Erin stares at her, feeling nothing but loathing.

'Let me go. You're not a killer, Erin.'

'Strange. Every email you've sent me over the past few years said the opposite.' Erin looks back at the mainland. 'I'm not letting you go. If you're lucky the police will be here any minute.'

Hewitt gasps something, but her breath snags.

'What?' Erin asks.

'They're not… coming. Didn't call them. I just cancelled the ambulance.'

'Shame,' says Erin. 'I bet you wish you had now.'

Hewitt's arm lashes out, trying to grab her, but she succeeds only in brushing the hem of Erin's coat. She screams in frustration, breath misting the air.

'That's right,' Erin says softly. 'I'm in control now.' She touches her head and examines her fingers. The wound is sticky but seems to be stemming, perhaps because her racing pulse is beginning to calm. 'Feels good, doesn't it? Being in control. Not something I'm familiar with, actually. I've mostly felt the opposite, these past twenty years. But I expect control is something you'd know all about.' She pauses. 'The first time I got sent shit in the post I had no idea what I was opening. It got right under my fingernails and even though I scrubbed them till they bled I still thought I could smell it for days. You must've felt powerful every time you did something like that.'

Hewitt's face shimmers with sweat. 'You deserved it.'

'Maybe.' Erin stares past the car, in the direction of the island. Aidan will call the police again when they don't turn up, she knows this. He will be distracted, thinking of her, but the flashing lights will come this way eventually. It's possible now that the tide will beat them. 'But Kitty didn't deserve what you did to her. Neither did Bee.'

'Bee deserved exactly what she got.'

'Did she? Tell me about that night.'

'I'm not telling you shit.'

'No? You were pretty chirpy just now. Perhaps I can change your mind.' Erin stands, lending her weight to the bonnet directly over the wheel.

'Stop!' Hewitt screeches. '*Stop it, you vicious—*'

'Vicious?' Erin gets off the car and looms over Hewitt. She

catches a faint whiff of urine. Hewitt has lost control of her bladder. 'No. Vicious would be force-feeding you these tiny pieces of glass.' She sweeps her arm across the bonnet, showering Hewitt. 'And then slitting your throat.'

Hewitt turns her face, avoiding the deluge of glass.

'What were you planning for me?' Erin asks quietly. 'Another "accident"? How were you going to get your revenge?'

'It's not even about revenge.' Hewitt closes her eyes, grimacing. 'It was about you taking the fall. Your confession, your suicide. It was about putting an end to this. You're not the only one who's been looking over your shoulder, Erin. I wanted it to be over, and if anyone has to take the blame, it should be you. Child A kills Child B. I'm pretty sure that would've been enough to stop them searching for anyone else.'

'So, what, then?' Erin asks. 'You thought you were going to drive me home, over two hours away, and I wouldn't have noticed anything amiss? That I wouldn't have fought back?'

'Not if you were unconscious.' Hewitt's breathing is shallow. 'There's a drive through coffee place right by the bed and breakfast. Hot tea, good for shock. My treat, with a little something extra slipped in.'

Silence lapses between them as Erin contemplates this. 'Aidan would've known,' she says finally. 'You were supposed to go back to the island.'

'I would've called him. Told him you'd forced me to take you home. That you'd become hysterical and threatened me.' There's a whisper of a smile about her now.

Erin stares at her. 'You're a fucking psycho.'

She returns to the car and removes the key from the ignition, pocketing it. The headlights go out, leaving the causeway in darkness. The sky is thick with cloud, but on the mainland tiny lights wink like eyes.

'*This* is how it ends,' Erin says. 'I'll give you a choice. If you tell me about that night, I'll go back to the island for help. If you don't, I'll sit here until the tide starts coming in. Then I'll get in your car and keep driving until I'm off this causeway. By the time anyone else gets here, all this – and you – will be underwater.'

'You know what I did to her. It was in every news outlet in the country.'

'I want to hear it from you.'

She feels Hewitt's eyes on her and senses she's about to yield her last bit of power.

'Another lie,' Hewitt says. 'What you want to know is whether what you did – you, Kitty and Mira – led to what *I* did. But deep down, you know the answer. Don't you?'

35

OCTOBER 1996

Charlotte has no idea who Belinda West is at first. All she's been told is that she left her last college in the midst of a scandal, plus some scant details. Her hair is very red, Charlotte thinks. Like blood. It's almost as though Belinda West *wants* to draw attention to herself.

Charlotte is well-practised in not staring. During her time as a teacher she's become adept at ignoring certain things in a professional manner: the sweat patches on colleagues' shirts in the staffroom, enormous zits on students' faces, the tone in a parent's voice that suggests they're going to be a problem in the near future. She even manages not to stare at Erin Sinclair *too* much, despite having known exactly who she is for weeks. But she's having trouble not staring at this new girl and her scarlet hair. She tells Paul she'll do the introduction. He's been oddly cagey since they arrived on the island and she wonders whether Tori has been giving him grief about coming on the trip, or if it's to do with having a new student who's made allegations against a previous teacher. Paul hadn't wanted the newcomer on the trip, arguing that she should be allowed to settle in first. Charlotte had been the one to push for it. It made sense after another student had pulled out, and she felt it might help the girl find some friends.

'This is Belinda West,' she says brightly, addressing the rest of the students. 'She's just transferred to us and will be in Paul's group when we return next week. I hope you'll all make her welcome.'

The other students look at her curiously, particularly those who travelled on Callaghan's minibus. Charlotte had listened to the chit-chat between Belinda and the others as she drove, but there had been no hint any of them knew the reason for her transfer – or that she intends to reveal it.

Paul starts reading out cabin allocations and Charlotte's gaze moves from the new girl to settle, as it so often does, on Erin. Like the others, Erin is staring at Belinda – it's impossible not to, with that hair – but she's gone quite grey in the face, and it seems to Charlotte that there is shock there. Does Erin know something the other students don't?

Charlotte has made it her business to watch Erin ever since she discovered who she is. After Nicky's death she had built up a picture in her head of the two children involved from the names and descriptions given by a couple of people her mother was still in contact with after she and Charlotte left the estate. The names – Webb and Morton – were securely locked in her memory. The descriptions had been sketchy: a thin, sullen child with lank brown hair, still new to the area when it all happened. Once, she was sent a copy of a class photo showing the other girl, by a parent of another child in the group. This girl was dark-haired and smiling, from a seemingly decent family – up till then, at least. What the photo hadn't shown was the eye defect which, the other parent had explained, made the Morton girl easy to identify.

Charlotte hadn't planned on returning to Essex, but then the job came up offering better pay, prospects and facilities than her existing position. The college is far enough from the estate to avoid any old memories and, while it fleetingly occurred to her that there was a small possibility either girl might still be in the area, she'd dismissed it almost instantly, believing they were hardly the kinds of youngster to enter higher education.

Fewer than three weeks into the second academic year of her post she'd been proven wrong when she overheard hushed staff-room speculation that a student was one of the 'two little liars' in 'that Pemberton case'. There'd been a change of name, from Morton to Sinclair, but the eye defect was unmistakeable.

Since then, she has watched Erin with a mixture of curiosity and loathing. There is fear, too, that her own identity and link to Nicky will be discovered – but overwhelmingly Charlotte believes she is safe. She can be a chronic over-sharer in some respects, but she doesn't speak about this part of her past to anyone. Not friends, not colleagues, or even boyfriends – not that any of them have lasted long. When they'd moved away Mum had drummed into her the importance of never mentioning Mick Pemberton or where they'd come from, both before Nicky's murder, and even after Mick went to prison. She has learned to keep her mouth shut and stay invisible, not that that has ever been a problem for her. Having a different surname from both Nicky and her mother afforded her an extra layer of anonymity and, while in some ways she regrets changing her surname by deed poll to that of a girl she'd admired at uni, she's grateful of yet another barrier to her past identity.

When Paul announces that Belinda is to share a cabin with Erin, Kathryn and Mira, the look of worry on Erin's face turns to outright panic. Charlotte's curiosity is piqued. She has noticed Erin's shy attempts to befriend Kathryn – or Kitty, as she prefers to be known – and wonders if Erin is afraid the new girl might steal the limelight. She watches Erin for as long as she can without it being obvious as the group disperses, then turns to follow Paul back to the minibuses.

'Man, I am *knackered*,' says Paul, once they're out of earshot of the students. He yawns, stretching his arms up over his head, and his thin sweater ripples across his back. When they reach the minibuses, he kneels, grumbling, to examine a puncture sustained on the rutted causeway. Charlotte feels a tug of longing as she glimpses his toned shoulders and tanned neck. God, what she wouldn't give to feel his weight on her, just once. Charlotte has never had sex with anyone she's been particularly attracted to. Her lovers have been few, and mainly a case of doing it because it's expected. She's always wished for a partner who'd intuitively ravish her, yet somehow she ends up with the type who prod her with morning glory and a 'knock-knock?'. Paul is a world apart from the last man she slept with, a former colleague whose soft, pasty body sprouted hairs in nonsensical patches. The memory of him makes her slightly queasy.

'Late night?' she asks casually, unable to help picturing him pinned between Tori's thighs. Tori, with her silky blond hair and revoltingly good figure even after two babies. Charlotte was thrilled to find out she's a nag. Clingy, too – always ringing Paul's office, demanding to know what time he'll be home.

'The twins are teething,' he replies, rubbing his eyes.

'Ah,' she says. 'So, you've come away with a load of other people's kids for a bit of peace? Nice one, Callaghan.'

He laughs and she feels a warm glow of pleasure. She enjoys making him laugh. She can't imagine Tori ever has anything amusing to say, judging by her permanent sour-puss expression.

'Miss,' a voice says. Charlotte and Paul turn to see Erin behind them. She's red and blotchy in the face, clearly troubled.

'What's up, Erin?' she asks. 'And you can call me Charlotte, you know. You're at sixth form now.' She waits while Erin struggles for words. The sight of this fills Charlotte with a vindictive glee.

It's strange, she thinks, how she can stand before this girl who irrevocably changed her life without reaching out and throttling her. Gratifying, too, that Erin has absolutely no idea who Charlotte is. In those first weeks of learning Erin's identity, Charlotte had been paralysed with hatred every time she saw her and had spent dark hours fantasising about pushing her down a flight of stairs or running her over outside the college gates.

But as time has passed the hatred has become marginally less potent. It's clear Erin is no troublemaker. She's quiet, diligent and, according to her subject teachers – particularly in art – her work is outstanding. She has noticed how Erin hovers on the fringes of the other students, rarely joining in.

'It's the… the room arrangements,' Erin says.

'What about them?'

'Can I switch?'

Her eyes are mesmerising. Charlotte hasn't had many opportunities to see them this closely. Erin is clearly conscious of them and usually avoids eye contact, but now Charlotte can see how the pupils appear to bleed into the iris, like black ink. She checks the cabin list and does her best to sound concerned. 'Is there a problem?'

'It's Bee… the new girl.'

'Belinda?' Paul asks, a little cagily.

'I know her. She lived on my street. We… we had a falling out.'

Paul sighs and turns away, but Charlotte barely notices.

'A falling out?' she repeats. And it's as though her body senses it before her brain does, because her guts twist. *I know her.* 'When? What happened?'

'We were ten. She… something happened and it affected a lot of people. I'd… rather not say any more.'

There is a rushing sound like static in Charlotte's ears as she tries to grasp what Erin is saying. The words repeat on a loop in her mind.

Something happened… affected a lot of people.

Charlotte bites down slowly on her lip and doesn't stop until she feels the skin break.

This girl, she thinks. *And that girl.* Morton and Webb, now Sinclair and West.

Child A. Child B. *It has to be.*

Charlotte is not a religious woman but it strikes her that if she were, this could only be a sign of divine intervention. *These girls have been brought to her for a reason.* She finds herself speaking mechanically, saying things she doesn't mean.

'It was long time ago, Erin. Children do silly, hurtful things sometimes. You're nearly adults now – can't you put it behind you?'

Still Erin persists, but slowly and persuasively, Charlotte shuts her down. She is reeling, simultaneously giddy and horrified. The only thing she's clear on is Erin's desperation to escape Belinda, and that's one thing, one *luxury*, that Charlotte will take the utmost pleasure in denying.

When Erin finally slinks off, defeated, Charlotte's head's spinning. She's startled out of it when Paul speaks. It's the first time since knowing him that she's ever forgotten he's there.

'Is it me,' he says in a low voice, 'or is there something really weird about her eyes?'

Charlotte shrugs, heart racing. 'Can't say I've noticed.'

The revelation throws her off-kilter. From the moment this trip was arranged she's planned to use it to get closer to Paul, but now she's struggling to think of little else but those two girls. All she can do is obsessively watch them, grimly fascinated by how Erin is plainly disturbed by Belinda's presence. A few times she catches herself and pulls it back, afraid Paul will notice, but he's quiet, stewing on something. She allows herself to dream that he's fighting with himself internally; conflicted between straying with her and staying faithful to Tori. He must get propositioned all the time, but it'd need to be someone special to turn his head, she's sure. Someone warm and intense. Someone who can make him laugh.

When evening comes they agree to oversee the students in the games room, where most of them have loosely arranged to meet up. Charlotte showers and dresses in new lacy lingerie and a navy wool dress similar to one she's seen Tori in. The bronzing lotion she puts on her legs is a little streaky, but in low lighting it shouldn't matter. She sprays herself liberally with perfume, the same one she'd found in Paul's cubbyhole – a gift for Tori, she thinks. She curls her hair, but by the time she arrives at the games room it's flattening and she's dismayed to glimpse herself reflected in a window only to realise the dress is shapeless and ugly. She's further put out that Paul's in the same clothes he's worn all day and hasn't even bothered to shave. In fact, he smells a little stale. Seduction is clearly the last thing on his mind.

Her mood continues to sour when Erin and Belinda arrive with Kitty and Mira. All four look relaxed, flush-faced and pretty. Heads turn as they circle the room. Charlotte stiffens as the girls notice her, sure Kitty's just said something which incites sniggers from the rest. *Obnoxious little yank.* In her flashy, expensive clothes, and car that's been handed to her. Charlotte would love to smack her one, but tonight she's more concerned with Erin and Belinda.

'Looks like they've been drinking,' she murmurs to Paul.

'They're seventeen,' he replies with a shrug. 'But I think most of them are pretty sensible.' He rubs his chin, looking oddly haggard. 'You head back, if you like. Get an early night. I'll stay a bit longer.'

'Yeah,' she says, crushed. He hasn't even noticed her hair. 'Okay.'

Back at her cabin she puts on the TV and sits in the dark, sinking a glass of red wine. The sight of those girls enjoying themselves and being admired, plus Paul's indifference, has left her somewhere between fuming and depressed. Prior to this weekend she's dreamed up all sorts of schemes to be alone with him, yet even though she doubts she'll get another chance like this any time soon, her mind keeps spiralling back to the two girls.

How has Belinda ended up at the same college? Charlotte

is still incredulous that her own path has collided with Erin's, but *both* of them? Erin's discomfort is obvious. If it wasn't, Charlotte would suspect Belinda's transfer has not come about coincidentally but because of the pair somehow conspiring to rekindle their perverse friendship. But this doesn't fit with what she was told. During the legal proceedings it had been stressed that Child A and Child B hadn't been close friends. Despite calls from the public, the court had offered assurance that banning any future contact between the two was unnecessary. The girl whose father had gone to prison had soon relocated, and the other had been taken into care. Neither wanted anything more to do with each other.

Charlotte huddles under a heap of blankets on the sofa, too wired to sleep. She finishes the wine, pours a second, then pushes her hand between her legs, trying to imagine it's Paul's. It's useless. The lacy knickers are irritating her crotch, and all she can think of is Nicky and her mum.

She'd been four when Nicky came along. A sweet little thing, always smiling. Charlotte had loved him as much as she'd hated Mick. Mick who was never kind to her, another man's kid. As Nicky got older and it became clear he was different, and not the son Mick hoped for, that's when he'd turned cruel. *Thick Nick*, he called him. One day Nicky tried to stop him walloping their mum. Mick hit him instead. He was eleven. Mum swore to Mick if he touched either of them again she'd leave, but Mick had laughed and told her she was welcome to fuck off with her brat but if she tried to take *his* son, she'd be sorry. And then he'd beaten Mum up for good measure.

A few weeks later Mum turned up early at the school, claiming they had dentist appointments. Really, she'd stolen money of Mick's and bought one-way train tickets to Cambridge. They left with nothing but the clothes on their backs, heading to a hostel. A new school, a new life waiting for them. Mum was convinced if they were far away enough Mick wouldn't bother coming after them – but what she hadn't counted on was Nicky, and how deeply Mick had terrorised him.

On the train, he'd said he was going to the toilet. Instead, he'd got off at the next stop, begged money from a passer-by and called Mick from a phone box to pick him up. By the time Charlotte and her mum realised he wasn't on the train it was too late to go back. Mum knew Mick would flip.

Mum spoke to Nicky once. Told him she was coming for him, that he had to be ready. Then Mick came on the phone and said if she ever called again, Nicky would pay the price. If she tried to take Nicky, he'd find them and kill them all. If Mum involved the police, he'd hurt Nicky. She couldn't win. Mick saw it as a humiliation that she'd left. Nicky was a pawn, something for Mick to retain that last bit of control over her. She went into a deep depression after that.

Between looking after Mum and her studies, Charlotte managed to hold it together somehow; the glue being the promise she'd made to Mum and herself that once Nicky turned sixteen and left school, she'd go back and persuade him to join them, and Mum would get better. But none of it had happened that way and now the glue holding Charlotte together is not love, but spite and bitterness and, yes, if she's being honest, her fantasies of Paul, to some extent.

She drinks half of the second glass of wine, then decides she's had enough. The urge to see Paul is too strong for her to ignore. Pulling off the hideous dress and mentally consigning it to the bin, she tugs on a dark top and black jeans which are far more flattering. She puts on her coat and leaves the cabin without bothering to switch off the TV, feeling heady as she goes back in the direction of the games room.

As she turns out of one lane and into the next, the sight of a figure up ahead startles her. When she realises it's Belinda West, every hair on her scalp seems to stand on end. Charlotte watches, momentarily frozen, as the girl strides purposefully towards Paul's cabin. Breaking out of her reverie, Charlotte follows, unseen, wondering why Bee is alone and what she's doing. Has something happened with Erin?

From within a copse of trees she watches Belinda knock and Paul open the door.

She watches as they argue in a heated, familiar, gut-wrenching way. Watches as he grabs her arm and roughly pulls her inside.

She watches, and realises.

After, she doesn't remember how she got to the window, but she remembers seeing them – god, *seeing* them – and then hearing the approaching footsteps of others. She hides nearby. Reeling. *Seething.* The sight of Erin and Aidan grounds her, briefly. She feels a nudge of concern, wondering if there's trouble of some kind at the games room. She thought Paul had stayed behind to keep an eye on things, but clearly he had other plans.

When Belinda leaves, Charlotte is unable to follow while Erin and Aidan are there, and so instead, she tails them, hearing snatches of their conversation. He walks her back to her cabin and leaves alone. Charlotte remains outside, growing steadily incandescent with white-hot rage. Sick with betrayal. Paul was never hers, but she's lost who she thought he was.

Filthy fucking man-whore.

Charlotte is a fool. And that *girl*…

That girl is rotten.

If it were anyone else she'd call the police. Call the college governor. Paul's wife.

She does none of these things. She doesn't need to. Now Erin and Aidan know, the affair will not stay a secret. She waits, and waits, hardly knowing what she's waiting for. She sees Belinda return, and go in. Minutes later, the four girls step out into the night as if nothing has happened. As if they are friends. Charlotte follows at a distance, listening and observing. They head away from the cabins, down to the shore.

They are not friends.

'Float the witch', the American yells. 'Float the witch!'

They're going to kill her, she thinks. And when they don't, she is simultaneously disappointed and relieved.

Her hands are cold as she steps down from the road on to the shingle once Erin, Kitty and Mira have gone. She finds her leather gloves in her pocket. Puts them on.

Belinda doesn't hear her straight away. She's coughing and crying and shivering, but at the last second she turns, seeing Charlotte behind her. Her face crumples in momentary relief, and she leans in as Charlotte kneels and pulls the girl into her arms.

'Shh,' she says. 'Shh.'

'Everyone… *h-hates me*,' Bee moans through chattering teeth and sobs. There's a wild, hopeless misery about her that is the best part of Charlotte's night.

Really, it's about what needs to be done, like putting down a sick animal. It's what Charlotte's always believed should happen to terrible people, where there's no hope of redemption. This girl was born bad, and she'll carry on being bad. Charlotte could end it quickly, before Belinda even realises what's happening. She could.

But Belinda West has caused immense suffering.

It's only fair she experiences it, too.

'Yes.' Charlotte's lips brush the dripping red hair. 'Everyone hates you. But I hate you the most.'

36

OCTOBER 2016

'SHE BARELY STRUGGLED.' HEWITT'S VOICE is gloating with the recollection. 'Probably too surprised… She thought I was there to *help* her. There wasn't much fight left in her anyway after what you three had done. You sort of… *broke* her, I think. Made it easy for me. I held her under for a bit, and then pulled her up. She got weaker after I'd done that a couple of times – didn't want it over with *too* quickly but then she made this weird choking sound… and when I pulled her up again there was this chunk of silver glass stuck in her neck.' She shrugs. 'I must've pushed her down on to it. I hadn't *planned* it, I'd only meant to finish what you three had started, but the sight of it – the blood, it was like I lost it for a minute there. I wasn't even really thinking, but the next thing I knew I'd grabbed hold of it, started pulling it across—'

'*Stop.*' Erin's voice is thick with tears. 'Don't.'

'You asked. All I did was take the opportunity you gave me.' Hewitt writhes under the weight of the car, groaning. 'You know this. You've always known what you did played a part. You served her up to me.'

'We didn't want her *dead*. We just wanted to scare her. To… to punish her—'

'You hated her, and what she'd done and how she made you feel. You wanted her gone.'

'We stopped,' Erin protests. 'We stopped…'

We broke her.

'Mira stopped it. You and Kitty had already gone too far. I was there, I saw you. I saw everything you did, heard everything that was said. Bee was already on the brink.'

'No.'

Hewitt scoffs. 'Lying again. Why do you keep lying, even to yourself? It's just you and me here. I've told the truth. Now it's your turn. No more lies.' She grimaces through a sheen of sweat. 'Answer one question: were you glad she was dead?'

Erin's throat tightens as though an invisible hand is around it. Trying to stop the truth. She shakes her head. Hewitt makes a disbelieving sound.

'It's strange, but the hardest part was afterwards – the next day. I don't mean the pretending, or even the waiting for her to be found.'

'How did you know she'd be there?' Erin whispers. 'Why didn't the tide wash her away?'

'I thought about letting it, but I wanted you to see her. I wanted *Paul* to see her. So I'd floated her out to the jetty and knotted part of her dress round one of its legs under the water. I knew I had to enter the water to untie it, and I'd planned to be the one who spotted her. But actually, the difficult part was putting on the clothes I'd worn when I'd killed her.

'I'd rinsed them out for ages. Got all the mud and sand off, and washed them till they ran clear of blood. But I couldn't get them dry. I could only wring them out as much as possible. They were still damp when I put them on. Damp and *so* cold. If anyone had brushed against me… But it paid off. Running into that water gave me a reason for any traces of Bee or her blood to be on me. It meant I had no clothes to hide or destroy. So yeah, that was the hardest bit for me at the time. Then later, wondering if the whole thing would catch up with me eventually. But when I did it I knew that was the cost, and it was worth the risk.' Her voice is quieter now, and her face waxy pale. 'Clearly the hardest part for you is admitting the truth. Why don't you just say it? You were glad she was dead. Weren't you?'

'Yeah,' Erin admits at last.

Hewitt tries to smile, but her face contorts with pain. 'See?' She coughs. 'We're not so different. You knew, same as I did, that she was rotten. You knew she didn't deserve to live. Don't get me wrong, Erin. You were equally to blame for what happened to Nicky, but at least you told the truth in the end. And what you did to Bee went some way to atone for your part in it. Then there was your dad getting killed, of course.'

Erin had sunk to her knees while Hewitt was speaking, but now she gets to her feet. Her movements are shaky, yet her head is starting to clear.

'I *was* glad she was dead, at first. You're right, I hated her. Because I hated myself. She reminded me of the worst part of myself, the worst thing I'd ever done. But there were things I didn't know about her. Things I didn't want to see. She was a victim all her life, long before you ever got to her.'

'Don't you dare feel sorry for her!' Hewitt hisses. 'My brother was the victim, not that little whore. I thought you saw that, Erin. I thought you *understood*.'

'She wasn't a whore. She was a girl. A disturbed, unhappy girl. And Nicky wasn't innocent. He was dangerous in his own ignorant way.'

'No. He wasn't. He wouldn't have hurt anyone! He wasn't capable of it.'

'You don't have to be capable to do harm. You can stand by. Watch. Do nothing. Join in.' Erin is no longer talking about Nicky. 'I'm going back to the island now. The world's going to know what you did.'

'Is it, Erin? And will it know about what *you* did? Only fair, isn't it?'

Erin doesn't answer, for these are not really questions. They are taunts. Dares.

An air of finality crackles between them. Hewitt's breaths lapse into brittle little grunts. Unmasked, she's no more a monster than Bee was a witch, and yet an underlying edge of menace about her lingers. She is a sinister core wrapped in ordinariness.

'How long?' she asks. 'Before the tide comes in?'

Erin glances at her watch. It feels like hours since they left the island.

'Fifteen minutes, perhaps.' She brushes grit off her shins. Her clothes cling to her damply. 'I'll make it. I'll tell them where to find you.'

She stares at Charlotte Hewitt one last time. Then she starts to run.

The causeway unfurls in the darkness, ribboning away from her. It's hard to see, but not impossible. The black rocks edging it keep Erin on track, but every so often she staggers as a stray one catches her off guard. She moves swiftly. She has time.

Too much time.

She veers left, scattering rocks from the causeway's edge as she strays from it. It's not hard to lose her balance, falling into the mudflats. She hauls herself up, shivering. She stinks of brine and fish. Her nails are caked. Her clothes are heavy, damp. Hewitt was right, this *is* hard.

When she is perhaps twenty metres from the island, Erin pauses and looks back. It's too dark to see where Hewitt is now. She and the car are swallowed by the darkness, but they're out there still, unseen, like the silver bottle's malignant contents from long ago.

Erin is close enough to the island now that she could run and be there in seconds.

She pauses, thinking of Charlotte Hewitt and Nicky Pemberton. Of Kitty.

And Bee. She thinks of scabby legs, of spiteful mothers, and loving ones. She thinks of daisy chains pushed through a neighbour's door.

'I'm sorry,' she says into the empty air. Nothing answers her. 'I'm sorry for hurting you. For pushing you away. I'm so sorry, Bee.'

She waits, growing steadily colder. Waits until the space beyond the road begins to glisten wetly, until water begins leaking between the black rocks to fill the crevices and potholes as the causeway slowly floods. She sinks down, letting the water soak into her hair, her clothes, her skin. It's bracing, enough to rouse someone who is disoriented from a head wound, who might have been staggering about, in and out of consciousness while in search of safety. Losing valuable minutes.

When she finally steps on to the island her hands are shaking so much from the cold that it takes her a minute to locate the congealed cut on her head. With numb fingers she prises it apart, reopening the wound until she feels fresh warmth spreading over her scalp.

Now she will go for help and tell them where to find Charlotte Hewitt.

It will be too late, but she hadn't lied.

Erin is done with lies.

Epilogue

NOVEMBER 2016

Erin is in the process of starting to clear her inbox when the email comes in.

It's ten thirty in the morning and she has paused for a quick cup of tea that's come up via room service. While she's drinking it she goes to the window and looks out. London is beautiful today; crisp winter sunshine across frosted rooftops. Far below the hotel, on the pavement, shoppers are already out in force on their way to Bond Street and Christmas lights are up, even though it's not December for another three weeks.

Her laptop chimes, alerting her to the new email. She sets her cup aside and sits down to open it, experiencing the familiar fairground-ride drop of her stomach that always accompanies the arrival of a message. Old habits die hard.

It's from an illustration undergraduate called Riley Emerson, a fan of Erin's work, requesting an interview with her as part of a dissertation.

'You should do it,' Aidan says behind her, making her jump.

'I didn't know you were reading over my shoulder.' Erin swats at him. '*Rude.*'

He leans in to kiss her neck. 'I can do something ruder, if you like.'

'You already did, an hour ago.' She closes the laptop and gets up, turning to fold herself into his arms. They stay like that for a long moment, and he presses his lips to the top of her head.

The cut is healing well, now a thin, slightly lumpy red scar that will fade in time. She decides she'll reply to Riley Emerson later and accept the request, provided it's not withdrawn once the day's out.

'Sure you don't want a coffee before we go?' she says, and feels him shaking his head.

'I'll get one later,' he murmurs into her hair. 'You know, I'm not sure how much longer we can call this arrangement "patient aftercare". It's serious overtime territory now.'

'What do you want to call it, then?'

'I don't know. I mean, since you don't sign books I'm nearly out of ideas.'

'Yeah, well. Maybe it's time I started doing that,' she says softly. 'And we could just drop the "patient" and "after" and go from there.'

'Yeah,' says Aidan. He holds her closer. 'We could do that.'

Erin wears a well-cut dark suit. It's the same suit she wore a week ago to a memorial service for Kitty that took place in a little Essex chapel. There had been photographers there that day, stationed along the country lane and snapping the arrivals at what they must have deemed a respectful distance. The funeral will take place in the States next month. Erin isn't sure yet whether she'll go. It's a decision that, like many, will hinge on what happens after today.

Five minutes ago she got a message from Mira.

Here for you, it says. **Now, and on the other side of this.**

Three minutes ago, a text from her mum: **I love you, I'm proud of you.**

She takes Aidan's hand, ready to walk in.

'You sure about this?' he asks.

'I'm sure,' she says, as he runs his thumb over hers. But she is sure only that she has two choices: stay silent, keep hiding, and let Bee continue to be hated.

Or speak and try to be something to her in death that she never was in life.

It has to be both of us. They'll believe you.

'I've got nothing left to hide,' she says. It's not a lie, exactly. But if it were, it's one she can live with.

She wears the dark suit now for a press conference. As they enter the room a thousand flashes go off at once before she's even taken her seat, and they do not cease, the endless *click-clicking* of camera shutters rolling into each other.

They slow, but do not stop entirely as she takes out her prepared statement.

'My name is Erin Sinclair,' she says. 'Many of you already know my story. But there's another chapter I need to give you now. It begins way before Charlotte Hewitt confessed to two murders, before dying on the Blackwater Island causeway last month. And it's a chapter I share with someone else. That person was Belinda West, or Child B as she's also known.'

She pauses, and the cameras flash so fast and so bright that she doesn't think her eyes have ever been this dazzled except for maybe during that hot, arid summer of 1990. She blinks, and she's swinging high into cloudless blue under a baking sun, the cornfield ripe and waiting nearby.

She thinks of a daisy chain in small hands.

'I am Child A. I ask you to listen to what I'm about to tell you, about two girls. One who was loved, and one who wasn't. Perhaps, by the end you'll know whether or not you can forgive us.'

She will visit Bee's grave, just once, she decides.

She will take her daisies.

Acknowledgements

My first thank you is to my agent Julia Churchill, who got me through the early chaotic drafts of this book that I needed, so desperately, to write, and teased out the missing ingredients and a layer of sensitivity. We did a book for grown-ups – whoop!

Next, my editor Carolyn Mays. Thank you for crossing the causeway with me, falling in love with this story, and making it better. I'm excited for the next one. Thanks also to excellent copyeditor Kay Gale, and proofreader Dominique Gane.

My coven/family/Ethel Matchstick gang: Theresa, Janet, Carlene and Tanya – thanks for being my beta readers, soul sisters and advisors (yes, even when I don't take the advice). Sorry for all the swearing and sex bits… risotto, anyone?

My bookish friend Jenny Davies. Thank you for being one of the first to read and feed back on this story, and sorry there were no fairies.

I'm grateful to my friend Kirsty Chambers (and Simon!) for assisting me with my paramedic-related queries, and to PC Kirsty Williams, the most excellent officer, for advising me on the policing aspects. Any mistakes are my own.

A huge thanks to you, the reader, for choosing this book. I hope it provided an entertaining few hours and for some of you, perhaps, a nostalgic trip down a 90s memory lane.

Last, but never least, I must thank the witch who resides in the silver bottle in Oxford's Pitt Rivers Museum. From the moment we met you had me under your spell. Whatever the truth of your story is, you were the beginning of this one.

About the Author

Photo courtesy of Michelle Harrison

Michelle Harrison is the bestselling author of twenty books for children, published in twenty-five territories. Her debut novel, *13 Treasures*, won the Waterstones Children's Book Prize. Prior to being a full-time writer, Michelle was a bookseller for Waterstones and then an editorial assistant for Oxford University Press. She lives in Essex with her son and cats. *Two Little Liars* is her first novel for adults.

Scan the code below on Spotify to access the playlist Michelle made and listened to during the writing of *Two Little Liars*.

michelleharrisonbooks.com

Q&A with Michelle Harrison

Is Blackwater Island based on a real place?

Yes. It's inspired by Osea Island in Essex, accessible via a causeway at low tide. I spent a weekend there researching, and found the isolation both fascinating and eerie. The real island is located in the Blackwater Estuary, so my fictional island name is a nod to that. The causeway was built by the Romans and features in the film *The Woman in Black*.

Did you come up with the lie first and build the plot around it, or did the characters' motivations shape the deception?

The witch bottle actually came first, followed by the island setting, and then the lie. For me it's always plot, then character, but one tends to drive the other anyway. The lie was initially nasty and aimed at Erin, but evolved into something truly damaging as well as becoming a huge part of Erin's and Bee's identities.

Who was the most challenging character to write, and why?

Bee, but she was my favourite, too. In the early drafts she was wholly unlikeable, and even though I knew the reasons for that, those reasons weren't clear on the page. Her murder had to matter more to the reader, so it was about finding a balance in keeping her an unsettling presence while also gradually teasing out the truth about her past.

How important is it to you that your characters are likeable?

It's more important that they're interesting. Deeply flawed characters and unreliable narrators are the ones I enjoy best as a reader, and those are the ones who come alive for me the most. I love digging into why characters are the way they are, and the events that shaped them.

Given the chance, would you open a witch bottle?

Nope! I try not to be *too* superstitious, but something like that wouldn't sit well with me. As Kitty says: *it was the idea of it, the whole thing about there being trouble if it smashed.* I think there's a lot to be said for self-fulfilling prophecies! Having said that, I'd love to know what's inside the real 'witch in a bottle' at the Pitt Rivers Museum, and I emailed them to ask whether it's ever been opened or X-rayed. It hasn't.

Are you writing another thriller?

I am. It's called *I Let Myself In*, and it's about a woman in the early stages of an *almost* perfect relationship, except the man she's seeing seems to be hiding something. In a moment of madness she has a set of his keys cut and lets herself into his house – but nothing can prepare her for what she finds…

NO EXIT PRESS

More than just the usual suspects

— CWA DAGGER —
AWARDED BEST CRIME &
MYSTERY PUBLISHER

'A very smart, independent publisher delivering the finest literary crime fiction' *Big Issue*

MEET NO EXIT PRESS, an award-winning crime imprint bringing you the best in crime and suspense fiction. From classic detective novels, to page-turning spy thrillers and literary writing that grabs the attention. Our books are carefully crafted by some of the world's finest writers and delivered to you by a small, but passionate, team.

In over 30 years of business, we have published award-winning fiction and non-fiction including the work of a Pulitzer Prize winner, the British Crime Book of the Year, numerous CWA Dagger Awards, a British million-copy bestselling author, the winner of the Canadian Governor General's Award for Fiction and the Scotiabank Giller Prize, to name but a few. We are the home of many crime and noir legends from the USA whose work includes iconic film adaptations and TV sensations. We pride ourselves in uncovering the most exciting new or undiscovered talents. New and not so new – you know who you are!

We are a proactive team committed to delivering the very best, both for our authors and our readers.

Want to join the conversation and find out more about what we do?

Catch us on social media or sign up to our newsletter for all the latest news from No Exit Press.

f fb.me/noexitpress   **X** @noexitpress

noexit.co.uk